Tandem Cottage

Mackinac Cottages Series
Book 3

Tandem Cottage

Mackinac Cottages Series
Book 3

By

Carrie Fancett Pagels

Hearts Overcoming Press

COVER ARTWORK BY LORNA BRICCO

ISBN Number: 979-8-9928267-1-5

Hearts Overcoming Press
United States of America

Cover Design: Lorna Bricco, Bricco Designs, USA, All image rights reserved, Copyright © Lorna Bricco, 2024

DEDICATION

To:

Renata A. Kowal, D.C.

&

Michael B. Potter, M.D.

Two fabulous medical providers who have blessed

me.

Their skill and compassion have kept me going

to complete this work.

Endorsements
for Mackinac Cottages series

Butterfly Cottage
This lovely novel, centered on three generations of women as they face a summer of change, will resonate with readers long after the last page is turned.

> ~~Suzanne Woods Fisher, Bestselling author of *On a Summer Tide*

Lilac Cottage
Mystery, romance, inspiration plus deeply nuanced characters you will love, and enchanting Mackinac Island--Carrie Fancett Pagels delivers all these and more in her fascinating new book, "Lilac Cottage." Plan your life so you can read it straight through!

> ~~Kay Moser, Aspiring Women series

Tandem Cottage
In the gripping story, *Tandem Cottage*, author Carrie Fancett Pagels brings heartfelt emotions, hope, faith, and trust. The story captured me from the beginning and I couldn't stop reading. Everyday people with unique experiences. A great read that touches the heart and soul.

> ~~Melissa Henderson, Award-winning author

Tandem Cottage was such a beautiful book. It is one that I never wanted to end. I want to know, what happens next! Some books end far too quickly—and Tandem Cottage was one such book. I adored it.

> ~~Julia Wilson, International reader & reviewer, ChristianBookaholic.com

Character List and Pronunciations

Alyssa (Uh lis' ah) Teann (Tee ann') – 25
       Samuel "Sammy" Teann – Alyssa's son
Reverend & Mrs. Teann – Alyssa's parents
       Gayle – Alyssa's sister (married to Tony)
Evangelist Romelda (Rom ehl' dah) – Alyssa's great-grandmother
Gino & Jennifer – Sammy's biological father & his wife

Carter Parker – 24, computer programmer
       Kelsey (Kel' see) nickname Kels – Carter's daughter
       Abbi-Renae (Ab' bee Ren ay') Kelly – Carter's deceased
wife, Kelsey's mother
Hamp Parker & Maria Parker – Carter's father and stepmother
Hampton Parker III "Parker" – Carter's brother
       Jaycie Worth Parker (Jay' see) – Parker's wife
Kareen (Kahr' een) & Gianni Franchetti (Fran cheh' tee) – Carter's
grandparents
Tamara (Tam' uh rah) Austin – Jaycie Parker's mother and Susan
Mullen's friend

Susan Mullen – school social worker and grief group therapist
       John Mullen – Susan's husband
         Colby Mullen – Susan and John's son
Representative Daniels – Susan's mother
Sadie "Rachel" Dunmara Welling RN & Jack Welling – co-owners
of Lilac Cottage and hosts for the medical retreat
Clark Jeffries, Jr. – computer programming business owner (son of
Clark Jeffries, Sr., Mackinac Island Parks' Director)
Starr Bourne (Stahr Born) & Juan Pablo – seasonal workers &
more!
~

EUP is the letter abbreviation for the Eastern Upper Peninsula—
which Mackinac Island is part of, geographically.
Yooper is someone from the Upper Peninsula
Mackinac (Mak' ih naw) Island, Straits, & Bridge
Mackinaw City (Mak' ih naw) – this small city is spelled differently
Sault Ste. Marie/Sault Sainte Marie or "The Soo" (Soo' saynt Mah-
ree')
Tahquamenon (Tah kwah' meh non) Schools & Falls
Newberry (New' bear ee)

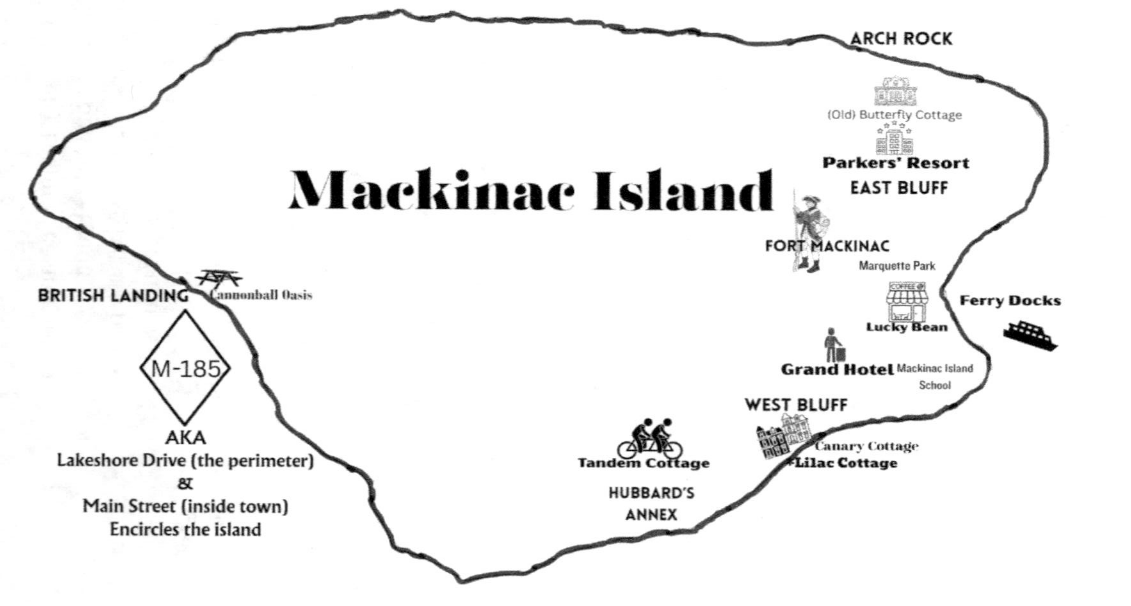

Mackinac Island
ARCH ROCK
(Old) Butterfly Cottage
Parkers' Resort
EAST BLUFF
FORT MACKINAC
Marquette Park
BRITISH LANDING
Cannonball Oasis
Ferry Docks
Lucky Bean
M-185
Grand Hotel
Mackinac Island School
WEST BLUFF
AKA
Lakeshore Drive (the perimeter)
&
Main Street (inside town)
Encircles the island
Tandem Cottage
Canary Cottage
Lilac Cottage
HUBBARD'S
ANNEX

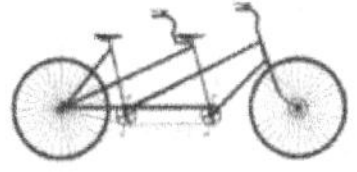

Chapter One

Tahquamenon Area Schools
Newberry, Michigan, February 2025

Cellphone vibrating, Alyssa's heart leapt—could this possibly be a call about a job prospect as a computer programmer? *God, make it so—for the sake of me and my son.* She pulled her cellphone from her pocket but didn't recognize the number. She'd sent out numerous job applications. Most had emailed back, but a couple had called to schedule her first interview. "Hello?"

"Alyssa, this is Gino."

She froze. Even after ten years, his voice made her skin crawl.

She hit the red end call button and shoved her phone back in her pocket as tremors worked through her entire body. After almost ten years he was calling?

No child support, no contact, nothing—not that she ever wanted to see him again. He was still what he was to her then—basically a stranger. But that stranger had left her with a child.

She whipped off her cafeteria apron and strode toward the library—it was almost three and her son would be expecting her. Sammy would worry if she was late.

Forcing herself to breathe in deeply, Alyssa marched toward the library. Sammy didn't have an aide with him anymore, like he'd had when he was in younger grades, but he still didn't handle less-structured events well. So, she'd offered to come sit near him during the special artist's presentation this afternoon—she couldn't let him see her like this.

The phone buzzed again, and she pulled out her ancient Android. *Same number.* Alyssa turned the phone off. Not going to let him interrupt this time with her son.

Get control—you can't go in there like this! Twenty-five years old and feeling like she wanted to roll up in a ball in a corner and cry like a little kid.

I can do all things through Him that is in me. She might not be able, but God was.

She pushed the library door open and then stepped in—quickly spotting her son in the back row. The presentation had already started and Sammy was stimming—bouncing in his seat.

The massive painting displayed in the front of the library—a tandem bike with a faint clock outline hanging in the clouds overhead—tugged at Alyssa's spirit as she sank into a chair, beside Sammy. Rows of children sat motionless in front of them.

Sammy leaned in. "Mom, you missed the intro," he stage-whispered, causing the girl beside him to giggle.

"Sorry!" Alyssa wrapped her arm around his shoulder to both comfort him, and to minimize his movement.

Why is Gino calling me? She fought the temptation to pull out her phone and check for a voicemail. Her cellphone service transcribed them into text—not always accurately, though.

The noted Upper Peninsula artist, Linda Anderson-Paine, was the guest presenter today. She stood beside her artwork, smiling at her audience. "Sometimes life is like riding a tandem bike where we," the artist pointed to the bike's front pedals, "turn one set of pedals, while God is applying the brakes." Mrs. Anderson shone an LED flashlight on the acrylic painting near the rear set of pedals.

Sammy leaned his head toward her and she touched his silky hair. *My sweet boy.* Different, but so smart.

The artist shrugged. "But sometimes, we're not pedaling at all, but He is."

Lord I could use that right now.

Mrs. Anderson waved her light over an hourglass painted in light blue on the darker blue background. "Anyone know what that is?"

"Hourglass!" an older boy blurted out from the front row.

"Right." She then beamed the light on the numbers one and zero in the upper right corner. "That's a ten, or decade, that I painted in there. Anyone have an idea why I did that?"

A ginger-haired boy sitting ahead of Alyssa and Sammy raised his hand.

"Yes?" A tender smile crept across the artist's pretty features.

"Because I'm ten?"

The other kids giggled.

The artist grinned. "Maybe. And there are more clocks hidden in the picture." She shone her light, illuminating several other timepieces.

Sammy wriggled. *Oh no.* Sitting like this for long was torture to him. As a child with Asperger's, it was super hard for him to hold back from blurting stuff out. His lips began to twitch.

It's coming. Watch for it. He's got to say something.

Alyssa tried to get her boy's attention by wiggling her fingers in their special signal.

Sammy ignored her. "He's your grandson, so I bet you put that in there because ten years is important to you." He thumped his chest, like he did when he was indicating something emotional. His lips moved like they did when he was chewing on the insides to keep from saying more.

"Bravo!" Mrs. Anderson clapped. "Exactly right."

The other kids gave Sammy the side-eye, and inside Alyssa wept for her son. But then, some kind of grudging admiration stole over their young faces.

"You see, art isn't just about enjoying what you're looking at—art can also make you feel something."

"And different people feel different things, right?" A blond boy in the front row offered.

"Right. When you see this bike, what do you think?"

He shrugged. "I think pretty cool—I want one of those two-people bikes."

"Tandem is what they call them." The artist motioned for her grandson to come forward. The sturdy boy jumped up and joined his grandmother in the front.

"What do you feel when you look at this?"

He crossed his arms. "Happy. I remember on my tenth birthday Mom took me to Mackinac Island, and we rode all the way around."

"That was a lot of fun, right?"

"Yup. The best!"

Alyssa averted her gaze. The time she'd taken Sammy to the island, on a field trip, he'd cried because of the horse manure odor and the strange sounds of horses' hooves. He'd only been in kindergarten then, but she'd not returned. Not only because of the many sensory elements but because they simply couldn't afford the ferry tickets, the bike rentals, and the food costs on the island—not on a school kitchen worker's scant salary. Thank God, though, that she had benefits and Mom and Dad didn't have to cover their insurance.

"How about you, Alyssa?" Mrs. Anderson called out.

Alyssa looked up. "Hmm?"

"How did this picture affect you?"

Her breath caught in her throat.

What did she see? *Time.* Time spinning rapidly by. One faint clock whose brushstrokes suggested it being turned rapidly and another clock-wheel operated by someone who seemingly wasn't there. God had different timing than humans had. *And ten years.* Ten years of her life. *Gone. All the struggles.*

As tears welled, she forced herself to breathe slowly, to compose herself.

One decision, but not really her decision, made over a decade ago had influenced how far she'd gotten in her life.

Nowhere.

Stuck in her hometown. Living with her parents.

Waiting to hear from someone if she might be offered a job with her new degree.

A thin, warm arm wrapped around her shoulders and her son leaned his head against hers.

"My mom is upset that she can't ride around the island with me because I stim too much."

Alyssa gasped. "No."

But hadn't she just been regretting him? That she'd made that mistake that resulted in him? This boy wasn't a mistake. He was her life.

He was her heart.

And they were about to start a brand-new life. A new adventure in another place. Soon. *God willing and if He'd start pedaling faster for me.*

She pulled Sammy in for a side hug, and he wiped the tears from her face.

"Your face is wet, Mom." He swiped his hand against his jeans—a pair from the church donation box. They probably had belonged to one of the kids in this very room.

Mrs. Anderson's sweet smile didn't quite meet her compassion-filled eyes. "I bet your mom is thinking how fast time goes and how in another ten years you'll be a grown-up and gone."

That comment made Alyssa's spine stiffen. Gone? Did Gino want to take Sammy? To claim rights? Why now?

He leaned in. "Are you thinking that, Mom?" he whispered.

He'd never been away from her for even one night.

"Mrs. Anderson, I'm going to three different summer camps this year, so that will help Mom get ready for me bugging out eventually."

The other kids giggled, and her boy looked around in surprise. He was perfectly serious, of course. Granted, he didn't realize his grandpa's archaic expression of 'bugging out' wasn't commonly used.

"Are you ready for that, Alyssa? For the summer camps?"

"We're both excited." *Did dread count as excitement?* Dread that she'd be called and have to go pick him up? Dread that the other kids would pick on him? She mussed her son's hair, and he patted it back in place.

"Yeah," her boy agreed.

"Well maybe they'll even have some tandem bikes at that camp." The artist scanned the boys and girls seated before her. "Wouldn't that be fun?"

"Yeah!" they chorused.

But all Alyssa could imagine was that boy on the back of her rental tandem bike crying his eyes out, wanting to go home.

Yorktown, Virginia

Standing beside his Trek, Carter clutched the offensive bike so tightly that his knuckles turned white. He stared at the community dumpster. If anything belonged in there, it was this fifteen-speed bicycle. Carter never wanted to see it again and he'd never wish his misfortune on anyone else. He knew he was being irrational, but he needed to clear things out—to get rid of what was holding him back. Probably his group therapy leader, Mrs. Mullen, didn't mean this type of thing. But he was going with it.

Carter bent, ready to heave this instrument of ruin upward, toward the edge of the dumpster.

"Hey man! Don't do that!" A kid—not a kid, but a guy with a floppy haircut who looked a couple years younger than Carter—half-jogged, half-ambled over to him, his hoody sagging open to reveal a Virginia Commonwealth University T-shirt. "I'll take that if it's not broken."

"No, man, it's not." The bike wasn't broken. *I am.* Irretrievably busted up inside with grief and walled off like a dumpster encased in concrete.

The guy, who looked a little familiar, squinted at him, and then at the bike, as Carter reluctantly lowered it to the ground. "It's got bad vibes." Just saying that out loud sounded kinda crazy. But that's how he was feeling.

"That's a Trek, man. Some of the best bikes out there. I like those."

Carter had, too. Once. Before. *Before everything.*

Scratching his face with one hand, the guy reached out and touched the front right handlebar. "You okay, dude, if I take it? Even with the bad mojo on it?" His voice had dropped lower, his green eyes full of something—a knowing. "These run close to six hundred bucks. Looks pretty new."

"Yup and it's yours." Carter pushed the bike, careful not to shove it toward him, even though he'd wanted nothing more than to hurl that bicycle away. *Far away.*

"You live in the house on the corner, right?" He angled his shaggy head in the direction of Carter's ranch-style brick house.

"Yeah." He cleared his throat.

"Sorry about your wife." His voice broke. "She was really fun to watch power walk—she was so into it."

Stiffening, Carter took a step backward.

His wife had been seriously into power walking, something she took up after they married. She'd had a lot of things she'd become obsessively involved with over the several years that he'd known her.

"Yeah, well, gotta go." Carter waved, turned on his heel and strode back to the house.

Each step called out a reminder of his wife. Hanging with her girlfriends, planning a wedding after she'd canceled their engagement, hours and hours in the lab working late, then the power walking—but never had her unadulterated attention been focused on their actual relationship.

Don't be looking at her deficiencies when you let her die! What was that verse—don't point out the splinter in your brother's eye when you had a log in your own? Only in this case, don't criticize your wife's stuff when you have your own big messes.

He swallowed hard as he headed to the steps to his house—stairs that he'd once bounced up in anticipation of being home.

The pink baby wreath hanging on the front door had faded from the bright Virginia sun and it now hung askew. He ripped the thing from its hook and flung it into the yard, then wiped his hands together. He'd really needed to throw something away today. Really had wanted to pitch that bike into the trash. Really craved to destroy reminders of what he'd lost.

Yet hadn't their marriage already begun to unravel before he'd lost his wife?

Stop it. Stop that. Things would have been all right. God would have gotten us through.

He shoved his hand through his hair. He was quick to credit God with things He could have done yet quicker to blame himself for the failure to save his wife.

The door swung open.

"What ya doing out here, Son?" Dad clutched baby Kelsey in one arm like a football, as he cast him a quizzical look. "And what's that baby wreath doing in the yard?"

Carter shook his head. "It's old."

"It can't be that old."

He shrugged and moved past Dad to go inside.

"I tossed all the pizza boxes you've collected, Son, and I ordered another case of formula."

Shame shimmied up Carter's backbone. He turned and extended his arms for his daughter. "Thanks, Dad."

"Yeah, no problem." Dad's mouth twitched like it did when he was about to launch into a list of complaints.

"Thought I had the Similac on auto-order."

"Maybe there was a glitch in the system."

There was a glitch. Actually, complete glitchiness ruled Carter's life—in his brain.

"Um, I stripped the sheets," Dad's voice was gentle, "and washed them while you were at your meeting."

"Thanks."

"Son, I think you should request remote work for this summer— come up north and we'll take care of you on the island."

"I'll think about it."

"That's all we can ask. Maria would love to spend time with the baby and so would I."

He stiffened and blinked at him in disbelief. "That's your high season." The family resort wasn't going to run itself.

"Your brother keeps talking about coming back from Switzerland and helping us again—him and Jaycie." Dad scratched his cheek. "Does he sound odd lately?"

Odd? Carter's whole life, his world was odd. And he was too consumed with his own stuff to notice Parker's oddness if there was any. "Haven't noticed."

There was a lot he hadn't noticed.

Hampton, Virginia

Susan Mullen forced herself not to gape at the newcomer to their grief group. That would be rude, especially because he was one of the few white guys in the room. She knew how it felt to be a minority person in a sea of white folks and get gawked at. But the realization struck her—Carter had to be the brother of her friend's son-in-law Parker. There were too many similarities to the twenty-something's story plus his distinctive name. She searched her memory for when she'd attended Jaycie Worth's wedding. Then a teenager, the younger brother, with his youthful face, only vaguely resembled this new group therapy client.

The young software analyst took a sip of his coffee. He must be in deep grief to tolerate the high octane brew the full-time staff made for them—that stuff could peel paper off the wall.

"Dude, you gotta take your meds or you're gonna end up like I did—over in the psych ward for a week." Antoine, the oldest in her group, nudged the guy sitting beside him.

The other participant shrugged.

Then Antoine focused on the newcomer. "Carter, man, we all been there and there's no shame in asking for help in this group."

"He's here, man, why don't you let him settle in?" Travis, a lean man in his forties, with skin so pale it almost looked translucent, scowled.

"Just tryin' to help."

"Thanks." A sliver of a grin tugged at Carter's lips.

This was him—Jaycie's brother-in-law. That was the beginning of the smile that she'd seen at the wedding. *No, no, no—I cannot keep him in this group!* Clinical objectivity and all that. Conflict of interest.

"You guys sound like my brother, Parker."

Susan pressed her eyes shut. Any leftover doubt galloped off like a Kentucky Derby horse out of the gate. Holding a Master of Social Work degree and certifications from the Commonwealth of Virginia, Susan took her obligations seriously, including avoiding any conflicts of interest.

"Ain't your last name Parker?" Antoine scratched his bristly chin.

"Parker Parker!" Travis barked out a laugh as the others joined in.

"That's your brother's name?" Paula Ecker, the lone female in their group, a middle-aged librarian who'd published a book on grief, straightened.

The Parkers were biological grandsons of a very famous Hollywood star, Wayne Stevens. The news had leaked to the media after his brother, Hampton Parker III, known as Parker, had visited their newly discovered grandfather. Parker went out to the movie star's ranch that previous summer. The news had jumped all over the Parker Parker thing—saying his name should be Stevens not Parker and maybe should be changed to Steven Stevens. She didn't need group members distracted further.

"Um, he's," Carter rubbed his nose, looking sheepish. "He's. . ."

"Contrary?" the woman asked, "or into that simplicity movement?"

"It ain't called that. It's Minimalism." Travis dipped his chin and pulled a smug face. "My old lady is into that."

Several of the other men hooted.

Antoine elbowed the member beside him. "Maybe she'll minimalism him out of the house."

Several of her long timers leaned in to high-five each other as they cackled. Look how far they'd come! They were laughing.

She cleared her throat. "I can see some of you are ready to graduate." She surveyed the group.

"I'm not graduating, Mrs. Mullen, but I am going to step back out until. . ." the librarian shrugged, "until the next wave hits."

Susan nodded. "You're always welcome to come back and visit with us." She admired how the woman had fit in so comfortably with all these men. Normally she'd run male-only groups, but that one had been opened up to women. Only one taker, though.

"Thank you."

Travis rose and grabbed the half-empty coffeepot and hoisted it aloft. "Anyone for a last jolt of sludge before we hit the road?"

Carter raised his mug, emblazoned with *Hampton Parks and Recreation*, the one Susan had brought in to substitute for the flaking Styrofoam disposables offered at the center. Travis filled the mug and Carter gulped several mouthfuls.

Yeah, Carter must be in deep grief because other than Travis, who was a longtime mechanic accustomed to what he called "dirt java." No one in their right mind drank that stuff.

I should call my friend, Tamara. And tell her what? *This retirement notion must be addling my brain because I cannot and will not violate confidentiality.* She should recuse herself from this group. But who would run it? *John.* Her husband could step in and do it. But this type of group wasn't really his thing.

Antoine clapped Carter's shoulder, the two men both still clutching their mugs for dear life. "You comin' back, dude?"

"Yeah, man." His earlier grin expanded. "For the coffee."

Travis laughed while Carter's lips twitched further upward.

Those two had nothing in common if you looked at the surface, and everything in common if you dug deeper. Everything that mattered right now. She couldn't take that away. She'd have to soldier on.

"Baby? You almost ready?" John startled her as he stepped into the room. When he attempted to sneak a kiss, she swiped at him.

"You know you're not supposed to be in here."

"It's over." He inclined his head toward the men dispersing.

This whole situation wasn't over though. She had to disclose to Carter that she knew who he was.

When the last member left, John locked the room's door.

Susan huffed a sigh. "If someone was your close friend's son-in-law's brother, would you let him into a group of yours?"

John made a face. "Do the friends all live here?"

"No."

"So no hangin' out with the client?"

She shook her head. "No. We met once."

"Would it do them more good or bad if you told the participant about the connection?"

"He needs this group."

She had her answer, and peace confirmed it. Carter Parker would continue in her group.

Lord have mercy.

Chapter Two

Newberry, Michigan, May

Either allow full summer visitation or my wife will set up a court date for a custody review—in which case who knows, we might have Samuel permanently." Gino's smug voice was bloated by second-hand confidence acquired from marrying one of Michigan's top attorneys. "Don't make me have you served."

That would be utter humiliation. *Why did I answer this call?* Because she'd still hoped to hear about a possible job, that's why. Alyssa pulled her cellphone away from her ear and stared down at it. She shouldn't have accepted the call when she'd not recognized the number. Clearly Gino was calling on a different phone than previously. Her thumb trembled over the red circle at the bottom of the screen, but she didn't touch it.

One of the other kitchen workers shot Alyssa a concerned glance as she hurried out of the otherwise empty cafeteria.

"You listening to me?" Gino's voice carried from the phone, accompanied by invisible smoke because his call was certainly straight from the pit.

I should have filed a complaint against him when I was a pregnant sixteen-year-old. Except for pride. Pride and fear had stopped her. Gino, then the friend of a visiting youth pastor and twenty-three years old, had offered her a ride home from youth group. She'd never seen nor heard from him again, until recently.

"You there?" he growled.

Alyssa sank onto a wooden chair outside the school cafeteria and pulled off her hairnet. Her voice, stuck in her throat, wouldn't emerge.

The Holy Spirit could intervene for her even if her tongue failed her. She returned the phone to her ear.

"Hey, you should be thanking Jennifer and me for giving you a break."

Seriously? He'd threatened to take away Sammy, and she was supposed to praise him and his new wife?

The school bell alarmed, announcing the day's end. She held the phone away from her ear and let Gino get blasted by the sounds of her world. How had she ever been charmed by this scumbag? Let him get an earful of her life.

"Hey!" His voice barely carried over the shrill ear-piercing noise. Then the phone screen showed he'd terminated the call.

Alyssa placed the phone in her skirt pocket under the heavy white apron as she stepped outside the doorway, hoping to get a glimpse of Sammy as he headed to the bus.

Doors opened along the hallway and children streamed out toward the bus queues. Alyssa waved at the little Williams twins and then stepped back into the cafeteria to grab her belongings.

As soon as she entered the brightly lit cafeteria, her phone rang again with the Nutcracker tune she used. It usually reminded her of happier days when she was young and enjoyed going to watch her cousin perform at Christmastime ballets—but right now the sound irritated her. *No doubt Gino calling again.* She huffed a sigh and pulled out her ancient Android.

The number was unrecognizable. Likely spam. But honestly, a spam call at this point would beat one from Gino. Unless it was one of the numbers from Gino's wife's law firm. Wrong area code, though—and not the one Gino had just called on.

Impulsively, she hit the accept button. "Hello?"

"Miss Teann?"

"Yes."

"This is George Ridley from Soo Township Schools." He gave a curt laugh. "I guess I should say Sault Sainte Marie instead of the Soo, but you being a Yooper know that, eh?"

"I do." She couldn't remember the last time she used the town's full name instead of the abbreviation.

"Did I catch you at a good time?"

She swallowed hard. She'd completed her course work for her computer science degree and had just begun sending out inquiries. "Yes, this is fine." She hurriedly headed to the far corner of the room, away from the doors and quieter.

"We received your resume and application and had a couple of questions."

"Oh, okay." That sounded silly saying just that. "I, um, I'm glad they came through okay." She'd submitted them electronically.

"Indeed, they did. Great GPA. But our team wondered if you'd done any internships."

She closed her eyes hard. Single parent, supporting an almost nine-year-old, working full-time during the school year and taking care of her son all summer long so she didn't have to pay childcare. "I'm afraid I wasn't able to do that."

There was a brief silence at the other end. "You're such a strong candidate. Successful intern work would have pushed you to the top of our list."

Top of their list? She opened her eyes and blurted out, "I've got some possibilities for this summer." *What?* Had she really just said that? Her so-called possibilities included potential for having her son taken away from her more than just the summer. *Liar, Alyssa the liar!*

"Well, that's super. Send us the name of the internship placement that you secure."

"Sure thing. Thanks so much for considering me for the position." And if she didn't get an internship—then what?

"Enjoy the rest of your day."

As if—but this call made it better. "Thanks."

The line went dead.

Alyssa brushed off the perspiration dotting her brow.

No internship—then no job. And no way to make a better life for her and Sammy if she didn't go out there and find one.

The phone rang again.

Gino.

Her head throbbed as she accepted the call and held the phone to her ear.

"Listen, you'll—" he let out a string of profanity and she jerked the phone away from her ear—"let us have Samuel this summer, or we're taking you to court immediately."

"Okay." What was she going to do? She certainly didn't have funds to fight this. And now she had reason to allow it, if only temporarily. If she could find an internship and get a position as a programmer, then she could support Sammy and herself more easily, without relying on her parents. *And then I could fight him and his new wife.*

"Okay take you to court? Or okay my son gets the best summer of his life?"

Defeated, she allowed tears to fill her eyes and then swiped them away. "Okay Sammy will go with you." She'd cancel all his summer camps. She'd lined up three that were free or that offered scholarships. He'd also miss his beloved VBS week.

"Glad you can be reasonable."

To use one of Grampa's expressions—*he had her over a barrel* and there was nothing reasonable about it.

Hampton, Virginia

Still another month of work as a school social worker, but Susan Mullen officially finished her group therapy sessions for the Hampton Community Services Program. That didn't stop her from thinking about her clients there. *Lord bless them all, especially Carter. He's too young to have lost his wife. Awfully young to raise a child on his own.* But God knew that, so why was she telling Him? Maybe because of the guilt she'd had for not only accepting him into her group but also not being able to say anything to her friend, Tamara, about her concern for the young man. Tam was his brother's mother-in-law and was very close with his father, too.

Her phone rang and she looked down and smiled. Tamara was great about checking in on her. "Good morning. How much snow ya got up there, girlfriend?"

"No snow. How's my challenge for you to trust God and take that leap and retire?"

Susan held her cellphone closer to her head, "I *am* trusting in God." If only Tam hadn't moved a thousand miles away, things might be easier. "I just don't know that the Lord cares about covering my insurance payments in retirement."

Susan moved closer to the coffee pot, on her kitchen counter, and poured herself another cup of decaf.

The bubbling laugh on the other end of the cellphone revealed that Tamara had heard her just fine.

Susan went to the fridge and grabbed her vanilla caramel creamer. "I know God cares about everything. . ."

"He does."

"But how do I know He's gonna stretch my budget or if He's expecting me to keep on workin'?" She poured a healthy dose of creamer into her mug.

"While you're pondering, I've got a proposition for you."

"Yeah?"

"Might help you add some options other than quit or not quit working altogether."

She didn't bother stirring the coffee but took a quick sip. *Perfect.* "Okay. Spill. Spill the tea!"

"You're using that new expression? Whatever happened to spill the beans?"

"I don't know, but my son is saying that one now, so I just picked it up."

"Makes more sense, kinda, doesn't it?"

"Yes. We all spill tea but beans—not so much. Of course, unless you're my husband, John." They both laughed. Susan took a long sip of her coffee and gazed out the window at a pair of cardinals flitting around her bird feeder in the backyard. "Tell me what you got sizzling for an idea."

"Here's the deal. You've always wanted to come up to Mackinac Island with me."

"Riiight," she drew the word out. Except that it was an incredibly long trip from Hampton, Virginia, to the Straits of Mackinac in Michigan—at least to this East Coast girl.

"This year Tom was invited to serve as consultant to a nonprofit that helps medical workers."

"That's nice. Different than dealing with. . . you know—"

"Cancer patients, right. This could be a nice transition in case he wants to do something like this later in retirement."

Carolina wrens flitted around Susan's dogwood tree, many congregating on the birdfeeder that John continually kept filled. "I'm glad Dr. Tom has this opportunity."

"Yes, the correct word, opportunity—that's what we want to offer you. What the board wants to present to you."

She set her mug on the counter, her hand wobbling slightly. "Explain, please."

"How'd you like to be our social worker consultant this summer—bring John, too, there's room—and hang out with Tom and me?"

Susan tugged at the neckline of her button-up, cornflower blue, blouse. "Yeah? Tell me more, girlfriend."

"Sure can." Tam laughed. "First of all, it pays, of course."

"It better."

"Yes, ma'am, I know your days of volunteering for anything outside of church are done."

"The group therapy program has financially been a huge blessing."

"Good. This pays well plus you'd stay on the island at a beautiful old cottage on the West Bluff—like those Victorian mansions I told you about." And had posted pictures on Facebook and Instagram.

Victorian mansions, not cottages. "I better sit down." Susan headed to the living room and sat in the recliner.

She could have sworn she heard a faint soft voice telling her to, "Listen well.'"

"We're distantly related to the owner of the cottage where it's hosted."

Hopefully not the Parkers. And hopefully no widowed Carter Parker there. "Old Butterfly Cottage?" Tamara's great-grandfather had owned the humble cottage on Mackinac Island, and Tamara's family owned the newer Butterfly Cottage on the mainland.

Tam laughed. "No. That's attached to the Parkers' resort, which is on the East Bluff on the other side of the island. This place is called Lilac Cottage."

"Nice." Especially nice that it wasn't Carter Parker's home.

"In season, the backyard is crammed full of lilacs. Smells like heaven. You'll love it."

When Tam was done explaining everything about what sounded like the most amazing job Susan ever could have, her friend said, "So you see—you have choices."

Choices.

Suddenly, her options for early retirement had expanded. God was providing.

As long as her former client wasn't there. It was one thing here in Hampton Roads, Virginia, with over a million people in the area to avoid running into the brother of her best friend's son-in-law, but it would be different on a tiny island with a circumference of only eight and two-tenths of a mile.

I never should have allowed him into the group—a conflict of interest for me to accept him. She valued her professional credentials and didn't want trouble from the Social Worker's Licensing Board.

But how in the world could I have turned that poor boy away?

Mackinac Island, Michigan, May

Carter resisted the urge to boom out the lyrics of Tauren Wells' song "Take It All Back" as he carried his daughter into her assigned nursery room—didn't want to wake her up. Not after that long trip up here. She'd been an angel herself, like the lyrics, on the flight from Virginia.

And now they were here. Fortunately, Parker Resort on the East Bluff hadn't been damaged by the severe ice storm that had happened a little over a month earlier. Canary Cottage, on West Bluff, which his stepmom, Maria, had inherited just a few years earlier, had been spared but lost many lilac trees. Carter and Kelsey were house-sitting this summer for friends at Tandem Cottage, in Hubbard's Annex. Plus he was working remotely. Once high season kicked in, Dad would be hopping. Maria was stepping back some from the hotel. She'd already promised she'd take her role as grandmother seriously. She was also voluntarily catering some of the events at Lilac Cottage's medical retreats, which were next door to Canary Cottage.

He lowered Kelsey into the expensive gold metal and glossy white crib. She stretched out on her back in her pink giraffe sleeper. He eyed the heavily padded rocking chair adjacent the crib. Maybe he needed an afternoon nap, too. This thing was super cush and looked expensive, like everything in this place. *No nap.* Too much to do. He left the room.

His phone rang and he answered his host's call. "Guess where I am?"

Cassandra Byrnes gave a full-throated laugh. "Since Colton hasn't had all the security cameras installed yet, but the front Ring camera is on, I know you're in the house, but not exactly where."

"I'm in the hallway outside the guest nursery. And since Tandem Cottage has eight bedrooms and what, sixteen rooms total—"

"Who's counting, right? We're just glad the house won't be vacant all summer."

"Thanks again for putting us up." He rubbed his hand over his cheek bristle. He and the baby were on the opposite side of the island from his folks. "Best that we're not at the resort."

There was a brief pause. "Colton thought it might be easier."

"Yeah." He bent his head. He did need some space. "How's your baby cooking?" Abbi-Renae and Cassandra both called their pregnancies that, but it still sounded odd to him. "And how're you feeling?"

The power engineer, now TV host, sighed. "If it wasn't for this contract for the Atlanta show, I'd ask HGTV to stop filming episodes. Baby doesn't like this heat."

He frowned. "How do you mean?"

"I'm on the struggle bus and I am inferring, via Mommy-Baby interconnect, that she doesn't like the heat and humidity either."

He exhaled in relief. "But nothing wrong with her nor mom—other than the summer AKA 'hell in a sauna' in Georgia like it is in Virginia?"

"Right."

"You gonna take a work break?"

"Hmm, at least a short one. Definitely after we get up there in late August."

"You won't regret it." His wife didn't get much time with their baby. *Barely any.* He gritted his teeth.

"We might also get sent on remote assignment to Alaska over the summer."

"Really?"

"Yeah, and we'll possibly be out of reach—with spotty internet."

"Wow." Was doing that during pregnancy a good idea? But Cassandra was still in the earlier months.

"You'll have to hold down the fort, or cottage in this case, while we're gone."

"Sure."

"Hey, before I forget—we hired an artist who's coming in to paint our nursery mural."

"No prob. We'll be here." *I'm going nowhere.*

"Super. We'll check in before we go off-grid."

"Okay. Thanks again and I'll talk with you later."

"Probably Colton next time, he wants to tell you all about the new car he got."

He laughed. "He's probably loving all those cars now that he's not living on the island." Cars had been banned on Mackinac since the 1890s. Only on the rare occasion was there an automobile on the island. There were emergency vehicles, though.

They said their goodbyes, and he headed toward the front of the house.

I need to tell Maria that I've arrived. Let Grandma know, too. His father was out west visiting his birth father, Carter's biological grandfather. *Dad sure earned that trip—I put him through it big time.*

Carter hoped he was on solid footing now. He wanted to be sure before he gave them the big news that he was allowed to work remotely on the island all summer. His grief support group facilitator, Mrs. Mullen, had instructed the members that when they made a big transition to allow themselves time to settle in first before sharing their news with others. The therapist had always acted a little wonky toward him. He chalked it up to him being the only guy in the group who wasn't blue collar—but she didn't act differently towards the lone woman, Mrs. Ecker, a librarian, who attended. Didn't matter now—Mrs. Mullen had helped him through the nightmare of losing Kelsey's mom.

Now the horror had dissipated, the depression lifted, and he was in the reality of single parenthood of a baby—at least that was what he told himself. His dad and his brother, recovering alcoholics, told him to "just put one foot in front of the other, one day at a time, because that's all you get."

Outside the house's large open windows, birdsong filtered in. If he was right, that was a cardinal making the loudest noise. Other than the noisy birds and the occasional sound of horses' hooves and carriages, the place was quiet, sitting back from the road on two wooded acres. This much land with a home was almost unheard of on Mackinac Island. The original owners of the cottage in the Annex had held the property for over a hundred and fifty years and hadn't sold off any land.

He checked the baby monitor on his phone. Kelsey splayed into the familiar starfish shape, indicating she was fully asleep. He headed toward his office area, where he'd set up his computers and screens, with the playpen, swing, and small toybox nearby. Fatigue oozed through him like thick honey melting through his brain.

Kelsey was getting older and her naps shorter. But his work hadn't gotten any less demanding.

I gotta find help.

Chapter Three

Nothing—not one single summer tech possibility or computer programmer internship listed anywhere in the online forums that Alyssa searched. But if she was to be hired in Sault Ste. Marie, she needed one. Seated at her parents' round oak dining room table, Alyssa closed the top of her ancient laptop. *I've messed up yet again.*

She recalled what her buddy from Advanced Programming class had told her. "Ya know, you waited too late to apply. Those internships are long gone."

Long gone. Sammy would be too, soon.

The song by Tauren Wells, contemporary music which Dad didn't allow in the house much less in church, came to mind. *God's not done with you, it's not over. . .*

Dad handed her the newspaper. "Lotsa work available on Mackinac Island."

"Computer related?"

He shook his head.

"Service jobs?" Of course they were. Just like she had now. *Pride cometh before a fall.* She set the paper before her.

Mom stepped in from the living room, the worry lines on her forehead prominently visible beneath the overhead light. The decades old wooden captain's wheel 'chandelier' with six glass covered dome lights glared down. "There's someone on the island looking for childcare."

That dug into her heart. Watching someone else's child or children, instead of her own son. That would be a constant reminder. She didn't dare reply to her mom's comment for fear of sounding ugly. Or resentful. Or any other of the many things she'd been accused of if she dared express negative emotions.

Alyssa opened the paper to the classifieds section.

"Yeah, there it is." Dad poked at the top center.

She glanced between her parents. Their expressions screamed that they'd discussed this. Did they want her gone for the summer?

CARE FOR INFANT. HOUSING OFFERED. SERIOUS CANDIDATES ONLY.

Baby wasn't as bad as caring for older children. At least not for her—because an older elementary school boy possessed her heart. "Let me look through them all."

Mom went to the coffee pot and poured herself a mug full. "Could be good for you to get away."

Her mother wasn't the warm fuzzy type, but she'd always been there for Alyssa. To hear her express what sounded like empathy surprised her. Maybe she'd picked up on how stressed Alyssa was about Sammy leaving—not that she'd dare express that sentiment directly. "Maybe so. I've had some friends who've worked there." The worst jobs were for maids. The best were waitressing at the high-end restaurants that liberally populated the downtown area. Housing, though, was a massive issue.

Dad tapped his fingers on the table. "If they'll put you up for that childcare spot, that's a big deal, as long as the dad seems *okay*." He raised his eyebrows.

She stared at him over the paper. Had he understood what had happened to her? Now that Gino was out in the open, Dad knew his part. Her father had invited the visiting youth pastor all those years ago and allowed him to bring his Air Force buddy to their group. *Look what happened there.* "Okay, Dad, I'll respond to the ad and see what happens."

Now, several days later after exchanging emails back and forth about positions and two text messages about three other job interviews, Alyssa had crossed the turquoise and sapphire expanse of the Straits of Mackinac by ferry, arriving on Mackinac Island with hordes of tourists. While those folks enjoying vacation were animated, she sat quietly, hands folded in her lap. She prayed that at least one of the jobs worked out. She intended to ask each employer after the interviews if they might also have computer work—two of them said computer skills may be needed. She needed something that she could use for the Sault Ste. Marie "Soo" Township job.

The first job interview went well even if it hadn't worked out. Doud's was the oldest continuously run family-owned grocery in the country which was impressive. *No housing.* The second interview, for restaurant openings, felt a little odd even before it had started. The owner, Mrs. Menteur, had promised her a ferry ticket and lunch. But there'd been no ticket waiting at the ferry office in St. Ignace. *Maybe she'll give me that at lunch, and I can use it when I return to begin work.*

She met Mrs. Menteur at Churrasco, her family's restaurant. The woman's deep tan contrasted sharply with her brilliant blue eyes and light ash blonde hair that had to have been hair extensions, since it reached almost to her waist. Her matching designer flared jacket and short skirt were straight off the cover of Vogue, which Alyssa occasionally stole guilty looks at in the library.

"Welcome, Alyssa. Have a seat." She gestured to a small booth to the left.

The scent of barbecued beef and pork wafted toward them. A server went by with a tray of beautiful salads. Alyssa swallowed hard. Another server, a trim younger guy with closely cropped dark hair, arrived and passed only Alyssa a menu.

"Take a look." Mrs. Menteur waved a French manicured nail toward the red leather covered menu. She arched her eyebrows at the waiter. "I'll have the usual."

"Yes, Mrs. Menteur." His dark eyes sparkled as he turned toward Alyssa. "What can I get you to drink?"

"Just water, please." She didn't want to take advantage of the woman's generosity.

"So, tell me about your work experience." Mrs. Menteur's condescending smile looked like one that had been painted on her.

Alyssa hesitated but then launched into an explanation of her work and her college training. She took a quick look at the menu. Thank God this woman was offering her lunch, because otherwise she couldn't have afforded this place.

The waiter returned and set his employer's sparkling water in front of her and then Alyssa's water.

"Thanks." Alyssa took a sip.

He took her order and quickly left. More guests were arriving and being seated around them. Mrs. Menteur offered all newcomers a serene, if fake, smile.

The waiter returned and set the soup bowl in front of Alyssa. Mrs. Menteur gestured for her to eat. For some reason, Alyssa didn't feel comfortable praying in front of this lady, although she normally would have. Instead, she lifted the spoon to her mouth.

"Is there any reason in particular that you decided to apply at my restaurant?" She asked this with a tone suggesting Alyssa had a nefarious reason.

She swallowed the delicious creamy potato soup hard. "I need a job." *I'm desperate.* "And you have openings."

"We do." She pressed her fingertips together, in front of her. "Beside the wait staff, we have a few others open."

Alyssa listened as Mrs. Menteur discussed the flat-out menial to those requiring a business management skillset. "Of course, you don't have the training to do the management jobs, do you?" Mrs. Menteur's mocking tone could have curdled the cream in the soup.

What was this woman playing at? *Bizarre.* And why, this being late May, hadn't she filled all those slots?

"But what do you think you'd be most proficient at?" Again, the mocking tone as she raised her wine glass to her lips.

"To be honest, if you have any need for computer skills, that would be ideal." *Why did I say that?*

The woman's steely gaze showed what she thought of that notion.

"But, since you didn't mention any, I imagine I could—"

The woman's iPhone rang and she tapped to take the call and held the phone to her ear and slipped from the booth and stood. Then she turned and walked away toward the back of the restaurant.

Alyssa placed crackers into the rest of her soup, afraid to have done so earlier, lest she make a mess or do something that went against etiquette, heaven forbid. She slowly finished her bowl of soup. The restaurant owner hadn't said anything about the ferry ticket. *I'll mention it when she returns.*

Alyssa finished her soup, and the waiter came and removed her bowl and spoon.

"Would you like to order anything else?"

"I don't think so."

He slipped a bill in front of her.

She raised her palm. "Oh, I believe Mrs. Menteur is taking care of this."

"She didn't say so. I just saw her back in the kitchen."

"But. . . she told me in her email that she would provide lunch." *As well as a ferry ticket.*

He shook his head slowly. "Her bill isn't on there, just yours. She said nothing."

"Could you go ask her?" She hated how desperate her voice sounded. *Whiny.*

"She's gone. Left for another appointment."

Alyssa gaped.

"Sorry." The waiter left the table.

From the booth in front of her, a handsome dark-haired man with tortoise square framed glasses swiveled to the side and looked at her. "Sounds like you've been Menteured."

She frowned. "I'm actually seeking a computer mentor, an internship."

He stood as his lunch companion also scooted out. The stranger was over six feet tall, and dressed in khakis and a light blue Oxford shirt. He extended his hand. "I'm Clark Jeffries and I overheard your convo about Mrs. Menteur stiffing you on the tab." He gave a curt laugh as the other person in the booth also stood.

"Oh. She really did say that she'd cover it."

"Yeah, she says that a lot. Doesn't she, Molly?" He gestured to his lunch partner, a full-figured woman with frizzy golden curls clipped up on the side of her head.

The middle-aged woman snorted. "She's pulled that so many times now, that we've got a betting pool going on over at Horn's Bar. What's it up to now, Junior?"

"Don't call me Junior unless you want to pay the bill." Clark crinkled his nose.

Molly waved toward Clark. "His dad is also named Clark and we used to always call this Clark 'Junior' to avoid confusion."

Alyssa cocked her head. "So you only identify yourself as Clark Jeffries, Jr., for professional purposes?"

"Yeah, or to avoid confusion. Molly isn't confused, she's being a brat."

"Back to Menteur and her numbers, Clark." Molly raised her eyebrows.

It's only May, but she's already had a dozen applicants who— just like you," he waved toward the check, "have been presented a bill for what they thought was a free meal."

"Is she. . ." She made a motion toward the side of her head. "A little off or something."

Molly guffawed. "That's one way to put it."

Clark raised his dark eyebrows. "She's a piece of work, that's for sure. I often wonder, when I see her in the church pew, how she can live with her dishonesty."

"Wow, she's a churchgoer?" Not that Alyssa had any right to point a finger. As Dad said—point one at other sinners and four fingers point right back at yourself.

"She is." Clark grabbed her bill. "It's on me this time."

Molly pulled it from his hands and examined it. Then she grinned at Alyssa. "Smart girl, you, only ordering soup and water."

"I'll do it as a business expense." Clark pulled out his wallet.

"But we haven't done any business together."

He grinned, revealing perfectly straight white teeth. "We did. I met you here and explained that unfortunately I don't have an internship available right now."

She blinked at him.

Molly poked Clark's arm. "He has the Eastern Upper Peninsula's premiere computer consulting business."

"Where are you graduating from?" He took the bill back from Molly and then handed her tab and theirs to the waiter as he passed.

"Just received my degree from Lake Superior State." She left off that she'd done it mostly online.

His features tugged in surprise. "You've already finished?"

She swallowed back embarrassment. "Yes. I'm very late to the game. But the one position that wants me also requires an internship—which I failed to get last summer due to other commitments." *Like parenting.* "Nothing available in Newberry."

Clark nodded. "Ah, right. I do some work over there. And who has got you on the hook but is waiting for a practice run?"

She chewed her lower lip. "The Soo schools."

"Yup. Schools and many others want to check the boxes, cross the t's and all that."

"Yeah, I could never work for a group like that." Molly patted her hair, which was sliding out of its clasp.

Clark laughed. "Don't I know it."

The other woman elbowed him. "Hey, watch it little cousin."

"If you're still here tonight, we'll be at Patrick Doud's Irish pub around eight."

Was he flirting with her? No. *Couldn't be.* "I'm afraid I'll have to head back." Because Sammy would have a meltdown if she didn't tuck him in at bedtime. Although he'd need to get used to that quickly. But she also couldn't afford dinner here.

"If that dragon Menteur hires you, come by our office sometime this summer." Molly winked at her.

The waiter returned, handed Clark his credit card, and had him sign the electronic payment device. "Hey, be sure to tell your boss that I paid the bill for her."

"Haha. Thanks, man." The waiter grinned at Clark, who must have tipped generously.

She smiled at the attractive programmer, too. "Yes, thanks. I really appreciate it." This guy was about her own age and owned his own company.

"It'll be worth it when Menteur hears she was foiled."

Clark handed Alyssa a crisp white embossed business card. "Our address and phone number. Email me your resume in case I hear of any openings."

"That's very kind. Thanks so much." Alyssa's face heated at this man's generosity.

"We EUP Yoopers look after our own." Molly nodded.

"Eastern Upper Peninsula rocks." She and Molly did a fist bump.

"And as you can tell, Menteur isn't a Yooper woman." Clark cringed.

Alyssa laughed. "I kinda got that vibe."

Molly's phone trilled a samba beat. "Oops, we better go. Got a meeting."

"See ya." Clark followed his cousin out.

Alyssa waited a moment in her seat, re-checking the time for her next appointment. *As much as I don't want to bother with this childcare job, I guess I'd better go through with the final interview.* Probably not much chance of computer skills usage with an infant.

She headed over to Market Street, to Lucky Bean, and went inside and inhaled the rich aromas of coffee beans and baked goods. Alyssa stepped to the back of the queue. She needed to fortify herself for the final interview. In an hour, she was supposed to meet Mr. Parker at a little bakery, The Christy Tea Shop, several doors down from the coffee shop. After she had her coffee, she'd scope out exactly where the tea shop was.

At the front of the line, a tall silver-haired man moved toward the register. Immediately ahead of Alyssa, a teenage girl in an adorable pink and silver mini-skirt, leggings, and sparkly top with matching flats took a step forward.

Behind the shiny glass cases to the left, a trio of baristas worked at a steady pace. That looked like a fun job. The gentleman at the front placed his order and stepped aside as the pink teen ordered a caramel frappe.

Alyssa scanned the board on the counter. *Love Potion #9? Interesting name for a drink.*

When it was her turn, she hesitated. "Um, what can you tell me about Love Potion #9?"

The cashier, a nice-looking dark-haired guy about her age, raised his hands. "I'm not sure. Rumor is the boss got engaged near the time the baristas came up with it."

"Oh, uh," she'd just wondered what it tasted like. "I'll try the frappe version."

"Sure thing. Name?"

She stared at him for a moment. She was about to say, 'Sammy,' then she caught herself. For so long, in her hometown, she'd had them put *Sammy's Mom* on the cup. "Alyssa."

"Alright, Alyssa, we'll have it up shortly."

She stepped aside and went to a rack where imprinted merchandise was displayed. A smiling barista called out, "Jeff!" and brought a cup out to the tall man.

She glanced through the front window, where a long carriage passed by, a tour group of about twenty people. Alyssa also scanned the tables out front, seeing none open. *Drats.* She needed to decompress before the last interview. Just a few moments alone at a table outdoors.

"Angel!" Another barista handed a frappe container to the teen.

Alyssa moved back toward the glass counter.

"Can you believe I'm making another Love Potion?" The barista, a muscular guy sporting a thick beard, winked at his co-worker, a beautiful brunette, who stuck out her tongue at him.

Alyssa tried to stifle her grin.

When the drink was finished, the bearded dude brought it around. "Alyssa?"

"That's mine." She smiled at him. He sported a new-looking thick wedding ring inset with multiple diamonds.

"Here's your Love Potion."

A little embarrassed at having this announced out loud, Alyssa took her drink and spun around.

"Whoops!" A handsome blond guy, with sad light blue eyes, grabbed her elbow before she ran into him and something else. With his other hand, he clutched a stroller. The adorable occupant, a baby about six months old grinned, revealing four little white teeth. Maybe closer to eight months old. She clutched a tiny unicorn that matched her pink unicorn shoes.

Alyssa was filled with gratitude that she'd not spilled anything. "Sorry."

"No problem." It looked like his lips were trying to twitch upward but failed.

"It's a cold frappe," she explained, "so baby wouldn't have gotten burned."

He blinked at her.

"She'd just have gotten a little messy. But babies, do, don't they? I mean they can go through like five outfits in a day!" She forced a chuckle. She was babbling. Why was she doing that?

Regardless, it was good the attentive father had kept her from tossing her frappe at the baby.

This time he did smile. A rusty laugh made its way past his lips. "You've got that right. She can out-mess the best of them."

"Have a good day." Alyssa bent and smiled at the munchkin, who was waving her toy. "You, too, little miss. You're so cute. Yes, you are!"

Then, cheeks hot with embarrassment, she headed outside, praying for an open table. *Yes.* A spot opened as a woman in an electric wheelchair and her two older lady companions departed, empty cups in hand. They tossed the cups in the nearby trash can. At home, Alyssa didn't allow herself the luxury of a frappe but today felt special, despite her disappointment with the interviews.

That little girl and her dad were adorable. Maybe that kind of job could be okay.

She slid onto the metal seat. *Better not act like such a goof when I do my interview.*

A couple rode by on a tandem bike. They laughed and looked like they were having so much fun. Sadness flitted in her spirit—Sammy had hated the tandem ride. Could have been from all the sensory stuff. Although his difficulties on the autism spectrum were mild, if he got an overload of input, he could shut down super-fast.

Two men with navy blue T-shirts with *Cross-wire Computers* emblazoned on the front sauntered past. Disappointment twanged within her. *No internship.* She may even have to wait another year before finding one. And the job in the Soo would likely be gone. And would her son be off with his father and new stepmother? Could they even manage a child on the spectrum? They'd pooh-poohed her concerns, but Jennifer had no children, and this was Gino's only child. How would they deal with regular kid stuff, much less Autism Spectrum Disorder issues?

I have to find a job and keep my boy with me.

Maybe Clark Jeffries and Molly could come up with something for her. A girl could hope.

She chewed on her lower lip. No wonder her boy had this same bad habit. Poor kid sometimes had sores from biting the inside of his lip.

The young father backed out of the coffee shop door and then carefully turned the stroller around.

She shouldn't have been staring at him—and why was she doing that—because he locked eyes on her. She averted her gaze and drank more of her frappe, which should have tasted amazing but suddenly seemed chalklike, although she didn't know why.

"Mind if I—if we—join you?" The hunky dad, who appeared close to her age, slumped into the chair beside her before Alyssa could respond. He immediately focused his attention on his daughter, who was tossing her toy to the ground. *Repeatedly.*

He leaned in closer to his daughter. "Uhn, uhn. I'm gonna keep baby unicorn then."

The little girl, who had striking dark gray eyes, grabbed for the toy and pulled it close to her chest.

Alyssa should go. Find someplace else to sit that was more private. Collect her thoughts. But maybe this was good practice for the upcoming interview to have this tourist and his baby hang out with her for a bit. Maybe God planned this so she could be ready. After all, this guy was probably much more approachable than the wealthy, likely older dad, who'd be interviewing her soon for a summer live-in spot. She began to relax.

The stranger pointed to the backs of the two men with the matching computer ad T-shirts and snorted. "Those clowns couldn't program their way out of a paper bag."

"You're a programmer?"

"Yup. And I don't have to wear a T-shirt that announces it."

"I'm also—well, I'm studying to be—a programmer." If she ever got a position. First though, an internship could sure help.

Chapter Four

That's cool." His Spidey senses zapped an alert. Why this sudden onset of angst? His wife had been a fellow computer science major, that's why. But he'd worked with other female programmers.

"I've been employed while completing my studies—and of course there was that little thing called a pandemic—so it's taken a while to finish." She sipped her frappe and averted her gaze.

"I took a year off school during the pandemic. Crazy times." He shook his head and then pulled his phone from his pocket and checked the time. Still had a half hour till the interview.

The pretty tourist reached over and pulled the side shade down on the carriage. "It's getting a little sunny." She lifted her gaze overhead.

"Right." He should have noticed. During the worst of the grief, he'd been too much into his own self. Too caught up in his depression. *This doesn't feel like that kind of distraction.*

Kelsey started wriggling. Hopefully, he'd not have to rush down to the public toilets to change her, but that was a distinct possibility. He bent and released all the straps that held her in the stroller and checked her diaper. No blue line on the front, so she was dry, and no landfill in the back—which she sometimes produced.

He pulled her into his arms. He'd never imagined how much he'd love being a dad.

"Do you mind if I hold her?" The woman extended her hands.

Carter hesitated, clutching his daughter more closely to his chest. What was this computer nerd gonna do—run off with Kelsey? This was Mackinac Island, and she'd get no farther than the harbor with the baby. Not only that, but the police were right across the street. "Sure." He passed his precious bundle over to the woman.

Her soft brown eyes widened as she took his girl into her arms and held her straight out in front of her. "Hello, precious! Aren't you the prettiest baby ever?" She leaned in and wriggled her nose. "Yes, you are!" Her voice had taken on a babytalk tone like his stepmother used. "Yes, you are the cutest baby on Mackinac Island if not the world. Uh huh."

Kelsey quieted. When the tourist rotated her onto her lap, The baby's gray eyes widened as she stared up at the woman and she giggled. His kid looked like she was in love with a complete stranger.

This was awkward. The woman looked way more comfortable with his own daughter than he was. She seemed very kind.

"So, are you two on a big vacay?" She smiled first down at the baby, who was still grinning, and then at him.

"Kind of." *Not really.* He wasn't going to discuss his personal business with her. *Then how am I gonna manage the upcoming interview for a sitter?* "How about you?"

A carriage rolled past, the huge Percheron horses' hooves making the sound that he'd recorded and put on his sleep tape for the nights in Virginia during the worst of the grief-induced insomnia. Horses' hooves, seagulls squawking, and Lake Huron's lapping waves were his comfort sounds.

"Oh. . ." She leaned over and adjusted the ruffle on the bottom of Kelsey's little dress. "I'm here for a job interview."

"Oh, wow. Mackinac Computer Solutions?" He'd seen their ad, but that was for IT. He knew his buddy, Clark Jeffries, had no openings, so it wasn't him.

Her cheeks flushed a pretty pink. "No."

Kelsey began to cry, and the woman raised his baby to her shoulder.

"Internship?"

"Nope. Couldn't find one this summer."

When had she started looking? Or were her grades bad? He had no room to judge, given that he'd almost not gotten one. "Sorry. Sometimes companies don't hire because the supervisors don't have time to do oversight." That's what had happened at his employer.

She frowned. "Maybe. But honestly, I started looking way too late."

"I get that." He finished off his drink. "What will you be doing on the island?" Likely waitressing, which could bring in big bucks during the high season.

Sunlight brought out the gold in her light brown hair as she rubbed Kelsey's back. "Believe it or not, I've got an interview for childcare work."

"Really?" *Definite Spidey senses happening.*

"Yes. In fact, as much as I'd be glad to cuddle little Miss Cutie Pie all day, I better go freshen up before my interview."

She adjusted Kelsey in her arms and held her facing Carter.

He didn't take the baby.

Although the attractive dad should accept his daughter back, he was typing something on his phone. Her Android buzzed, indicating a text message.

He pointed toward her phone, set on the tabletop. "Bet that's from me."

She raised her eyebrows and then she looked down at the phone. "You're Mr. Parker?" Not the forty-something guy with a dad bod that she'd imagined. On the other hand, she'd been only sixteen when her son was a baby. She'd had him beat for youthful parenting.

He smiled broadly, for the first time. "Me, my dad, and brother go by that title. And probably a lot of other Parkers out there."

She averted her gaze, down to the infant in her arms. *Yikes.* Thank goodness she'd not said anything stupid. Or had she? "Is this little Miss Parker, then?"

"Yes, after much negotiating with my wife, she accepted the baby having a singular rather than hyphenated name."

He needed childcare, though. Where was the wife? Would she be there, too? "Will your wife be joining us for the actual interview, then?" She knew her own smile was wobbly, but she needed this job. And maybe, just maybe, this guy could also help her with her programming stuff—who knew? She wouldn't push it, though. Not with him. There was a woundedness that she recognized, and she didn't want to upset him.

"Uh, no." He rocked back in his seat. "She's, um, in Virginia. She, uh, she's gotta stay there. At least for now." He grabbed for his cup and tried to drink, but from his expression it must have been empty.

Alyssa bounced the baby on her lap. "Sorry. That's not really my business."

"No. It's all right."

She bit her lower lip.

An attractive brunette, wearing expensive-looking oversized glasses, attired in a flowing midi dress approached them. Her high platform espadrilles looked uncomfortable but were stylish.

"Carter Parker!" The woman pushed her sunglasses up, revealing large expressive eyes. "I'm glad to see you've come home."

Home? He'd said he lived in Virginia. Where his wife had remained. *Strange.*

"Yup. My job let me work remotely. But I haven't let anyone know yet."

"Oooh. It's a surprise?"

"Yup." But the muscle jumping in his cheek suggested more. Much more than a surprise. A secret, maybe?

The woman drew her horizontal hand over her mouth. "Zipped shut."

Carter nodded. "Had to get a cup of your delicious brew first thing."

Alyssa frowned. The way he said it sounded like he'd only just arrived. But had he?

He gestured from Alyssa to the stranger. "This is Carolyn May, the owner of the famed Lucky Bean!"

Carolyn did an adorable little half curtsey. "I don't know about famed, but I'm grateful for the success we've had."

Alyssa pointed to her empty frappe container. "I can see why. My frappe was fantastic." Not that she regularly indulged. Not as a single parent working at a cafeteria and going to school.

"Thank you." Carolyn touched the baby's cheek. "So soft. She's adorable." There was a wistful longing in the beautiful lady's eyes.

"She is," Alyssa agreed. She looked to Carter, but he was staring past Carolyn, into the street.

"How old is she? And do you mind if I hold your baby?" Carolyn directed her attention directly to Alyssa.

Expecting Carter to respond, Alyssa hesitated, gaping. When he didn't, she closed her mouth and dipped her chin. The coffee shop owner knew him. But she didn't know he was the father to this baby. *More oddness.*

Alyssa had been floating the notion of passing herself off as not being a mom. Reinventing herself for just one summer. Trying on what it might have been like to be a twenty-six-year-old independent woman. She often wondered this at home, but now she'd have a chance to live it. Because of Gino. Her stomach soured.

As Carolyn took the little girl, Alyssa's arms felt empty. She rubbed them. If she got this job, she could be tight-lipped like this man. She could have a taste of what it might be like if Sam's father and his new wife got permanent custody. If she moved and didn't have her boy with her, she didn't have to explain his absence at every turn like she would have to do in her hometown. What would that be like? She'd never been on her own. But the future she'd planned had been with her and her boy—in another town—with a new start.

Like the Tauren Wells' song, she could hear the lyrics in her mind, 'God's not done with you.' Maybe God had a new start planned.

The coffee shop door opened and a woman peered out. "Hi, Carolyn. I thought I saw you."

"Oops, that's my manager. I better go." The shop owner's long dark tresses fell forward as she carefully passed Kelsey back to Alyssa.

"I'm Alyssa, by the way."

"Nice to meet you and your little girl."

Alyssa's mouth dropped open, but Carter said nothing.

When Carolyn left them, Carter took the baby, rechecked her diaper, and placed her back in the stroller. "Would you like to walk Market Street for a bit?"

"Sure."

"We could go up to the house, in the carriage, if you'd like to see where you'll be living."

Where would she be living?

"Am I hired?" She'd not said yes.

She'd not said yes to Gino, either.

He should have corrected Carolyn, but he couldn't. To say his dead wife's name always made it too real. He was in reality now but that didn't mean that saying her name didn't start some unwanted waterworks. And nose blowing. Mrs. Mullen and the others in group said it would come in time. *Nope, not going there right now.*

If Carolyn didn't know about Abbi-Renae being dead, did that mean Maria, Dad, and Gran had kept the news off the Mackinac gossip line? Had to be. Immense relief coursed through him. He could pretend she wasn't dead.

That she'd not bled to death in their bathtub while he'd been out for a joy ride on his new bike. *I should have been there.*

"Mr. Parker? Carter?"

"Um hmm?"

"Can you tell me more about the specifics?"

He pushed Kelsey on toward where the carriage was parked. He wasn't functioning as well as he thought he was. He'd been afraid this would happen. But he'd hoped that Mackinac would bring some healing. "Of course, I'm working remotely, so I'll be working from home."

Alyssa nodded.

He rattled off the pay, the hours, the end date.

She repeated back the salary and looked like she was swallowing hard.

He'd doubled it since the first two applicants turned out to be duds. And then he'd had no one else interested. Alyssa was his only person to answer his ad.

What else could he add? "Oh, there are all kinds of bikes at your disposal. You don't have to bring your own if you don't want. And since we're out from town, you'll have the carriage at your disposal on your off days." But who would drive her? He'd deal with that later. "And I can have meals brought in when you're working, or I'll cook. I don't want you to worry about that since I don't have a personal chef up there."

"A personal chef," she repeated, eyes wide.

"Nope. Don't have one there. Hope that's not a deal breaker."

She touched his arm. "There's just one thing."

Lord, I need some help here. You're supposed to send the angels in for me like that Tauren Wells' song says. Or were the lyrics that Carter was supposed to call the angels down himself?

"I really need an internship badly. Is there any chance your employer could sponsor me?"

He opened his mouth to tell her 'no, there's no chance of that,' but he clamped his lips shut. "I'll see what I can do." And what made him say that?

"Fantastic. I think I could come on board—definitely if you could get me that internship option, too."

She didn't sound fully committed. And how could he disappoint her with the truth?

And what about her references? He didn't call until after he'd done interviews. He'd need to call hers. Yet he'd already offered the position. He pointed to the nearby driveway, where his carriage was parked. "That's our ride." Funny how a shiny emerald-green carriage drawn by a couple of strong young horses was the equivalent of a souped-up sports car on the mainland.

"Really?"

"Yeah, we've got a driver for today." His friend Jason, who liked to gamble at the casino in St. Ignace, needed some extra cash.

Jason tipped his baseball cap to them.

"Let me take the baby for you while you put the stroller in back." Alyssa opened her arms for Kelsey as Carter shifted the diaper bag and removed his girl.

Soon they were all loaded into the carriage and heading up to Tandem Cottage.

As Jason directed the team on, Carter mentally reviewed the rest of his checklist. 1. Availability for summer—confirmed, 2. Good with Kelsey—excellent, not just good, 3. Not a raving psycho—verdict was out on that since she was a fellow computer science nerd.

He shrugged out the tightness in his shoulders. He'd found out quickly, after the wedding, just how many issues his wife had. He'd thought he knew her well. He'd been so wrong. Yes, she'd had her idiosyncrasies, and he'd thought she was possibly on the spectrum, like a lot of techies, but the marriage counselor's test results were an eye opener. That day, when they'd read each other's personality assessment results, had been a game changer for him. After the session, he'd stayed behind and asked the therapist if Abbi's results were someone else's or what. He'd watched her carefully complete the form. She'd not given her answers randomly. The therapist confirmed that she'd hand-scored them herself and that she'd redo them. Which she had. *Same results.* And he'd remembered the crushing defeat in his soul as he'd asked God to help him with his marriage and to change his wife.

Shouldn't be thinking ill of the dead. Grandma Kareen had put up with Grandpa Hampy for decades, but Carter respected that she didn't bad-mouth him.

Guilt, that horrible companion, crept up on him. Carter should have been there for Abbi-Renae. Shouldn't have gone for a bike ride. Should have put cameras all over their Yorktown house like Colton had suggested, to monitor the baby. But they'd not have placed one in their bathroom, regardless.

He wiped sweat from his forehead.

Alyssa pointed to the long bricked semi-circular drive and gaped. "Is this your place?"

"No, it belongs to some friends." He should probably tell her, on the off chance that she'd seen their show. "It's a Frank Lloyd Wright home redesigned by Cassandra and Colton Byrnes."

He saw no recognition on her pretty face. "Do you watch HGTV?"

"Too busy for that."

"They have a show about mixing function and comfort with high tech."

"Wow. That's wonderful. How do you know them?"

"Long story, but Colton is an islander who landscaped with me."

"Beautiful how this is landscaped with the lilac trees in the center and the hollies surrounding." Her eyebrows rose. "Either landscaping pays fantastic here or his life took a major pivot."

"Pivot." Carter would share the specifics some other time. "And their lives are changing again with the addition of a baby girl due later this year."

"Their first?"

"Yup."

"That is a big change." Her lips briefly compressed, then relaxed.

Marriage had been a bigger change for Carter than welcoming baby Kelsey. Because his wife was on the spectrum, and might never be as emotionally available to him as he wished, was tough. He'd wondered if she'd be the same toward their daughter. Maybe that's why he'd taken a bike ride that day. He'd been running away from figuring out how he'd insulate newborn Kelsey from her mother.

Abbi-Renae may have ended up overcoming her problems and could have become a great mom. On the other hand, might Abbi have become like her own toxic mother?

He'd never know.

Chapter Five

Hampton Roads, Virginia

Susan clutched the contract offer that Tam had sent through good old-fashioned snail mail and blinked in disbelief. Either the Mackinac Island Medical Retreat contract had an error in the number of zeros after the salary amount or her eyeglass prescription needed correction. Her heartbeat surged in agreement with the figure.

"John! Would you come look at this?" She slid her glasses down and pointed at the contract, printed on heavyweight creamy paper.

Her husband looked over her shoulder. He whistled. "They're gonna pay you that, honey? For only eight weeks of work?" He pulled a chair up alongside her.

She pushed her glasses back up her nose. "Unless it's a typo."

"Wooo." John leaned back. "I'd like to say, 'that's more like it,' but with us both having been social workers, I know that's not the usual pay." He rocked further back, holding onto the table.

She slapped at his hand. "Don't do that. You're going to tip over."

He straightened the chair's legs back down. "We could add more elder care for your momma."

Susan crinkled her nose. "Not that she'd accept more." But he'd hit on her main concerns about the trip. "What about our yard?"

Her husband of over thirty years pointed at the bottom of the page. "Don't tell me that won't pay for lawn service, too."

"And my medical appointments. What about those?"

"You know what this sounds like?"

She shrugged. "Someone being reasonable?"

"Sounds like a worrier, worrying her way out of this opportunity."

She had to agree.

"Sounds like all the excuses you've piled up about not retiring and doing some things with me now that I'm home."

"That's not fair."

He rose. "Seems God has thrown a great opportunity right into your lap, possibly answering your prayers, and you want to toss it back at Him." He pretended to throw a ball.

"All right." She raised her hands in surrender. "I'll call the elder care agency and see if my mother needs more helpers during our absence."

"And I'll get quotes on lawn care. Pat, next door, has great guys that help him out. Not cheap—but reasonable."

"Okay."

"When do you have to let them know?"

"Tam's husband, Dr. Austin, said within two weeks."

"I'll get right on this." He clapped his hands. "Early retirement, here my wife comes!"

Susan glared at him. "John Mullen, a summer's work doesn't mean I'm retiring early." *Gives me more options is what it does.*

"But it does mean I can finally see where all that fudge is made that Tamara sends us every year." Lines formed around John's eyes as he smiled.

"That'll be fun." She'd watched videos of confectioners pouring the hot fudge mix onto marble slab topped tables and then pushing it with a huge wooden turner. Not that she'd be indulging this summer with her new blood sugar issues.

"Guess what I've heard?"

"What?"

"They give you free samples." John patted his stomach.

She shook her head. "That could work. You eat the samples and don't bring any back to the cottage for me."

"Are we going?"

"Yes. We're going."

Mackinac Island

The bitter taste of stale coffee clung to Carter's tongue as he stared at his computer screen. His head ached. A giant marshmallow had apparently squished into his brain and was sambaing in there. Or maybe it was a rhumba. He and his wife had learned both at the dance classes they'd taken while she was pregnant.

He lifted the oversized white HGTV mug to his lips and downed the last of his caffeine for the day. If only he knew Carolyn May's secret coffee recipes over at Lucky Bean—maybe then he'd enjoy his cup of morning joe. Kelsey would wake soon. He set his mug down and rubbed his eyes.

I need help. And so far, I don't have it.

His phone pinged with a text message. *Alyssa.*

Although she'd given him a tentative "yes" and not the resounding one he'd hoped for, Carter understood why she needed to consider the offer. It was a big commitment. His ever-present state of exhaustion assured him of that fact.

May I call you? Alyssa texted.

Promising. He rolled his chair back from the desk and stood. He called her number.

"Hello?"

"Good morning, Alyssa, this is Carter." No doubt she had his name on the number, but you never knew for sure.

"Oh, thanks." She sounded breathless. "I just had a couple questions."

"Shoot away." He gritted his teeth. He was beginning to sound just like his dad. That TV commercial, about how to not sound like your parents, was aimed at people like Carter. He was a twenty-four-year-old going on fifty.

"First of all, I'd love to help take care of your beautiful baby."

"Awesome." He shoved his hand through his messy hair. *Need a cut.*

"And the package you offered was amazing."

He heard a "but" in her tone. "But?"

"I know you said even if you could get your work to agree, you may be too busy to sponsor even an. . . um, an informal intern."

He was glad he'd come clean with her on that before she'd left the island that day.

She'd been so disappointed. He'd seen that in her soft brown eyes. But he didn't have time to finish his own stuff much less ask the company for an intern—and their slots had been filled for months and assigned. "Yeah, I'm sorry, I don't know how I could do it."

There was a long pause. He turned and surveyed the large open concept space, which had become a monster mess since he'd arrived. He'd have to hire a housekeeper, too. And if Alyssa didn't take care of Kelsey, then how would he get any work done at all? "What if I try to use my contacts to pull in . . . at least a brief internship that you could do in your off hours?" *Please, dear God, I need some help.*

"Oh, wow, that would be so amazing."

"Could you promise you wouldn't bail on me if I find you something?" Where, though, he had no idea. Clark Jeffries wasn't hiring nor accepting interns. It would have to be someone who'd accept a remote intern at this late date. *Unlikely.*

"Absolutely."

"So have I sealed the deal?"

"Yes. If you can do that for me, I'll let my parents know."

"Great. When can you come? I can send someone to pick you up from the ferry if you give me the day and arrival time."

"How about the three o'clock Arnold Line tomorrow?"

Star Line had been purchased by the new owners of Shepler's and now renamed to Arnold's, which had been a long-running ferry service in decades earlier.

"Arnold ferry tomorrow at three, then?" He scratched his cheek. He needed a shave. A shower. Actual clothes and not pajamas before she arrived.

"Tomorrow too soon?"

"No, no, that's great."

"I'll text the arrival time."

"Great."

Instead of the sound of Percheron horses plodding toward the Annex, Carter imagined a calvary stampeding toward him, with Alyssa on the lead stallion. He must have been watching too many of his grandfather's old movies.

But the relief he felt had to have been like those of the people in the fort who were about to be rescued.

Newberry, Michigan

Attired in a snug-fitting, black pinstripe two-piece pantsuit with four-inch black patent stiletto heel pumps, Gino's new wife, Jennifer Fredda, and Alyssa's son's new stepmother, couldn't have looked more out of place in Alyssa's neighborhood had she tried. Although maybe the woman had. *Maybe that was the point.*

Alyssa couldn't help but overhear Jennifer's strident whisper to Gino, "Seriously? That's it? The kid doesn't have anything else he's bringing with him?"

Heat shot up Alyssa's chest to her scalp. How dare she refer to this precious boy as *the kid*! If she'd said it loud enough for all to have heard, Alyssa would have called her on it. When Jennifer looked in her direction, Alyssa crossed her arms and glared, sending a definite message that the attorney had been overheard.

At least she had the decency to blush.

Her son's stepmom, in person, appeared older than her pictures suggested, with heavy wrinkles on her forehead and around her eyes and mouth. "That's everything then?" Condescension weighted down her voice. Apparently, her embarrassment had been fleeting. Very fleeting. *Very lawyerlike.*

Dad stepped forward, carrying the two old suitcases that were ordinarily used for mission trips or church conventions. "Yup. He's all set."

The black Lexus SUV hogging all the free space in their driveway was plastered with bugs on the front grill, giving Alyssa a perverse sense of justice. The Northwoods, and its insects, couldn't be traversed without acquiring a thick layer of bug goo.

Jennifer's nose crinkled as she followed Alyssa's gaze. "Is there a car wash near here?"

"It's just going to get covered again on the trip back," Gino told her.

"But I want it cleaned, now!" she snapped.

Alyssa stiffened. If this woman acted like that toward her husband, how was she going to be all summer? Did Sammy stand a chance?

Gino saluted Jennifer. "Yes, ma'am."

Dad set the bags down, his eyes conveying disapproval.

Sammy ran back from the SUV and wrapped his arms around her. This was her boy. She didn't want to share him. Not with these people. Not with this dad who had barely been involved in his life. Nine more years till adulthood. Nine more years of this. Nine years till he was eighteen and could make his own decisions. Her friends had told her that a lot of judges let kids decide at sixteen, or even younger, if the child wanted to continue visitation. Maybe only seven more years then.

Mom wrapped her arm around Alyssa's waist, a rare action. "Sweetie, God will be with him."

Of course He would. That was a given. Alyssa resisted the urge to give a retort. Sometimes it felt like her mom thought Alyssa was still a child. Maybe it was because Mom had basically co-parented with her.

She turned toward Mom, suddenly realizing how she might be taking this whole situation. "Mom, you're finally an empty nester."

Mom blinked at her. "Just for the summer." It looked like she was chewing her inner lip. She was holding back.

"Right." But if somehow Carter Parker could get her an internship and then Alyssa got the job, both she and her son would be moving out.

"If those two creeps keep him all summer, I'll be a monkey's uncle." Mom gave a curt laugh.

She grinned at the archaic expression her maternal grandpa sometimes used. "A monkey's aunt, Mom, not uncle?"

Mom shrugged.

"On the other hand . . . Jennifer," Mom said the woman's name with disgust, "strikes me as the type who won't accept any kind of failure. So maybe they won't give up easily. Maybe it will just be me and your dad all summer all alone. Except that your sister and her family will have their RV out at the lake for the month of July."

Alyssa gaped. Gayle had never mentioned she was coming, much less with her entire family. Neither had Mom nor Dad. Not even when she'd shared with them about her job on the island and that she'd be gone the entire summer. "When did Gayle decide that?"

"Just today."

Probably after Mom had told her that not only would Sammy be gone, but Alyssa, too. That hurt. It hurt almost as much as watching her child be taken away from her. *Not taken away.* But it felt like that. *Just for the summer.*

She tried to process her mother's words. No wonder she and Dad had seemed just a little weird this morning, a little smug almost. Their oldest child was coming to spend time with them. They weren't going to be encumbered by their youngest daughter, who'd gotten pregnant as a teenager, and her illegitimate child.

Stop. Stop that. Stop telling yourself lies. Her parents had been good to her, helping her to raise her boy and complete college.

Time to leave the nest. "Okay maybe not an empty nest this summer—but a different kind of nest, Mom. Maybe when Sammy and I move, we'll also be able to come back and visit."

"You'll only be up in the Soo, honey. Daddy and I can always drive up there to see you." Mom waved her hand in dismissal.

Stunned, Alyssa crossed her arms across her body. Did she understand that message correctly? *Don't call us, we'll call you?* Had Mom and Dad been waiting for the day when she and her son would be gone? Clearly, Gayle had been anticipating just such a moment, for her to change her plans for a Yellowstone trip and now come up north.

Sammy didn't get into the vehicle but ran back to Alyssa and clung to her. Tears pricked her eyes. How she loved this boy. She ran her hand over his thick silky hair. They'd never been separated. This summer had been the first one that they'd planned for him to go away to summer camps.

A pain, like a pulsating glob of raw biscuit dough throbbed in her gut making her feel ill. "Love you, Sammy Boy."

He drew back. "Love you, Mom."

She bent and kissed his forehead, inhaling the scent of him. Freshly shampooed hair, grass, a whiff of Tide laundry detergent from his T-shirt all formed the scent of nine-year-old boy. "I'll miss you. But we'll talk every day."

He patted his pocket. "I'll keep the phone safe."

She'd splurged and added him to her phone plan, and her friend Aida had given her an older cellphone that she no longer used. She bent so her face was closer to his. "The best thing you can do for me this summer is to have an awesome time."

"I know."

"They have a lot of fun things planned." But if she had to put up with Jennifer and Gino, she wasn't sure she could stand it.

"But you won't be there."

"I will be when you come back."

That was if these two didn't try to take her boy away from her permanently.

She wasn't going to let that happen.

Chapter Six

Mackinac Island

A buzz of spastic energy, mixed with anxiety, enveloped Alyssa as she slipped as far into the left ferry seat as she could, next to the window. *Alone.* All around her couples and families chatted and laughed. No Sammy. No Mom and Dad with her. Just herself. Freeing, but also a little scary. She pressed her back into the vinyl seat as an older couple slid in beside her, at the edge of the bench seat. Like Alyssa, the blonde woman wore a dress. However, the stranger's was a maxi dress of pink and purple topped by a matching sweater. Alyssa's drab grey and navy plaid cotton print dress hit just below her knee. She'd worn the garment out of respect for her father, who'd driven her to the dock. But as soon as she arrived at the cottage, she intended to change into the shorts and T-shirts that her friend Aida had passed on to her.

The ferry departed the dock and they moved out of the harbor. Then the ferry skimmed through the vibrant blue waters of Lake Huron to get to Mackinac Island's town area, which was on the far side, away from St. Ignace. As they neared the entrance to the island's harbor, she peered out at the hillside, topped with beautiful Victorian mansions. Then the prominent white structure of the Grand Hotel, with its gorgeous front porch—the longest in the world, came into view. She'd ride by it every time she needed to go into town for something.

A thrill of anticipation worked its way through her. Just a single woman on her own arriving on the island to work. That's who she was. Not Sammy's mom or the reverend's daughter. Well. . . she was still a mom and a pastor's daughter. But she was starting to feel a little more than those parameters as the ferry arrived at the dock and they all began to depart—the noise abuzz with excitement.

When she reached the luggage area, she spied her bag and bent to take it.

One of the dock porters, a guy in his late teens with a mop of nut-brown hair and matching dark eyes reached for Alyssa's suitcase, but she held fast. "I'm going to a private cottage. They're coming to get me and my luggage."

Carter Parker might be surprised to see how little she brought, though. Did he really need to send a private carriage down to get her? Why not take one of those horse-drawn taxis? But he'd refused to let her call one.

Dressed in a polo-shirt and khaki shorts, the dock porter wore the same attire dock porters had back when she'd brought her son years earlier. *Probably the same for decades.* He raised his hands. "Sure thing, ma'am," he drawled and placed two fingers on the tip of his baseball cap.

Ma'am? Yikes, did she look like a ma'am? And what was someone with a Southern accent doing working on the island?

She weaved through the other passengers clustered on the dock.

Carter had instructed her to wait by the street. The sounds of horses' hooves and people laughing and talking were interrupted by the sound of a ferry horn. She jumped. Around her others did, too, and she didn't feel so embarrassed. *Better get used to that sound.*

She pulled her blue Samsonite roller case down the walkway. What a blessing it had been to find this gem, with three-hundred-sixty-degree wheels, at the thrift store. There was no way she was going to show up here with Mom and Dad's thirty-year-old duffel bag. That thing belonged in a dumpster. But God had provided just when she'd had the need.

"Where you goin', miss?" Another dock porter came alongside her, also with an accent sounding very deep South. This guy was a little older, with a coffee-toned complexion and some gray threading his wavy hair.

She waved him off. "Tandem Cottage, a private place." She'd been told the porters didn't generally transport to most of the private residences.

"The Byrneses is back?"

Alyssa stiffened, surprised someone knew the owners. "Um, no." Carter had specifically cautioned her to not tell anyone he was there. It was a strange request, but she saw no reason she couldn't honor that.

"*You* stayin' there instead?"

"Yes." She pressed her lips shut.

"Tha's one big ole house for one little lady." He laughed.

A carriage pulled up, with Carter driving. He pulled into a spot nearby. Kelsey was secured in a baby seat strapped in the back. "Hey, Alyssa!"

"Oh me oh my, you must be Mr. Carter Parker's baby mama. We heard that on the down low about him gettin' hitched. So tha's who's in the Byrnes's place."

"Yes." What? Had she just said that to this stranger? Why had she said that?

But before she could correct her untruth, the man was waving at Carter and hauling Alyssa's suitcase to the street and up into the carriage like it was a down pillow. "Carter Parker, you do beat all! I just met your little missus. And look at that little sweetums you hidin' back there!"

Carter's eyebrows rose but he didn't say anything back to the porter as Alyssa stepped up into the carriage, cheeks hot. She sat beside the baby and touched her silky cheek.

Carter bent toward the older man. "You doin' good, Roy?"

The man stepped back and raised two thumbs up. "Blessed. Always blessed."

"Awesome. Me, too." But Carter's voice lacked conviction.

"See ya!"

As Carter directed the horse out into street traffic of bicyclists, pedestrians, and carriages and drays, Roy called after them, "Hey, Carter, Miss Starr is back in town! I'll tell her where you stayin'."

Carter pressed his spine into the seatback.

Who was Miss Starr? Obviously, the porter thought Carter would want to know.

He blinked a few times, looked over his shoulder, and then they made a turn up a side street.

"Just FYI, Starr is a barista with a ministry, and she's got almost as many quirks as my wife." He clamped his mouth shut.

Not a very nice thing to say about his spouse. "A coffee ministry? We have that at our church." A tiny congregation, with an equally minuscule coffee ministry, but very sweet people—and all equally as conservative in clothing and thought as her father.

He shook his head. "She's an actual barista. Here on the island when I met her—at Lucky Bean. Then Starr worked a coffee truck when I was in my last year at UVA in Charlottesville. When I got my job in Yorktown, she showed up working at the Starbucks there near our home. She even babysat for me a little bit."

"That's a lot of coincidences." Dad would say there are no coincidences just God incidents.

"Yeah." He puffed out a breath. "She's been a good friend and she's always helped me get connected with whatever church she was working with, too."

"You don't think. . ." No, she wasn't going to say it. He'd think she was a loon to suggest this woman was his guardian angel.

"Well, I do wonder if she has a thing for me, yeah. But she knew I was engaged and then married. Although that doesn't deter some women." He straightened. "And I kind of had an attraction to her when I first met her, but it wasn't like um, you know. . ."

"You were drawn to her, to something about her. Maybe the Holy Spirit in her—I've had that happen with people I've met." *Like maybe with you, dude, but married is married—nix to that for sure!*

Carter pulled the reins as a group of four bicyclists darted in front of the horses.

"Good thing you have quick reflexes."

"The horses are accustomed to those kinds of idiots—of which I used to be one." He turned and smiled at her. "Starr worked here before and loved it and no doubt wanted to come back. Great seasonal work and way better here in the summer than in Virginia. 'Hell in a sauna' is the daily July through August forecast down there."

"Gotcha." But Alyssa couldn't wait to meet Starr and make up her own mind about her motives—especially since Carter's wife wasn't there. "I'd think your wife would want to be here, too, instead of in that heat and the humidity."

A muscle in his cheek jumped. *Uh oh. Touchy subject.* She shouldn't have probed that sore spot.

"It's best she stays there." His voice was so low, she barely heard him over the horse's hooves.

They turned up a back street. All the gardens were so lush and beautiful.

They turned again and baby Kelsey squealed.

"I think she likes this street best because of the trees on each side of the road."

"Those maples really are pretty." Alyssa swiveled toward the baby. "I agree with you, little Kelsey."

"I should tell you a little bit about how I now have the cottage situated."

"Sure."

"We'll have access to almost all the home, except the owner's private suite and their storage room. But the kitchen, living room, back patio, and so on are open to us. The place does not have a water view nor a pool. But there is public access across the street."

He'd said she'd have a private bedroom and bath and that the room door locked. "Is the situation for me the same as you planned?"

"Yup."

They rode on and the expansive outline of the Grand Hotel came into view. She sucked in a breath. The place was truly spectacular with a white columned porch that went on and on.

"Largest porch in the world." He turned toward his daughter. "Right, Kelsey?" When he wriggled his nose at her, Carter looked adorable. What would it be like to have a husband like that? A father like that for her son.

Those thoughts were chased away by the reality of her situation. *Never gonna happen.*

But wasn't there God's perfect timing for Alyssa's own special someone? Gino certainly hadn't been that person—not that she'd ever really thought about getting married. She'd planned a life as a professional woman. She'd be a computer guru someone in a big city, living on her own, drinking lattes whenever she wanted, unencumbered by anyone's needs or wishes. Yeah, look how that fantasy had worked out for her—she'd not even managed to get an internship.

They rolled past the Grand Hotel, as guests, most attired in what she'd consider business casual, some in casual resort wear, moved up and down the steps toward the grounds below. A massive pool area dominated the grassy knoll. "That kind of surprises me that the pool would be so, well—"

"Gargantuan?" Carter laughed. Grandma Kareen hadn't been a fan and had written multiple letters to the Town Crier newspaper about her sentiments. "Yeah, it surprised a lot of islanders, too. They replaced the old historic pool with what looks like a kiddie park but I'm guessing that my little Kelsey is gonna love it when she's a little older."

She quirked her eyebrows upward. "Yeah, there's always that."

"Giddyup." Carter clucked his tongue to get the horse, which had almost stopped, to move on again.

They continued through the area with stone or brick stacked columns on either side, marking the beginning of the lane on the West Bluff.

Carter inclined his head toward the Victorian houses up ahead. "I sure cut a lot of those lawns over the years." That all seemed a million years ago after what he'd been through.

"Oh, look at that one!" Alyssa pointed toward about a dozen people, some attired in medical garb, who milled about in front of the beautiful Victorian home, with a circular porch and a turret. "Is that a medical facility?"

"Nah, it's a place they've now set up as a retreat for nurses, doctors, and so on. To give them a break after all the stuff during Covid, ya know?"

"Wow, that's great."

"Yeah. They call that one Lilac Cottage because of all the lilacs out back." He pointed to the driveway beside the home, which led back to the budding trees. "My mom, umm, my stepmom, Maria is supplying some of the food to the medical retreat group. Her Mexican food creations are stellar."

Carter bit his tongue hard. He didn't want to share that his stepmother, as a descendant of the Swaine family—albeit only recently discovered—owned the yellow Queen Anne cottage beside Lilac Cottage. That was on a need-to-know basis, and Alyssa didn't need to know. *Not right now.* Nor did anyone on the island need to know his wife had died.

But now with Roy—by nightfall everyone would hear that Carter, his "wife" who Roy believed Alyssa to be, and baby Kelsey were at Tandem Cottage. He closed his eyes for an instant. Too late to do anything about that. But it could work for him. Or it could bite him on his backside.

"Hey, listen, even though we're a ways out from the town area, you can always call the Goughs and get a carriage when you need— if I can't drive you."

"The Goughs?"

"Yeah, the taxi. I can drive you when I'm free—like today. And I could teach you how to drive."

"Oh! I don't think I could."

"It's not that hard. Bitsy and Amos are a team and could probably drive you to town and back up here all by themselves."

She clasped her hands in her lap.

"You have to get downtown so you can mix with the fudgies."

"I'm not a fudgie, but I'm still offended on behalf of them." She placed her hand near her neck. "After all, what's the point of all that fudge if you can't consume it on vacay?"

"Truth that."

Soon they'd arrived at the beautiful Frank Lloyd Wright cottage. The place seemed very out of place for the island. "Do you think that maybe the builders of Tandem Cottage sat it back underneath a bunch of trees, almost like hiding it in a mini forest?"

Carter shrugged. "We should ask someone who might know. Molly Jeffries is into all that stuff—I could ask her."

"I met her." Warmth surged through Alyssa at recognizing the name of an islander. "And Clark Jeffries, her cousin and business partner." She didn't share that she'd sent the computer consultant a resume.

He shot her a surprised look. "Clark knows all that geeky history stuff, too. His dad is the head of the Mackinac State Parks."

"Really?"

"Yup." He gave her the side-eye again. "And Clark is one of the island's most eligible single guys."

"Noted." She tickled Kelsey's tummy. "But if you get that internship for me then I won't have time for socializing."

"I sent out a ton of requests, so let's see if we get you something." Carter parked the carriage and helped her out and then removed Kelsey from her seat.

Before long, they'd entered the spacious foyer which smelled of a spicy potpourri combined with baby formula and. . . sweat? She may need to purchase some heavy-duty room spray. Would Doud's Grocery even carry that stuff?

"I've got you in the south wing. Kelsey will be in the north wing with me."

This place is so big it has two wings? "Any word when that artist is coming?" He'd told her that an artist would be doing a mural for the Byrnes's nursery in the north wing.

"Cassandra is out of touch right now, but I'm guessing whenever they have an opening in their schedule."

"Ah." Hopefully, the muralist wouldn't be too intrusive.

"She did say it should only be a two-day job."

That was a relief.

He gestured toward the far end of the room where there was an archway. "Your room is the first one on the left down that corridor. "Sorry but I'll leave you to get set up because I have a diaper to change." Carter made a cringey face and half-jogged off with his daughter to the other side of the house.

Alyssa crossed the terrazzo floor of the huge square receiving room, pulling her bag behind her, and entered the corridor to the far wing. Her room was the first one on the left. This room gave a nod to its rustic roots with wallpaper resembling bark and a dark brown ceiling. A chandelier of deer antlers hung in the center of the room and thankfully not over the bed. The hardwood floors were stained a soft gray-green and a deeper green wool area rug screamed 'expensive.' The four-poster bed was formed from pine tree trunks wrapped in deep brown leather strips. She'd never seen anything like it. This was like cool Up North vibes on steroids.

After she'd unpacked her belongings, Alyssa sought out Carter. What kind of wife stayed home when she could be with this adorable dad? She sure wouldn't have stayed away.

Alyssa followed Carter's voice. A woman's tinny voice interrupted him, "And why do you think that's okay to take Kelsey up there so far away?"

"We've discussed this." Carter's voice held a steel edge that Alyssa had never heard before. "Repeatedly."

So apparently his wife was not on board with this decision. She stiffened.

"And you're not even going to tell me exactly where you're staying?"

Whoa. Alyssa's eyes widened. She stepped backward and swiveled to head down the hall to her wing again.

Maybe her thoughts about Carter Parker had been far too generous. Sounded like he'd taken his daughter and was keeping her hidden from her mother. *Oh no.* What kind of legal issues could arise from that? Had she jumped out of her own frying pan and into Carter's fire?

Not my business.

Her own son was her business, though, and she needed this job. She could do this job. She'd stay out of whatever drama Carter was going through, to the best of her ability.

Dear Lord, I don't know Carter's situation, but you do. Please help him and little Kelsey.

And help me.

After that aggravating call from his mother-in-law, Carter needed something to wash the toxicity out of his spirit that Nancy had just tried to deposit. He grabbed his iPhone and opened the YouTube channel to find one of his favorite songs.

Jireh. That was what he needed. He put in his earbuds and started the music by Elevation Worship. He closed his eyes and rocked slowly back and forth. *Jireh, You are enough.* God, Jireh God, was more than enough to handle this situation. He could get Carter through the loss of his wife and the harassment by her mother.

He began singing along with the lyrics. One of the best things he'd gotten from his weeks in grief therapy was being pointed toward this song. He closed his eyes, raised his hands heavenward, and rocked along with the music. His grief counselor had recommended this song to him, and Mrs. Mullen had been so right. He lowered his arms and crossed them over his chest and sang the verse.

Like the Bible said, and this song, if God watched over the sparrows, how much more did the Lord care for him? When Susan Mullen had asked that, in group, there were a lot of nods of agreement. And the tissue box got passed around twice. This anthem was both freeing and cathartic, releasing some of the pent-up pain they'd collectively held amongst themselves. He missed the people from the group. There were a few who, like him, had experienced multiple losses that had built up into a complete melt-down in their functioning.

What would I have done without Dad?

Thank God, his earthly father had gotten sober and had stepped in when Carter had needed him most. And now, he had Alyssa to help him.

He opened his eyes.

Alyssa stood there, eyes wide.

His face heated and he gave a nervous laugh. "Well, you caught me at it!"

"Oh?"

"Yeah, I like to rock out in private sometimes."

"But that was Christian music, right?" She looked quizzical.

"Yeah. I love that song. Jireh runs almost ten minutes and once I've listened to it—"

"And sung and danced to it?" She cocked her head at him.

He ran his hand through his hair. "Yeah, all that." He wouldn't apologize for it. "And you'll catch me doing that with baby Kelsey, too, singing her some good praise music. Anyway, that's something that helps me get through this thing called life."

Great, now he was sounding like some kind of know-it-all who was older and wiser than Alyssa, who was maybe a couple of years younger than him. How old was she anyway?

"My dad's a preacher." The way she bit out the words sounded like she'd announced that her father was a terrorist. What was that all about?

He raised his hands. "Well, I'm no preacher, but like I said—don't be too surprised if you catch me with my ear buds in and rocking out with praise worship."

"Does your wife like the modern praise music, too?"

It felt like she'd slapped him, and he pulled in a sharp breath. Abbi-Renae was in heaven now and hearing praises to God all day long. "She's totally into praise music. Every day all day."

It was true.

But it felt like a lie.

Chapter Seven

Alyssa tried to superimpose this image of Carter worshipping with one of him arguing with Kelsey's mom—and couldn't. Maybe Carter's wife wasn't on the phone earlier then. But who else would think they had an absolute right to know where he and the baby were? How could he be worshipping like that, singing, then claim his wife did, too, if he'd left her?

People did some weird stuff.

And people lied.

Boy, do I know that from experience.

Not my business. How many times was she going to have to remind herself of that fact?

There was a vulnerability she'd sensed in Carter that made her care more than she should. She was a sucker for the underdog, after all she'd gone through with Sammy, and it had made her more sensitive to others who were struggling.

Maybe he felt guilty for leaving his wife. Maybe he wanted a separation to work things out. She'd pray for them.

"Um, I was looking for the rest of the baby stuff."

He stared at her. "Should have all been there in her nursery."

"It's a gorgeous nursery."

"Yeah." He rubbed at the scruff on his face. "We didn't have time to get ours ready before baby came and it never really happened other than the crib and changing table."

"So she was early?"

"Yeah." From the twitch in his cheek, that wasn't something he wanted to discuss. Maybe his wife had been upset that he'd only done a minimalist nursery. Maybe the two of them were into that, though, given the lack of baby toys.

"So, I did look through the drawers and the closet but I didn't see any toys other than her stuffy in the crib."

"Oh, yeah, well, we have the stroller."

She bit back the urge to tell him that yeah, that was a given.

He slapped at his forehead. "Oh, let me show you her playpen."

She grinned. "I knew you must have had her developmental toys somewhere." Relief coursed through her. "I was wondering how I was going to keep her busy if I couldn't find all the infant stimulation stuff like. . ." She almost said, like she'd had with Sammy. "Like you need to have."

His golden brows bunched together as they walked down the hallway. "I, um, we, well you'll see."

She followed him to the open living area. There was a large empty room adjacent to his work area, which consisted of multiple computers, a long desk, and a rolling chair. "I see the Pack 'n Play."

He gestured toward the small portable crib. It had a changing table insert on the top and a raised mattress with a blanket.

Alyssa stepped toward the Pack 'n Play and looked inside. A couple of stuffed animals, a ball, several rattles, and a shape sorter were all that she saw. "Where's the rest?" She heard the accusatory tone of her voice and apparently he had, too, because his cheeks turned pink.

Maybe his wife hadn't wanted to send all the developmental toys up. Maybe it was simply too much. But. . . "I hate to say this, but babies need all kinds of play stuff. I mean, I can make up some things and we can go to the park—"

"Yeah, we do that a lot." He shrugged and circled the Pack 'n Play. "We take lots of walks. She loves the outdoors."

"She's got some outdoor toys here, eh?"

He pressed his lips tightly.

"A swing?"

Carter shook his head.

This could be way more challenging than she'd thought—especially if he didn't want to spend anything on his daughter's needs. Maybe one reason he was here was because his friends let him use the place free. Carter did wear the same clothes over and over—like a uniform. Maybe the guy was either on a tight budget or truly was a minimalist.

She raised her hands. "No worries! We'll find some things we can do that don't require a bunch of extra *stuff*." She intoned the last word as if a curse and wrinkled her nose as if she, too, wasn't a fan of toy clutter—she wasn't, but developmental toys to stimulate growth were in their own special category. Somehow, she'd have to find things she could borrow or could make.

Carter went to his desk and grabbed a small note pad and a pen and jotted something down. Then he pulled a rose-colored MacBook

Air off the smaller desk. So much for her theory of minimalism. If she'd noticed, she'd have realized he had every computer gizmo needed for his own workstation. And why did he have a rose gold Mac with him?

He motioned for her to join him, and he handed her the note pad. "That's the login and password for this computer." He tapped the Mac. "And the next set of passwords are for the Amazon account."

"The Amazon account?"

"Order anything you think Kelsey needs."

Had he been clueless about what stuff an eight-month-old needed or did his wife not have a clue? Why hadn't she made sure the baby had what she needed?

"Um, are you sure about this? You know you'll have to take it back or ship it back to Virginia later. We could probably borrow some things." From whom she wasn't sure.

"Positive." He shoved his hand back through his hair. "I've been too distracted to keep up with some of those things—the developmental toys and all that. So you're doing me a huge favor. Order away!"

No mention of his wife. He'd said he'd not kept up. "Thanks! And I won't overdo it."

She'd never been more tempted to Google someone than she was right now.

No stalking your employer or his wife!

Carter pointed toward the entrance to the next room, a living area with a sumptuous looking white leather couch and a massive television. "Check out the family lounge and start adding some things Kelsey needs to the Amazon basket."

"Sure." Sounded like she was already on the clock.

"I'm gonna go check on Kelsey." He pulled his cellphone from his pocket and looked at the screen. "She's starting to wake up."

He headed off and Alyssa slowly crossed the massive room, the white oak floor immaculately stained. Artwork liberally sprinkled throughout on the walls. The colors were straight out of the women's magazines she read in the pediatrician's office. Alyssa entered the family room, and the lights automatically came on. Overhead, a chandelier that looked like chains of small lights, cascaded down from a vaulted ceiling. Inside, the lounge was much bigger than it looked from the office area, maybe twenty feet by thirty. The ivory overstuffed chaise had two matching couches on two of the other walls, and there was another oversized television on the back wall.

Three black-and-gold rugs, each with a different, but complimenting pattern, overlapped on the floor.

"Potential tripping hazard for me," she mumbled aloud. A glass table with a gold rim and gold interlocking rings base was surrounded by gold and ivory velvet side chairs. She pulled one out and daintily sat down, almost expecting the thing to scream that she shouldn't be sitting on this very expensive piece of furniture.

She puffed out a breath as she slid the MacBook onto the glass tabletop and opened it. She checked the notepad for the ID and the password. The ID, Abbi must be his wife's name. Why would she let him take her computer, though? Or had he grabbed it out of spite? The password, not surprisingly, was Kelsey followed by a dot and the numbers twenty-four and seven. No doubt her mom thought about her every day and all day—why then wasn't she here?

The log-on worked. The screen saver was an image of Carter with his arms wrapped around his very pregnant wife. The pretty young woman smiled at the camera, but her eyes and her smile were off just a bit—like she wasn't quite there.

She reminded Alyssa of someone.

Sammy.

Something in her spirit lurched sideways as she examined the picture again. That same absent, "in their own head" look, and smile—same as Sammy and some of his Asperger friends often displayed.

"Oh, Abbi," she softly exhaled the young woman's name. "What has happened?"

A shiver went through her, and she rubbed her arms. It almost felt like a chilly column of air formed around her. This may be a Holy Spirit thing. Was his wife. . . no, she wouldn't allow herself to even consider that nudge her spirit was sending. *No.*

Had Carter married his wife only to realize he couldn't cope with someone on the spectrum? Had Abbi found parenthood too overwhelming? Suicide risk was higher in neurodivergent people— especially the doubly so, like a gifted person as Abbi no doubt was. *Is.*

And Sammy.

She shook off both thoughts, shivering.

Again, she found herself praying for Carter and his little family.

Her text message alert sounded, and she checked her phone. *Sammy.*

They won't let me call said I have to settle in. Can you call me?

It's already starting! The stuff she'd worried about. She stared at the phone, outrage building. They'd agreed to nightly calls. But she didn't want to get him in trouble with his dad and make things worse for him.

She sent a quick text message. *Set the ringer off so that it just buzzes.*

After waiting a moment, she called the phone.

"Mom, mom," he whispered, "they lied to us."

"What's going on?"

"They didn't lie about their pool—it's big but they don't get in with me. I swim by myself while they drink wine all night."

She drew in a deep breath through her mouth and closed her eyes. *Lord have mercy.*

"Stay safe in the pool, and don't take any chances."

"I won't." It sounded like he was sniffing back tears. "Mom, that summer camp—it's not a camp. It's daycare."

"Why do you say that?" Gino and his wife had described in glowing detail all the perks the camp offered.

"There's babies there, Mom!" his wail grew louder. "We're all in this big cement building that looks like an old school that closed down. There's babies in cribs and that's where the daycare ladies mostly hang out."

"Babies take a lot of care."

"Yeah. And they don't go to summer camp, do they?"

"No, Son, they don't."

"But I made a new friend there."

"Yeah?" She'd prayed and prayed that he'd make a friend.

"He's in high school, and the judge made him come work at the place. But Drew is really nice."

She closed her eyes hard. A kid in trouble with the law was her son's new buddy? "I'll talk with your dad tomorrow." After she sorted out what she was going to say.

"Mom?" He sniffed loudly. "Do you still love me?"

"Oh my gosh, of course I do!" She rubbed her forehead.

"Then you can't let Gino keep me all summer. And I don't wanta call him Dad."

Muscles in her chest spasmed. She wouldn't make false promises. "Let me see what I can do, and let's both pray that God helps us."

The next day, after tossing and turning and praying, Alyssa decided to check out the second nursery in case Cassandra Byrnes had purchased any baby toys Kelsey could use. She headed down the long hallway which was carpeted in a leaf-patterned dense wool.

This wasn't even the couple's main house, and they weren't expecting twins, but they'd set up not one but two designated baby rooms. Who had so much money that they could have two rooms dedicated as nurseries in their vacation home? Alyssa entered and stood inside the completely empty second nursery painted a soft buttercream. Painters tape, in an X, marked one wall—presumably where the mural would go. Kelsey slept in her crib in a matching sized room on the opposite side of the sprawling house.

Footsteps padded down the hallway.

What would it be like if Sammy could come here, too, and stay with them? No point imagining that, though.

"Whatcha doin'?" Carter, his hair sticking out in a million directions, attired in knit blue shorts and a matching T-shirt, leaned against the door frame. Clearly, he hadn't showered and changed yet. "You trying to order toys for this other baby, too?"

"No." She arched an eyebrow at him. "And FYI, I don't intend for Kelsey's playtime to be in her room." Oops, that sounded like her bossy mommy voice.

He laughed and saluted her. "And where will my little empress be living her developmentally best life once the dray guy delivers everything from Amazon?"

"First of all, I haven't ordered yet, because I wanted you to approve."

He crossed his arms. "I saw the Amazon cart and ordered."

Her jaw dropped. "All of it?"

"Yeah."

"I put in a ton of stuff, some duplicates or variants of the same types." Ack, already making mistakes. "I'm sorry—I thought we'd go over the cart before we placed the order."

"We can either gift the extras to Cassandra and Colton's baby or we can donate them."

She pressed her lips together. She'd put over seven hundred dollars' worth of items in that cart. And it hadn't been hard. Not like going to the thrift shops in the next towns and spending hours picking through stuff like she'd done for Sammy's baby toys. And the church ladies had been good to her, too, bringing in their kids' and grandkids' things they no longer needed.

"Thanks, Carter. Anyway, I thought I'd check out this other nursery right now," she held out her phone, which had Kelsey on monitor display, "while your princess sleeps."

"Wondered if she'd ever go down last night, little stinker." He rubbed his eyes.

"She just needed a good old tummy rocking session."

"Thanks for helping. And who taught you that?"

"My grandma." Maternal grandmother—not the paternal one she'd been kept from. The previous night, when Kelsey kept crying, Alyssa had checked on father and daughter. Carter was pacing with her and the baby had gas.

"Wow, your grandma came to where you were babysitting and showed you?"

Alyssa rolled her lips in. *Shouldn't have said that.* She wasn't ready to talk about her son. "Sure worked for your little pumpkin." Maybe she should tell him about Sammy. *Nope.* This whole notion of just being herself—just Alyssa—was too compelling right now.

"I'd never have thought to put her on my legs, tummy down, head away, and rock her and rub her back."

"You got a reward, though."

He laughed. "Hugest burp I've ever heard from her."

"There ya go, then, eh." She shoved her hands in her shorts' pockets. How nice not to have to wear a dress or skirt.

His phone chimed, and he pulled it from his shorts pocket. "Wonder who that guy is." He frowned, then swiveled the phone toward her revealing the activated camera video from the front door.

She shook her head. "Nobody I know."

Carter tipped his head back and groaned.

"What?"

He lowered his head. "Cassandra and Colton's artist maybe?"

"Do you think that's him?" Alyssa cringed. "He does have the grungy artist look." Albeit he looked nothing like her friend, Linda.

Carter touched the screen to talk with the man. "Hello. Can I help you?"

The guy looked down at a piece of paper in his hand. In his other hand he held a flat case almost the size of a briefcase. Maybe artists' tools or paints? Linda sometimes used markers, held in a case like that one, to first outline her work before painting. The guy's old-fashioned large dark glasses reminded her of some her grandfather had worn in pictures from the eighties. "Is this Tandem Cottage?"

"Yes. Who are you?"

She raised her eyebrows. Carter was getting right to the point.

"Cassandra told me to come here." He looked directly at the surveillance camera. Appeared to be maybe in his early forties. Clean-shaven, floppy brown hair, a Hawaiian shirt and cargo shorts, he looked like he should have been going on a trip to the tropics. But, then again, most of the artists she'd ever met, other than Linda, were eclectic dressers.

"I'll be right there." Carter ended the contact and shook his head. "Thought the painter was coming later."

"Well, he's not actually a painter. He's a muralist, so he might want you to refer to him as an artist."

"Whatever." Carter made a guttural sound. "I can't believe this."

"Where will he stay?"

"I assumed they'd stay in the south wing, but I didn't realize it was a guy."

This is already getting complicated.

Susan touched John's arm and then pointed toward the harbor. "I can't believe it's nine o'clock at night, and it's still light outside here on Mackinac Island." They were seated side by side at Marquette Park with few others there now since most of the day-trippers had departed. Across the street, yachts were moored in the harbor. Pedestrians walked down the sidewalks and bicyclists sped down the road.

"We better go grab those things from Doud's Market and head back up." John raised his eyebrows.

"Spoilsport."

"All good things must come to an end."

"Well, the summer has only just begun."

"Right, but my tired old knees are ready to finish biking and get into that big old bed up there at Lilac Cottage."

She laughed and walked across the lane to the store on the corner. They entered the brightly lit grocery store with beautiful wood floors.

John tilted his head back to look up at the high old-fashioned ceilings. "We aren't shopping at Kroger's, are we, honey?"

"Nope. But look at all these goodies in the refrigerator case." She pointed out some gourmet items.

As they headed down the right side, she caught sight of a familiar figure turning the corner, and she grabbed John's arm.

Couldn't be. No. No way. Not here.

"John, I think one of my clients is here."

"The young guy whose folks have a resort here?"

She shook her head. "No, no, that client is back in Virginia—his company doesn't allow much off-site work. That was something I had to fight for to get him to work from home while in therapy."

"Who, then?"

A guy in a Yacht Club T-shirt, wearing sunglasses this late in the day, moved past them. He leaned over and raised his left arm to his mouth. "Can't confirm National Treasure."

"Oh!" Susan ducked around the corner in the opposite direction. Her bizarre client, Leland, had referred to himself as a national treasure several times. The others had always laughed it off. Susan had taken note of that expression because she'd heard it many times in her family—in reference to her mom.

From farther back, by the pizza counter, she heard a commotion. Someone started fussing and fretting with someone else.

She looked down each aisle, then turned and spotted her former client self-checking out at a register. Then he scurried out the door, reminding her of a sand crab skittering across a Hampton beach.

John joined her. "That was the weird dude from your fall group, wasn't it?"

"Yes." She gave a low groan. *As long as I don't acknowledge him as a former client, I'm okay.* If Leland declared that himself, she was covered. Confidentiality could be a tricky thing. To be honest though, this client had always given her the creeps, so there was more to it than client-therapist privilege.

From the back, the sunglass guy stormed toward them, his jaw set. As he tried to push past John, her husband swiveled and his foot turned out, tripping the man.

John tried to catch the guy as he fell to the hardwood floor. "Sorry, man." He extended a hand, but the guy, whose sunglasses had fallen off, shook his head in disgust.

"Was that deliberate?" the stranger demanded.

John straightened to his full height. "I was trying to get out of your way."

The guy's narrowed eyes seemed to take them both in and assess them.

Military? *Police?* Just a guy who thought he was better than everyone else?

He shook his head and stomped off out of the store, leaving Susan and John cringing.

"We better get our stuff, John, and get out of here before something else happens."

"Agreed."

They got their few items and went to a register with a cashier. The pizza counter guy had come up front. "Hey, did you two get caught up with that pompous. . ."

Another worker shook her head at him.

"I had customers in line for pizza, and he almost jumped over them and shoved a lady aside."

"Entitlement makes people do some funny things." The other employee, wearing a green shirt embroidered with 'Doud's', bagged their items.

Entitled, that was the word she'd been searching for.

"Gotta say—this is the first time Shane White has pulled a stunt like that in here."

"He almost ran over you two, didn't he?" The woman inclined her head toward Susan and John. "I'll have the owner say something to Mr. White."

"Oh, and tell him the dude at the self-checkout left cash on the machine and didn't use a card."

Sure enough, when Susan looked to where Leland had bagged his items, there was a wad of cash.

"Life's interesting here on the island in the summer." The two workers high fived each other.

John laughed. "If this is the extent of your bad behavior at the store, then I'm all in."

"Me, too." Susan grinned.

"Where ya live?"

"Virginia, and the crime in Hampton Roads makes me not want to read the paper or watch the news." John crinkled his nose.

The worker shook his head. "The big news today was a bear that got loose down in Petoskey and knocked a bunch of trash cans over downtown."

Susan laughed. "I'm not sure I'd want to deal with bears in my backyard."

John nodded.

They paid and headed out of the store to where their bikes were locked.

"What do you think your client is doing up here?" John put the bag in his bike's basket.

Susan donned her helmet. "I have absolutely no idea."

"This is one of the most popular vacation sites in America right now. Maybe that's it."

"I wonder if he brought his mom with him."

"Huh?" John made a face of incredulity. "She's dead—right?"

She shook her head slowly. "Um, yes, she is, but he constructed an image of her for his home." She lowered her head, waiting for his response.

"What? Susan!" Eyes wide, he blinked at her. "It's just creepy. Like Norman Bates creepy."

She mounted her bike. "Exactly. Which is why I didn't tell you."

"Disturbed clients like him are why I want you to retire and forget doing these groups, too."

She exhaled a sharp breath.

"Did you ever figure out what the guy did for a living?" John got on his bike and pulled up next to her.

"Nope." And she'd never told her husband that Leland, who rode a bicycle over ten miles through city traffic to get there, was often followed out of there by a black SUV. She'd never been sure if it was coincidence until the night when in pouring rain, the SUV driver, wearing a trench coat, grabbed the bike before Leland could get going, and threw it in the back of his vehicle. Then Leland got in and the two men drove off. "Don't know and not sure I want to know. But I do know that the people who set the group therapy up for him were his employers and paid for it."

"But who?"

"I don't know—Brenda takes care of all that."

"Right. But you never asked her?"

A carriage rolled past them and a string of bicyclists.

"Nope. But we better get going."

The two of them merged out at the end of the traffic. *Funny to think of this as traffic.* No motorized vehicles on the island save for emergency ones.

"On a different topic, the obstetrics nurses are arriving tomorrow," she called to John.

"They asked me to do a sub-group with the male nurses who have recently lost patients."

"Yay!" She'd been bugging Tam and Dr. Tom to make use of John's skills, but they weren't sure they had the space. "Where are you meeting?"

"Under the lilacs out back on the benches."

"Rough place to work, ha ha."

"We better get pedaling." John started going faster and turned right to head toward Market Street.

She pushed harder. "Hey, what about your tired old knees?"

"I'm getting ready for my retirement."

And soon she'd be ready to retire, too.
Right, God?
What about her mother? Frail, elderly, and unwilling to listen—yet still a force to be reckoned with.

Chapter Eight

That artist reminds me of the shadow wraiths in the movie last night—poof, a glimpse in the hallway, and then he's gone." Alyssa sat on the leather bar stool at the kitchen island, next to Carter, and set her Newberry Indians coffee mug, from home, in front of her. The cup, so out of place in this gorgeous home, reminded her that she, too, was only a temporary occupant.

"Saw him bicycling off, that's about it." Carter slid a plate of oversized blueberry muffins toward her.

She took one and set it on a napkin.

"Glad you've accepted my habit of eating certain things on napkins."

She laughed. "You were right—less dishes to wash."

Carter chomped a bite of his muffin and swallowed. "Jack Welling is on my 'good guy' list for bringing these over from the Mackinaw City Bakery yesterday."

"Why did he claim he was your uncle and then cackle like he did?" Jack Welling was a funny guy. Engineers, like computer nerds, possessed a different kind of humor.

"It's complicated. I've known the 'golden boy' Jack most of my life. His wife Rachel is not technically my aunt—she's my grandfather's biological daughter. Her mom basically, um. . ." He raised a hand. "I don't want to get into details. And my dad isn't my Grandpa Parker's biological son which makes Rachel no relation to me."

"There's an unusual family connection and he was trying to aggravate you, eh?"

"And succeeded." He raised what was left of the baked good, as if toasting the absent Jack. "But I forgive him since he brought me, us, a treat."

Alyssa raised her eyebrows. "This is almost as good as what my mom bakes."

"Yeah?"

Homesickness twinged her heart. "My mom is an amazing baker. Our little church sells her muffins, cookies, and breads at bake sales for fundraisers." Sammy loved all his grandma's treats. So did she. This would be her very first year not having one of her mom's sky-high birthday cakes on her special day, which was coming soon. *I need to think about something else before I start crying.* "Hey, on a different topic—I've got a question about the mail."

"Yeah?"

"You know how Amazon Prime orders can take three to four days to get here?"

"Or more." Carter swiveled toward her.

"The same in Newberry sometimes. I don't know why I thought it might be better here." Because she thought with all that money on the island they might get preferential treatment.

"Boondocks effect up north." He scratched his chin. "But here ya get used to Boondocks plus island equals delays."

"Is the mail slower, too?" She'd not yet received a letter from Sammy. She nibbled her lip. Gino had refused to let him call, despite their agreement. Her son was supposed to send letters, and she'd mailed him several. No replies to her texts either.

"Mail is about a day or two behind the mainland."

"Not that much then." Her message indicator pinged and her heart leapt. Maybe that was Sammy now.

But the message was from her sister. Because of her text settings, she could read the beginning.

Gino is a jerk don't let him ruin your life

Heart hammering, she quickly hid the message.

Carter's sheepish expression suggested he'd seen the message.

Carter watched Alyssa's complexion go ashen after she'd gotten that text. What kind of control did this Gino have over her that he could ruin her life? Had he blackballed her from getting an internship? A few years back, a professor at UVA had shafted his older pal Clark Jeffries and impacted his job search. Was this the same situation? But why refer to a prof by his first name? *Probably a romantic problem.*

But it was Sammy she said she loved. Didn't Carter have many people he loved, though? Those people had gotten him through this awful time. Who wouldn't love Alyssa? His baby girl sure did. He found her warm, kind, funny, and intelligent. And beautiful. Why wouldn't she have boyfriends? Or more.

Alyssa was unmarried, she had confirmed. But maybe she'd finally split from a longtime boyfriend and that was ruining her life. She did seem sad sometimes. But not wrecked. Not the destroyed person he'd been. Not the ruin that Dad had come in and rescued.

Carter scooted his stool back. "I'll pick up the mail after lunch. Meet you and my little angel here at noon?"

Alyssa laughed. "Or whenever she's ready for her food. We're trying smooshed carrots today."

"Hmm, smooshed?" He laughed. "Is that a new Gerber product?"

"Nope." She pointed to the mini food processor on the counter. "I cooked the carrots last night and I'll puree them."

Baby sounds emerged in stereo from their side-by-side phones. "Aha! The princess awakens." Alyssa's eyes were bright, and her voice full of false cheerfulness. Clearly the text about Gino still bothered her.

The only person who'd ever accused Carter of being a jerk was his brother, and it was usually when he'd dumped Parker's hidden liquor stashes.

Why had his sibling only come home once in the past eight months since Abbi had died? Not that everyone's life should revolve around Carter, but he'd needed all his family's support.

Maybe Parker was right, and he was a jerk. After all, what kind of guy went for a bicycle ride while his newborn baby and wife were sleeping? A nice long ride. That hadn't ended nicely at all. No, he had no room to be thinking about anyone else being a jerk. If he'd stayed home, Abbi might still be alive.

A buzz of excited voices surrounded Susan and her friend Tamara at the Jockey Club, where they stood in line waiting to be seated. Finally, they were getting a lunch out by themselves. Susan angled toward Tam. "That's really nice of your mom and dad to collate all those program notes while we're out."

"Whew, yes. Our volunteers extraordinaire." Tam ran the back of her hand over her brow. "I'm thrilled Mom and Dad finally returned to the mainland Butterfly Cottage."

Dawn, Tamara's mother, was a dynamo. "Her energy is a lot like Momma's."

"I disagree." Tam dipped her chin and raised her eyebrows. "Your mother has everyone's mother beat."

Susan laughed.

The line moved, so they took several strides forward. The aromatic scents of herbs, freshwater fish, and potatoes wafted from a nearby table. So much for her intention to have one of their spectacular salads that Tam had raved about. Her stomach growled, as if nudging her toward the whitefish selection.

Tam turned and pointed toward the road behind them. A white carriage pulled by four white horses carried a bride and groom toward the Grand Hotel. "Seems like only yesterday Jaycie and Parker were getting married."

A frown tugged between her eyebrows. The young couple had suffered several miscarriages in the past five years. A lot of prayer had gone up for them, but Jaycie had told Tam that they had stopped trying for a baby.

"Ladies?" The waiter motioned for them to follow him to a round table topped with a bright yellow umbrella.

Tam leaned in. "This place is almost always busy."

Situated adjacent to the Grand Hotel's lush green golf course, Susan could see why. She took her seat. "This is fantastic. To sit outside in late June, on a sunny day, with a little breeze, instead of the furnace-like heat and humidity I left in Virginia."

"I gotta admit I don't miss that summer torture." Tamara shook her head.

Their server arrived. He reminded Susan a little of her son. He was a tall, handsome, twenty-something with an athletic build, his dark skin so smooth. How was Colby doing now that he'd returned to New York? If she retired, could she travel there more frequently to attend his performances?

"Ladies, here are your menus, and may I get you something to drink besides the water?" Their server even had a beautiful smile like her son's, and she offered a big smile in return.

"Arnold Palmer for me." Tam took a sip of her water.

"Just water for me, thanks."

"I'll give you some time to look over your menus, ladies."

A young mom in a stylish white and navy tennis set determinedly pushed a stroller past, followed by an older woman with matching light blonde hair. That had to be her mother. No one led them.

Susan frowned. "Tam, I didn't see those folks in line, did you?"

Tam glanced at them. "Some of the regulars have standing reservations and dine inside." She inclined her head toward the building at the end of the walkway.

"Oh." What would it be like to have so much money that you could eat there every day? *Rich people have their own problems, too.*

"Before I forget, did I mention that there's a formal event at the end of summer?"

Susan's jaw tightened. "Like a tux and a formal gown?"

"Dress suit and a long dress, but some people wear fancy gowns. It's a fundraiser and where we announce the winner of internationally known designer Cassie Browne's gorgeous gown."

"Is there dancing?"

"Yes and lots of food. All the biggest chefs on the island contribute their favorite dishes."

This sounded expensive. She drank some of her water as nearby seagulls swooped near the lush green lawn.

"Best of all, we have free admission tickets for staff."

"The very end of August?" She was due back to her job by then.

"Yeah, I know, you're needed back at the school. But if you listen to John, maybe you'll still be here." Tam winked.

The waiter returned with the lemonade-tea mixture and handed it to Tamara. "Ready to order?"

Tamara cringed. "I think we're gonna need a few more minutes."

As Susan perused the items, she couldn't help but overhear the two women at the next table.

"I'm orderin' me a big ol' margarita right off the bat." The woman's deep Southern accent sounded South Carolinian. "Just got another text from that awful lawyer I've been dealing with. Lord have mercy. She's a handful."

"The custody case?" The other woman's words were more clipped. Maybe northern East Coast.

"Right." The stranger made the word sound like 'rot.' "Just because I shared my cell number with that broom jockey, she thinks we're buddies."

Broom jockey? Susan stifled a laugh as she realized the woman meant witch.

Susan forced herself to tune out of the private conversation as she selected a yummy-sounding whitefish sandwich and fries. She and John had been enjoying the freshwater fish that they couldn't get down in coastal Virginia.

"Why share your private number then?" the Northern woman asked.

"Honey, I do that for witchy-poos likely to make big noises if I can't deliver the goods." She emphasized the last three words and laughed. "Sugar, let's face it—that happens *beaucoup*."

"If they think they are special to you, then they complain less?"

"You got it, baby!" It sounded like the Southerner had slapped the tabletop.

Glad I don't deal with this woman in my line of work.

The waiter returned. "Ready?"

Susan and Tam gave him their orders.

Tamara's phone rang. "It's Jaycie. I better take it."

Susan nodded. Jaycie had gone quiet in the past month or so. "I know you've been concerned."

"Excuse me." Tamara pushed away from the table, stood, and took the call. "Jaycie, how are you?" She headed toward the restaurant's entrance.

The two women nearby placed their drink orders. "Make my marguerita extra-large, honey."

The waiter headed off.

"Can you believe the convention's luncheons and snacks got pawned off on us? Cheapskates."

"Probably figured we wealthy social workers could afford it."

They're social workers like me? She cringed.

"If my honey-pie wasn't splurging on me, I'd be in a room with y'all. No offense, but four gals in one room is way too much for me."

"Yeah, but back to that attorney. Is she the one who nearly lost her license last year? The affair with the female judge?"

"Yes, ma'am—surely was. Miss Witch got in a fix 'cause folks believed her lover-judge threw cases in her favor because of their relationship—not because of being gay."

"Detroit area, right? But she kept her license."

"Yes ma'am. Married an air force officer right quick and grabbed his kid from the custodial momma for the summer. Needed to remake her image as a family law attorney."

"But what's that got to do with social services?"

"Claims the momma is neglectful." The woman cackled. "Not one little bit of evidence for that. But what I do have evidence of is her hubs being a predator."

"Seriously?"

"As sure as her name is Jennifer Fredda."

Susan would never have discussed a case over lunch, much less stated the client's name.

As Tamara returned to the table, Susan relaxed again.

Tam took her seat. "Jaycie isn't telling me something."

"What's going on?"

"Parker has been ill." Tamara sipped her drink.

"Sorry to hear that."

"Speaking of hearing—her phone call was clearer than any we've had from Switzerland."

"Got a new phone?"

"I don't know." Tamara ran her hands over her face.

Susan leaned in. "What is it?"

"Something is wrong. We don't talk about the baby situation anymore, but I wonder if she lost another but wouldn't tell me."

"Is that mother's intuition?"

"I hope not."

Susan took her friend's hand. "Let's give it to God." *And Lord, take my retirement plans, too. Although that awful social worker at the next table makes me want to cling to my profession, I don't think that's the message You're sending me.*

When is that artist gonna get out of this house? Carter ran through his options as he laid Kelsey to bed—none of which seemed good. He dragged his hand down his face. He'd go check on Alyssa in a minute and ask her opinion. This situation with the painter was bad. So bad. For some reason, he'd been expecting a sweet older woman who would show up just as he was leaving the island. That wouldn't have presented him with the issues he had now.

The older guy, maybe in his early later rather than early forties, was very closed mouthed. He hadn't disclosed much in their few encounters. As much as he wanted to know more, Carter didn't want to disturb Colton and Cassandra—probably couldn't even reach them at their remote location. Maybe it was a mistake putting the artist on that side of the house with Alyssa. When the guy told them that under no situation could they go in the nursery once he started, Carter almost kicked the guy out. That was super weird, but Alyssa attributed it to artistic temperament.

He exited Kelsey's room and headed over to the south wing. Good thing Cassandra and Colton weren't there yet because they'd not be happy with some of the messes he and the baby had made. Alyssa had been a champ about helping pick up. She'd even been washing Kelsey's baby clothes and bedding. Although Kelsey had loved the pureed carrots, she'd launched them all over her clothing and Alyssa had them soaking in some kind of enzyme solution in the laundry room. How did she know to do that? Must be a girl thing.

He quickly texted Alyssa about coming by her room.

She replied, 'k.'

When he got to her room, she unlocked the door.

"Yeah, better keep that door locked with him down the hall." He jerked his thumb in that direction.

"He's not even here."

"Where is he?"

She shrugged. "He took his bike and rode off about an hour ago."

"Does he go off riding every night after dark?"

"Yup, I think so."

"Not uncommon on this island, but for some reason it strikes me as odd." He rubbed his cheek again. Needed to shave.

"Me, too. I hope it's not me being ageist or something."

"Nah." He rubbed his eyes. "Sorry he's been here this long."

"I hardly ever see him. When I've gotten up in the middle of the night to go to the kitchen, the light has been on under the nursery door, and I hear music, but it's not too loud."

"Whatever he's eating in the kitchen, he always cleans up after himself."

"I've mainly seen granola bar and peanut bags." She shrugged.

"Is he bothering you at all?" Carter would definitely have words with him if he was.

"No." She shook her head. "He's like what I imagine a hallmate at college would be like. He must be a night owl and sleep during the day."

"I don't really understand these creative types."

"He's different from any artist I've known. But like I said earlier—it'll be all right." She stepped out into the hallway.

Standing this close to her, something floral, maybe roses, wafted from her. *I shouldn't be thinking about how good she smells.*

Carter rubbed his neck. "I thought he could knock it out in a day or two, but we're going on a week now."

"Maybe he'll finish soon."

He wasn't sure he could handle having the guy there much longer. "Let's hope so."

"Let's hope and pray for the best."

"Agreed." And he also agreed that he shouldn't be standing this close to her, wanting to lean in, inhale her sweet scent, and—

Her phone rang. "I gotta take this."

"Sure. Goodnight."

As he turned and walked down the hallway, he heard her fervent words, "I love you, too, and I miss you so much, Sammy!"

What would Sammy think about his girlfriend being here on the island living with another guy? Maybe Carter should offer for her boyfriend to come visit. But then again, she'd not asked to leave for the mainland to see anyone. And she'd never mentioned who Gino was either. Maybe she had a bunch of boyfriends.

Something in his spirit nudged him.

Couldn't possibly be jealousy.

Chapter Nine

A thousand butterflies seemingly fluttered in her chest as Alyssa talked with her dear boy. She loved him so much. Missed him like a part of her had been torn off. "How are you? Did you get settled in at the camp?"

"It's daycare, Mom. I told you that." His words came out as an accusation.

She knew Sammy didn't mean to be rude, but it took a moment for her to readjust to his manner of speaking. He'd offended a lot of people over the years but those who understood that he was on the spectrum usually gave him grace. "Yes, I forgot it's not summer camp. I'm sorry."

"It's not your fault, it's theirs. They're awful people."

She scrunched her nose. She wanted to tell him to not say that, but she felt the same way.

"Mom, I'm gonna hitchhike home. I've been watching all kinds of YouTube videos on how to do it safely, and my friend Drew said he'd come with me." The words all rushed out of her son at such a rapid pace that she needed a moment to process them.

"Don't you dare even think about hitchhiking, do you hear me?" She used her best Mom voice.

He sniffed. "Yes, Mom, but you have to get me outta here."

"Have you talked to Grandma and Grandpa?" She nibbled her lower lip. As stiff and straight-laced as they were, her folks loved her boy and her. Sometimes it didn't feel like it. But they always came through in a pinch.

"Um, I'm not supposed to tell you, but Grandpa drove up with Grandma and saw me at daycare."

"How?"

"They walked around the outside of the playground when we were sent outside. I saw 'em." He blew his nose loudly, and she pulled the phone away from her ear.

That was over a six hour drive round-trip for her parents. "Son, is this true?"

"Scout's honor—even though I dropped out of Scouts, it still counts, right?"

She sucked in a breath. Dropped out of Scouts, out of soccer, out of softball, out of 4-H, and would have dropped out of Sunday School if her dad would let him, which is something she wouldn't let him do either. "Yeah, it counts. What did they say?"

"Said they were praying and asked how I was. I said 'rotten' and Grandma started crying, so I said a few good things I'd done."

Her stoic mother had cried? That made tears come to her own eyes. "Anything else?"

"They were working on something to get me back home early. Said Auntie Gayle had a plan if Gino refused."

What was their plan? She should call her sister back. But her text message said that their camp site had no signal, and she'd call her when she was back in town.

So her parents and her sister were working to get her boy away from Gino while she did nothing? That was going to end.

Would it mean leaving her position here? She'd have to pray on that and take action.

Lord, I thought you gave me the green light on retirement—but this roof repair in Hampton is giving me the red light. Susan gripped her cellphone tightly as she listened to the contractor.

"Had to replace far more plywood underneath where the old shingles were." The roofer cleared his throat, sounding like iron rods grating together.

"How many more pieces did you have to add?"

He worked the math out loud for her. When he shared the additional expense amount, she stared up at the plaster medallion on the ceiling. She knew plywood was expensive, had seen the line-item amount in the emailed quote. This was exactly why retirement really couldn't happen right now or anytime soon. *Red light. Expenses. Unplanned expenses.* "All right, then. Do what you have to do."

"Yes, ma'am. We'll get after that as soon as we finish up in Kings Mill this afternoon."

She ground her teeth, knowing exactly what that meant. Kings Mill, an upscale community in Williamsburg, about a half hour from Hampton, was where contractors said they'd be working when they had no intention of coming back that day. "My roof is all covered and protected though, right?"

"Yes, ma'am, we've tarped it down." He coughed, that sound a pack-a-day smoker made. "Y'all come on now!" he called out—apparently to his crew.

"Thanks for letting me know."

"No problem, ma'am." The call ended.

John sat beside her on the couch. "Was that the roofer? Is it done?"

"Yes, and no." She raised her eyebrows. "Sounds like almost all the plywood had to be replaced on the front."

"From losing three little shingles in that storm?"

She released a long sigh. "That's what he said."

John pulled out his cellphone and jabbed at the screen.

"What are you doing?'

"I'm texting my buddy across the street from us. He'll go check it out."

Susan laughed. "He'll no doubt tell us if they don't actually replace all that wood."

"You got that right."

"We have an older house, honey. That means more repairs, maybe even costlier ones, in the future."

Jack Welling, the owner of Lilac Cottage and husband to Rachel, the program director, ambled toward them. "Thought I heard you mention old houses." He jerked his thumb toward the huge yellow cottage next door. "A couple of summers ago I helped my family make the repairs to our cottage. That place was built well over a hundred and fifty years ago."

John grinned. "Ours was built in the sixties."

"The nineteen sixties," Susan clarified.

The dark-haired man laughed. "That's almost a new build around Mackinac."

John raised his eyebrows. "I've heard barging stuff to and from the island for repairs is a nightmare."

Jack nodded.

"Maybe I should be grateful my roof repair is being done on mainland Virginia?" Susan cocked her head as she met Jack's hazel gaze.

Jack winked and gave her a thumbs-up. "Hey, just FYI, the neurology bunch is downstairs getting their coffee before their first presentation. Are you part of that one?"

"Nope." She would avoid that one like the plague. How on earth had yet *another* of her clients shown up on Mackinac Island? Paula Ecker, the librarian from her winter group, who'd published a book on grief, was here presenting to the neurology contingent. Her daughter was a neurosurgery nurse out west somewhere and was also attending. A few days earlier, Jack's wife, Rachel, had shared that a speaker was from the Hampton Roads area and asked if Susan knew her. Luckily, Susan's former client was staying at a bed and breakfast on the island, with some relatives. So all Susan had to do was stay clear of the meeting area when she was speaking. "I'm afraid I have other plans this morning."

"No problem." He gave a dazzling smile and then left them.

John covered Susan's hand with his own warm one. "Honey, I have my own FYI."

"Oh yeah?"

"That roof repair." He lifted his chin and then lowered it. "FYI, I put aside extra for just such expenses."

"Do what?"

He wrapped an arm around her shoulders and pulled her closer. John pressed a kiss to the top of her head. "I put the roof allowance into the budget last year and padded it some."

She pulled away. "You did?"

He squeezed her shoulder and then released her. "I'm sorry I didn't get this done sooner. Maybe if I had, then we wouldn't have needed that extra I put aside."

Laughter echoed from the nearby hallway and Susan straightened and patted her hair. "If you hadn't set it aside, though, we'd be paying almost ten percent for a home improvement or equity loan now with rates going up."

"And that's how we're going to have to plan in retirement for both of us."

She leaned back in and grabbed a quick kiss before anyone entered the room. "You're so smart."

"Glad you think so, 'cause I've got a great plan for this afternoon for us."

"What's that?"

"Tamara said we could take her and Tom's places on that Sip-N-Sail cruise."

"Oh, I've been wanting to go, but I never got us tickets." *Too busy.*

"Get your phone fully charged 'cause I'm sure you'll want lots of pictures."

If only they could come back every summer. Wouldn't that be great?

Alyssa steeled herself as she entered the kitchen and approached Carter. She reached Kelsey in her highchair and bent and kissed her silky head. Carter looked up, warmth in his eyes. She was about to quash that, though. "I hate to ask again, but have you heard anything about any internships for me?" *Like your boss letting you give me an internship?* Since she'd spoken to Sammy, she'd searched the internet, the government databases and spoken to her professors about positions available without an internship. In her sleep, she was even dreaming about job applications. After she went into town to pick up a few things, she planned to spend the afternoon updating her resume and applying to anything and everything that she could find.

Carter stirred some peaches into Kelsey's baby cereal. "Sorry, I'll keep trying."

But would he? She'd been there almost two weeks. "Okay. Thanks." She needed to take matters into her own hands. Clark Jeffries had said to look him up. She'd do just that.

Her phone buzzed her eight o'clock alarm. This was her day off and Carter's stepmom couldn't watch Kelsey, so Starr should be there shortly.

"You still riding into town?"

Kelsey stuck her tongue out and her cereal dribbled down her chin. Carter wiped it off.

"Yeah." First, though, she'd visit Clark's office.

"Could you drop something off at Lilac Cottage for me?" He pointed at a lime green tote stuffed full. "Those are the reusable plastic containers that my stepmom brought food in for us."

"She's a great cook. I've never had Mexican food like that before—so delicious and all those different seasonings she uses."

"Yeah, she's been spoiling us."

Normally she gave Carter and his stepmother lots of space when she came over. Alyssa ate outside on the far back deck. But he always saved her some food to eat later.

"She and Dad are gonna watch Kels—that's my nickname for her—soon so you and I can get out of the house at the same time."

Why? She felt her eyes widen. "Oh?"

He locked gazes with her and his cheeks reddened. "Told them I wanted to show you some great places off the beaten track."

Maria came over a few times a week already, in the early evening. And Starr was Alyssa's relief worker now, too. If Alyssa was going to explore the island it should be with a single guy—not a married one.

Carter handed the tote to her. "Thanks for dropping this off."

"No problem." But was there a problem? She was going to have to be careful. Maybe Clark Jeffries might show her around the island. If Clark didn't have a job for her, maybe he might accompany her if she hinted strongly enough. He was single, wasn't he? Not that she understood how all these dating things worked, since she'd never actually been on one.

Soon she headed toward Lilac Cottage. She waved at another rider traveling in the other direction but the guy, who looked about her age, ignored her. He was one of the wealthy summer family members who lived across the street from them. *Oh well.*

As Alyssa pedaled out from the Annex, sunbeams broke through the clouds and warmed her face. Glorious. Such freedom here. Was this what it was like to be childless? Go where she wanted. See who she wanted to see. Free time to read, to watch television, to possibly go on a date? Was it selfish to be relishing this opportunity?

This was temporary. She'd have her son back soon. She'd have a great job. They'd move into their own apartment. Gino would not keep her boy. *No. Not happening.* She had enough money saved now that she could hire an attorney just in case he and Jennifer tried to keep Sammy after August.

She soon spotted Lilac Cottage and pedaled up the drive between it and the impressive yellow cottage alongside it. Maria emerged from the gorgeous adjacent home and waved at Alyssa, motioning for her to come over. She braked and rolled the bike to a bicycle stand nearby, filled mostly with ten-speed comfort seat bikes that were popular on the island.

Alyssa carried the tote toward Maria, who was attired in a bright purple, red, and white capri set.

"Hola!"

"Good morning. Carter had me bring your containers."

"Wonderful! I'll bring them over to my *casa*."

Her casa? Didn't that mean house? Did Carter's parents own this huge mansion? *No.* He'd driven her and Kelsey over to the Parkers' resort on East Bluff. And he'd shown her the original island Butterfly Cottage. No mention of another property.

Alyssa passed the tote to Carter's stepmom. "Thank you again for all the wonderful meals you've brought over. Carter has shared with me, too."

"De nada." She waved toward the yellow cottage. "Soon my grandsons will be here, and I'll be cooking every night for them. I hope you and Carter can bring little Kelsey over to see them. I'm so glad I have a place to put all of them when they are here. Our resort is fully booked during high season."

Alyssa nodded dumbly. The homes on the West Bluff were in the multi-millions. These people did not live like she did, nor would she ever live like them other than for this season. Maybe Carter felt sorry for his humble little childcare worker and didn't want to rub her nose in his family's wealth. Her heart sank, although she didn't understand why.

"Let me take these to my kitchen and I'll be right back. I want to talk with you about our plans for the fourth of July."

Why would his family include her? Would his wife finally show up and join them?

"Sure." Fourth of July? In two weeks? And she still didn't have an internship.

She swiveled to see Clark Jeffries step from a carriage by the curb. Just her opportunity. She'd beg if she had to. She absolutely needed an internship, even if it wasn't paying.

Alyssa hurried down to greet him, trying not to run full out like an idiot. She waved at him and then stopped, realizing she looked like a schoolgirl. "Hi, Clark."

His dark eyebrows quirked upward beneath his glasses and then he smiled in recognition. "Good morning. Are you running away from Mrs. Menteur again?"

"No, thank goodness." She still cringed, thinking about that woman.

"Are you here for my presentation?" He looked down at his watch.

"Um, no, but I'm glad to see you."

"I'm afraid I'm late for my talk."

As he hurried up the drive, she tried to keep pace with his long strides. "I hate to bother you, but I was wondering if possibly you have room for an intern yet?"

"No. Sorry."

Desperation nudged her. She and Sammy needed their own space. She needed a full-time job. "What about a free one, a volunteer?"

A striking brunette emerged from the side entry to Lilac Cottage. With long chocolate brown hair and matching dark flashing eyes, she pointed a slender finger at Clark. "Better get in here before this crowd revolts and goes golfing instead of hearing your technology presentation." Her sensuous languid smile was one Alyssa would never be able to pull off. *Ever.*

Alyssa turned to see Clark's wide eyes and expression of adoration. *Whoa, he has it bad for whoever this medical professional is.*

"Yes, ma'am." He saluted the brunette.

Clark jogged toward the tall woman.

He didn't even look back.

So much for my plans.

Maria shuffled toward her as fast as her heels would allow. "Plans for Independence Day?"

But Alyssa wasn't independent. If she didn't get an internship and a job, she'd be back at home with Mom and Dad. None of her job inquiries had produced any possibilities other than the one in the Soo. Her sister, Gayle, was looking for positions in Virginia for her, so Mom must seriously want Alyssa and Sammy out of the house to put her up to that. "I can't make any plans for that day because my parents will want to celebrate my birthday." How had that untruth slipped so blithely past her lips? That wasn't technically true, but they had always made a birthday cake for her special day.

Maria's red lips formed a pout. "Oh, I'm sorry we won't have you with us. How many candles this year? Twenty-two?"

"Twenty-six."

Was that her imagination or had Maria's face registered confusion and disbelief? Did Carter also think she was only twenty-one?

It didn't matter. What mattered was she had to push harder and spread the net wider to get a last-minute internship or a job that would accept her without one.

But how far would she have to move? And who would help her? Poor Dad, he was always helping his small flock who had to leave far from Newberry for work.

Would she be the next one to fly off?

If Mom and Dad had driven all the way to Marquette to check on Sammy, then might they show up over here on the island? *No. Too expensive with the ferry trips and all.* But might they ask her to meet them in St. Ignace?

Why were her lips tugging into a smile at the thought of spending her birthday with her parents? Would her sister and her family join them, too?

"Are you all right?" Maria touched her arm. "You seem a million miles away."

"Just missing my family."

The older woman pulled her into a hug. "We're so grateful you're here helping take care of Carter and his little family. God bless you."

When they pulled free, Maria's face shone with spilled tears. Apparently unable to speak, she compressed her lips tightly, then turned and headed back to her yellow mansion.

Why hadn't Carter stayed there? Why was his stepmother so distressed?

This wasn't Alyssa's world—she was there only temporarily. She pulled her phone from her pocket and scanned her emails. Two were from friends who were creating apps and had invited her to join their groups, and she'd not yet responded. Another was a message from the leader of a bigger group forming to create a state-funded app for animal crossings near highways. Carter had participated in a similar volunteer group in Virginia. She'd accept anything that might help her get a job. She'd ride somewhere and respond to the messages.

Her phone rang. *Gayle.* "Hello."

"Oh, glad I got you." Gayle sounded out of breath. "We're in Curtis and found Wi-Fi and have internet access."

"Great! How are you enjoying yourselves?"

"We're doing fine. But my husband wants to speak with you about Gino. He thinks you still have a case to charge against him."

Chapter Ten

Have you told her yet?" Starr Bourne arched a platinum brow at Carter as she rocked Kelsey on her hip.

Carter refilled his coffee mug. "Told who what?"

"Told Alyssa about Abbi-Renae."

He swigged back Starr's delicious coffee until warm liquid ran down his chin.

Starr handed him a napkin. "Things are getting. . . you know." She rocked side-to-side.

He shrugged. "No, I don't know."

"You like her," she said in a singsong voice.

"Of course I like her—Alyssa is great with Kelsey." But he knew Starr meant something else. Feelings for his daughter's caregiver grew stronger every day.

"If she's picking up your vibes, then she's going to feel guilty if she feels the same way." Starr pushed back her acid green and bright blue hair over her ear.

"Why do you always have such strange hair?" He slugged back more coffee. Yeah, he was being rude, but she was being intrusive.

She patted her hair. "You're changing the topic, but it's fun to have uniquely colored hair."

"I'll take your word on that." He snickered.

"It's like when you're in. . ," she blinked, "when you're where I'm from. We have every color imaginable there. We're all unique."

He cast her a sideways glance. "How much espresso have you drunk this morning?"

"Anyway, you should tell Alyssa because if you don't, you know someone else will."

He couldn't even say his wife's name out loud. How was he going to announce that she was dead? And her passing was his fault. "Let them tell her." *Maybe that's what I'm hoping.*

"That's not fair, and you know it."

"Do I?" He shrugged. "Gotta get back to work."

"Tell Alyssa soon so she doesn't get a shock—you know." She waggled her hand and then pulled it back as though receiving an electrical jolt.

He shook his head and then left the room, waving over his shoulder as he went. Today he'd sent out another dozen inquiries for internships and jobs for Alyssa. His boss was still procrastinating about letting Carter host her as his own intern but was considering her for a position in Virginia. Carter wouldn't share that, though, until there was an interview offered.

Why did the thought of Alyssa, him, and Kelsey all in Virginia, make him want to smile?

"What are you grinning about?" Starr closed her eyes hard, her lips twitching. "It's about Alyssa."

"Lucky guess."

"Is it?"

Seated on the cushy seats on the Lilac Cottage front porch, Susan extended her phone toward her husband. "Those pictures Colby took of the new roof look great, don't they?" Colby had snapped the pics after he'd performed in a concert at the Ferguson Center in Newport News, Virginia. He had stayed at their house, only twenty minutes away from the venue.

"Looks darned good—ought to since it's roofed with architectural quality shingles."

"Right. And Colby said they didn't leave any nails in the yard, either. They'd used a magnetic thingy to pick them up."

"As they should, for what we paid." John raised his eyebrows. "On a different topic, have you heard from your mom?"

"God bless the USA." Susan feigned waving a flag. "She's still coming here with her contingent."

"Glad we don't have to deal with all that."

She swatted at his hand. "John! That's mean."

"Well, you know. . . she'll have her friend with her."

"I'm relieved Evangelist Romelda is accompanying her. And that entire group they'll be with."

"Yeah." He chuckled. "Romelda won't let your mother pretend she's able to get up out of that scooter. Can't have her try a walker like she did on her last big outing."

"Right. That was a fiasco. She could have broken so many bones if she had fallen."

"That's what all those bodyguards are for."

"Oh my goodness, no, that's not why the government pays for them." She swatted at him.

Seagulls swooped down on the lawn and gobbled up bits of broken bread that the latest medical provider group had scattered. No matter how often Rachel and Jack asked them not to do so, each group had at least one person determined to disobey. The seagulls squawked before they flew off.

"But we won't have to pay for her caregivers to come to the conference. Government can take care of that." He handed her phone back.

"True. But can we trust those Secret Service people? They almost lost her in Las Vegas when she decided to play the slot machines."

"No gambling at the Grand."

"But I always wonder what those lawmakers get up to when you have that many politicians together."

He shrugged. "I don't want to know."

Down in the street, a string of carriages drove past. She imagined Secret Service agents hanging off the side when Momma and her bunch toured the island. Momma would insist on touring—as she did at every political event she attended. Susan exhaled a loud breath of frustration just as a breeze from the Straits carried onto the porch.

Her phone rang. *Brenda from work.* She answered it. "Hey, girl, how you doing?"

"Fine." Her voice was curt. "Hey, I hate to bother you with this but I, uh—I have to."

Susan stiffened. She touched John's hand and then put the call on speaker phone. "What's up?"

"Remember the guy you had all those questions about?"

"Leland?"

"Yeah, him. That's not his real name, by the way."

"Oh?"

"FBI is looking for him as is the CIA."

"What?" Susan squealed, took the phone off speaker, and held it to her ear.

"You need to contact them if you hear anything from him."

"Why? What did he do?" Brenda had never told her what the guy's situation was for work or anything about Leland's referral.

"You know how Leland said he was a national treasure?"

She huffed a laugh. "Well, yeah."

"Susan, he was—he is. He's considered a national asset and he's gone missing."

But he wasn't.

He was somewhere there on Mackinac Island.

"Break time," Carter announced. He took Kelsey from Alyssa's arms. He set the baby down in her new play pen area, which was so huge Alyssa called it "the enclosure." Kelsey crawled over to her favorite toy, a battery-powered piano and began pounding on it.

Alyssa laughed. The two of them sat on the nearby custom leather lounge chairs.

The piano's musical tones were interrupted by a *ping-ping-pingetty-ping* machine gun sound. Carter cringed as Alyssa's eyes widened. His mother-in-law's text message was meant to sound cringey and it worked. He'd custom set it, which he now silenced. He'd looked at the message in the privacy of his room later—when he could throw the phone down on the bed after he'd read the text. The sooner he could prove how well he was taking care of his daughter the sooner he could get Abbi-Renae's mom off his back. She sure had a lot of nerve threatening to take legal action against him.

He shook his head. "Ever have someone so toxic that your eyeballs steam just looking at their messages?"

She gave a curt laugh. "Why not block them?"

Carter ran his tongue over his dry lips. "Hmm. I mean people you'd love to ghost but can't? Anyone like that for you?"

Her nose crinkled the way it did when she was irritated. "No steaming of the eyeballs, but my brain locks up when I read their messages."

"Yeah, it's those 'have to' people," he crinkled his nose in distaste, "that are the problem. 'Have to' deal with them because. . ." He didn't finish the sentence. Didn't need her knowing his family problems.

She fiddled with the button on her blouse. "Sometimes, though, people cut someone off because they just disagree with them. Like my dad has done with his grandmother."

"Yeah?"

"Yeah." She fixed her gaze on him. "My great-grandmother was the first woman ordained as a minister in our church denomination."

"Wow. But how's that a problem?"

"It was when the ordination was basically by accident."

"What?" He gave a low laugh.

"I'm not sure. But she got ordained and then the church renounced it."

"Yikes."

Alyssa's face flushed pink. "Not only that but she ended up parenting my dad."

"Your grandmother died young?"

"Yes and no." She raised her eyebrows. "My father was illegitimately born."

He shrugged. "Not his fault."

Alyssa locked eyes on him. "Yeah, but back then it was a major problem."

"Did your great-grandparents take him away from her?" Carter leaned forward.

Kelsey turned and looked at them, likely expecting appreciation for her performance. He and Alyssa clapped. Kels crawled over to her multicolored educational bunny, which had all kinds of learning activities programmed on its many soft-touch buttons.

Alyssa crossed her legs. "No. I guess Dad's mom was kind of wild, which he blamed on his grandmother."

"Why?"

Alyssa frowned. "My great-grandmother was unconventional. She was all about female empowerment back before there even was such a concept. My dad blamed her strong female orientation for his mother acting out."

"Doesn't sound fair."

"Probably not, but I live under his roof." She waved at Kelsey.

"You don't see your grandmother, I mean great-grandmother?"

"My grandmother died when Dad was twelve but she'd not lived with him in years."

He straightened. "And your great-grandma?"

Alyssa took a deep breath. "I only see her on television if I sneak and watch her."

He raised his brows and locked gazes on the beautiful woman beside him. "Whoa. Who is she?"

When Alyssa said her name, Carter pushed back further in his chair. "My grandma likes to watch her in the morning. Says Evangelist Romelda has a huge ministry."

"Yup. And my dad is the son she refers to when she asks viewers to pray," she waggled her hands and laughed, "for reconciliation for her with him."

"That's crazy." His jaw dropped. "And your dad is a preacher, too?"

"Yes. But he preaches a different kind of religion than I've found in the Bible—and in my great-grandmother's messages."

"Wow. Sorry."

"Yeah. Me, too."

"Hey. You oughta come with me and Kels to our church."

Alyssa pushed her hair back. "Is it a hellfire and damnation kind of church?" She sure didn't want to attend one of those.

"Didn't think they even had those anymore—except maybe in some of the rural areas in the South." He tapped his fingers on his chair.

"Um, oh yeah they do have them—just go listen to my dad sometime."

Kelsey plopped onto her bunny, which caused it to count to ten. The baby squealed in delight.

"And people come to hear your dad anyway?"

"That's part of the problem. It was bad enough before the pandemic, but now attendance is abysmal." How were Mom and Dad going to make it in the coming years? That had been another reason she'd wanted to get started working as soon as possible.

"No doubt."

"Thank God they have the small parsonage near the church." She pulled at the bottom of her shirt. "But there haven't been any improvements to it in decades." *Other than Dad's rare attempts to repair things.*

"But they have a place to live, right?"

"Unless the church folds—which it could." Alyssa laced her fingers together on her lap. "Another reason why I've got to get some more programming experience so I can get hired on in the Soo."

"I need to push my boss about internship options for you again. And can you do both that and take care of Kelsey?"

"I have to make time. I need that experience. I'm sending out job applications but so far no other bites than the one in the Soo."

He stood and jerked a thumb toward his work area. "I've gotta get back to work. But I'm sending another request to my boss right now."

"Thanks, Carter."

"De nada."

What a strange phrase to use. The Spanish expression of it being nothing, or not a bother, was just the opposite of how she felt. She was bothering him.

It's everything to me and my son if I can get us moved this fall.

Her phone rang and Gino's number showed. "Hello?" She wanted to launch into a tirade about how he wasn't letting her son call her.

"What do you do when your son locks himself in his room and he's in there rocking back and forth and making some unearthly sound—like a high pitched Nazgûl squeal?"

Oh no, that hasn't happened in a long time.

"Yeah, like a Ringwraith from Lord of the Rings!" Jennifer must have taken the phone. "He's driving us nuts with that noise."

Her heart rate soared. "Let me talk with him." *As you should have been letting me do.*

"All right." Gino must have grabbed the phone back. "But we've got guests coming and a swimming party tonight. He needs to get his act together."

"That's entirely too overstimulating for him!"

"Then he can stay in his room, out of sight."

Kelsey popped off her toy and scurried over to her blankie, grabbed it, and rolled onto her back. Alyssa needed to talk with Sammy before the baby had to be fed and put down for her nap.

"Your mom is on the phone, Samuel." Gino sounded like he was stating that a skunk had entered the room. She imagined his nose curling.

Sammy's pitiful high-pitched whine slowed to a panting sound, like a wounded animal. She'd heard that sound many times before they'd gotten all his treatments straight.

"Here! Talk to her."

"Mom?" Her son's gravelly whisper was one she'd not heard in ages. He must be stressed out of his mind.

"I love you, Sammy boy."

Silence.

A tear rolled down her cheek. "I love you so much, and I'm praying that God will bring you peace. And help."

"Mom, I wanta come home, home, home." It sounded like he was slapping himself.

"Stop that right now!" Jennifer barked at him.

"Sammy boy, let's sing our song now, okay?" She launched into 'Jesus Loves Me' and he gradually joined in with her. Usually, he'd rock back and forth and sing this song many times through with her until he calmed down after a meltdown.

"Jesus loves me, this I know, for the Bible tells me so." She stood and paced as she sang, keeping one eye on Kelsey who was laying suspiciously still. Oh no, that meant a diaper change was imminent.

Alyssa continued on, as they sang the song again several times. "Little ones to Him belong—"

"Mom? Do I have to go to their party?"

"Let me talk to—" She couldn't say 'your Dad' –"to Gino."

"Yeah?" Gino's gruff voice set her teeth on edge.

"Tell your guests that your son is unwell." *True enough.* "Allow him to eat in his room tonight."

"Noted."

"And re-read all those instructions I emailed about handling his Asperger's problems."

The phone line went dead just as a foul odor wafted from the play area.

The whole thing stank—baby and Gino and poor Sammy.

Susan strolled into the cottage's backyard, where John's group would be meeting shortly. The lilacs canopying the place enveloped her in a heavenly scent. She punched in the numbers to the FBI agent and made the call.

"Agent White."

Susan tried to make her lips move but couldn't.

"Who's calling? Where'd you get this number?" His voice was just as grouchy as the last time she spoke to him at the grocers.

"Susan Mullen, social worker from Virginia."

"Mullen. Yes. Good. Thanks for calling." Now he was sunshine and roses. "Whatcha got for me?"

He sure cut to the chase. She'd do the same. "I saw Leland here on Mackinac Island."

A pause. Sounded like he was inhaling on a vape or something.

"Knew it. Thought I saw him, too."

"Doud's is where my husband and I saw him."

"Is your husband the big dude who tripped me?"

"He didn't trip you; he was trying to get out of your way," she put some bite in her tone.

"Whatever. Same result and he interfered with me following my target."

"The pizza guy said you got into an altercation in the back, too, Agent White."

"Wouldn't get out of my way," a whine crept back into his voice.

"Like us? We tried."

"Sorry." But his voice was anything but sorry. "So you thought that was Leland, too?"

"Absolutely. It was him. I got a good look at him at the register."

"Register? We have no paper trail on him. No ATM receipts, no credit card trail."

She rolled her eyes upward. "He tossed cash on the machine and took off."

"Cash? Yeah, that makes sense." This guy's voice rose and fell like a roller coaster ride.

"Doud's wasn't too happy about him using self-checkout and then tossing money at the machine." Susan made a face as she remembered. *Nor had they been happy about Agent Shane White's behavior.*

"Yeah. Know any reason why he'd be up here? Anyone from your therapy groups he might contact here?"

"I did have a client from the island, but he's in Virginia. Or should be."

"You can say the name—I got a court order for all the names of clients."

"He wasn't in any group with Leland, though."

"Carter Parker?"

She hesitated. "Yes, but to my knowledge they never met. There was a two-month gap between their groups."

"All right. We'll ferret out the connections. But if you think of anything—anything at all—or if you see him again, contact me ASAP."

"Will do." She felt like she ought to salute or something.

She spied Maria coming up the walkway with some of her scrumptious Mexican breakfast pastries. "Hola!"

Susan stiffened. Once she'd had learned that Maria's last name was Parker, and that she was Carter's stepmother, Susan had avoided the woman.

Now, as the dark-haired woman waved at her, Susan waved back. *Should I ask her about whether the family knows Leland?* Why would they?

Not only that, but wasn't that Agent White's job?

It was.

Chapter Eleven

Frozen by the possibilities of what to do with her free time, Alyssa stood at the kitchen sink staring. Exhaling loudly, she pulled down the gold-plated faucet and filled her water bottle with the filtered water. Although limited to the eight-mile circumference of the island, that felt immense. She might be a preacher's kid and a believer, but she wasn't perfect. Having this little bit of distance from her son right now, she could admit that she sometimes begrudged her son's claim on her time. Now was her opportunity to take care of herself and get some exercise.

A text pinged. Gino. *Meltdowns continuing.*

She rubbed her forehead.

"Big plans for your day off?" Carter entered the kitchen and jostled baby Kelsey on his shoulder.

Alyssa forced a smile. Her other free day had been so consumed with job applications—ones not requiring an internship—that today she only had one thing planned. She'd already scheduled a consultation with an attorney. Had to have a plan for Sammy.

She turned off the faucet. "Haven't decided." Was that a lie of omission? Just like not telling him she had a son.

When Kelsey fussed, he swayed her side-to-side. "Could gorge on fudge. Just bring some back."

"Nope. Long lines, I imagine."

"Could run over to Lilac Cottage and ask Maria to send me tamales and Mexican rice for lunch." He winked.

"Or not." She raised her eyebrows and gave him a pointed look.

"Yeah, or not. Could bike to the Ice House, order brisket nachos and ride them back." He tried to make a begging face but the effect failed.

"I'm sensing a theme." *Should I offer to make the poor guy breakfast?*

"That three in the morning bowl of cereal is long gone."

"I wonder if the artist's granola bar is holding him?" She grabbed a wrapper he'd left on the counter and tossed it in the trash.

"When are we gonna get rid of that guy?" Wide-eyed, Carter shook his head, which made him look adorable.

Why wasn't his wife here? Whatever the reason, Alyssa could take care of Kelsey's daddy a tiny bit.

"Sit down." She pointed to the padded chair at the table. "Scrambled eggs and toast. In exchange for advice for my day off." She'd still keep her call to the lawyer private.

"Deal."

She strode to the Thermador fridge and pulled out a carton of eggs. She grinned remembering how she'd not wanted to touch the refrigerator when she'd learned it cost over fifteen thousand dollars.

"Thanks, Alyssa." He jostled the baby on his lap and pretended to be a horse, making neighing noises.

Soon breakfast scents filled the kitchen air. Sunlight filtered through the skylights overhead as Christian music played through the speakers. Her favorite one by Tauren Wells played. Like the lyrics suggested, she needed to take back what the enemy stole. *What Gino stole.*

"First, bike around the island."

"That's my plan."

"Could stop at the Cannonball."

She looked over her shoulder. "Cannonball?"

"About halfway around the island. Great ice cream and fried pickles."

She blinked at him. "No more suggestions until you've eaten."

He dipped his chin, but not before she'd caught the mischievous glint in his eyes. He shifted Kelsey on his shoulder. "Butter and raspberry jam on my toast, please."

"Sure thing." Once she'd plated the food, she slid it in front of him.

"You're not eating?"

"Already did." She extended her arms for Kelsey. "Come here you little munchkin." The baby giggled. She felt so warm and cuddly. She smelled good, too. Alyssa had taken pity on Carter the previous night when she'd found him almost nodding off after dinner. She'd bathed Kelsey and washed her hair, which had grown even in the short time she'd been there.

Carter tucked into his food.

"That infant bike carrier should be a great way to get Miss Kelsey out and about a little bit more, eh." She'd been concerned that

Carter didn't usually leave the house with his child, other than taking her out into the backyard and on a few trips to her grandparents' resort.

He lowered his fork. "Got a text that the bike carrier arrives today. Supposed to have an easy on and off attachment. So we can transfer from mine to your bike." He took a bite of toast and chewed.

Funny how he considered the women's bike hers now.

"Best times for long rides are before the ferries arrive and early evening when there's less traffic."

Her appointment for the attorney call was mid-morning. "Maybe I'll wait till later to bike. Which means delaying all the foodie stuff you suggested. Right, Kelsey?" She waved the baby's hand and then kissed her tiny fingers.

He used his index finger to trail a fake tear down his face. This guy was so loveable—how could his wife abandon him? But then he crammed a third of the toast into his mouth and ruined the effect.

"Okay, I'll do one of the foodie things you recommended, but only one." She couldn't believe the pushback she was giving her boss. There was something about him that made her feel easy and at home. *Getting a little too comfortable.*

Carter wiped a crumb from his mouth. "Lucky Bean—get a cup of coffee. You said you're dying for another of their frappes."

Kelsey squeaked as if agreeing with her dad. Alyssa bounced her.

A cloud passed over his handsome features. "Wonder why Starr wasn't picked up by Carolyn for this summer's crew." He forked some eggs into his mouth.

"But Starr has helped us out a lot. You'd be overwhelmed otherwise." Starr came in a few times a week. "I'll caffeine fortify at Lucky Bean and give everyone your regards."

"I sure miss Juan Pablo. He was a great barista—my favorite. He and Starr had a ministry at the park—open to anyone."

"Where is he now?"

"Starr said he's busy helping his father out—but he never mentioned his dad when he was here."

She shrugged. "Maybe he did but you missed it."

"Maybe."

She jostled Kelsey on her lap. "Maybe you and I can ride over to Marquette Park in your new bike carrier."

"I hope Amazon isn't wrong about its delivery time. It's probably more of a suggestion than actual time."

"I'll still go to the park. I like to check out the places before I take Kelsey out." To find where she could easily do diaper changes. Where a stroller could easily be managed.

"One of my favorite rides is behind the fort, and then a short walk to Anne's Tablet. The cannons are too loud inside the fort for her." Carter used his fork to cut the rest of his egg into pieces. "If you take her inside Fort Mackinac, check the cannon firing schedule and take Kels when it's quiet."

"That's what I would have to do for—" She clamped her mouth shut. She'd been about to say, 'for Sammy.'

He angled his head at her. "Sure thing. Do that before you bring Kelsey near Fort Mackinac."

She nodded. "Today, I'll enjoy the last of the lilacs. And visit The Island Bookstore to buy a book." She'd not read a novel in a long time. Since before college classes.

"That reminds me. My aunt will be here for a book signing later in the summer." He took the last bite of his toast.

"Your aunt?" She blinked at him. "She's an author?"

"Yeah, Mimi Vendue." He made air quotes with his hands, "Tagline the Parisienne Dabbler."

She gaped. "You're kidding me! I loved to sneak and read her books when I used to have time to read." *Before I became a mom.*

His lips twitched. "College and working can gobble up reading time."

As did childcare and helping with chores. She moved Kelsey to her shoulder. "That's so cool that she's your aunt. Which means you're related to that movie star, Wayne Stephens, too, right?" She suddenly felt shy. Her employer had some amazing connections. Why was she surprised, though, when they were in this gorgeous house because of his friendship with TV show hosts? And with his stepmother owning a mansion on West Bluff.

"Yup. Wayne's a great guy." He cast his eyes down.

He looked like he was holding something back. She wanted to ask what their exact relationship was, but she bit her tongue.

"Hey, I can schedule a private carriage ride for the three of us tomorrow afternoon after church. And I can point out some places that might be good for you on your own, or if you want to take Kelsey. How does that sound?"

"Amazing. Thanks."

"And you're welcome to join us for church."

An opportunity to listen to someone, in person, other than her father preaching. During the pandemic, they'd watched various preachers on television—none of them doing a good enough job by Dad's standards. She'd planned to sleep in this Sunday.

I think I'll pass. "Sounds great." How had those words just slipped past her lips?

Lilac Cottage was crammed full of physicians, EMTs, and a few nurses who dealt with cardiac issues. This wasn't exactly Susan's area of expertise, but she'd been trained in trauma, grief, and self-care for support personnel, so she was focusing on those issues this week.

Rachel Welling, RN, the director of the program and owner of this beautiful cottage, stood at the front of the spacious training room. Beside her stood Dr. Tom Austin, the medical advisor, as did Susan. Rachel gestured toward her. "Mrs. Susan Mullen, our clinical social worker, will be addressing you later today. You've seen her impressive credentials in the brochure."

Susan silently exhaled a sigh of relief as the cardiology health providers smiled at her and nodded. She returned a tentative smile.

Dr. Austin rocked back on his cowboy boot heels. "I hope one of the tasks on our list this week won't stress you too much," he drawled, his Texas twang making her smile grow larger.

The students shifted on the massive couches they occupied.

A hand shot up. "I thought we were here to de-stress."

Murmurs agreed.

Dr. Austin nodded. "That's a big part of the plan. But besides herding all the cows, a cowboy has to do some other things."

Rachel turned her palms up and then made an inclusive circle with her arms. "Like take care of yourself."

A few of the attendees sank further into their seats. Susan took a step forward and wagged a finger at them. "Don't get too comfortable, because I've got a task for y'all to do."

Definite groans from the back row.

She put her hands on her hips. "This morning y'all need to get on out front, into the carriages waiting, and head into town."

"For real?" The slim red-haired guy who'd asked the question shot to his feet.

Dr. Austin displayed a rubber band wrapped stack of admission tickets. He tossed it into the air and caught it, then laughed. "We've had generous donations. Got some tickets to the fort, restaurant vouchers, coupons for a free half pound of fudge and so on."

"Woohoo," someone called out from the back and Susan laughed.

"Each day this week," Rachel took half the packets and motioned for group members to come forward, "we'll send you out to do something."

Susan raised her arms. "Today you're all tourists! Hooray!"

"Welcome to Lilac Cottage—our health retreat summer program." Rachel grinned as she passed out the vouchers.

"The carriage ride is paid for and we'll be tipping the drivers upon their return." Dr. Austin pointed to a blonde woman in the middle of the queue that was forming. "And don't be making like a cowgal and gallop through town using that voucher from Cindy's Stables."

The pretty forty-something woman rolled one shoulder in and made a teasing expression. "Aw, why not, Dr. Austin?"

"She's got routes laid out. You'd best follow them if you know what's good for you." Tom Austin feigned a stern facial expression.

What was the route God had laid out for Susan? In her spirit, she felt that nudge to retire earlier than she'd planned. Especially with her mom getting so frail. A fragile elderly lady who would not retire her position in Congress.

When her mother and her political contingent arrived on the island, Susan would try one last time to convince her to step down from office. She had to give it one last try. And if Momma agreed, then Susan would submit her retirement request to the school district.

Wasn't that like giving God a challenge, though? To do something with her mother to make her own decision. You do this, God, and I'll do that? Not only that, but as a therapist, she knew you didn't make behavioral plans based upon someone else's behavioral choices.

She knew it was wrong.

But so was continuing to represent constituents when you were heading toward ninety.

The oldest member of Congress. The taunts from members of the media that Momma should step down, rather than die in office, increased monthly.

Momma loved serving her country.

Susan loved helping people, too. God was pulling her away from her school job, though, and a tug in her spirit had become more like one of those lassoes that Dr. Austin liked to mention.

The image of God lassoing her and pulling her toward home and her retired husband made her want to laugh, but she restrained herself as the participants streamed out of the room.

Tom moved alongside her, elbowed her gently and handed her a packet. "One for you and John, too. So skedaddle and have some fun."

"Just for the morning, though." Rachel winked at her.

"Yes, ma'am." She riffled through her packet and found the coupon for Lucky Bean. She had a big presentation this afternoon and some caffeine reinforcement couldn't hurt—especially when it tasted so good.

With her latte in hand, Alyssa exited Lucky Bean and headed down the street, looking for an empty bench. *Nothing.* Excited tourists crowded the sidewalks. She spotted a Hispanic man rolling back a wooden faux street front façade decorated with flowering trees, mostly lilacs, and roses and hydrangeas. Why had she never noticed that before? Maybe because the artwork on it was unbelievably meticulously done. So much so that it looked real. *Great optical illusion.*

Was the nursery artist trying to achieve something similar? Was that why he was still there at Tandem Cottage?

"Hola!" the man, in his mid-thirties or so, brushed his hands together. "Are you looking for the Christy Tea Shop?"

She gritted her teeth and held up her frappe. "Sorry, no." This was where she was supposed to have first interviewed with Carter. *Funny, I've never noticed this place before.*

"You're welcome to sit in our courtyard if you wish."

"Oh, I, um, no I shouldn't."

"Sit," he drew out the word and made a comical face. Something about him made her feel ridiculously comfortable.

"All right." But would this be a good place to make her call if the owner was hovering around?

He waved toward the glass storefront, which could have been plucked right out of the late eighteen hundreds. But then again, so were many places on this island. "I'll be right in there if you need anything. I've got to get some baking done in the back, but if you call for me, I'll come."

"Thanks." She took a seat at an ornate metal table with a matching chair sporting a pink and white striped cushion. *Very comfortable.*

She sipped her yummy frappe, a coconut mocha mint confection. At the appointed time, she called the attorney, who answered immediately.

After the introductions and pleasantries on the call and an explanation of fee structure that almost had her swallowing her tongue, the attorney explained how the initial call would go.

"Okay, I think I understand." Alyssa retrieved a small notepad from her fanny pack.

"So tell me, what is the main purpose of the call?"

"I have a nine-year-old son whose father recently asked for summer visitation. He'd never even met him before and things aren't going well."

"Out of the blue, he shows up?"

She moistened her lips. "He'd gotten married—to an attorney in fact—and they'd wanted him with them for the summer."

"After ten years?"

"I never told him about Sammy."

On the sidewalk, people passed by, but absolutely no one looked in her direction, which seemed odd.

There was a long pause. "He didn't know? Paid no support?"

"No and no." She compressed her lips. She wanted to spill out the whole story. And then she did, like a runaway railcar. When she finally finished, she forced herself to breathe normally.

Tourists continued to stream by, but still not a one looked toward the tea shop.

"Wow. So you weren't yet sixteen and it sounds like no actual consent was given."

She wiped away tears she'd not realized were rolling down her cheeks. She grabbed a tissue and gently blew her nose.

"You still there? That's statutory rape, at a minimum, if not outright rape." Disgust tinged the attorney's voice. "How old was he?"

"Twenty-four."

"So eight or nine years older."

"Yes. I don't know his birthday. I honestly don't know much about him."

"Then he and his new wife just grab your son for the summer. Unbelievable."

Yes, it was. "Right."

"What's her name?"

"Jennifer Fredda. She used to work downstate, but now she's in Marquette."

He muttered a few profanities. "You've got to be kidding me."

"No. Why?"

"She just barely survived a major scandal this past year. Almost lost her license."

"Oh?"

"And she'd be an idiot to be pushing any demands if she knew about the um, circumstances, of Sammy's conception."

Alyssa gripped the phone tighter. "I doubt she knows."

"That," he ripped off a few more choice words, "woman surely can work out math. Husband is thirty-four and son is nine while you, the mama, are only twenty-five."

"She doesn't know that."

A seagull squawked as if disagreeing with her.

"No? But she knows Sammy's birthdate and that it takes forty weeks, give or take, to produce a baby." It sounded like he was crumpling up paper.

She gave a curt laugh.

"Drop that little bombshell on her. I'd have your son Sammy tell her your twenty-sixth birthday is coming up."

"I couldn't have him do that." It was putting him in the middle.

"It's the truth, isn't it?"

She scrunched her eyes. "Yes."

"If he makes a big deal of it with his father, it should register with him and that nasty witch he married."

Sounded like the attorney had history with Jennifer. "Is that your professional opinion? I could send them an email about how much I'll miss him on my birthday?"

"Stipulate twenty-sixth birthday." Sounded like he'd tapped his desk hard with something metal.

"I'll pray about it."

"Whatever floats yer ore boat."

She smiled. "I like the ore boat reference."

"My office is near the Soo Locks. I see those beautiful freighters coming through all day."

"I'm hoping to move to the Soo myself."

"Great place to live."

If only she got the job. "Thanks for your help."

"Call me back if you need more help." He coughed. "She may be nasty, but Jennifer isn't dumb."

"Nothing personal—but I hope I don't have to call you back." Because she sure couldn't afford his fees.

"This is one of the few times I have to agree about that. I'm hoping you get your kid back soon."

"Thanks." She ended the call.

Thankfully, no one had entered the courtyard during her call. At the street, tourists continued to pass by, not a one of them looking this way. On a whim, she waved toward a trio of silver-haired women. No response.

"All done with your call?" The proprietor held the tea shop door open. "Come pick up some treats to bring to Carter and the baby."

"You know them?"

"Oh yes, Starr has told me all about little Kelsey." He turned. "Haven't you, Starr?"

Oh, wow, she must have gone in the back way to the place because Alyssa hadn't seen Starr enter the shop. Pink and purple spiky hair peaked out from beneath Starr's visor, which was embroidered with silver and gold thread that sparkled in the sun. Starr waved, her fingers fluttering. "Hi there. I'm glad you met Juan Pablo."

So this was him, the guy Carter said he missed. "He didn't introduce himself."

Starr shook her head at the man. "You know you have to say things out loud here."

The look he shot Starr would have made Alyssa's cheeks flame.

"Oh!" Starr rapidly crossed her hands over each other. "That came out wrong."

Or had it come out right? Alyssa had read stories of the afterlife in which people didn't have to speak to one another to communicate. *Like telecommunication.*

Were these two something different? Angels?

"*Si,*" Juan said to her.

Yes, was he an angel who had read her mind?

"Si, yes, I should have introduced myself and no, I do not think Miss Alyssa would be able to hear me if I simply talked to her in my mind." Again, he shot Starr a glare.

He mumbled something to himself and despite her poor Spanish skills, it sounded like he told her the student should not correct the teacher. But she'd probably mangled her translation.

"Come try these new cookies out." Starr motioned her toward the shop's interior.

"I better go."

"Bring her some." Juan Pablo's voice was firm, authoritative.

Starr gave him a little bow and hurried off.

"Um, I heard you and Starr used to do a ministry in the park."

"Oh, si, yes, we still do. But we've been keeping that limited."

"How long have you been here this summer?"

"Not long." He rubbed his jaw.

"I know Carter would love to see you. He misses you being at Lucky Bean." Probably shouldn't have said that. *TMI.*

"I'll be working some here," he waved toward the building and courtyard. "And I'll also be the new barista for the Lilac Cottage medical support program."

"Oh, wow, that's exciting." Wasn't Starr doing some part-time work there, too?

"Those medical personnel who worked through the pandemic are very special people." He pressed a hand to his chest. "I am truly honored that I was selected to minister to them at this time."

Ministry through coffee? Well, he was supposed to be a minister, but they'd hired him for something else. "That's, um, that's very nice."

Starr returned, a plate of white powder covered cookies in one hand and a frosted white bakery bag in the other. "Try this and bring the rest to Carter."

"And the baby. She's old enough now." Juan Pablo, hands clasped at his waist, watched as Starr presented her the goodies.

"Thanks." Alyssa took a bite of what looked a lot like a Christmas cookie that they'd once received in the mail from someone, but with no return address. Surprisingly, Dad had let her and Gayle try them. Snowball cookies? But the taste in her mouth was like citrus, coconut, macadamia nuts and chocolate all rolled up in one— her favorite cookie flavors all in one single cookie. She took another bite. It was as if eating sunshine that filled her with hope. And courage. She examined the remainder of the simple round cookie. "This is amazing."

"It's an angel food cookie." Starr rocked on her hot pink satin shoes.

"It doesn't taste anything like angel food cake." She frowned.

The two exchanged a quick glance.

"This is the Evangelist Romelda's cookie recipe. Special flavors from a special lady."

Before she could tell Juan that Romelda was her great-grandmother, he'd joined her at the table. "You know, it's a shame her grandson has frozen her out of his life and that of her grandchildren. And that he has ignored Scripture that says we aren't to do that to those who have brought us up. People should honor their parents, and she certainly was a parent to her grandson." He gave her a long look of concern with those dark eyes of his, as if he could see right inside her thoughts.

Alyssa rubbed the side of her head. Had they put something weird in this cookie?

She needed to go.

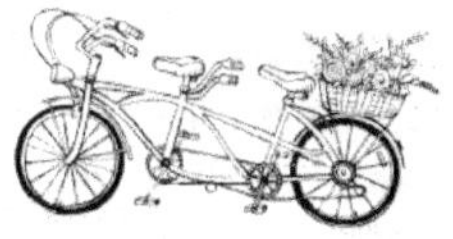

Chapter Twelve

Right now she felt more like Alice in Wonderland than Alyssa on Mackinac Island. She rose hurriedly and stumbled toward the sidewalk by the street.

A little dizzy, she leaned on a metal newspaper vending machine.

"Look at that." Nearby an older woman with obviously dyed black hair, sporting round blue plastic frame eyeglasses pointed at Alyssa.

She straightened as the woman and her friend, another older woman but with natural silver hair, moved toward the newspaper box. "Look! Romelda is coming to Mackinac Island soon. I want to see her in person."

"Me, too."

Neither put any money into the machine to get a newspaper. But as the two walked off, Alyssa opened her wallet and put the coins in to buy a *Mackinac Island Town Crier* copy and opened the box to retrieve one.

She tucked the paper under her arm and swiped her hand over her face. Her conversation with the attorney must have upset her more than she'd realized. But he gave her hope and courage to go forward with her next steps. Was it him, or something or someone else? Light-headed, she headed toward her bike, in the rack by Lucky Bean.

She should go sit in one of the many churches on Mackinac Island and ask God's wisdom about her situation. *I need to confront Dad about his behavior toward my great-grandmother.* Regardless of what he chose to do, Alyssa would meet Romelda in person when she spoke at the Grand.

"Excuse me." A petite Black woman with threads of silver streaking her hair pointed to the newspaper. "Isn't that the Evangelist Romelda on the cover?" The lady had a Southern accent.

The man holding the lady's hand leaned forward. "Sorry to trouble you, miss, but my wife's momma is best friends with Romelda. Aren't you, Susan?"

Alyssa gaped at the stranger.

"Sure as the sun rose this mornin'." Again, that Southern sweet accent. Would Alyssa have a similar accent if her father hadn't left Virginia and his grandmother behind? He'd worked hard to project a very Northern-sounding accent.

"I know this probably sounds crazy, but she's my great-grandmother. But I've never met her." Alyssa rubbed her temple. That cookie was doing strange things to her head—and to her mouth. Why had she shared this information with two people she'd just met on the street?

The couple exchanged a look. The woman moved closer. "My momma is Congresswoman Daniels. Those two are thicker than thieves."

Congresswoman Daniels was her great-grandmother's best friend. Dad had described them both as two meddling old ladies who had no business telling other people what to do—which was very rude of him. Alyssa would remind Dad that the Bible urged children, in his case grandchild to Romelda, to honor those who'd raised them.

"We're the Mullens." The man extended his hand and she shook it. "John and Susan, from Virginia."

"Would you like to sit down with us for a minute?"

"Sure. There's a spot near here where I just drank my frappe." She motioned for them to follow her.

But when they reached the place where the little courtyard and tea shop should be, she couldn't find it. "I'm sorry. I thought it was right here." It had to have been. She'd only walked a short way up Market Street.

John swiveled around and pointed back toward Lucky Bean. "If we get a move on, we can grab that table."

"Come on." Susan waved Alyssa back toward the coffee shop, where a round table with three chairs had just freed up.

They half-jogged back to the café.

John pulled out Susan's seat for her and then did the same for Alyssa.

"Thank you."

"You're welcome." He pointed to the entrance door. "There's a big chocolate muffin in there calling my name."

Susan leaned back and gazed up at her husband. "Is that right? Maybe a couple of those chocolate chip cookies might be calling our names, too." She motioned to Alyssa and herself.

"No thanks for me. I just had the strangest cookie I've ever eaten. And someone was just speaking to me about my great-grandmother before I ran into you."

Susan cocked her head. "Isn't that something? I don't believe in coincidences."

"Nope. Sounds like a God-incidence to me." John nodded at them and then headed into Lucky Bean.

Alyssa set the paper atop the metal table. "I wish I could meet my great-grandmother."

"Lord have mercy, that needs to be fixed. Um hmm."

"I agree. But can you help me?"

Eyes rolled heavenward; the older woman gave a tight shake of her head. "I can, but it's gonna involve my momma."

"Fine by me. I'd love to meet Congresswoman Daniels, too."

Susan locked gazes with Alyssa. "First we have to get past her security guards and the Secret Service."

After that meeting with sweet Alyssa, and learning of their family connection, Susan had been too wound up to join the others for dinner. All the way back from town, she and John had discussed how they could connect the young woman with her great-grandmother. But that would also mean a call to Momma. *Later.* After her evening Bible study time.

"Let's grab those pre-packed meal bags and eat on the lawn." Susan pointed to the counter at the end of the dining room.

"Sure."

Soon she and John were outside, seated in Adirondack chairs. A huge ore boat passed by in the Straits of Mackinac, which felt a little surreal. "We sure don't see those down South, do we?"

"Not like that."

"Plus, it's still light out, a comfortable seventy degrees, and we can enjoy a picnic dinner outside." She opened her bag.

"Is that what you call this sub and chips?" John unwrapped his sandwich. "Barbecue chicken, some baked beans, coleslaw, biscuits and your sister's apple pie—that's what I call a picnic."

She cast him a grumpy look. "Fine. I'll just eat my delicious turkey sub and check my Facebook messages while you imagine what our picnic could have been. And picture us sweating in the ninety-degree heat." Susan opened a personal Facebook message from a work colleague. *Another political link to something violating my personal beliefs.* She definitely wasn't in the mood for this.

Maybe she was just tired after their conversation with Alyssa and her presentation in the afternoon. But her nerves sat on edge after being sent something that her pal knew she vehemently disagreed with.

John set his Diet Coke can down. "What's up? You look like you swallowed a frog."

"Well, the person who sent this acts like a toad." She shook her head. "Feels like I can't get away from some of the nonsense."

"Don't open those social media apps."

"You're right." But it was nice staying connected to other people. "Lately, I've been questioning some of the so-called friendships I've had at work."

"Honey, that's why they are work friends, not friend friends."

"Yeah, but some of these are longtime friends from college days."

His thick salt-and-pepper eyebrows rose. "I bet I know who you're talking about."

"Um hmm."

"Sweetie, I told you years ago, when she used to call and talk *at* you and not to you, that there was something up with that woman."

Once, while Susan was lying in a hospital bed recovering from major surgery, the college pal spent over an hour bemoaning her own woes.

"Remember that time she didn't even ask you about your breast cancer but just dumped on you about her momma being put in a nursing home?"

"I do."

"And the time she came for our son's graduation and insulted you at least a half-dozen times?"

She had let the bad behavior go. "I was trying to extend grace."

"I call it failing to cut ties."

"I think it's me sweeping things under the carpet." Like getting on God's timeline for retirement.

"You ever think, babe, that leaving your school job is like that?"

She turned to face him. Was this a God thing that her husband was thinking exactly what had just occurred to her? "John, I think I'm going to unfriend her—and maybe my job, too."

He made a quizzical face. "You gonna unfriend work?"

"Maybe so. Maybe soon." Susan took a bite of her sandwich as a seagull landed nearby and stared at her accusingly. No way was that bird getting any of her sandwich.

"As far as that gal, I almost sent her packing from our boy's party, but didn't want to cause a scene. I'd have chased that devil off."

"In contrast to that frenemy, I've been blessed to have known Tamara thirty years. She's never said an unkind word to me. Honest, though, when she's disagreed with me."

"Don't I know it. And Tom's like that, too—but always has a Texan saying to make the truth funny."

She pushed some stray hairs back from her forehead. "I've sure missed seeing her at the elementary school."

"If you're up here every summer, you'll see her more."

Susan looked down at her cellphone and went to her soon-to-be ex-friend's personal page. Her finger hovered over the Friend/Unfriend button.

The seagull squawked and she startled. Not far from them, three gulls dove down toward the yard. No matter how many times Tamara told the medical guests not to feed the birds, there was always one who wouldn't listen.

You're not listening.

That voice had come from deep in her soul and tears pricked her eyes.

John reached for her hand. "You okay?"

She dipped her chin.

God had been tapping on her shoulder about retirement. Like the nurse who loved to toss leftover bread to the gulls, Susan had ignored what she was being nudged to do.

"It's like this," John opened his bag of kettle chips, "when you ignore what God is telling you to do, there's gonna be consequences."

"I know."

"What's He telling you to do?"

"Unfriend my pal." Like usual, Susan deflected whenever her husband pushed her on this topic.

"And you didn't do that right now, did you?"

She sipped her soda. "No."

"And now you'll continue to get obnoxious links and messages from her."

"I will block her and I'll call that accountant tomorrow."

"What?" John flexed his shoulders.

"What we're really talking about is my inaction on retirement."

He took her hand and squeezed it. "You know what they say—it's the way you do the little things that translates to the big things."

"And the stupid annoying link and my inability to cull that relationship is an example of how I put stuff off."

"It's okay. But I'd sure love having you home with me—or rather on the road with me, if you retire."

She nodded. "I'll call and get the retirement review process started."

"Great. I'm proud of you."

She laughed. "Wait till you see what she tells us, before you get too happy."

What if the numbers suggested she should slog away at work for another ten years?

"Tonight, first though, I'm gonna call my mother and let her know about Alyssa wanting to see Romelda." Susan laughed. "All these years she's been praying with her best friend that one day Romelda's family would open their hearts to her. And now we get to be part of that." She pressed her hands to her chest. "It's a humbling feeling."

John wagged a finger at her. "Just remember, maybe Romelda's son had a reason to 'unfriend' her."

"From everything I've heard over the years, he went off the deep end when he got to that ultra-fundamentalist school. That place demanded students to cut off anyone who wasn't conforming exactly to their standards."

"None of us is perfect. But God extends grace."

"If you're gonna go by God's Word, then don't twist it so that no one gets grace at all. Seems like Reverend Joseph Teann has judged and convicted his grandmother despite all the many people she'd helped lead to Christ."

"Or maybe because of it." John shrugged. "He can't abide a woman preacher, just like those people who kicked her out of her congregation back in the day."

"Regardless of whether he disagrees with her preaching, he should show her respect. I'm not a fan of Momma continuing to be out there in Congress—Lord knows how much me and my sisters never got to see her at home. But that doesn't mean I'd cut her off."

"Maybe you could tell your momma once in a while that we appreciate all she's done to represent us."

She nodded. That would be showing respect and honor. Maybe she and Reverend Teann had a few things in common.

Back from her busy day, after checking her emails Alyssa sprawled on the king-sized bed. Her phone chimed, indicating a call from Mom. "Hello."

"Alyssa?"

She was tempted to ask who else it would be. "Hi, Mom. How are you and Dad doing?"

Silence.

"Mom?"

A loud exhalation on the other end. "We're good. But I need to talk with you."

"Is it Sammy?" She pushed herself up off the cushy mattress and set her feet on the plush green rug. "I heard you saw him."

"Yes we did, that sweet boy. But he's fine. At least for now."

"What's going on?" The woodsy papered walls surrounding her felt like a forest closing in on her.

"Your sister and her family visited today."

"Great. Are they enjoying the lake?"

"Oh, yes, the kids love it, and Dad and I have gone for a bonfire."

Michiganders loved their bonfires. "Wonderful." She was waiting for the "but" to come.

"I wanted to ask you something."

Wait for it. "Okay." Was she going to ask her to move out of the manse even if she didn't get a tech job?

Mom huffed another sigh. "I wondered something."

"About what?" It always felt like Mom was holding back from telling Alyssa she should get a small apartment on her own.

"You know your sister hasn't come up in a very long time."

"Right." Ever since she'd had Sammy, her sister hadn't come home. Mom and Dad had flown there a few times, when Gayle and her husband had bought tickets.

"And we'd love to see her and the kids more. I'm thrilled to get some grandma time with them before they're grown up." Mom sure wasn't sounding like it.

Alyssa squared her shoulders. "When we move to the Soo, on our own, Gayle will probably come up more." It hurt that her sister avoided her and Sammy.

"You think her absence has been because of you?"

She blinked a few times. "Well, yeah." She wanted to add, "Duh," but refrained from being a smart aleck.

"No. She doesn't want to visit because she's upset with your father and me."

She dropped the phone from her ear and stared at it. She pressed the speaker button and set the Android atop the bed. "How so?"

"Well, because. . ." It sounded like she was sniffling. "Because we didn't do what she wanted."

This is news. "Which was what?"

Definite sniffing. "Report Gino to the police."

Alyssa pulled the scrunchie from her hair and let it fall. It had always felt as though her sister was furious that Alyssa had gotten pregnant. "But how could you do that when I refused to tell you who the father was?"

"Gayle said she was sure it had to be Gino."

Dad pushed for a DNA test to be done, and Alyssa hadn't allowed it.

"Well now we know she was right." It sounded like Mom was blowing her nose. "Tony is adamant that we should have him charged."

Her brother-in-law, a police officer, was to laws as Dad was to religious rules.

Alyssa stood, hands on hips. "I decided not to pursue things."

"He said, as an officer of the law, that he should have reported it."

"What?" Alyssa's voice came out a little too loud. "He doesn't even live in Michigan. They live in Virginia."

"I know, I know. But you were only fifteen."

"A month away from turning sixteen." And Gino had been twenty-four—the age her employer was now. She couldn't imagine Carter hitting on a teenage girl, much less. . .

"Now that their own kids are getting older, I think she's softened in her judgement against your dad and me."

Alyssa had always thought her older sister had passed her judgement on her—not on Mom and Dad. Being away from Sammy had been like an ache deep in her soul—how had Mom felt when Gayle became so distant? At least Alyssa had little Kelsey to take her mind off the loss. "I hope you can get your relationship back, Mom."

"I've prayed for this for a long time."

She moved toward the wall and straightened a picture of three turn-of-the-century lumberjacks felling a giant white oak. "Do you want me to talk to her?"

"Not right now."

"It might help."

"I just wanted to hear your voice."

"What?" Hadn't Mom heard her voice every day for all these years?

"I miss you. I miss Sammy." She sniffed again.

"I miss you, too, and Dad and Sammy."

"I. . . I finally realized what it was going to be like to have an empty nest," she ended with a choked cry.

This was so unlike her reserved mom, who wasn't the warm and fuzzy type. Tears pricked her own eyes. "If I get that job we'll only be a car ride away." She'd thought her mom and dad would be ecstatic.

"We wanted to come see you on the island this week—the whole family."

Genuine shock coursed through her. "Really?"

"Yes, but Gayle said she and Tony want to come alone. So we're going to watch the kids. Take them into town and to the movies and bowling. And your sister is supposed to contact you about coming on your day off."

This summer was getting weirder by the moment. "That's not for another week."

"Oh no. I don't know if that will work then."

She exhaled sharply. "I'm working. And I was just picked up for three programming volunteer jobs. I'm sorry."

"Oh my. You'll be awfully busy."

"I need to prove myself to future tech employers."

"That makes sense." It sounded like mom had pulled a wooden chair out in the kitchen and had sat. "I hate to ask you, but what if those horrible people try to keep our dear Sammy?"

"Not happening!" Her loud voice made her flinch. "Sorry, I didn't mean to snap."

"It's okay."

Alyssa took a fortifying breath. "Mom, I consulted an attorney about Gino and Jennifer."

"You did?" Her mom's voice whooshed in relief.

"Yes."

What a day it had been. She'd come home to find her email inbox showed acceptance for all three volunteer programming assignments. She'd met a sweet lady whose mother was best friends with Romelda, and she would arrange for Alyssa to finally meet her great-grandmother. She'd gotten great—and free—advice from the attorney.

Alyssa would send that email to Sammy about her birthday. And one day soon, she would have a talk with her father about responsibilities that children had toward their parents or in his case, toward a grandparent, who'd raised him. "Tell Dad I'm going to call him when he's at the church office this week."

"Sure."

She still had to work out with Susan Mullen, though, how they were going to get her dad and his grandmother together again.

God worked in mysterious ways—she just had to trust Him and the process.

"I met some nice people today on my day off." Even though they were closer to her parents' ages than her own, they already felt like friends.

"I'm glad. And I bet you'll meet some interesting people in those projects you're joining."

"Thanks. I'm hoping so."

"Love you."

"Love you, too." As the call ended, for the first time in a very long time, she wanted to talk with her mom again soon.

Chapter Thirteen

Lord, I give all these matters to you. . . A cellphone call interrupted Alyssa's morning prayer time. She reached for her phone and saw the number. "Sammy?"

"Mom! Mom! Mom!" Sammy's staccato shouting on the phone sent off all kinds of alarms.

"Son! What's wrong?" Sweat broke out on her arms. Was he injured?

"They, they, they. . . stopped giving me. . ."

No. No. They couldn't have stopped giving him his meds. But from the anxious panic in his voice, they had. "Your meds?"

"Yeah, yeah, yeah." His repetition only reinforced why his pediatric psychiatrist, a one-hundred-mile drive away from the rural area where they lived, had prescribed them several years earlier. They'd relieved a lot of his Asperger's anxiety and improved his depressed mood. Lots of work to adjust his dosages.

And now Gino and his wife had messed that up.

"I'll send him a message right away." Now wasn't the time to ask Sammy if he'd mentioned her birthday to his dad. "Have you been practicing your breathing?"

"I, uh, yeah, at school, at camp, I mean, at daycare." He sniffed loudly. "But they make fun of me."

She closed her eyes. Baby Kelsey began making sounds on the intercom, a sign she was waking. "I'm sorry, Sammy. I love you and I'll see what I can do."

"Let's, let's pray, Mom."

"Yes. Lord, we love You, we trust You, we praise You." Kelsey's babble increased. "We give all our concerns to You. In Your precious name, Amen." The baby squealed. She had to get to her. "Call me tonight if you can."

"I will." He sounded a little better. "Love you."

"Love you more." She was about to say goodbye but stopped. Kelsey happily vocalized, sounding almost like she was singing a song. "Hey, did you get my message last night?"

"Yeah, yeah, your birthday is coming up. I'm going to miss that. I hate, hate, hate that."

She chewed her lip. "Sammy, I give you specific permission to tell Gino that it's my twenty-sixth birthday and that. . ."

"What?"

"That I want to see you soon." *How am I going to pull that off?*

"I wanta see you too. I wasn't sure I should tell him because that's personal stuff and our rule is we don't share personal stuff with strangers, and Mom, he's more like a stranger than a dad."

Kelsey was babbling happily.

Alyssa rubbed her eyes. "Well, you have permission to tell him and also Jennifer, okay?"

"Okay. Bye. I gotta go." The line went dead.

What if Gino's wife flipped out and sent Sammy back, like the attorney thought she would? She should call Mom later and prepare her for that possibility.

Kelsey's baby sounds grew louder. Uh oh, that was the "maaaa" sound she did when she was getting upset. She'd been saying "dada" since Alyssa had arrived, but the "ma" sound was new.

She hurried out of her room and headed through the house and to the other wing. Carter, wearing headphones, gave her a thumbs-up as she passed, then continued with his phone conference call. She went into the kitchen and used the Baby Brezza machine to make the baby's bottle. Then she hurried to the nursery. She almost glanced into Carter's room, since his door was ajar, but didn't. Why was she tempted to do that? *Silly girl.*

She turned on Kelsey's smart light, which adjusted from dimmer to bright in the span of a minute. She loved that light. Great use of technology. She set the bottle down by the rocking chair. The baby sat up in the crib and grinned at her, revealing a new little tooth pushing up.

"Oh my!" Alyssa pressed her hands over her mouth in exaggerated delight. "Look at you, Miss Kelsey! You've got another little tooth, don't you?" She lifted the little darling from the crib, kissed her, and then brought her to the changing table.

Once she had a clean diaper on Kelsey, she carried her to the rocking chair. "Lights dim!" she called out and the smart light lowered to fifty percent. She offered Kelsey her bottle. This reminded her so much of when she'd rocked Sammy and fed him. That feeling of warmth and connectedness. Even with the lower lumens, she could clearly see little Kelsey staring up at her in what looked like adoration. The baby stopped sucking on her bottle, grinned, and cooed. Then she began drinking her bottle again. So adorable. When Kelsey had emptied it, Alyssa burped her and carried the child down the hall to where Carter was removing his headset. He stood and opened his arms for his daughter.

"Guess who's getting a new little pearly white?"

"Do you have a new tooth?" Carter pressed his forehead against his daughter's, and she giggled.

"Ma!" Kelsey pointed her index finger at Kelsey, and Carter's features tightened in shock.

Alyssa rushed to comment, "She's just making a sound. She doesn't think I'm her mother."

Did she?

She extended her arms. "Time for some smashed bananas and teething biscuits this morning."

Alyssa shifted Kelsey onto her hip and then pretended to be a horse galloping. Not too fast though, she didn't want baby to spit up her milk. "Neigh! I'm a horsie."

Kelsey made a sound that sounded a little bit like a horse.

"Look at you! You're making horsie sounds, too!" She touched the baby's tiny nose. "Your mom is missing out on all these moments."

Her phone rang, but Alyssa didn't answer. It could go to voicemail. She got Kelsey positioned in her highchair and then opened a grape-flavored teething biscuit—her favorite—and handed it to her.

Kelsey eyed the flat easily dissolvable biscuit as though she'd found a diamond in a coal mine. Alyssa chuckled as she grabbed a banana from the counter and peeled it. She took half and smooshed it with a fork in a small melamine bowl with a picture of Bluey on it. She found a baby spoon for Kelsey to hold and one for Alyssa to feed her.

"Mmm." Kelsey grinned.

"You sure love those biskies, don't you? You're gonna get your nanners next."

She peeled the rest of the banana and ate it, then removed the juice cup from the fridge and handed the cup to the baby. "You're ten months old soon, aren't you?"

Carter strolled into the kitchen, hoisting his mug aloft. "Empty. I need a refill."

"Good timing. When's Kelsey's birthday? She's ten months old soon, right?"

Her employer froze, his eyes glazing over.

"Carter?"

"I, um, yeah." He turned on his heel and left, without refilling his mug.

What had she said? How hard was it for him to simply state his daughter's birthdate?

She was tempted to go after him, but with Kelsey in the highchair, she didn't dare leave her.

Her phone made a sound indicating that a voicemail had been received. She glanced down at it. As the attorney had predicted, Jennifer had responded to the info about Alyssa's birthday. She listened to the message.

"Is this a joke?" Jennifer shouted. Alyssa held the phone away from her ear as the woman continued to yell, "You're turning twenty-six? Call me!" The voicemail ended.

A nerve had been struck with Carter and with Jennifer. What next? The attorney had advised her to wait to see what Gino would do. *I sure don't want to call Jennifer back.* She shuddered. On impulse, she texted her.

Correct. 26 on next birthday.

Alyssa sent the message.

"Hola!" Maria's cheerful voice carried from the front entrance. "Where's that baby?"

Kelsey's eyes widened. She tapped her spoon on the highchair tray. Maria had been singing some of her favorite Spanish songs with her granddaughter and teaching her to tap her hands or a wooden spoon while they sang. "Tah, tah!"

"Did you just say, 'tap tap'? No way, you little smartie pants." Alyssa patted Kelsey's arm.

"Tah, tah, tah, tah, tahhhhhh." Kelsey's tonal changes sounded a lot like a Christmas song.

Maria strode in and opened her arms. She began to cha-cha and executed a perfect one-footed spin. *"Feliz Navidad, Feliz Navidad, Feliz Navidad próspero año y Felicidad."*

Alyssa pressed her hands to her mouth. "Oh my gosh, that's what she's been trying to sing."

"You wonderful girl." Maria kissed the top of Kelsey's head, narrowly missing a spoon in her eye. She motioned for Alyssa to move, and Maria took the seat by the highchair.

"Tah, tah." Kelsey picked up the last smidge of her teething biscuit and offered it to Maria, who shook her head. The baby then popped it into her own mouth.

"I think you're Grandma Tap Tap." Alyssa smiled.

Maria turned to look up at her. "I always wanted music in my house and dancing."

"Kelsey is taking after you. She likes praise music, too."

Carter ambled into the kitchen, again with his mug. "Are boys allowed in here?"

"Only daddies!" Maria wagged a finger at him and then spooned some banana into Kelsey's open rosebud mouth. "Like that sign you put on her door at home—'No Boys but Daddies,' it says."

Kelsey hoisted her spoon. "Da!"

"I think she agrees." Alyssa tilted her head.

Maria made some shooing motions. "You two go and play. Grandma Maria is here for the day."

Carter took his mug to the sink. "So that new Italian guy is working out? The manager that Parker suggested."

"He's divine." Maria wiped a bit of banana from Kelsey's cheek. "The guests as well as the staff love him. Which means your dad and I can relax a whole lot more this summer. Your dad is coming over later after check-out time, which can get busy."

"Why don't we take a bike ride together, Alyssa?"

"You deserve a break." Maria waggled her fingers toward Carter. "I'll pay you twice what Carter does so I can have this sweetie to myself—"

"We get the hint, Mom." Carter bent and kissed her cheek.

Alyssa eyed his blue-and-green plaid pajama bottoms. "How long do you need to change?"

He tugged at his T-shirt and then bent his head to look at his pajama pants. "Don't these match what you're wearing?"

"People who leave their houses usually don't wear jammies." Alyssa couldn't believe she'd just scolded her employer.

Maria hooted. "You tell him."

Baby Kelsey's eyes grew wide, and she began to cry.

Maria began fussing in Spanish as she removed the baby from her highchair. "Sorry I was so loud." She jostled the baby and began to sing "Feliz Navidad" again and Kelsey quieted, then grinned.

"We better make a break for it." Carter jogged off toward the north wing.

Alyssa touched Maria's shoulder. "In the fridge, there are two little bowls of chunky pureed chicken—which she isn't a fan of—and carrots and rice, which she loves."

"I've brought tamale innards and some soft beans and rice for her. And some extra tamales for you and Carter tonight."

"Thanks." Luckily the baby's tummy had managed Maria's spicy food in the past, so hopefully today would be no different. Should she thank her for giving her a break? No, she didn't need a break and frankly wasn't sure she wanted a full day with her boss, a married man. This could be a little weird, even though they got along well.

I'll just think of him as another computer nerd, and we'll be fine.

"De nada. Don't forget to take a water bottle."

"Right." Alyssa made one up for herself, and for good measure, she filled another, an orange and navy plastic UVA bottle, for Carter. Then she headed to her room to grab her backpack, wallet, and other personal items she'd need.

Once inside the Up North glam room, she shook her head. How was she going to accustom herself to a minimalist apartment after living in luxurious Tandem Cottage? She was getting a little too accustomed to having all her free time to herself. When Sammy returned, they'd form a new routine in the Soo. For now, she'd enjoy the bike ride with Carter while Abuela Maria spoiled little Kelsey.

Alyssa gathered her things and then strode across the terrazzo to the front of the house. "See you later, Maria!" she called out.

"Don't rush back!"

How sweet. Mom had not ever, not once, said those words in reference to Sammy. She'd just stalwartly done everything that was needed to be done to help Alyssa and Sammy.

Outside, Carter's voice carried from the side yard.

"No! I've told you! I'll never relinquish custody to you!" He'd never sounded so angry.

She froze in place. Had Carter and his wife decided to make the separation permanent, but she wanted custody? *Lord God, have mercy and guide them.*

"You know it would be for Kelsey's best!" the angry woman's voice carried on speaker phone. "Especially after what you did. It's all your fault that—" the woman's voice silenced.

Carter threw his phone into the grass. Another couple of inches and it would have hit the hard driveway surface.

Alyssa took a slow deep breath and continued forward, hands shaking. She bent and grabbed the phone and jabbed at the end call button. "You're lucky. The screen protector didn't even crack." She took several steps toward him and handed him the phone.

"Thanks." His face held a mix of disgust, irritation, and fear. "I don't know how some people can call themselves Christians and yet behave so badly toward others."

Was his wife like that? A superficial believer? Still, that wasn't grounds to leave someone and take a baby with you.

"My nasty mother-in-law, Nancy, who never bothered to come see me and Kelsey after. . ." he swiped his hand through his hair. "She never helped us with anything."

"But she wants custody?" Was this the time to ask about Kelsey's mom again?

He shook his head tightly. "I'm not taking her calls anymore. Gonna block her." He shoved his phone in his pocket. "She can talk to my lawyer next time."

Had Alyssa's consultation with the lawyer helped, or was it causing problems for her son today? Hopefully, those two nutjobs wouldn't take out their issues on Sammy—but Jennifer's text showed she was riled.

"Ya know what?" Carter splayed his hands. "Let's forget about my horrible mother-in-law and go for a nice ride.

"You sure you're okay?" Part of her wanted to disclose her own custody problem, but she fought it. Today, she could be simply Alyssa Teann, a single twenty-five-year-old woman, on an outing.

They mounted their fifteen-speed bikes and soon sped out of the Annex and down West Bluff. Sunlight sparkled off the turquoise Straits of Mackinac to their right. Would she ever tire of this beautiful sight?

A group of equestrians approached; three older women in immaculate riding attire. From their postures and confidence these were their own horses and they were well-acquainted with being in the saddle. The front rider inclined her head toward Alyssa.

She dipped her head in return.

Once past them, Alyssa called to Carter, who rode ahead of her, "It's a lot easier riding without groceries on the back."

"That baby pull cart is coming in handy, doing double duty." Carter called over his shoulder.

"It is." Her frequent trip to Doud's Market, for little extras like spices, were strengthening her legs, too.

Carter slowed and gestured for her to bike alongside him. "Maybe you should stop making us such great dinners and we'll eat out."

She almost stopped pedaling but then hurried to catch up. If she went with Carter and the baby out to dinner, wouldn't that send the wrong kind of message? Not only that but it was expensive. "That's all right, boss, I can't afford to splurge on dinners out."

"Works for me." He laughed. "I'm enjoying all your experiments. Don't you make them for your folks?"

She laughed. "Mom doesn't usually let me cook at home. It's her kitchen, after all." And although Alyssa worked in a school cafeteria, the "cooking" there was usually reheating what the government had sent them. Only when Mom and Dad were on mission trips had Alyssa been able to practice her cooking skills.

"I can't decide which I like best—your Moroccan stuff, the Italian pasta dishes, or the French recipes with the cream sauces."

"Even if it means you have to order fancy ingredients?"

"No problem. You've seen some of the spices Maria gets off-island."

"True. She's found some pretty cool ingredients."

"I think you mean hot, as most of her spicy concoctions are."

"Right."

When other bike riders headed toward them, Carter pedaled faster and she slowed to move back behind him. As they biked past the Grand Hotel, empty carriages stood ready to return departing guests to the docks. Other Grand Hotel carriages arrived full of new guests. A little dark-haired girl in a pink sundress waved at them and Alyssa waved back.

"Care if we stop at Lucky Bean first?"

"Sure." Although Carter kept great coffee at the house, nothing compared to what the coffee shop offered. Starr's coffee making skills spoiled them when she was around, but that wasn't every day.

Soon, they were headed up Market Street, toward the café. The back streets were almost empty this morning. A lone man exited the coffee shop.

Carter slowed the bike a little abruptly, even though she could see no obstacles other than two slow-moving drays. He aimed the bike toward the curb, almost a block from Lucky Bean. "I may rethink this." He dismounted and she stopped her bike and got off, too.

"Why? Anything wrong?"

They stepped onto the sidewalk.

Carter turned his back toward the coffee shop and jerked his thumb over his shoulder. "Just spotted someone I don't want to see."

Alyssa squinted. Attired in a navy polo shirt, open at the collar, and light-colored khakis, the guy had a stiff, almost military, bearing. He clutched a newspaper in his left hand and a cellphone in the other. "Okay. Who is he, and what's the dope on him?"

"Shane White. Ugh."

She laughed. "Did you just say, 'ugh'?"

"Yeah, I reserve that just for him." Carter huffed a sigh, something he didn't often do.

"Come on. Spill the tea. Or the coffee. Or whatever."

"He's one of the big shots who shows up here every summer. Hangs out at the Yacht Club. I have no idea why he's friends with the coffee shop owner, Carolyn. Can't believe she doesn't see through him."

"And that bugs you, why?" There had to be more to it. "Did he steal one of your girlfriends or something?" She hastily added, "Before you met your wife?"

"Real secretive guy. I don't trust him—especially since Carolyn, the shop owner, got married a couple of years ago and is a new mom."

"Huh? What's that have to do with anything."

He frowned. "Too much a pretty boy. And his last big flame was a married woman."

"Oof." Alyssa cringed.

"He used to hang with this big-shot social influencer, Bunty Braeburn, who was secretly married to an actor."

"Maybe he didn't know."

"Had to have known. They were super tight. A supposed longtime couple." He snorted. "A couple of cheaters is more like it."

Alyssa shrugged lightly. "In this world we live in, if they aren't. . . saved," there, she'd put it out there, "then what can we expect?"

His nose crinkled, as it did when he was thinking. "Unsaved? You mean 'not a Christian'?"

She nodded. "Are we going to let handsome cheater dude keep us from our well-deserved awesome caffeinated treat?" She crossed her arms and tapped her foot. "I think not."

He laughed. "Come on, then." He swiveled around and for just a moment, it looked like he might offer her his arm, but then he pulled it closer to his side.

As they walked toward the shop, Shane's sweeping glance seemed to be taking in the entire street. His stance suggested he was rooted firmly to the cement sidewalk, yet his posture also indicated he was ready to bolt at any moment.

Vigilant. That's what he was. He was waiting for someone or something.

As they neared, she spied sweat dotting Shane's tanned brow, even though the day was cool, and he stood in the shade. And she could have sworn she'd heard him whisper, "No national treasure," which was odd. She must have misheard. Maybe Shane believed Carter thought too highly of himself—like he was special. *A treasure.* Which Carter was becoming to her, and she absolutely could not allow.

Shane's eyes widened. "Carter Parker. How are you doing? How's your Aunt Rachel?"

"Fine. You could see for yourself. She's up at Lilac Cottage. With her husband." He stated the last three words almost like a threat.

What's going on here?

"Lucky man." Shane quirked an eyebrow. "And I'll be heading over there this afternoon."

"I'm sure you will," Carter mumbled.

Definite history there with this guy.

Alyssa extended her hand. "I'm Alyssa Teann. The babysitter for Carter's daughter."

His handshake was warm and firm—perfect—pretty much what she'd expected from him. "Nice to meet you."

"What brings you here since there's no yacht race?" Carter sounded like a petulant teenager.

"You as part-owner of an island resort ought to know Mackinac is *numero uno tourista* destination this summer." Shane reached into his pocket for something.

Part-owner of a resort? Did he mean the Parker's resort? But that was his family's resort, not Carter's.

Shane handed Alyssa his business card. She accepted it but shot Carter a glance. He scowled.

The minimalist card had Shane Wade White and his phone number imprinted on the front. But when she flipped it over, there were strange numbers and doodles on it.

"I represent techno artists and am on the watch for rising stars. Any chance you're an artist?"

"No. What's all that stuff on the back?" The crazy drawings resembled differential equation formulas.

Carter leaned in and grabbed the card. "Looks like somebody on crack vomited up a multivariable calculus textbook."

"Carter!" Alyssa made a shocked expression.

Shane flipped his hands over, showing his palms. "I'd agree, but my customers love this stuff. All the trend in Los Angeles. So much that they're offering big bucks to acquire more pieces."

"Ya never know what kind of junk people will put on their walls." Carter tried to hand the card back to Shane, but the good-looking guy raised his hands, then dropped them.

"Keep it. Just in case you see anything like it out there." He pulled out another card and passed it to Alyssa. "And you can call me any time that you're free from your babysitting duties." He winked. "Show you around the island."

With that easy grin, who could resist him? She couldn't help smiling back. Maybe Carter was being too harsh.

"She's busy. Doesn't have time." A muscle in Carter's cheek jumped. "She's also doing a computer internship after babysitting hours are over."

"Oh. I see." Shane cast her a glance as if asking for confirmation. Computer internship?

With whom?

Chapter Fourteen

R ight," Carter repeated, astonished with himself for making stuff up. He was headed down a slippery slope, lying for his own advantage. He didn't want to lie. He genuinely did want to help Alyssa. He'd explored supervising her so Alyssa could have internship experience—but his boss hadn't approved it yet.

Alyssa gazed at him expectantly. He was such a heel. How was he going to pull this off?

Carter took her elbow. "We're gonna get our coffee now and talk geek stuff."

Shane raised his fingers to his brow as if in salute. Was that guy ex-military? Carter didn't think so. Maybe he was just mocking Carter—that seemed more likely.

Carter firmly guided Alyssa toward the entrance. The door opened and coffee scents flowed out. When he glanced back, Shane was sauntering off, his phone pressed to his ear.

"I don't like that guy," he hissed toward Alyssa.

"You don't say." She chuckled and rolled her eyes. "You're not too good at hiding your feelings, boss."

He grimaced. "Stop calling me that. Makes me feel old."

"I thought I should, since we're out in public and you're my boss." She quirked her eyebrows upward. "All right. I'll call you Mr. Parker."

"Don't call me that, either." He crinkled his nose. "Stick with just Carter. We're on the island—Mr. Parker is my father."

She crossed her arms over her chest. "Okay, Just Carter."

But Shane had helped Rachel and Jack out. Carter knew that, but he didn't know how the dude had assisted them. *And why*. The too good-looking interloper just seemed to be in the thick of things at awkward times. Jack and Rachel wouldn't tell him what Shane had done besides initiating the clearing out of Lilac Cottage's massive basement, now used for their medical retreats. Weirdly, Carter's offer to help with labor had been refused. Shane had insisted they call in a specific clean-up crew. "I'm telling ya, that guy is trouble."

"Maybe I'm trouble, too." Her lips formed a perfect pout.

He resisted the urge to sigh. Dad had always been after him to break that habit.

Someone tapped him on his shoulder. He had the awful feeling that Shane had come back to harass him. Fisting his hands, he turned and looked into bright blue eyes identical to his own.

"What the heck you doing away from the resort?"

Dad threw his arms around him and lifted him up a few inches. "Is that how you greet your old man?"

Why was moisture filling Dad's eyes? Of all the horrible things since Abbi-Renae's death, that concern about whether Dad would pick up a bottle again was the worst. Grief from Mom's overdose death had rammed his father further into addiction all those years ago. *Is Dad stressed for me and my loss, or is this something else?*

"Maria told me you were biking, and I knew you'd stop here first." Dad released him and looked at him hard. "You heard from your brother lately?"

"Yeah. He texts me every few days. Why?"

Dad's lips pinched shut.

The line moved forward and the three of them continued into the shop. The baristas shot Carter a strange look, but maybe he was imagining things. Dad tilted his head forward and grinned at Alyssa. "Good morning. I hear my granddaughter is in good hands."

"Nice to see you, again, Mr. Parker."

"Sorry I had to keep running off when you guys visited our place." He shrugged. "High season keeps me jumping."

"I can imagine."

The night they'd stopped by, a couple had been arguing in the lobby and Dad had to help. Then Parker had called from Switzerland about something to do with permits. Growing up at the resort, Carter had been amazed his grandparents possessed so much energy, and they had Dad and Mom to help them. Now Grandpa was gone and Grandma Kareen remarried to Grandpa Gianni and retired. "How's your new manager coping?"

"I'm sure glad your brother and Jaycie sent him over here to us." Dad rubbed his eye.

Yet another mention of Parker. They'd lost several pregnancies. Was Parker in danger of a relapse? He'd sounded good the last time they'd talked on the phone. Preoccupied but okay. "What's going on with Parker and Jaycie?"

His dad stiffened and blinked. "I don't know. Hoped you did. Your brother's sounding more distant. Says he's taking a break soon. Thinking about coming home."

Marital problems? *No.* But all those pregnancy losses may have finally caused a crack in their solid relationship. "It's been a while. Maybe there are things he needs to take care of here. Jaycie coming?"

"He wouldn't say."

The coffee line moved forward, and they inched closer to the register.

"Listen, I'm not here for the caffeine, Son. I'm on my way to Lilac Cottage to see Tamara and Tom Austin to bring some coupons for our resort." He dragged his hand over his square jaw. "I better run."

"See ya later then."

Dad smiled at Alyssa and then left.

"Your dad is so nice."

"Sobriety can do that to you." Why couldn't he resist blurting out inappropriate things? Maybe because his wife had allowed him to do so? *Nah, couldn't blame it on Abbi-Renae.*

Alyssa's raised eyebrows nearly reached her bangs.

Should keep his mouth shut instead of talking about his family's issues in recovery from alcoholism. Sobriety was powerful, though.

And God is powerful, too. But where was God when Carter needed Him? When his wife was dying? He'd seemed far away from him then.

He pressed his eyes closed for a moment, trying to block out the memory.

"You okay?"

"Yeah."

The older couple in front of them, attired in matching neon yellow T-shirts and holding hands, moved forward and so did Carter and Alyssa.

"So how about that internship I'm doing?" Alyssa looked hopeful, but skeptical.

Truth time. He had to get off that slippery slope and onto a solid ledge. "I actually did put in, with my employer, for you to do an internship under my supervision."

She blinked at him. "And? I can tell there's more to this."

He scratched above his lip. "I haven't heard back from them yet. And. . ."

"So there's no actual confirmed internship?"

"Not yet, but there may be." He stretched his neck.

"And what else?"

"I told them you may be willing to work for free."

"What?" She cocked her head. "Without confirming that with me?"

He shrugged. "You sounded desperate for an internship. You did offer unpaid at one point."

Disappointment painted her even features. "Yeah, I guess I did. And I am desperate. Thank you for trying."

"Hey, maybe they will approve it, and maybe they'll even pay." He left out the part where he knew all their paid internships had been long gone.

She playfully pressed a fist to his shoulder. "You have to pay for my coffee, at least, if I'm maybe, possibly your new intern."

"Sure thing."

It was their turn to place their order. Andrette Herron's eyes widened. "Carter Parker! Why are you hiding up at the Annex all the time?"

"I'm not on vacay. I'm working remotely." His flat tone was meant to convey his lack of interest in this topic.

"Oh. I must have forgot that." The manager raised her index finger. "But I have to tell you this before I do forget. Juan Pablo is back, and he is going to pinch hit for us, taking the weekend afternoon shift."

"Alyssa, here," he pointed at the woman, who was becoming more important to him by the day, "told me she ran into him recently at some tea shop. I was hoping I'd see him."

"Go to the park this Sunday, and he and Starr will be preaching up a storm."

The guy behind them fake coughed. Probably annoyed they were chatting and holding up the line.

He gave Andrette his order, and then Alyssa ordered her frappe. He paid for both.

"Good to see you, Andrette."

"You, too."

They moved out of the way. The line now formed out the back door and into the street, maybe twenty people deep.

"Good thing we got here when we did."

"This place is so popular, but it's no wonder, eh." Alyssa inhaled appreciatively. "Their coffee is the absolute best."

"It is."

"Do you see Starr?"

"Um, nope." He glanced around. "Woulda noticed her spiky hair with pink glitter strands."

Alyssa pointed behind him and he turned.

He raised his eyebrows as Starr half danced, half ambled, toward them, waving a pink and purple sparkling pinwheel thing in her hand. "Hello, baby daddy and fellow babysitter."

That strange feeling of wonder, warmth, but also weirdness filled him as it always did when he encountered Starr. "I hear you and Juan took back your preaching gig."

Starr raised her pink glittered eyebrows. "*Absolutement!*" Starr pulled him in for a quick hug, and he smelled the almost incense-like perfume she wore. "Juan is back, and you know what that means." Suddenly her expression changed, as though she'd said too much.

"Which is?" he encouraged. Juan Pablo had been there during Rachel's and Grandma Kareen's difficult time. He'd not seen him since.

"Um," Starr turned toward Alyssa. "How about that internship?"

Alyssa cocked her head. "I'm about to start doing an internship with Parker's company and gosh, we may need you to watch Kelsey a bit more. . ."

"Of course." Starr jumped, like a kid, and clapped her hands. "Let me know."

"That artist is still there." Carter moved further aside as more customers crowded them.

"Not for long." Starr sounded very sure of that.

"How do you know? Have you talked to him?"

"No." She poked a sparkling pink and lime green nail into her pale cheek. "I heard through the grapevine."

He'd love to know exactly what her grapevine was. He suspected it wasn't the Mackinac Island gossip line, but something a little more mysterious.

Shopping on Mackinac was nothing like shopping in Hampton Roads. Susan held John's hand as they strolled down Market Street toward where she'd recently spotted a gorgeous dress. She'd love to wear that when they dined at the Grand Hotel, later in the month.

As they neared Lucky Bean, John gently elbowed her. "Not till we're on our way back. They're not gonna let you take coffee into the dress store."

She laughed. "You must have been reading my mind."

"Married all these years—I ought to know by now."

She cast him a playful faux irritated look. How she loved this man. If only she could trust that covering the health insurance would allow her to retire earlier than sixty-five, which was in another four years.

As they passed the café, the scent of coffee and pastries wafted out. Movement at one of the outdoor tables caught her eye. She flinched. Was that him? Leland? Either that was him or he had a twin.

Susan turned to her husband. "John, I swear I just saw that guy the FBI is looking for, from my group."

John stopped and she did, too. But when he whirled around to look, she tugged on his hand. "Don't gawk!"

"You want me to go back and see? Maybe get us some coffee now?"

"Give me a moment and I'll look. Maybe it's my imagination. I've been watching for him." Slowly, she turned until she could get a good look at the man. *Similar features. Similar build.* But when he removed his hat, he was balding. "Nope." She turned back around.

John shrugged. "You know they say there are something like three people in the world who may look just like you. What do they call that?"

"Doppelgangers." She laughed. "Yeah. Well, this guy could have been if he had more hair."

A young couple with a stroller came behind them. "Excuse us. Sorry."

"No problem," Susan said as she and John stepped aside. The baby was so cute, dressed in a little cherry printed outfit with a matching headwrap. Alyssa had told them she was babysitting an adorable ten-month-old baby girl.

Then a lithe young man with thick blond hair exited the coffee shop. *Oh no, no, no.* That was Carter Parker, her former client. And beside him was Alyssa Teann.

As she took John's arm and spun him around, she hissed, "That's my client from this winter, Carter Parker."

John covered her hand with his as they hurried in the other direction. "If these eyes are right, that was our new friend, Alyssa, with him."

"Um hmm."

"Wonder what those two are doin' together."

"I don't know, but I do know I don't want to run into him."

"Well, let's go get your dress and circle back for coffee after."

They continued to the intersecting street and turned left. Once they hit Main Street, they turned left again and found more tourists on both the sidewalks and bicycling in the street. Carriages were filling up by the carriage tours line. They arrived at their destination, and Susan entered through the open door to the dress shop.

Inside, the faint scents of lilac and roses mixed with something musky. "I heard this place is new, and islanders don't always like change."

"Some change can be great, though. Like this place." He gestured around. "And big changes can be good—we're asking your mom's friend to meet with Alyssa. Hopefully, Romelda can see her son, too. That's a big shift for that family."

"You're right. That huge change, if successful, could bring healing."

John followed her in as she went to the window, where the elegant gown was on display.

She looked up and saw the man from the coffee shop on the sidewalk. Now wearing his bucket hat and oversized sunglasses, the man's prominent features and the way he moved, so erratically, still reminded her of Leland. Had her client worn a toupee?

Through the window she spied a middle-aged woman, arms full of bags, who rushed toward the man. "Kenny, can you take some of these things?" Then she gave him a huge smooch on his cheek.

"Definitely not Leland." She couldn't imagine him accepting a kiss from anyone but his mother. "I want to help Agent White, but I haven't seen Leland again. Although now I have another client to worry about running into—especially when we see Alyssa again."

"Honey, we're not here to be spies."

She touched John's arm. "Wait. Remember when we met Jack's father? He said he was a retired cop or something."

"He said law enforcement. He was vague."

"Anyway. You want to ask his opinion about this situation?"

"He's retired. And I thought Agent White said to keep this to ourselves."

"You're right."

"May I help you with anything, folks?" The store manager, a red-haired woman dressed in a caftan-like garment covered by a flowing pink vest, gave them what looked like a pained smile.

There were a lot of customers milling around, and it looked like she was the only one working right now.

"Yes. I love that gown." Susan pointed.

"The burgundy one?"

"Yes."

The woman leaned forward and removed the dress from its display and held it out for Susan. "It's beautiful, isn't it?"

"The right size, too." Susan touched the soft fabric.

"Sold!" John grinned and pulled out his wallet.

They followed the shopkeeper to the counter, and John paid for the transaction.

When they stepped out into the sunlight again, a carriage drawn by a team of six Percherons rode by. The clip-clop of the hooves had become a comforting sound this summer.

"I'm gonna miss this place."

"Maybe we'll be back. I just happened to enjoy a soda in the sunroom while Rachel and Jack Welling were in the lounge area. Did you ever notice that you can hear right through that glass?"

"John, you know it's not nice to eavesdrop. But what did you hear?"

"They want to offer me a position next year. And bring you back as a permanent staff member. With a nice fat bonus if we both stay through the summer."

"Maybe eavesdropping pays off sometimes, but don't make a habit of it." She nudged him with her elbow.

"Don't say anything to Tamara about it. I might just have imagined something I wanted to hear."

"You'd like to come back?"

"I would. But only if my sweetie is with me."

"Sweeten me up a little more and take me back to Lucky Bean." She grinned at him.

"With a fudge stop en route."

"We are gettin' way too used to this, aren't we?" She laughed. But it was true.

Alyssa kissed Kelsey goodnight and set her in her crib. What a day it had been. So much fun biking around with Carter. She couldn't help but imagine how it would have been if Kelsey had been in the baby cart behind her dad and Sammy on the back of a tandem bike with her. Good thing she would be leaving here the end of August.

As she stepped out from the hallway onto the terrazzo floor in the foyer, the front doorbell rang. Carter was in the middle of an evening Zoom meeting with his colleagues, so she went to the door. She checked the outdoor camera. Standing outside was a heavily pregnant brunette with dark circles under her eyes. She had a rolling carry-on case beside her. One of the Gough taxis was pulling away in the drive.

"Hello."

"Can you let me in, please?" Her pleading eyes and voice tugged at Alyssa's heart. Was this Carter's wife? She looked a little older than him. And she didn't look like the few pictures of Abbi-Renae that Alyssa had seen.

She slowly opened the door. The woman did look familiar. "May I help you?"

"I'm Jaycie Parker." The woman craned her neck to look around Alyssa.

"Carter's sister-in-law?" Carter had shown her a picture of his brother and sister-in-law from a recent visit with them. Alyssa stepped aside and Jaycie entered the cottage. "He never mentioned you were coming, and he's in the middle of a conference call."

"I didn't tell him, and I won't interrupt. But can you point me to a bathroom?" Jaycie smiled and patted her belly. "Baby is sitting right on my bladder."

"Sure." Alyssa moved past her, to the right and then gestured to the front bathroom. "Right there."

"Thanks." Jaycie did the pregnant lady duckwalk to the bathroom.

She turned to see Carter, jaw dropped open, raising his arms, palms flipped over in the sign of confusion. In a couple of minutes, he terminated his session and strode over to her just as Jaycie emerged from the bathroom.

Carter pointed to Jaycie's belly, which looked about seven months along. "What?"

The pregnant woman began to cry. "We didn't want to say because of the other times. . ."

Carter had only said his brother and his wife had experienced some struggles. From Jaycie's comment, Alyssa inferred they may have lost one or more pregnancies.

"It's why I remained behind in Switzerland when Parker came to see you."

Switzerland? Carter hadn't mentioned that. Just like he'd not shared his folks owned a mansion on West Bluff. What kind of lives did these people lead? *Not like mine.*

"How far along?" Carter sputtered. "When?"

"About two months away, depending on if she comes early."

"She? A girl?" Carter whooped.

"Congratulations." Alyssa offered her a warm smile.

Carter pulled his sister-in-law in for a hug. "Baby Kelsey will have a little girl cousin to play with."

Alyssa tried to excuse herself by moving away from the two, but Carter touched her shoulder. "Stay for a minute."

"Okay."

"Jaycie, this is my right-hand gal, Alyssa. She's taking care of Kelsey and she's a fellow programmer."

Alyssa raised her palms. "Not quite yet." But Jaycie was doing a double take between the two of them, her eyes slightly narrowed.

Carter's phone rang. "Have to take this. Be back in a few." He jogged off toward his workstation.

Jaycie pointed to the nearby chairs and the two of them sat.

The pretty dark-haired woman leaned back into the chair. "I really hate to ask, but how's he doing, Alyssa?"

"What do you mean?"

Exhaling hard, Jaycie shook her head. "After everything that happened, we're worried about him and Kelsey."

Alyssa's breath caught in her throat. *Oh no.* That feeling in her spirit when she'd been on the MacBook—that Abbi-Renae was gone. What had happened? She schooled her face into a placid expression—one she used for Sammy, so he'd not see how upset she was. But Jaycie wasn't looking at her, but around the expansive room.

Carter jogged back over to them. "Did you get any dinner earlier, Jaycie?"

"Yes, me and baby girl are fed." Jaycie patted her belly.

Alyssa pointed to the one piece of luggage. "Is that all you have?"

"It is. Parker is bringing the rest."

"Parker is coming home?" Carter shoved his hand back through his blond hair.

"He stayed behind on the mainland to take care of a few things. But I wanted to see you first." She spread her arms overhead. "So here we are."

Alyssa flipped her palms over. "Let me leave you two so you can talk."

"Not yet. I have great news tonight. I have. . ." Carter made a drum roll sound and pretended to bang a drum, "a new intern!"

Her heartbeat surged. It was finally happening. Grinning, she took a step toward him, almost ready to hug him and then caught the look on Jaycie's face. A wariness tightened the woman's pretty features. "Mr. Parker, boss, sir, thank you!"

His face twisted into a goofy expression of disbelief. "Um, internship withdrawn, unless you call me Carter. And since I finally got your date of birth info off your application to my company, I perhaps should call you, ma'am, since you're almost two years older than me."

"Good idea. Call me ma'am." Alyssa crossed her arms sent him a look that dared him to do it.

He crinkled his nose. "I think I'll call you Commander."

"You think I'm in charge?"

"If the title fits. . ." He made his mouth wide as if he was shocked.

Alyssa grabbed a pillow from the couch and tossed it at him.

Jaycie's eyes widened as she brought her index fingers together and then pointed toward each of them. "How about Nerdy Carter and Minion Alyssa—the two programmer geeks?"

Carter crinkled his nose. "Could work."

"She called it." Alyssa fist-bumped Carter.

"You two." Jaycie shook her head. "I swear I feel like I just met a female Carter clone."

"Can't be. A clone would be same sex, right, Alyssa?"

"Yup, her analogy is wrong." They fist-bumped again.

Jaycie yawned. "Somebody lead me to my bedroom. I gotta crash."

"Sure thing." Carter grabbed the carry-on bag and toted it off to their wing.

So would he start them on an internship project that night? Would he explain to her about her duties? She had to let Mr. Ridley know she'd grabbed an internship.

Praise the Lord! She'd have to tell everyone! She'd be sending emails all night.

Her phone pinged for a text.

> Mom why are they mad and yelling about your birthday? I called Grandma and Grandpa and they said to stay in my room and be quiet so I did. I want to see you for your birthday. Can I? Can you come and get me? Grandma and Grandpa want to come but they said you have to say it's ok. Mom, please tell them it's ok.

Oh boy. Heart hammering, she quickly texted him back.

> It's ok and I will tell them. Praying for you. Love you. xoxo

Carter ambled back into the room. He stopped several feet away from her. He was wearing the same expression that she imagined was on her own face—shock and upset.

"I, um, Kelsey's mom. . ." He rubbed his face. "My wife died suddenly and tragically and that's all I want to say about it right now."

She couldn't find the words to respond.

"Goodnight." He turned and stalked off.

Chapter Fifteen

Alyssa had tossed and turned all night, after talking with her folks, who were contacting Gino today to arrange pick-up of Sammy. She rubbed her eyes and prepared a morning cappuccino for herself and for Jaycie, who'd insisted her obstetrician allowed caffeine.

"I heard Carter told you about Kelsey's mom."

"Died tragically and suddenly, he'd said." Alyssa repeated dumbly. Heat flushed her chest.

Poor Carter, poor little Kelsey.

Jaycie accepted her mug. "Didn't he say before?"

"No," her voice emerged as a whisper. So much for hiding her emotions.

"Wow, he's in worse shape than I thought."

"He's never even said her name," she blurted out. He'd written it on the computer information paper, though.

"Wow, he won't even own what happened? I hate to do this TMI thing when we've only just met last night, but this is what I am here for—to check on Carter and to take care of my baby." She sipped her cappuccino.

Alyssa added more sugar to her mug. "No. He'd never said."

"It must be too painful."

Shaking her head, Alyssa bit her tongue.

"Hey, I want to help with Kelsey and get to know her, but I can't do a bunch of lifting. Just in case. But I can hold her, rock her, and feed her."

"Just no lifting?"

"Nope. I'm going to focus on Carter and getting him to open up."

She thought back to the few things he'd said. His wife sang praise songs all day long. *In heaven—that's what he meant.*

"I'm going to pull in the big dogs. Maria and Hamp. Have my mother-in-law and father-in-law been here much?"

Alyssa gave a tight shrug. "It's high season, plus Maria is helping cater the healthcare providers' seminars."

"Maria and Hamp are going to have to get more involved. I bet they thought he'd told you about her death."

"I only knew her name from her Amazon account," she blurted out. *Probably shouldn't have said that.*

"Oh my gosh. Poor Carter. He's been through so much. His mom—did he at least tell you about her and about all the addiction in the family?"

She nodded.

"Well, Hamp lives and breathes that resort in the summer, but Parker and I are ready to come stateside. So that should help."

She liked Jaycie already and she didn't even know her. It was as if some invisible bond was already forming.

"You know, I feel like I've known you forever, but I think it's us both having the Holy Spirit." Jaycie gestured between herself and Alyssa. "You're a born-again believer, aren't you?"

"My dad is a preacher, and I made a decision for Christ as a young girl." And Sammy had made that profession of faith, too. *I miss him so much.*

"Let's pray that the Lord helps us crack Carter's grief shell."

"Interesting way to put it."

"Yeah, I can't take credit." She tilted her head and pressed long splayed fingers near her neck. "My father-in-law invented the term. He said Carter was in a cement shell of grief and he couldn't crack it—but that his therapist had made a big dent."

"Wow, I didn't even notice the shell—to even take a crack at it." She shrugged.

"I know I'm oversharing, but if you'd known him before, then you'd know he's not the same guy right now. His phone calls, his texts, the family Zoom meetings—it's like the Carter we all knew and loved is gone." Tears trickled down the woman's pretty face, and she swiped them away. "Well, not gone, but like a grayed down version."

"Like making a psychedelic image and then turning it to grayscale?"

She gave a rich laugh. "Maybe not psychedelic but close."

"So I probably don't even know who the real Carter is then, eh?" That stung for some reason.

Jaycie drained her cappuccino mug. "Describe him in five words."

"Hmm. Serious, determined, great father—that's two words but I'm counting as one—restrained but maybe that's like serious, and kind."

"That's only half of our sweet Carter." Shaking her head, Jaycie raised her feet from the floor. "Look at my swollen feet."

"Yikes. This is early in the day."

When Jaycie shot her a questioning look, Alyssa pointed to the living room. "Believe it or not that sofa over there has a secret recliner."

"No way, but hurray!" Jaycie carefully stood and moved to the creamy leather sofa and plopped down at the end. She groped for the button, pushed it, and the foot section raised.

Alyssa beamed. "It's pretty cool because it's all one piece. I guess some kind of designer trick, so you can't tell it's actually meant for comfort."

"Fancy! But I love it."

Alyssa slacked her hip. "Mind if I ask what Carter was like before?"

"Oh, the other half of him was the best. The zing. Funny, happy-go-lucky—even given all the Parker men have been through. Always reminded me of the kind of kid who could sail through anything."

Alyssa nodded. "He's not a kid anymore."

"Nope. My husband was a young alcoholic. Thank God, he's staying sober."

"Yes, praise God for that."

Jaycie locked eyes on her. "I'm glad you're a believer. Carter always had a strong faith, but oh my goodness, one person can only take so much loss."

"Someone with less faith and strength of character may have broken down."

"He did for a while. But Maria and Hamp took care of him and Kelsey in Virginia until he could cope. He got help."

"He said he'd been in therapy, too."

"Yes." She pressed her head back. "Before Abbi passed away, Carter was the family's rock. He was like that Energizer Bunny in the commercials. He just kept going, and you could count on him to be steady."

Alyssa raised her index finger. "That's still the same. He's a very steady kind of guy who you can count on."

"Yeah. I think we didn't see that. He was a kid still, the baby in the family, but he was the one everyone leaned on emotionally. He was the happy guy. But he was also the one everyone could go to for a pick-me-up."

"Still steady, but no longer the bluebird of happiness."

"Right."

"But he's still there, Jaycie." She bit her lower lip. "And lately, even since I arrived here, he's telling jokes and laughing more. And he takes joy in the baby's activities. When I first got here. . ." She cut herself off, not wanting to tell Jaycie that he'd not even had proper baby items for Kelsey.

"I think I know. Maria said he arrived with like one or two toys for Kelsey, and you got after him about it."

"I did. But he was taking care of her basic needs—just not the developmental play stuff. But he's got me for that now."

Jaycie gazed at Alyssa like she was taking her in. "Maria was right about you. You're just what Carter needed."

"I think you mean what Kelsey needed." She needed to re-direct this conversation fast. "I'm her babysitter. Mrs. Parker is very gracious."

"They both need you, and it's probably good you didn't know about Abbi-Renae. Carter never could stand someone feeling sorry for him." She gave a curt laugh.

Carter wasn't his old self, which was to be expected. And he wasn't sharing about his wife's death. What exactly had happened?

"Alyssa, how's his Lupus doing? We've been worried he'd flare again. He got pretty bad right after Abbi died, but then said he'd improved. It's a non-subject now—he won't discuss it."

"Lupus?"

Jaycie raised her dark eyebrows. "I'm guessing he didn't tell you about that, either."

"Nope."

"But that can also mean it's being well-managed. Maria thinks it is."

"I have seen no sign of him being in an autoimmune flare and no rashes that are visible. I have an older cousin who has it. Kind of a scary disease."

"I'm sorry for being literally a 'Nosy Parker' as the Brits say, but we really wanted to know from someone other than Maria."

Her baby monitor app came on and Kelsey came into view on her phone. "Guess who's up and ready to see her auntie?"

Susan displayed her phone for John to see the weather info. "It's ninety-five degrees at home and effective temperature of one hundred five."

"Good thing we're here."

Tam headed toward their table, coffee pot in hand. "Good morning."

"Good morning." Susan grinned at her friend. "Can you sit?"

"You better believe it." Tam set the coffee pot down and pulled out the chair across from Susan. "And Tom is joining us, too."

One of the kitchen staff rolled the breakfast cart toward them. On top, an assortment of baked goods, including her favorite low-carb strawberry muffins, tempted her. Fruit cups, bananas, apples, and oranges filled the lower portion. "Would you like something hot, too, today?" the young woman asked as Susan, John and Tam chose their selections.

"Can I get a Denver omelette?" John's voice was silky sweet, and he winked at the server.

"Of course, sir."

Susan raised her eyebrows, but her husband pointedly ignored her. Tam looked like she was stifling a laugh.

The worker moved on to the next table, and John leaned back and patted his stomach. "I sure do love this place."

Susan shook her head. "Thank goodness for all those bike rides and walks we take or we'd both need a new wardrobe when we get home."

Tom, waving a folded newspaper, slid in beside Tam and kissed her cheek. "Mornin' sunshine."

"Good morning, sleepyhead."

Tamara grabbed the paper and shook it open. "Let's see what passes for news around here."

"Better than murders and all manner of crime like at home." Susan took a bite of her muffin.

"So true," John agreed.

Tam gaped at the newspaper, her brow crinkling.

Tom leaned in. "Isn't that—"

"Yes!" Tam cut him off and passed the re-folded paper to Susan. "Look."

Susan took the newspaper and read.

Congressional Leaders to Gather at the Grand Hotel

It felt like a cannonball from Fort Mackinac had landed in her gut. "She's the most stubborn person I've ever met."

Tamara poked at Momma's name. "But doesn't she have to have a nurse with her most of the time now?"

"She does. John and I just spoke with her, and she confirmed her nurse is coming."

"But didn't her personal care attendant just quit?" Tam rolled her eyes upward.

"She did." John shook his head. "But her friend Romelda and her crew will be with her."

Momma liked the idea of Romelda meeting with Alyssa, but she'd told Susan she'd have to make the call. *Hopefully she'd remember to phone her friend.*

Tom rapped his fingers on the tabletop. "I thought her doctor said she needed to stay in one familiar place if she was to finish carrying out her duties."

"He did. But like any of us here," Susan motioned around the table, "or anyone in the world, Momma knows best."

Tamara laughed. "Sounds like Mrs. Daniels all right."

Quiet settled over their table, as Tom ran his fingers along his jaw, Tam stared down into her coffee mug, and John clasped his hands together on the table.

Susan's head began to pound. "She's coming to the Grand Hotel, and if I had been the one making," she made a motion as if shoving someone, "her go there and work for our country, I'd have been reported for elder abuse."

"Yup, you would. Virginia hotline for senior abuse." John's warm hand covered hers. "But not a one of us, or her constituents is making her show up in Congress on any given day either."

Tom chuckled. "She's not alone. One of my buddies says the pharmacies there send bags of anti-dementia meds up there every day to Capitol Hill."

"Scary, isn't it? When Momma comes home, John and I have to do everything we can to make sure she's safe. Make sure all the caregivers are there, and she's getting all her medical needs met."

"Then she turns back around and runs up to her place in DC and operates like she pleases." He used his free hand to cup around his mouth. "But we've got cameras in the front, in the back, in the kitchen, hallways, and even the living room in case something happens to her. And we've got some caregivers there, too."

"And we go up, and Colby checks on her when he visits from New York. And the caregivers give us their reports each night."

"Do you think she has dementia?"

"No!" Susan covered her mouth, her cheeks heating. "Sorry, that was too loud. I think she's a cantankerous, frail, very elderly lady who would be safer at home. Every day I wonder if she'll fall and break something."

"From what I've seen of her on TV, she's a force to be reckoned with. I mean, those eyes and that face, when she's interrogating people." Tom did a great imitation of Momma's intense stare of scrutiny, and she and John laughed.

"Nailed it!" John high-fived Tom. "That's my dear old Mother-in-law."

"Her friend, Romelda, often talks on her show about her own estrangement with her grandson, whom she helped raise. I wonder if she's as hard-headed as your mother." Tamara cocked her head.

John exchanged a long look with Susan.

She huffed a hard breath. "Actually, we are working on reuniting Romelda with her granddaughter, who is on the island right now."

"And Susan is calling Romelda tonight, aren't you honey?" John knew her tendency to avoid difficult situations, and he was calling her out. "Because you know your momma isn't gonna remember."

The server brought their food. As she passed John's omelette to him, Susan reached for it. "That's mine, isn't it honey?"

Everyone at the table, and the server, cast Susan a look of disbelief as she tucked into her husband's breakfast.

The rest of the food was laid out.

Susan handed back the plate. "That was pretty good penance payment."

"Penance payment?" Tom's lips twisted into a comical expression. "Is that some kind of Southernism we don't use in Texas?"

"I get exactly what it means." John waggled his eyebrows.

Tam cast Susan a knowing look. Her friend knew John's little trick of putting her on the spot, and how she'd make him pay later.

But she would make that call. She owed it to Alyssa and it would bless Romelda, and Alyssa's father, too.

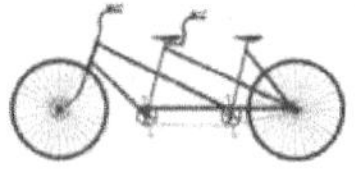

Chapter Sixteen

If this time spent with Carter developing a new app was supposed to be "work," then Alyssa was going to love her job in the Soo. Mom confirmed they'd brought Sammy home from Marquette. She and Dad were boxing up some things for their move in late August. Carter and she had spent the past day getting Jaycie settled in and adjusting to baby time with the new intern time. Things were moving along on all fronts.

"Little angel is in bed," Alyssa told Carter, who was staring at his large middle screen. "As is her auntie."

Carter's mouth twitched into a grin. "Pregnant ladies need lots of sleep."

"Yup."

He turned and his eyebrows pushed together. "You sound like you know something about that."

Heat crept up her neck. She didn't want to lie. "I know Jaycie was exhausted when she got here, and she's been catching up on rest."

"Yeah, but she says not to worry. Her doctors, and mommy friends, have told her to sleep whenever she feels like it. Especially after a transatlantic flight."

"She's snoring loud enough to wake the dead." She cast a guilty look at him. "Oh, I'm sorry. I shouldn't have said that." *Awkward.*

He motioned to her seat beside him. "She couldn't possibly wake my wife. She's been gone over ten months. Abbi-Renae is in heaven."

He said her name. "I'm really sorry. But that explains a lot."

"It's not something I've been ready to discuss."

"I'll let you bring up the topic when you're ready." She flexed her hands upward. "Until then, we've got lots of other things to discuss."

He swiveled around and reached for his coffee mug. "You're right about that."

"With Jaycie here, I imagine she'll want to catch up with you." She longed to ask about his Lupus but wouldn't push it.

"I imagine Jaycie will feel better soon. I slept almost twenty hours after I flew to Switzerland when I graduated." His face contorted briefly. "Abbi-Renae wouldn't go."

Alyssa shifted in her seat. "But your wife was pregnant then. That was probably why she didn't want to go."

"Nope." A muscle in his cheek jumped. "It would have interfered with her race-walking routine."

"Huh?" She crinkled her nose, trying to picture a twenty-two-year-old woman power walking while pregnant. "What do you mean?"

He drained his coffee mug. "Abbi race-walked through our neighborhood before and after work."

"She couldn't skip it for a few days or do that in Switzerland?" For someone who didn't want to talk about his deceased wife, he'd finally opened up.

"She could have." He raised his eyebrows. "But then it would have unraveled her for a few days. Better to not rock the boat."

Had Abbi-Renae suffered from autism like Sammy?

He jerked his chin up slightly. "Best to not speak ill of the dead, as my grandma would say."

She nodded.

He turned and scanned the images on the screen. Dark circles under his eyes made him look far older than his twenty-four years. "All right, back to this program I want to show you."

How were they going to work out an internship when the guy was already exhausted from his day job? And grieving his wife. Maybe she should let him out of his promise. Why had he allowed Shane to goad him into saying that she was his intern, anyways?

"Okay now, watch for it." Carter leaned in.

A spinning top of rainbow colors appeared on the computer screen and zig-zagged across the images, till they all disappeared.

"Wow, that's cool." She'd never seen anything like it.

"Done!" Carter raised his hands, grinning. He pushed back his chair, stood, and began to open his arms—as if to hug her. Then he suddenly moved his arms to his side, his cheeks reddening. "Finally, got this project to work."

"Congratulations." She high-fived him. "How long you been working on it?"

"Ah. .," he closed one eye and leaned his head to the side. "Not sure I want to say."

She laughed. "But it's done now, so that's what counts."

"If only it were that easy my little Padawan" He stretched and yawned. "But time is important to our clients, that's for sure."

"You sure you're ready for our evening session?"

"Yeah, let me run grab that last cup of coffee—unless you want it."

She waved a hand. "I'm good." She wasn't just good—she was almost giddy.

Carter strode off toward the kitchen.

We're doing this. I'm getting internship credit. The school district can seriously consider my application. Sammy and I can move. All of this can happen because of Carter.

A text message sounded on her phone, and she checked it. Her jaw fell open. Shane White asked her out to dinner. A real date. She swallowed hard, knowing Carter didn't like the guy. But she needed a distraction. Now that she knew Carter was. . . available, all kinds of early warning alarms had been going off in her head. A date with Shane could silence those.

Alyssa pulled her chair closer to the desk. She had the sudden sense of the unreality of this moment. She'd just been asked out to a super nice restaurant. She responded to the text. *What time?* He responded with the time and that he'd meet her there. Shane wasn't sending a taxi. She'd have to get her own or bike into town. Still. . . a date!

Life was getting exciting. She opened the file they were working on. She was doing the work she needed to be doing. She could actually make money at her dream job. She wouldn't have to be on her feet most of the day like she was at the cafeteria. She'd have better and more hours. Much better pay. And it was all at her fingertips.

Carter carried two mugs back into the room. "Whoa, you look deep in thought."

She laughed. "Kinda. And what's that second cup?"

"Herbal tea." He passed the steaming mug to her. "With one teaspoon of honey in it."

"Why thank you, kind sir," She used a faux Southern belle voice.

"You know they don't talk like that in the South anymore, right?" He gave her a skeptical look.

"I was channeling my inner Scarlett."

"Scarlett O'Hara?"

"Why, yes, dear sir." She fluttered a hand to her throat. "Are you acquainted with my story?" She didn't know any guy who'd watched *Gone with the Wind*, unless their mothers made them.

He sipped his coffee and sat down next to her. "One of my projects at UVA was to make an app that would take the user all over Scarlett O'Hara's world. So, yes, I did watch the movie. Many, many times." He pretended to gag.

"Whose idea was it?" It had to be a female classmate.

His facial features softened, and it looked like he was poking his tongue into his cheek.

His wife. It had to be his wife, for him to look upset.

Distract! She wasn't going to let this go bad before they'd ever even started. She waved her hands. "No worries. Doesn't matter. But I'll get that app working as well as this new one, right?" She gestured to the empty screen.

He blinked at her. "Yeah, it worked." He pulled in closer to the desk and typed in his password.

"That was so super cool that spinning top that erased the screen."

He turned and grinned at her; his earlier anxious expression gone. "Well guess what?"

"What?"

"I'm going to walk you through creating a similar app."

"Truly?"

"Good thing I got that one to finally work."

"Um, yeah." She quirked an eyebrow at him. "Or were you expecting that I'd help you solve it?"

He shrugged. "Could be."

The screen opened, and Carter quickly opened the document with the code for the app.

"This is so cool." She shivered.

His cellphone vibrated and an image of Kelsey, moving in her crib came into view. Carter watched the image. "Looks like Kels is wiggly tonight."

Oh no. If the baby woke up, would they even get a chance to get a good start on their first night of professionally supervised programming?

Her own phone vibrated in her pocket, but no way was she going to pull it out and look.

Carter's screen saver came on. This different set of pictures, one she'd never seen before, included a much older couple with a very-pregnant Abbi-Renae. In this photo she didn't look at the camera, just like the other one Alyssa had seen. Next appeared a photo of baby Kelsey, Maria Parker, and an incredibly disheveled looking Carter floated by on the screen. He looked horrible. His hair stuck out in a gazillion directions, his gray T-shirt sported multiple spit-up stains, and the circles under his eyes put tonight's dark rings to shame.

He'd lost his wife, had become a single dad, and then later had to go from office to remote work. And now this grieving dad was giving up some of his down time to sponsor her.

But when he learned that Shane White had texted her earlier that day and she'd accepted his offer of a dinner date, would Carter flip out? How had the artists' agent gotten her cellphone number, anyway, since she'd not texted him? Had Carter given it to him?

Why would he? She chewed her lower lip. She was going on her first date.

"Hey, my mom and dad are coming over tomorrow to hang with Kels and Jaycie tomorrow night, and I'm going out with some friends."

Was he encouraging her to get out of the house? She already had plans. "I think that's great. I've got some things I'll be doing, too." She gave him what she hoped was a warm and confident smile.

Her high heeled shoes had arrived that afternoon, and they were about to go out on the town tomorrow night.

She'd been asked to dinner. A real date.

What could go wrong?

"It's about time you came out with us." Rachel Dunmara Welling tugged Carter's arm as they headed down the sidewalk toward Mary's Bistro.

Main Street was bustling with tourists, some crowded elbow-to-elbow in the line outside the restaurant.

Jack Welling mussed the back of Carter's hair. "Can't have my best man dodging my texts."

Best man at the wedding seemed a decade earlier, not the couple of years that it had been. Carter had had a little crush on Rachel, and they'd become good friends before he'd learned she was his Grandpa Parker's biological daughter and sort of his aunt.

Families sure could be complicated.

"Hey, I have to hang out with the old folks now and again—a little pity visit, ya know!" He hoped his cocky voice and smirk would convey that he wasn't gonna put up with being treated like poor, widowed Carter. That wasn't a vibe he was going to tolerate much longer from family members.

"As if! We're not that much older than you, ya goofball!" Jack swiped at him but Carter leaned back.

Rachel turned, sporting a shocked expression.

"Close your mouth, you're not a trout." Carter crinkled his nose.

"A trout?" She elbowed him.

Jack snickered. "But she's quite the catch."

"Aw, Jack, you're so sweet." Rachel made a kissy face.

"Too bad she hated you for so long." Carter couldn't resist the dig.

Rachel moved closer in as another couple passed them on the walkway. "Hey, I didn't hate him."

"Yeah, ya did hate me," her husband disagreed.

"No, I just. . ."

"Hated," Carter and Jack said in unison. "Him," Carter said. "Me." Jack patted his chest and laughed.

"You, two. How am I going to make it through dinner without you two guys picking on me?"

"We weren't picking on you," Carter raised his index finger, "just pointing out the truth."

Jack quirked a dark eyebrow. "Your version of the truth."

"Truth is truth."

Jack moved ahead and opened the restaurant door for them, but a group of people, six in total, traipsed out the entrance door.

"Thanks," the guy who'd barged past first, told Jack, whose wide eyes indicated his surprise.

The rest of the group looked between Jack and Rachel and Carter, some with understanding on their faces. Those exiting were supposed to use the other door.

When the strangers finally got past, Jack waved Rachel and Carter through. They had a reservation, so they didn't have to wait in line outside.

Inside, the scents of fresh whitefish, lemon, baked bread, and fresh veggies co-mingled. How many times had Carter eaten at this place? So many, he couldn't count. But tonight was the first time he'd been there as a dad, with a kid at home, and as a widower. *A widower.* It sounded bizarre just rolling that word in his mind. He'd never noticed the two highchairs at the back of the restaurant nor the fact that there weren't many kids, and no babies, in this place.

The hostess, new this season, gave Jack the eye, and he lifted his left hand and began twisting his wedding ring around. Jack, with his dark hair and flashing hazel eyes was just a little too good-looking. The hostess's gaze followed the ring, and her perusal of Jack stopped. At least some women were deterred by a wedding band.

Carter flexed his fingers, the overhead light flashing on the three diamonds in his ring. Was that why he'd not removed it yet? Because even though it may not deter all females, it would stop most from considering him available? Emotionally, he wasn't.

If he was being honest, Alyssa was becoming more than a friend.

"Jack, do you see who's here?" Rachel ground out her question in a low voice.

"No." Jack, who was taller than Carter by a few inches, looked around. "Oh. Yeah."

Rachel waved her hands. "We're not staying. I'm sorry."

The hostess frowned.

"Come on." Rachel gestured for Carter to go.

He saw them then. *Shane White seated with Alyssa.*

No way. After he'd warned her off him? Women seemed to fall for jerks and not good guys, like he was trying to be.

"Let's go to the Pink Pony." Jack inclined his head toward the exit.

Carter knew that Shane had struck a nerve with Rachel and Jack a couple of years before, but obviously there were still issues.

"Is your dad here?" Rachel hissed toward Jack.

He scowled. "No. I don't see him."

She patted Carter's arm. "We're still going to Pink Pony. I don't want to be around Shane. Especially after he had the nerve to show up at Lilac Cottage uninvited."

"You oughta be grateful for him," Jack said as he opened the front door, but the exit door this time. "Saved our bacon." He waggled his hand and made a sizzling sound.

She shook her head. "Doesn't mean I want to see him or be reminded."

"Are you two ever going to tell me exactly what happened with him?"

"Nope!" Rachel snapped. "And Alyssa should stay away from him."

Jack cast a quick look back. "He's not a bad guy."

"She should still stay away from him."

Yeah, Alyssa should stay away from Shane, but maybe not for the reasons Rachel had.

A real date. Alyssa was on a real date. And with Shane White, an attractive guy who'd previously been linked with Michigan's biggest social media influencer, Bunty Braeburn. Bunty's tentacles reached far. Alyssa's Mobile App Development professor gave students a project to create an app based on Bunty's multi-varied approach.

That whole assignment Alyssa and her fellow computer science students spent ninety percent of their time working out the bugs. Not that such a situation was unusual—which was the faculty members point in assigning them the project. Nothing glamorous about social media app development. Computer programmers just had to get used to working out the bugs.

Maybe dating was sort of like that.

"Have you ever been to Mary's Bistro before?" That mega-watt smile put a dimple in Shane's cheek making him, if possible, look even more appealing. His dimple wasn't quite as cute as Carter's though—but why was she thinking that?

Because I know he's not married, poor guy, Carter's a widower.

"Um, no, haven't been." She compressed her lips. Every extra bit of money she had was being put aside for her apartment in the Soo—which now looked possible because of Carter. *Thank God for that man.*

"They've got a more compressed menu than in previous summers, but still some favorites." That grin again.

She could see how that smile could make a girl's knees go weak. Thankfully, Alyssa was sitting. "What's your fave?"

"Whitefish with crabmeat and the zoodles on the side with lemon butter sauce."

Sammy loved zoodles. On the rare occasion when Mom let her cook, Alyssa would sit at the table after work and spin the zucchini through her machine to make the vegie noodle strands. Then she and Sammy would melt the butter, add lemon juice from the bottle, and throw in some Italian herbs. When they moved to the Soo she'd cook all Sammy's favorites.

Shane leaned in. "You okay?"

Alyssa blinked. "Yes, sorry, I was just thinking." She forced a smile. "I'd love to have that." But when she found it on the menu and saw the price, she pulled in a little breath. He was paying, right? He'd asked her here. This was a date. But what if this was like she'd heard some guys did things—they asked you someplace then split the bill? Was he like the restaurant owner, Mrs. Menteur, who had interviewed her earlier that summer?

"Order whatever you'd like." Those words and his warm eyes conveyed her answer. "I'm so glad you were able to come out with me."

"Very glad to be here." Her heartbeat ticked upward. This guy had no clue that he was her very first real date. *Ever.* Maybe when they got to the Soo, she'd meet more people. Guys who didn't know her parents. Who didn't mind a child.

But a child with special needs?

She'd enjoy this while she could pretend that she wasn't the single mom of a child on the spectrum. No, not pretending. There was no need to know in this situation. She'd never see Shane after he left the island.

The waitress, whose pretty face was covered in piercings, arrived at their table. She looked vaguely familiar. "Ready to roll?"

Shane saluted her. "Yes, ma'am, Ms. Waitress Extraordinaire, two whitefish with crab, zoodles on the side, and a coke for me."

The young woman nodded, her lips twitching. When she turned toward Alyssa, her eyes widened and she smiled, revealing teeth that could have used years of orthodontia.

Recognition hit hard. It had been several years since the girl had graduated from Tahquamenon High. "Shalley Woods? How are you doing?" Alyssa and the other cooks had always snuck the girl extra servings of milk and whatever dessert they were having to the rail-thin girl.

Oh no. Would Shalley ask about Sammy?

"I'm doing great. Lovin' life." She gestured around to the busy restaurant. But her features had tightened.

"Shalley's my favorite waitress, aren't you Shalley?" Shane winked at her.

Shalley laughed. "If you say so, Mr. White."

"Hey, when are you going to start calling me Shane?"

She shrugged. "Um, never! Not until you stop calling me Ms. Waitress Extraordinaire."

He raised his palms. "Not happening."

"Then de nada it is."

"Nothing doing, huh?"

"That's right. Nothing."

His lower lip curled in.

Alyssa glanced between the two. Was there something between them? Something more than just playful banter?

Shalley pointedly swiveled toward Alyssa. "Hey, Alyssa, tell me what you want to drink and I'm sure it's not *milk*, right?" She winked hard at Alyssa, and she thought she understood the unspoken message—don't say anything about Shalley's impoverished and difficult childhood to Shane. *Maybe Shalley has a crush on Shane.*

"Got it. No milk like in our cafeteria days—let's never speak of that again—and I'll have a Coke, too." Alyssa quirked her eyebrows.

The tension eased from Shalley's face and Alyssa's gut. "Matching orders. Isn't that cute?" Her nose crinkled as she locked eyes with Shane, then turned and left the table.

Awkward. Beyond awkward. She had to turn the conversation around. "I'm the best zoodle maker in the world, by the way."

Good humor flooded his tanned face. "Yeah?"

"A weekly thing for me, when they're in season," and if Mom allowed her. "I've got a lemon butter sauce to die for."

"Hopefully not literally. That would be a bummer for your guests." Creases deepened around his eyes and on his forehead.

"Nope. I make the recipe myself. I eat it a lot," she extended her arms, "and as you can see, I haven't died."

He took a long drink of his water. "Would you believe I once took a sauce-making class in France?"

"No way."

"Yes way."

She leaned in. "What was your fave thing you made?"

"Crème Sicilian with Chef Shane's extra punches."

"Yeah? Do tell."

Shane explained what was in the sauce, in detail. *Maybe a little too much detail.* From his enthusiasm, he truly enjoyed cooking. Too bad it wasn't her specialty—but she was improving now that she had a chance to cook for Carter.

"Okay, now I told you, Alyssa. So spill—how's your zoodle sauce made, what are the secret seasonings you add?"

She laughed. "You got fresh ingredients from the markets in Paris and I use whatever dried herbs and spices are on sale from the local grocery store."

"In Newberry? Not much there, I bet."

She cocked her head. "Have you been there?"

Quick as a flash, something in his expression changed, tension tightening his forehead. If she'd not been staring straight at him, she'd have missed it.

"Who hasn't? You have to drive through to get to the Tahquamenon Falls."

Actually, you didn't have to do that. There were other ways, especially coming from this direction. But she wasn't going to start arguing with her date.

Shalley carried a tray with a half-dozen drinks on it. She bent and handed Shane his first.

"Your pal, Mr. Welling, just reserved a table for midnight."

"Is that so?" Shane rapped his fingers against his Coke glass.

The restaurant closed at eleven. It said so on the menu, on the sign out front, and on Google.

Shalley passed Alyssa her pop. "Be careful around this guy. He's a real charmer."

"Yeah, yeah, Ms. Waitress Extraordinaire." He pressed his hand to his chest. "If you'd only agree to let me marry you and sweep you away to my island in the tropics, then you'd not say that anymore."

A genuine smile lit the waitress's face. "I'd still say it to any chick who'd listen."

Shane shook his head.

With Shalley standing closer to her now, Alyssa could see that some of the piercings looked odd—possibly fake. Like those magnetic ones that people used, thinking they looked cool. Usually, though, it was just one, maybe two. But she had multiple ones. *Weird.* But given what Shalley had grown up with—a drunk for a dad and a mentally ill mom—it was amazing she'd turned out okay at all.

Alyssa touched the girl's arm. "I'm so glad you're enjoying it here on the island." She hoped her words conveyed more than that. Even though they were only a handful of years apart in age, Alyssa had always felt so much older than that frail girl who the lunch ladies all doted on.

"Hey, I'm enjoying life here." She pointed at Shane. "But when Mr. White finally jets me off this island to Tahiti, I'll be better yet."

Surely normal dates weren't like this, were they? Alyssa's friends had talked about bizarre situations but usually it was because they were bored out of their minds and couldn't wait to get home and rid of the guy. One friend had described her dates with her now-husband as comfortable, fun, but with zing. Was charm the zing factor? Shane had that in spades, as Mom would say. Nope—zing was something different.

An unbidden thought raced through her mind—was zing that feeling she got anytime when she sat down next to Carter Parker? Her face heated.

Shane shook his finger at Shalley. "You're embarrassing Alyssa."

"I'll be back in a moment with your food, sir."

He saluted the young woman.

He had to have been military.

"Which branch of the service were you in, Shane?"

He straightened. "Semper Fi! Marines forever."

"A former marine who studies sauce-making in Paris—you're an interesting guy."

"Why not? I don't want to be a bore like Carter."

Her spine stiffened and her jaw almost dropped. "He's not a bore." Anger rushed through her. This idiot reminded her of the bullies who said awful things to Sammy at school. *What a jerk.*

He splayed his fingers. "Sorry, sorry, I didn't know you felt so strongly about your boss." But something other than remorse played across his face. A cunning, calculating, wariness. But why?

This guy was not to be trusted.

Just like Carter had said.

Chapter Seventeen

Suddenly, Alyssa wished she was back at Tandem Cottage, spending a comfortable evening with Carter and his baby girl. She took a drink of her Coke, her hands shaking. She couldn't, she wouldn't, make a scene here at this popular restaurant. Shane was goading her on, and she'd taken the bait. She wasn't going to sit there and take anything more. But this adrenal surge, similar to what she always got defending her beloved son, had her ready to flee her first real date.

"You'll have to excuse me, but I need to. . ." she slid toward the end of the bench, pointedly looking toward what she thought was the bathroom area.

"Oh, yeah, sure."

As she left the table, he'd pulled out his cellphone.

She moved purposefully through the tables of happy customers. On one hand, she wished she'd told Shane off right there on the floor, but she wasn't going to give him the satisfaction. Her father and mother had always told her to leave if she was uncomfortable somewhere—just like she'd told Sammy. She stopped at the edge of the bar area and caught the eye of a bartender. She pulled a fiver from her wallet. "Is there a back way out of here?"

The dark-haired guy, about her age, leaned in. "Go past the bathrooms." He inclined his head to her right. "And that black metal door is an exit to the alleyway at the side. But you'll come out onto the dock. Turn right."

"Thanks." She passed him that hard-earned money, more appreciative than she'd ever imagined she'd be for directions to an exit.

She walked carefully in her high heels around and toward the exit. She stopped to draw in a deep breath. Was she being childish? What would Carter say if he heard this?

He'd already warned her about Shane. He didn't like him. *At all.*

Now how was she going to make it back to Tandem Cottage in these high heels? Ugh. She brushed her hand against the floral summer dress she'd worn. The dress and the heels were both brand new—the first fancy outfit she'd ever owned. She walked down the boardwalk, a breeze ruffling her hair, worn loose around her shoulders.

Couples strode past hand-in-hand. A group of people, obviously related given their similar facial features and tall heights, gathered beneath a maple tree. Several teenaged boys sat on a bench sharing images on their phones. No one even noticed her. She'd certainly not wanted Shane to see her leaving, but now she felt almost invisible.

Options? Walk barefoot. Ow—no thanks. Steal a bike—a definite no. Walk in her new heels and ruin them or twist her ankle and break it. *Definite no.* She could try to buy a pair of inexpensive sandals but she'd still be in danger of a foot fiasco.

A cab? She'd have to.

She dialed the number and gave Gough's Taxi the info, then ended the call. She'd be picked up in thirty minutes in front of the Pink Pony, where the cab was headed next. She exhaled a puff of air then headed toward the popular restaurant down the street. She merged in with a large group as they passed the entrance to where she'd just left, and she kept her head down.

Her track record maintained—she couldn't label that a date. *Dateless Alyssa.*

Once safely past the restaurant, she raised her head. There were a ton of people out. She'd never come downtown this late. Even with the day trippers gone back to the mainland, the place was packed. Overpacked if she compared it to her hometown. Hard to believe it was only an hour away. It was like a different world altogether.

She peeked in at the souvenir shop on her right. Sammy would love that Mandala coloring book. He was getting interested in art. If the muralist working at Tandem Cottage wasn't so odd, Alyssa would have talked with him a little bit about art and how he got started. Maybe she'd still try.

When she arrived at the Pink Pony, there was nowhere to sit out front, to wait. Maybe she'd go back to the shop.

The door to the restaurant opened.

"Alyssa?" Carter's voice caused that zing that she shouldn't be experiencing. He joined her on the sidewalk. "Whatcha doin' here?"

She'd not told him about the date, of course. "Waiting on a taxi."

He surveyed her from head to foot. "You're sure dressed up tonight."

"Yeah, well, I've got a new outfit to show off." Her stomach growled.

"Don't waste it. Come join us. Rachel and Jack are here."

"I can't."

"Come on." He took her arm.

"I already called a cab."

"Goughs won't care. Happens all the time."

"No, that would be rude."

"To cancel the cab?"

"Well yeah, plus to elbow in on your dinner with the Wellings."

Carter pulled his phone out of his pocket. "I'll call the taxi company and cancel. I have a direct line number."

A private carriage rolled past, and the driver inclined his head toward Carter, who waved.

Amazing how many people he knew. She wasn't going to butt in on this private dinner. "No, I'll go back."

"We'll talk a little business—some internship stuff, and I'll write it off to the company."

"That's a *wayyy no*."

"Seriously. Do you know how many so-called lunches I've had with customers who just ordered liquid beverages, if you know what I mean."

"Oh."

He put the call through and spoke rapidly with someone. "Thanks, man." He slipped his phone into his pocket.

A striking woman with large gray-blue eyes and thick dark wavy hair came through the door and waved them forward. "Come on, the hostess is seating us right now."

"That's Rachel," Carter whispered as he wrapped an arm around Alyssa's shoulder, and again that unwanted sensation burst through her. This was her boss. Her internship supervisor. This was ridiculous. *It's fine, I'm leaving end of summer. I'll never see him again.*

She drew in a steadying breath and entered the Pink Pony—yet another place she'd heard about but never seen. Loud laughter and chatter filled the large room. The adorable painting of dancing pink ponies on the wall made her smile. A band was setting up on the front right stage.

The scents of fish, something sweet, and beer and wine filled the air. Diners' tables were covered with food that looked amazing. Her mouth watered.

"This way." The pretty blonde hostess motioned them on.

Before long, they were led to a table and were seated.

"Jack," Carter gestured to the good-looking dark-haired man, "this is Alyssa. She's my intern and also Kelsey's babysitter, like I told you."

Jack assisted his wife into her seat and then extended his hand. "Good to meet ya."

Carter held Alyssa's seat for her. "Thanks, boss."

"Don't call me that or Jack will make me call him Uncle Jack and that would make me sick. It's just Carter."

A grin tugged at Rachel's red lips. She was gorgeous enough to be a model. She reminded Alyssa of one of the top cover girls from back in Mom's day. *Selma something.* She'd google her later.

Their waitress, with a shaved head and long dangling fish skeleton earrings stopped at their table. "Drinks?"

Jack pointed to himself, "Coke," and then to his wife, "French press coffee."

"Sure thing."

Carter touched Alyssa's hand. "What would you like?"

Diamonds in his gold band glistened and reminded her yet again why she needed to take care with her heart. He still wore his ring, and it hadn't yet been a year since his wife had died. "I'll have. . ." something different from what she'd ordered at the other place. "Tonic water with a twist of lime, please."

"Coffee for me. I've got night shift duty."

"Got it." The waitress turned just as another server came through with a tray loaded with beer bottles.

With ease, the other server raised the tray over her head as their waitress pulled back, narrowly avoiding a collision.

"Wow, she made that look easy, didn't she?" Alyssa had once dropped an entire tray of orange juice on the floor during a large school staff meeting.

"I was thinkin' the same thing," Carter said and grinned.

"We have got some amazing catering staff this summer for our program at Lilac Cottage." Rachel opened her menu.

"Speaking of staff, did you actually hire Starr?" Jack flicked his menu at Carter.

"That's how I know I'm on night shift."

Alyssa gently elbowed Carter. She'd not seen Starr all day, and his parents were taking care of Kelsey. "What do you mean?"

"She texted me, right before I saw you out front. Said Kelsey may have an ear infection."

"Oh, wow, I should have recognized the symptoms." Alyssa blurted out.

Three pairs of eyes locked on her.

Rachel frowned. "Why should you have known?"

"She worked at a school." A muscle in Carter's jaw jumped.

She'd asked him not to disclose that she'd been a cafeteria worker, but now she felt silly that she'd been ashamed. Alyssa wasn't going to disclose that as a mother, she'd nursed her boy through multiple ear infections. "I was a school cook and served kids grades K through twelve."

"And probably babysat a bunch of those kids over the years, too, I bet." Jack rubbed his cheek.

"I did." Until she had her own. Was it Jack Welling or his father who Shalley had told Shane about coming at midnight?

Not my business.

Carter tapped his fingers on the tabletop. "I don't know why Starr believes Kelsey has an ear infection, since she's not been at the house in the past twenty-four hours."

"Maybe Starr is there with Jaycie and your folks."

A group of middle-aged men sporting matching touristy bucket hats passed, their raised voices drowning out all other sounds.

"Regardless," Rachel leaned in and spoke loudly, "If she does end up sick, we've got a full house of pediatricians this week at Lilac Cottage."

One of the bucket hat men looked at Alyssa, and she gave him the evil eye that she reserved for kids in the cafeteria who were misbehaving. The silver-haired man raised a finger to his lips and elbowed the much shorter man beside him. "Shhh! Be quiet!" Then he turned and gave her a thumbs-up. She couldn't imagine her father ever behaving in that manner. Maybe she should be happy she had a reserved preacher for her father. But at least these guys looked like they were having fun. Dad could use a little joy in his life.

"Yeah, I'm sure one of those baby docs will enjoy running out to look in your kid's ear, while they are on a medical retreat." Jack's funny expression made it clear that he doubted that was true.

"I didn't notice any signs, like Kelsey trying to pull at her ear." Alyssa better stop, or they'd ask how she knew about babies rather than school kids.

"She didn't feel hot either." Carter ran his hand over his jawline. "But she was fussy in her sleep last night. Anyway, I can call the island doc instead of bothering your gang."

"They won't mind. We've got a great bunch right now." Rachel covered the heart-shaped glass stone on her necklace.

"We do. And the best cook on the island." Jack winked.

"Don't let my mom hear you call her a cook. She takes great pride in having been a medical office manager for over twenty years."

How does a medical manager own a cottage on West Bluff? Clearly there was a lot about Carter's family that she didn't know.

"Maria's food is the absolute best." Rachel took Jack's hand.

"She says that's because she does it all with love—that's her special ingredient." Jack kissed his wife.

Carter made a sourpuss face. "She even has a sign to prove it in the Butterfly Cottage kitchen."

"That's so sweet." Alyssa leaned toward Carter as the people being seated at the next table bumped into her.

A tall heavyset woman in the trio turned. "Sorry, y'all, I didn't mean to intrude in your space," she said in a deep Southern drawl.

Alyssa straightened and gave her a quick nod.

"My mom says making food for special people is like breathing." Carter continued. "Essential for her."

The waitress returned with their drinks and slid them in front of them.

"Orders ready, eh?"

Jack rubbed his cheek. "Loquacious as ever, I see, Laura."

"Yup." She arched her brows right back. "Order?"

"Usual."

"Yup. And the missus?"

"Same."

How often did these two come here? These prices weren't cheap.

"I'll have the whitefish au gratin with a side salad." Carter handed her his menu. "Any Oreo cheesecake tonight?"

"Yup. I'll set your cheesecake aside as claimed."

"Thanks."

"And your missus?" Laura cracked a smile as she waited for Alyssa.

"That's not my wife." Carter's clipped tone made Alyssa flinch.

"But I heard from Andrette over at Lucky Bean that ya got hitched."

Jack's lips curved into an 'O' as Rachel shook her head, which the waitress caught.

"I'm his employee." Alyssa kept her voice firm. "And I'll have the same as Mr. Parker. Thanks."

"Sure thing, hon." The waitress made a hasty getaway.

"Sorry," Carter whispered.

Mrs. Carter Parker she was not. "No prob. Sorry about her mistake."

"Not your fault." He extended his hand towards hers, as if to cover it, but then stopped.

"So, Alyssa, what do you think about Mackinac Island? Do you like it?" Rachel stirred sugar into her coffee.

"Or has Carter put you off the whole place?" Jack waved as an older couple passed by.

"Haha. I'm shocked you didn't put Rachel off permanently just by," Carter waved in a circle toward Jack, "by being you."

"Hey, I never had anything to do with Rachel being off island, and you know that. She had to finish her nursing training."

"Boys, boys," Rachel rolled her eyes upward. "Try to behave."

"This is a side of Carter that I've never seen before." Alyssa chuckled.

"This is the real him." Jack crossed his arms. "Annoying. Immature. Always making a joke at someone else's expense."

"Um," Alyssa shouldn't say it, but she could simply not resist. "That sounds an awful lot like you, Jack, from what I've just observed."

Rachel and Carter hooted, and the patrons at several tables around them turned to stare. The Southern lady who'd just bumped Alyssa raised her penciled-in eyebrows. If they weren't careful, the bucket-hat old guys would come back and reprimand *them*.

"Good one!" Carter high-fived Alyssa and then Rachel.

Jack reluctantly uncrossed his arms and did the same. "Ouch, that hurt."

"Not as much as your wisecracks hurt our ears." Carter touched one ear.

Rachel frowned. "Now that's just mean, Carter. You're going to injure poor Jack's feelings."

Carter's face showed mock horror as he pressed his hands to his cheeks and pushed in. "Oh my goodness. I didn't know Jack had feelings. Poor widdle baby!"

"Where has my boss and internship supervisor gone, and who is this man?" Alyssa poked her index finger in her cheek.

"Oh, I assure you this is the real deal." Rachel sipped her tea. "This is Carter, the magnificent, in all his glory."

"Listen, I see Carter talking on the phone with his brother, and how he is with his baby and his parents, and he's nothing like this."

"It's the drugs." Jack looked serious.

Rachel elbowed her husband. "You know better than to say that."

"Oh, yeah, sorry." Remorse tinged his words. His cheeks turned pink.

"If anybody is on drugs it's you, Jack. In fact, I suspect that is the real reason you have the medical hospitality thing going. You simply hope to get in on some kind of illegal drug scam." Carter pointed at Jack as he turned toward Alyssa. "Not a philanthropic bone in his body, so I'm thinking he didn't go along with Rachel's scheme because of any smidgeon of niceness."

"Smidgeon?" Jack cackled. "Who says smidgeon? What did UVA do to your brain?"

Alyssa held up her fingers an inch apart. "Anyone with a smidge of sense can see that you are the catalyst for Carter's personality change."

"It's not a change. It's a normal reaction by anyone with a smidge," Carter mimicked her hand gesture, "of allergenic response to Jack's form of humor."

"Which is?" Alyssa made her face a blank expression. "I haven't noticed any actual, genuine humor demonstrated yet. But we could probably make him an app for that, don'tcha think?"

As she and Carter laughed, Rachel and Jack eyed one another.

"Ohmygoodnessgracious," Rachel slurred her words together. "She actually gets him."

Jack held his arms up in a cross sign. "That's dangerous. Back, back, you two deviants."

"Of course I get him, we're both computer programmer nerds." Alyssa sipped her tonic water. She had to admit this was the most fun she'd had in a while. *A very long while.* Most of her school friends were now married and many had moved away.

"Yeah, but so was Abbi-Renae. . ." The unspoken sentiment, Rachel omitted, seemed to be that Abbi didn't jive with her husband.

Jack jumped in. "You do understand," he intoned, "that if you fathom Carter then you are probably—"

"Carter!" A glamourous silver-haired woman dripping in diamonds, on the arm of a very tall, older, smartly dressed gentleman, rushed toward their table. "You're here!"

With clothes and styled hair that screamed "wealthy," the woman wrapped her arms around Carter from the back and repeatedly kissed the top of his head. The man stood back, seemingly holding back a grin. "I have missed you so much, and when I heard about—"

"Grandma Kareen!" Carter's eyes widened. "Grandpa Gianni, good to see you."

His grandmother stood back then gaped at Alyssa. "You must be her!"

Grandma Kareen might reveal his crush on Alyssa. And there might not be anything he could do about it. *Dear God, help me now.*

"Why, yes, I'm the babysitter." Alyssa's tone, so perfectly even, assured him that she would help this situation. "And you must be Kelsey's great-grandmother. I've heard wonderful things about you."

"Oh, you're the childcare person?" Her voice held disappointment.

"Right. I watch your beautiful grandchild."

"And Alyssa does a great job, Grandma. How are you doing?"

"I'm fine, but what about your new intern? Are you going to listen to me about—"

Jack exchanged a quick look with his wife. "What did you tell him, Mrs. Parker?"

"It's Mrs. Franchetti," Gianni said.

"Sorry, Mrs. Franchetti, what did you tell Carter to do?" Jack smirked.

Carter tightly shook his head and glared at Jack.

"That as wonderful as his new intern sounded, he should ask her out."

Carter closed his eyes not wanting to see the expressions on the faces around him. "Grandma Kareen, that's not what I said."

"I know, but you should listen to your old Grandma and start looking for a new mother for that precious baby girl."

"Yeah, Mrs. Francetti, you're right." Jack winked at Alyssa, who looked confused.

"A grandmother always knows these things." She pressed another flurry of kisses to the top of Carter's mortified head. "Ask that girl out sometime."

Alyssa raised her hand, as if in a classroom needing permission to ask a question. Grandma Kareen had that effect on people. "Mrs. Franchetti, I'm also Carter's new intern. I'm delighted he's giving me a glowing review. I think he's just practicing for when he writes up my review."

Grandma took a few steps toward Alyssa, then raised her reading glasses, dangling from a diamond-encrusted chain to her eyes. "Oh, honey, as pretty as you are, my grandson would have to be as blind as a bat to not notice."

"That's right," Jack agreed. "She's almost as gorgeous as my bride." He kissed Rachel.

Alyssa touched Grandma's arm. "Oh, and we're not on a date."

"Well, what is this then, hon? A cribbage game?"

Her husband did smile then. He stepped forward and took his wife by the elbow. "Good evening, everyone. Stop by our private booth before you leave, and let's set up some plans."

That guy did have cavernous pockets. Only the wealthy could afford the private booths in the far reaches of the restaurant.

Now if only Carter could slide under the table and then disappear.

As Grandma walked away, Alyssa patted his shoulder. "Thanks, boss, for the recommendation. I'm glad to get a super early review." She pointedly smiled at Jack and Rachel, whose somewhat shocked expressions had softened.

"Your grandmother means well." Rachel shrugged. "At least you still have yours. I miss my grandmother so much." She pressed her hand to her chest, covering the necklace again.

"She was a great lady." Jack pressed his lips together.

Sadness washed over Alyssa's pretty face. "My paternal great-grandmother, who raised my dad, will be on the island soon. I've never met her."

"Perfect chance to ambush her." Jack waggled his eyebrows.

"Jack!" Rachel scowled. "Why have you never met her?"

Alyssa flipped her hands over, palms up. "My dad didn't allow us." She clamped her lips shut.

He jumped in, "That's crummy when families are broken, and Rachel and I know all about that."

Rachel nodded. "But will you try to see her?

"I hope so—I met a couple people who personally know her." She pushed her hair behind her ear. "Believe it or not, Evangelist Romelda is my great-grandmother."

"What?" Rachel's red lips formed a perfect circle. "I watched her with my grandmother all the time. She's such a great preacher."

"I agree." Alyssa grinned.

"Wait." Rachel pressed her palms on the table. "One of our staff, Susan Mullen, a wonderful social worker, was talking about meeting Romelda's granddaughter."

Mrs. Mullen was here on the island? Carter's breath caught in his chest. She'd seen him at his worst. Sweat broke out on his forehead.

Jack elbowed Rachel. "Were you eavesdropping again?"

The pretty brunette blushed. "I was walking by the Mullens' table and couldn't help overhearing Mrs. Mullen say she was helping Romelda meet her granddaughter who was on the island." She pointed at Alyssa, "Which has to be you."

"I met Mr. and Mrs. Mullen by a paper stand, believe it or not." Alyssa laughed.

His stomach soured. The grief group therapist knew all about his lapse in judgement about his wife. He pushed back from the table. "I better get back to Kelsey because of that ear infection." He wasn't going to be a bad father even if he'd been a lousy husband.

"Your mom and dad are there, kid." Jack groused.

"I'm not a kid, Jack. I'm a dad. A dad with a sick kid." He gritted his teeth.

"Come on, stay," Rachel pleaded.

He pulled a wad of cash from his wallet and set it on the tabletop. "This should cover Alyssa's and mine. I gotta go."

"Don't be that way, man. Sorry I called you a kid."

He waved away Jack's response, turned on his heel and left, his heart hammering. He'd grab the extra bike behind Lucky Bean and return it in the morning. Should be home in under twenty minutes. It would take more than that to find a carriage, plus the drive up to the Annex.

Outside, he smelled horses and sugary fudge—a unique Mackinac Island scent. Too much sensory overload for Abbi-Renae. She'd stated emphatically that she'd never return to Mackinac Island.

And she'd been right.

Too bad it had been his fault.

Chapter Eighteen

Which version of Carter was Alyssa going to get today—Dr. Jekyll or Mr. Hyde? Last night, Jack claimed Carter was in a snit because he'd treated him like a kid. Alyssa wasn't so sure. As soon as he'd received the text about Kelsey, all his little nervous gestures had ticked upward. But now, in the days since his rapid departure from the restaurant, Carter had barely spoken to her. Once the doctor confirmed Kelsey's bad ear infection, Carter provided her sole care. But he asked her to represent him on his business meetings as his intern.

Her senses buzzed, and it wasn't from the ginormous mug of coffee she was chugging—being able to participate in a genuine computer programming business team was a rush. This morning's team meeting had centered around assigning tasks to each member and explaining an upcoming project.

The meeting was ending but the manager hadn't assigned her anything. She tapped her toes, waiting. "Alyssa, glad to have you here. You'll assist Carter on his assigned work."

"Sure thing." Last night, on the Charlottesville Codes Project, she'd been given her own work to do. And her other project, assisting a friend in designing a new app, had also tasked her with a specific chunk of coding. Maybe she should be grateful Carter's manager hadn't asked her for anything extra.

"All right, crew, that's a wrap."

The session ended and the screen went blank. Alyssa closed her laptop and swiveled around. A disheveled Carter dragged the back of his hand over his eyes. "I gotta shower, it's been a few days."

She bit back a snarky comment.

"Can you pick up some grub from Maria for us? She's got that big picnic for the Petoskey medical staff and is trying to empty out her second fridge."

"Where and when?" His stepmom seemed afraid to step foot in the house. She'd called Alyssa and asked about Kelsey and had said Carter had yelled at her about the ear infection. Maria believed it was because he was afraid something would happen to his baby, and he'd already lost his wife. She was probably right.

He placed his hands on his hips. "Lilac Cottage and now."

"Oh." She stood. "Guess I better get going."

"Thanks. Kels is down for her nap." He turned on his heel. "We'll go over later to the picnic. My mom's grandsons got here last night. They're just a little bit younger than me."

Outside, she grabbed the bike. Another glorious day on Mackinac. Blue sky and puffy clouds. Too bad poor Carter was on overcast mode. She biked to Lilac Cottage, mulling Mom's phone call from earlier. Mom and Dad enrolled Sammy in summer camp and he was doing well. Sammy got on the phone and agreed, predicting he'd win a prize for remembering Bible verses. Definitely sounded better than he had at Gino's.

Laughter carried up the back drive, as Alyssa dismounted the bike and walked toward Lilac Cottage. She hoped the large basket on the front would hold Maria's empanadas, tamales, and burritos.

As she neared the tall hedgerow between the yellow and the white Victorian mansions, she wiped her brow. Mom promised that she and Dad would bring her a home-baked birthday cake. How wonderful it would be to see them and her boy.

"Son, I understand," came a man's voice from nearby, "and I'm on it now, too."

Alyssa looked around, trying to locate the other person, but saw no one.

"We've got a possible situation," the man's voice grew serious, "that matches up with your targeted agenda."

What was that about? She froze. What if she stepped on a twig and the caller heard her? And thought she was listening in—which she was?

"Male identified by former therapist. Reliable witness."

She needed to walk away.

"Yeah, I know that, Shane."

Alyssa's spine stiffened. Was that Shane White on the phone? Shane wasn't a very common name. *Still.*

"Not my fault they called me in. You've had more than enough time to track our national treasure down. What the heck have you been doing with your time here?"

Alyssa rolled the bike slowly ahead, cringing when the wheels rolled over some twigs. She hurried on. Would the person who was talking jump out of the bushes at her? As she reached the end of the trees, she spied Maria's grandsons. Maria had said they'd finally arrived and had texted her a few pictures of her *nietos guapos*—handsome grandsons. Three of them were setting up for the picnic lunch. She peered around the huge backyard, looking for the man on the phone. *Nobody.*

Maria emerged through the back door, carrying platters piled with steaming food. "Hola, Alyssa!"

"Hi, Maria."

Maria set the platters down and then hurried to Alyssa and gave her a hug. "Thank you for coming. I've got a box made up for Carter—and you, too. And that artist, if he ever comes out to eat anything!"

Alyssa laughed. "We've only seen remnants of power bars and Red Bull cans. A tuna pack here and there."

Maria clucked her tongue. "If this doesn't entice him out of his lair, you'll have to carry some into that nursery for him!"

"Yeah. I'll do that."

From the dividing treeline, a middle-aged man moved toward them. As he drew closer, he looked familiar.

Maria waved toward him. "I don't think you've met Jack's father yet, have you?"

"No."

His posture suggested restrained tension, with a muscle in his face jumping even as a tentative smile formed. He moved toward them slowly, limping slightly.

Maria gestured toward her. "This is Alyssa, she's babysitting my new little granddaughter this summer."

He extended his hand. "I'm Pete Welling."

His was the voice she'd heard. She stiffened. "Nice to meet you."

Maria smiled. "We were just discussing how that artist up at Tandem Cottage never eats my good food." She made a face of mock horror, framing her face with her hands.

Mr. Welling didn't so much as chuckle. "Artist?"

"Yes, he's supposed to be painting a mural in the nursery." Alyssa shrugged. "But he sure is taking his time." And was making her nervous being in her same wing—not that she would complain to Carter about it.

"All he eats is junk food." Maria shook her head.

"Ah." Welling nodded slowly. "Nice to meet you, Miss Teann, but if you'll excuse me, I have a quick call to make."

Maria hadn't said her last name. How had he known? Unease coursed through her. Didn't someone say he was in law enforcement?

"I've got to load Alyssa up with food and get this picnic ready for the medical staff." Maria clapped her hands. "Boys! Bring me out that box for Carter."

"Box? I've only got the bike with the basket."

"De nada. It's a small one."

When she went to leave, Pete Welling had disappeared again. And who was he calling?

Carter's phone lit, displaying the front camera which showed Alyssa struggling with the overloaded bike. He jumped up and headed outside.

Even with red cheeks and sweat plastering her bangs to her forehead, she looked beautiful.

He grabbed the box from the basket and took a steadying step. "What did she put in here?"

"Way more than we thought she would, obviously." She raised an eyebrow.

The scents of all the goodies made his stomach growl. "You didn't tell her about Jaycie, did you?"

By her scowl, she hadn't.

"Sorry, I just feel protective of her."

"I understand. But that ends today." She wagged her finger at him like a schoolteacher. "Either you or Jaycie tell everyone, or I do."

"Scout's honor."

She cast him a doubtful look. "I did get to meet Jack Welling's dad."

"He's there?" Something must be going on with Jack.

Alyssa's phone rang and she looked at the caller ID. Mixed emotions flashed over her pretty face. "I've gotta take this."

"Sure." He swiveled to face the house.

"Hi there!" Alyssa's voice was tinged with joy, but anxiety, too.

Was it Shane White calling? Had she agreed to go on a date with him after all? And why was that any business of his? *It wasn't.* Maybe that was where she'd been the other night. Maybe a date with him first? Early dinner? A very short early dinner. Heck, if he was eating with Shane, he'd keep it short, too.

"I love you, too, Sammy." Her voice held a depth of emotion.

He slowly walked away. This Sam guy was pretty lucky.

"I can't wait to see you, too." She sniffed. "And I'm so sorry about everything."

A weight settled in his chest. Alyssa wasn't his girlfriend. She was his babysitter and intern. He had no business feeling jealous of the guy she was in love with nor envy him the time they'd get together. But if she was so crazy about him, why didn't she go meet up with him on the mainland on her free time?

Jaycie opened the door, her long dark hair in a fluffy mess. "What all did my mother-in-law send over? You didn't tell her I'm here, did you?"

"No, but you don't get to touch one tamale unless you call her today." Alyssa was just as stern with her as she'd been with him. She sounded an awful lot like a. . . mom.

Jaycie raised her hands. "Will do. But if I know my baby heartburn—it's not going to take kindly to Maria's cooking."

"Oh, I hadn't thought of that. Maybe not." His wife couldn't eat anything spicy during her pregnancy, not even her favorite Asian dishes that her mom made for her.

That cloak of despair threatened to land around his shoulders. He'd dodge that garment before it enveloped him. "So cool that you'll have your daughter soon. And I'm so blessed that I've got my sweet Kelsey." *Focus on the positive, not on what isn't there anymore.*

He smiled even as moisture welled in his eyes.

Grief was a strange thing. You could be laughing one moment and crying the next. Sometimes at the same time.

Chapter Nineteen

Grief work is different for everyone," Susan slowly made eye contact with the participants in her talk, "and as Dr. Mary Svendsen just said, bibliotherapy is one excellent intervention technique." She inclined her head toward the renowned psychologist.

"Thank you, Dr. Svendsen." Tamara, who was seated beside Susan at the front of the group, began clapping. The participants joined in as Mary Svendsen, Ph.D., the podcaster and internet therapy sensation waved her goodbyes and headed toward the back.

Dr. Austin, also seated in the front, held a new iPhone and a pair of ear buds aloft. "These are a giveaway to someone in this group session from one of our generous sponsors."

Tamara stood and gestured toward Susan. "Now Mrs. Mullen is going to share about another intervention you can suggest to your patients."

Susan snuck a quick drink of her tea and then set the china cup back in its saucer. "My topic today is the use of music for grief. If you'll open your handouts, you can follow along with me."

The rustle of papers ensued.

She launched into her topic. "I've run grief groups, often focused on men, for the past five years, through our community outreach program."

"Men are often an overlooked group." Dr. Austin patted his broad chest. "I know that from personal experience."

"Yes, and another intervention, music, can soothe the soul for both sexes."

"Right." Tamara elbowed her husband and the two exchanged a kiss.

Susan cast them a stern look. "Okay, enough of that PDA, y'all, or we'll have to send you out."

"We're going!" Tamara took her husband's arm and pulled him away as the other healthcare providers laughed. Half of the attendees for this week's summit were from his oncology department at the hospital. They may appreciate a little bit of privacy. A strange mix this week—the other half of the group worked obstetrics.

"All right," Susan began again. "I want you to start by thinking of several songs that have brought you comfort. You don't have to share."

The room quieted again as the participants wrote their answers. She gave them a few minutes and finished the rest of her ginger tea.

A pretty young Hispanic woman with bold strands of white hair framing her face raised her hand. Susan inclined her head.

The young woman pressed her hand to her chest, her rhinestone encrusted fingernails flashing under the chandelier light. "Do you have a story to share about someone who this may have helped?"

Susan drew in a slow breath. She had to be careful of confidentiality. "I do." She looked around the group, a bit unsure if she should share the next part. Not everyone was a believer, and her song was all about faith. "A client asked me to recommend a song. Was the only one in a group this size," she gestured to include them all, "who couldn't come up with their own 'anthem'." She made air quotes with her hands.

"What did you do?"

"I asked the individual to stay after group and offered to play my favorite song. It's a worship song."

"Amen to that," one of the obstetrics nurses called out.

"This person was so devastated from the loss of their spouse, and lost a mother to drugs, and grandfather recently to alcoholism." She shook her head slowly. Poor Carter Parker had been in a deep well of shock and grief.

Many group members' eyes widened, and some made low comments to each other.

"*Vaya! ¡Eso es trágico!*" The young nurse pressed her hands to her mouth.

Another participant called out. "What happened to the spouse?"

"She'd experienced a horrible condition, very rare, that causes a new mom to bleed out days after birth."

It was as if the entire room gave a collective gasp.

Oh no! She'd revealed too much.

"So he had a newborn baby at home?"

"Yes. And he blamed himself for his wife's death even though it wasn't his fault whatsoever." She shouldn't have said that, but it slipped past her lips.

"I lost my first patient to that. She was in the hospital, and we still couldn't save her." A slim blonde woman lifted her thick eyeglasses to swipe at her eyes. "The hemorrhage was too severe."

Maria entered the room, but unlike usual, she had no coffee cart nor snacks. She looked troubled. "He thought it was his fault, what happened, this father?" She mumbled something in Spanish and made the sign of the cross.

One of the oncologists asked, "What was the name of the song?"

Susan's mouth went dry, and she couldn't respond.

Carter Parker appeared as if from out of nowhere. Dizziness threatened Susan's reserve.

He looked right at her. "It was Jireh."

"By Elevation Music and Maverick City?" a nurse with a short Afro asked.

"Yes," Susan squeaked out.

Carter clapped his hands. "I'm so sorry to disrupt this talk, but my nephews finished their grilling a tad too early." He squeezed one eye shut and made a face of regret. "Lunch will start earlier rather than later."

Saved by the bell. Or by the burners. "Thank you for letting us know," Susan forced a smile. "We'll continue after lunch," Susan managed to say before the healthcare providers rose from their seats.

The Hispanic nurse approached Maria. She rapidly asked her questions in Spanish, and Maria frowned. Then the pretty young woman wrapped her hand around Carter's forearm. "This is you, si? The one Mrs. Mullen speaks of?"

Carter dipped his chin as he gently removed what looked like fairy talons from his arm. The healthcare worker had a strong grip despite those long nails.

"Come with me." Dark eyes flashing, the young woman waved toward a silver-haired man, who was struggling up from his chair. "That's our head obstetrician. He's also a University of Michigan professor."

Carter took a step backward. But there was something kind and compelling about the older man's gray eyes that held him fast.

"I'm Dr. Woody Noland." He tilted his head. "Please tell me that's not your story we just heard."

Carter compressed his lips and nodded as those blasted tears rolled.

"Come on over here for a minute." He gently took Carter's arm and led him to the far wall.

Thankfully, everyone had left.

"Angelina, come sit with us. She knows this story."

"What do you mean?"

"You tell him, Angie."

She splayed those glittery nails across her chest. "This happened to me."

And she was alive. He glanced between the two of them.

"I've worked obstetrics for forty years, and most of our patients with hemorrhagic bleeding don't survive. Those in the hospital have a small chance but those at home. . ." He grimaced.

"It's why I became a delivery ward nurse. I was at home when it happened to me." Her tawny complexion paled. "It's a miracle I'm here today." She made the sign of the cross.

"Angelina was home alone with her baby. Her husband had an emergency at work."

"He left you?" Carter demanded. "Alone?"

She waved her hand. "Only for an hour. He came back just as they were taking me to the hospital."

If only his wife had had that chance.

"Angie was the top student in her class. She recognized the indicators immediately."

"If I hadn't, and if the paramedics weren't only two blocks away when I called, and if I hadn't done several things I knew to try. . ." She swiped at a tear.

"It's nearly impossible to have all those things come together. Unfortunately, by the time most new mothers figure out what is happening, it's too late."

"I looked down at the water and saw the blood. If I had closed my eyes and just rested, I don't think—"

"I wonder if that's what my wife did." Carter shook his head. "I found her like that, as if she'd fallen asleep."

"And it looked like there was a tub full of blood?"

"Yeah." He whooshed out a breath.

Dr. Noland's lips compressed into a line. "It looks like that when blood and water mix, but I assure you, it wasn't."

"Si. I was alert, and when I saw that first trickle, I reacted. You poor man, to have discovered her like that."

"It can happen so fast. If your wife had her eyes closed, she likely wouldn't have called for you, even had you been home." His lips thinned.

"No one really explained much of anything to me. I was in such a state of shock. I'm not sure I'd have understood what they were saying." Those early days were such a fog, and he was in terrible shape—so Mom and Dad came to take care of them.

"But you understand Dr. Noland, si?"

"Yes. Thank you both." He shook their hands.

"Best get Angie over to the picnic. I heard there will be music in her native language."

"My nephews have their own little band."

"Your *sobrinos*?"

"My stepmother's grandsons." He winked. "Don't speak Spanish too rapidly to them. They're third generation, and I'm not sure they totally understand those Mexican pop songs they sing."

"Haha! Now you make me want to try that."

"Behave yourself, Angelina." The doctor waved goodbye as the two left.

Someone tapped him on his shoulder, and he turned. Grandma Kareen opened her arms for him. He gave her a big hug.

She stepped back from him, examining his face. "No picnic for you. You're coming with me."

"I am?"

"Yes." She headed out of the room.

"What's going on, Grandma?"

"You'll see."

When they arrived outside, a carriage awaited. Inside, sat Parker and Jaycie, Dad, and poor Grandpa Gianni, who had to hunch a little because of his height. Parker waved and made a goofy face. It seemed like it had been so long since he'd seen him—grief did that to you.

Grandma gazed up at him with expectant eyes. "We all had planned a big surprise for you and then. . ." She blew out a breath. "Then Maria called."

"Ah." His heartbeat was only just now calming down from what had happened at Lilac Cottage.

"She said you needed us right now." She stopped walking. "Are you going to be all right?"

He touched his left thumb to his wedding ring. For the first time since her death, he somehow felt Abbi-Renae releasing him—but it was probably his own guilty conscience setting him free. "I'm gonna be okay."

"Good." Grandma started walking again, the rhinestone embellishments on her silver and white sneakers glinting in the sunlight.

"You need to get Kelsey a pair of matching shoes." He pointed.

She laughed. "First she has to take steps and then we'll see."

They reached the carriage and Dad scooted over to make room beside him for Grandma Kareen. Parker grabbed Carter's arm and almost pulled him onto his lap, before shoving him into the seat beside him.

"Did I miss you, bro?" Carter shook his head. "I must have been delusional."

"I'm sure you were." Parker took Jaycie's hand in his. "Because I didn't miss you at all."

"Ha!" Jaycie leaned forward, her belly touching her bent knees. "I heard about you every day."

"Not every day. Maybe once a month."

"Every minute, actually." Jaycie straightened. She winced and then groaned.

Gianni's tanned face showed alarm. "Are you all right?"

Parker scooted to the end of the seat. "Stop the carriage?"

Jaycie crinkled her nose and then laughed. "No, I'm fine—just a little muscle twinge."

"But you're okay?" Carter reached across Parker to take Jaycie's hand.

"Yeah. I think it's no biggy."

Parker wrapped an arm around his wife. "Good."

The carriage continued toward the curve as West Bluff ended and wrapped into Hubbard's Annex.

"Are you taking me to your new place?" He smiled at his grandmother and her husband.

"We are, but we have a big favor to ask." Grandma touched the gold necklaces at her neckline.

"I thought this was a surprise."

His step-grandfather flashed a grin. "We thought you were doing a great job caretaking the Byrnes' cottage."

"But Gianni and I thought you might need a place of your own." Grandma Kareen patted her husband's hand, both her and his ring fingers sporting large gold and diamond rings.

"As long as we can spend summers up here with all the grandchildren—my family, too." Gianni pointed to the massive white Victorian structure near Pontiac Trail. "That's our new place, but we were hoping you'd live there. Fifteen guest rooms. Fully winterized."

"When did that happen?" Carter frowned. "That old place was only a summer home. Not in use for many seasons now."

"We evicted many ghosts. Woooooo! Ghosts of the past horrid décor style." Grandma waved her hands around. "And Gianni had three crews working all winter to get this place ready."

"If ya got Wi-Fi, then I'm in. But is it childproofed?"

"The surprise is—we have an entire baby, toddler, and parents' floor." Gianni beamed. "My daughter and her family just tested it out for you. They're waiting for us now."

Parker arched an eyebrow. "And did they give it a five-star review?"

"Ask them when we get there." Gianni chuckled. "Probably a little quaint compared to their homes in Martha's Vineyard and New York."

"Carter is quaint. Aren't ya, Son?" Dad tapped Carter's knee.

"Yeah, sure."

Jaycie stretched. "Once Parker and I sort out our options, we might claim some of that floor."

"When we're off duty from the resort." Parker wrapped his arm around Carter and rubbed his fist on his head. "We're staying back in the States, little bro."

Dad cast him a wary look. "Maria and I are swapping hotel operations with your brother."

"You're moving to Switzerland?" Carter raised his eyebrows.

"We sent our new manager over there for now, but yes. That's the plan."

Plans.

Plans had a funny way of changing.

Chapter Twenty

Arrival Alert flashed on Carter's phone, and a low chiming sound echoed in the foyer. He'd just returned to Tandem Cottage. His phone screen displayed one of Gough's taxis pulling up the drive. He turned to the screen at the entry door. When the carriage stopped, a woman exited. She was casually dressed in mom-style travel clothes.

Someone in the taxi handed a small duffle bag down to the stranger and a square black case with a handle.

Alyssa joined him in the entryway and pointed to the display screen. "She looks familiar." She leaned in.

"No idea." Carter went to the door. "Gonna find out. Stay here."

He stepped outside. The woman paid the driver as the other taxi occupants stared in admiration at the property—some taking pictures.

Their visitor, an attractive blonde in her late forties, smiled at Carter. "Hi there. You must be Carter Parker. I'm Linda Anderson-Paine."

He stopped walking toward her and rotated his head slightly to the left and raised an eyebrow. Mom called that his 'and that means what?' look.

"I've been commissioned to paint the Byrnes' nursery." She pointed to the black case. "Would you mind carrying my art case in?"

A faint ringing sounded in Carter's ears. The guy in that room wasn't the artist? He forced himself to breathe. Before Abbi-Renae had died, he'd never had a panic attack. His heart pounded in his chest, threatening a new one.

As the taxi drove off, Mrs. Anderson left her bags and moved toward him. "Are you okay?"

"Yes." He raised his hand. "Just give me a moment." If the guy in the house wasn't supposed to be there, then was he a menace?

She passed him her business card. "On the back is the number Cassandra said to use if you have any questions."

He flipped it over. It was the same number he had. *I'm an idiot.* He should have asked the strange man for identification when he'd arrived. Should have called Cassandra. Had he endangered them all? Sweat broke out on his brow. He ran his hand through his hair. "Stay here. We have a situation. There's someone here who claimed he had this job."

"What? No. I'm doing the mural." She pursed her lips. Linda pulled out her phone as Carter headed into the house.

He pointed at Alyssa. "Go outside, now please. There's another artist here, and I think ours is a scammer." *Or worse.*

"Oh!" Eyes wide, she left the house.

He swooped into Kelsey's room and pulled the sleeping baby from her crib. Then he grabbed her bag and fled the house, Kelsey squealing.

Carter jogged toward the two women.

Alyssa pointed to Mrs. Anderson. "Linda is a family friend and an amazing artist. We've known her for years. So, when she says she's the Byrnes's muralist—she is."

"I couldn't reach Cassandra, but Colton said he has no idea who that guy is." Linda shook her head emphatically, her long earrings swaying.

Should have called them myself, weeks ago.

Kelsey lifted her head from Carter's shoulder and whined as she reached for Alyssa.

He had to do something. "I'll call 911."

"The scammer is gone right now." Alyssa took Kelsey in her capable arms. "He went into town early this morning."

"What? The guy has never left in the morning since he got here."

"Not that we know of."

"I saw him take a bike and head out super early. And he's not come back."

Carter shook out the tension in his neck.

"I think we should go back inside." Alyssa jostled Kelsey. "Someone has a wettie diaper." She put her face close to the baby's. "Don't you?"

Mrs. Anderson removed her sun visor. "I wonder who is impersonating me."

"Not impersonating per se." Carter took the artist's bags. "Now that I think about it, the dude just said Cassandra sent him. Maybe I'm panicking for nothing. Maybe she's got him working on something else?"

Alyssa shot him a disbelieving look. "Don't you remember we showed him to the nursery? And he had all those art pencils and markers with him."

Linda frowned. "Gosh, I hope Cassandra didn't hire someone else and forget to tell me or her husband about it. But I can't imagine Colton wouldn't know. They've got the renowned Mary Lou Peters painting watercolor portraits for both hallways and the master suite."

"I love her work and yours." Alyssa opened the front door and then went inside.

Carter set the bags down in the foyer. "Let's go see what he's been doing back there. Something weird going on, and I'm like two seconds from calling the police."

"Let's check it out." Linda shrugged. "I'll give you my professional opinion."

He and Mrs. Anderson headed down the corridor on the right. When they reached the nursery door, he pulled it open. "This is it."

"Whoa, Nellie." Linda stiffened. "What the heck is that?"

Carter gaped as he surveyed the once pristine walls, now covered in complex mathematic formulas from the ceiling to the floor. The case of markers lay open, the contents scattered.

"That's not artwork." Linda rocked back on her heel. "At least not anything I am familiar with."

A recollection niggled at his memory. "Wait. I know someone who is looking for specific weird art like this."

Mrs. Anderson placed her hand over her chin. "Someone who wants this kind of thing?"

"Yeah." Now to get pretty boy Shane White's card and call him.

She surveyed the room. "Are you sure?"

Footfall sounded in the hallway.

"Carter?" Mr. Welling's voice carried.

What was he doing there? Carter swiveled. Jack's dad, a gun holstered around his midsection, and Shane White behind him, the outline of a pistol visible beneath his jacket entered the room.

"Is he in there?" Shane called out.

"No." Carter scowled in his direction.

Shane's nostrils flared. "Everybody out."

"What's going on?" Carter stepped toward Shane. "Who are you to tell me what to do?"

Shane flashed a badge at him.

Welling motioned for them to leave.

"Forget you ever saw those formulas," Welling told Carter, as he ushered them out and closed the door.

"Definitely not artwork—like I said." Linda's voice was so deadpan that Carter couldn't help but huff a laugh.

"Now that we have confirmation, there'll be a team here as soon as they can get from the mainland. But you need to pack up and go elsewhere."

"Go elsewhere?"

Carter resisted the urge to grab Shane by the shoulders. Instead, he pointed at him. "If you think I'm gonna pack up all these baby things and leave with my daughter just so you can paint one room in that wing—you've got another thing coming."

Before the agent could respond, Mr. Welling nodded. "Just that corridor would be fine."

Shane scowled. "This is my case. I say everyone leaves."

"Do you have any idea the heat you'd take and the people who'd be on our tails if you do that?" Welling gave a curt laugh.

"Especially the owners of this place, the Byrnes. You'd better not let your clean-up crew use anything toxic on those walls." Carter moved closer to the two men. "Cassandra and Colton need to agree on whatever you do."

"Yeah, they may even want to have the walls re-drywalled." Welling tapped his loafer on the floor. "I'm no 'safe paint' expert but I know for Leland's walls in Yorktown—"

"He's done this before?" Carter gaped.

"Immediately before he came north. That clean-up job took a week to get the proper paint to cover everything permanently."

"A week?" He couldn't put Alyssa out for a week either.

"Gianni Franchetti is in town," Welling said to Shane in a low voice. "He throws a lot of weight around."

The mention of his grandfather made Carter take pause. He could ask to move everyone over to Cardinal Cottage.

Baby Kelsey in arms, Alyssa moved up the corridor toward them. "What's going on?"

Shane raised his palm. "Stop right there."

Carter motioned them forward, with perverse pleasure.

"The fella staying here isn't an artist." Welling tapped his foot. "He's a nationally renowned physicist who went missing this summer."

"Oh." Alyssa blinked hard.

Baby Kelsey said, "Ohhhhh," too, and he couldn't help smiling.

Carter went to her. "Shane's trying to kick us all out, and I told him to pack sand." He took the baby from Alyssa and waved Kelsey's hand. "Isn't that right? Say 'pack sand'!"

"Saaaa."

He kissed her soft cheek and she giggled.

"Actually, I had a favor to ask." Alyssa crossed her arms. "My great-grandmother has asked if I could stay with her for a few days at the Grand Hotel. She's arrived early."

Alyssa packed her overnight bag, tension vibrating through her. *Shane White, a federal agent.* Their "artist" Leland actually a missing physicist. And the Byrnes had commissioned her friend Linda as the muralist. Linda, fortunately, had been hired to do another mural on the island so she headed off to the Jeffries' cottage to work on theirs. Had Clark Jeffries formed a relationship with the brunette she'd seen him with at Lilac Cottage? Funny how God worked things out. She'd prayed so hard that Clark would find her a spot, but that was not to be.

Carter entered through the open door. "Hey, Alyssa, I let my boss know what's going on. If you're able to work in the daytime, then come over to Cardinal Cottage. That's my grandparents' new cottage."

"Let me see what my great-grandmother says. I'd imagine Romelda has got a bunch of things she has to do for her viewers. I'll ask her."

He raised his hand. "No worries. I'm sure we'll be back here soon."

But would they?

And if she couldn't get her internship hours in, then what? "We'll make this work somehow, Lord willing."

He headed back out. She heard him speaking with someone farther down the hall.

A fresh-scrubbed looking young woman with immaculate makeup stopped at her door. Arms akimbo, she was attired in a white blouse, khakis, and tan loafers.

"Shalley? Shalley Woods?" Gone were the multiple piercings, the overdone makeup, and casual waitress clothing.

"Agent Shalley White." She grinned. "Mom to the most adorable toddler on the planet."

"That whole restaurant charade makes a lot of sense now." She shook her head. Shalley's husband was supposed to be Alyssa's first real date—that ended up not being a date.

Mr. Welling stuck his head in the door. "Better hurry along, Shalley, we've got work to do here and need to section this off."

"Yes, sir." Shalley took several steps toward Alyssa and pulled her into a hug. "Do you have any idea how you and the other lunch ladies blessed me?" She released her.

"I'm so glad." She twisted her lower lip. "I'm guessing Shane isn't the. . ." she wanted to say 'jerk' but didn't, "way he acts on the island when he's at home."

"When I met him, he'd just gotten off a summer of pretending to be yachty guy," she waggled her shoulders, "dumped by society media princess. He was so happy to be back to normal old Shane. I was in my last year of college in criminal justice. He sort of date-recruited me for my job." She laughed.

"Shalley?" Shane bellowed down the hall.

Seriously, she didn't consider that *jerk* behavior? But then again, considering her family's home life, he was a saint. Footfall carried toward them.

Shane entered the room, and Shalley rolled her eyes at him. He glanced between the two of them. "You two ladies have five minutes to finish your conversation."

Shalley crossed her arms and slacked her hip. "Oh yeah? Says who?"

He laughed. He extended his arms making tickle fingers. "Says the tickle monster!"

As Shalley ducked behind Alyssa, she assumed her best cafeteria voice, "No tickling on my watch, mister!"

The former school misfit ducked back out and chased her husband out of the room, both of them screaming as they ran down the hall.

What had just happened there? Shalley and Shane? And he had a different personality. Thank God that girl made it through okay. What a hard life she'd had.

She turned toward her bag. Excitement about meeting her great-grandmother swirled within her along with a dose of anxiety."

What if she doesn't like me?

Later, when Alyssa arrived at the Grand Hotel, she almost bolted. The place was decorated in such over-the-top colors and patterns that it sent her already rattled nerves on edge.

"May I help you?" A young Asian woman in a white blouse, a dark jacket, and tailored pants offered her a tight smile.

"Um, Romelda," was all Alyssa could croak out.

Then she spied the television evangelist, striding down the hallway, surrounded by a half-dozen people. *My great-grandmother!* Romelda looked much as she did on the screen, but a little frailer. She was an elderly woman, after all, despite her beautiful and current fashion wardrobe.

The hotel staff member followed Alyssa's gaze. "Oh, yes, she's very famous."

Alyssa stood there, as her knees began to shake. "My great-grandmother," she whispered.

Romelda's eyes locked on hers, and she pressed her hands together in a praying position, raised them to her mouth, and bowed her head. Tears were rolling down her cheeks and now Alyssa's, and she strode toward her great-grandmother.

Romelda opened her eyes and her arms. "Girl, give me some sugar before I keel right over."

Laughing, because Dad had schooled her on some Southernism, she hugged her great-grandmother and kissed her cheek.

"Well, if you don't beat all." Romelda stepped back and surveyed Alyssa from head-to-toe. She turned to a middle-aged man nearby, with a neatly trimmed beard. "Roger, don't she look like your ma?"

The man nodded.

"That's your cousin, and his five boys are playing in that kiddy water park they've got out yonder."

Sammy would have more cousins—and boys at that. "Nice to meet you, Cousin Roger."

He extended his hand and then gestured to some of the others. "These folks are your kin, too."

"And there's a passel more of 'em over on the mainland visiting the Tahquamenon Falls."

"That's near where my folks and I live."

She raised her eyebrows. "Don't I know it. They all want to hop in and see your daddy, but I told 'em I got a plan. I'll tell you all about it tonight while you and I get to know each other."

Dad would finally see his grandmother, the woman who raised him. She began to cry again and Romelda pulled her into her arms.

"Grandma's here, honey, and I reckon between God and you and me, we'll get your daddy to a family reunion, real soon."

"Amen," she said.

For the second time that day, Gianni and Grandma Kareen pulled up in a carriage to get Carter. This time, though, Parker and Jaycie weren't with them. They'd gone over to the mainland with Dad. Romelda had sent a taxi for Alyssa earlier. Gianni and Grandma were already out riding in the carriage and offered to come back and get him and Kelsey. Carter had hastily packed her diaper bag and clothes and his own overnight bag and his shaving kit. Funny how quickly Tandem Cottage had come to feel like home. Would Cardinal Cottage feel the same?

Carter handed Kelsey off to Gianni and then climbed into the carriage.

"You'll be back inside here in a few days." Gianni's brown eyes lit up. "I've got several teams flying in to manage this, uh, problem. Welling has been told."

"What about Agent White?"

With a deep belly laugh, Gianni adjusted Kelsey to his other knee. "Grandpa Gianni has friends much farther up the chain than Shane White has."

"I bet." Carter high-fived Gianni's free hand.

"What perplexes me is that most physics problems today are solved in groups collaboratively—not individually. But Welling claims this guy has never worked well in group." Gianni flexed his shoulders. "So, if his superiors knew that, they should've realized there's a whole lot more going on with him—which there clearly is."

"Some things with computer programming you have to work on in group, just to weigh in on all aspects."

"Welling said good old Leland memorized a group-presented problem of national importance. He wasn't supposed to be working on it outside the group."

"But he did."

"Not only here, but at home in Virginia. Which, by the way, was in your neighborhood."

"What?" Carter stiffened. "Never heard about it."

"And you weren't meant to." Gianni touched the side of his nose. "Only certain people learn about those things."

Grandma Kareen reached across and patted Carter's hand. "Just like you don't need to know about how Gianni knows and how he makes stuff happen." She snapped her fingers. "Like that."

"Taa." Kelsey clapped.

"You are such a little talker, baby girl. I'm so proud of you."

"She's changing the subject." Gianni clutched her as the carriage turned and pulled up beside the largest mansion on the bluff. "Which was a great tactic."

"My little great-granddaughter is learning the ropes." Grandma crinkled her nose.

The white manor-style home gleamed as sunrays poked through the clouds. "I can see how you cleaned this place up. You can't really see it from the road."

Gianni arched his eyebrows. "And we like it that way."

"We do," Grandma agreed. She tickled Kelsey's chin. "Don't we? No 'Lookie Lous' for us."

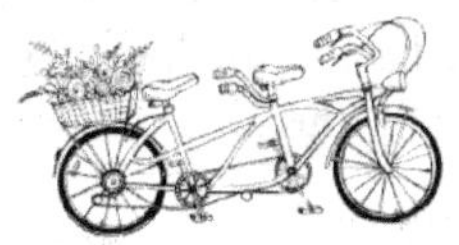

Chapter Twenty-One

Susan held the cellphone close to her ear to tune out the cheerful voices of tourists enjoying Windermere Point and to hear her mother's voice better. "You're here early, Momma?" She motioned for John, who was watching some kids flying their kites, to join her and Tamara at the picnic table. Tom Austin remained staring overhead as a red dragon kite, over ten feet long, swooped.

"Tha's right, honey, me and Romelda got both our digs all straight. Her doll baby granddaughter is with her, too."

"Alyssa?"

"She's real sweet. We want you two to come for dinner down in that big ol' dining room with all of us."

She cringed. She and John would be in the middle of a bunch of politicos and that would turn her stomach. But did she and John need to provide her mother assistance? "Momma, are all of your people with you?"

"My people?" Her mother cackled. "If I brought all our people from Virginia, all those I represent, there'd be no room for all of 'em."

"Momma, you know what I meant—your caregivers."

"Oh, they comin' soon. But I got a passel o' folks helpin' me, so don't worry none."

She blew out an exasperated breath. "We'll come."

"Six sharp, you hear?"

"Yes, Momma."

"All right." Her mother ended the call.

"She hung up on you, didn't she?" Tamara laughed as Susan gazed at her phone in disbelief. "She's consistent, I give her that."

John stood across from her at the picnic table and flipped his hands over. "What's going on?"

"My mother can't make anything easy."

"Nope." John unclasped his hands and slapped the table. "That woman just won't listen to people, and she refuses to retire."

She refuses to retire. The resentment in her husband's voice wasn't lost on her. His choice of words likely included Susan's decision to keep working. Maybe he wasn't talking about Momma.

Tom returned to the table, one hand on his navy-blue cap as the wind picked up. "Thought those kids' kite might not come back down."

Susan smiled. "It sure was pretty but that rapid descent looked like it might break that poor dragon."

"Humph, I hope your mom doesn't have to crash to make her retire." Tam ran her hand over her lower face. "Your mom takes her duties seriously."

"Not sure congressional leaders call it retiring. Resign from service. Not seek re-election?" Tom offered. "Get bucked from the bronco?" He grinned at his last offering.

"Tom!" Tamara gave her husband the stink eye.

"Probably she's like the rest of those elderly lawmakers." Tom shrugged. "If she steps down, then her state won't have the political clout they want. Then again, any other state is just half of Texas. So, since she doesn't live there. . ."

Tamara shook her head. "Not everything needs to be compared with Texas, my dear Thomas." Her friend only called her husband Thomas when he was edging toward her bad list.

"Sure does." He wrapped an arm around his wife and kissed her.

John joined her on her side of the table. "Are you going to check on her once she arrives?"

"She's already here." Susan rubbed her temples. "We're supposed to have dinner with her tonight."

"What about her Secret Service detail?" Tamara pulled sodas from her insulated pack and passed them around.

"This had to be on the docket for a while." Tom popped the top on his Coke. "I imagine reshuffling wasn't a happy task."

"No doubt." John's curt tone held disgust.

Tam sipped from her can of cherry cola. "Mrs. Daniels is an entity unto herself. She's got tremendous influence."

"I love my mother, but I just don't get it." Susan tapped her fingers on the top of her Diet Coke. "Why not spend her last few years relaxing?" What was Momma's resistance all about?

In her soul, conviction spread.

Fear. Fear of being separated.

Fear of not enough.

In Momma's case, it was fear of not being enough to so many people who were her constituents. At least Susan didn't have that notion. Or did she? Was she worried that if she left, then her shoes wouldn't be properly filled?

"You never know, though, what could happen." Her mother's fearful favorite saying smacked Susan's consciousness. Who exactly did know what was going to happen on any day? Only God knew.

"You look deep in thought." Tamara eyed her knowingly.

"I'm thinking I am my mother's daughter."

Tom exchanged a quizzical look with John.

Seagulls swooped overhead, squawking.

"Momma has to make her own peace with God about what she's doing."

"You'll not try to rescue Congresswoman Daniels from herself?" Tom winked at her.

"Nope." Susan gave her head a hard tight shake. "She usually chooses to disregard everyone's advice anyway."

Just yesterday, John had said that God had provided everything they needed for Susan to retire. He asked what else the Lord would have to do besides smack her upside the head to realize that He had given her just what she needed.

"I'm retiring next year," Susan blurted out and then pressed her drink to her lips. Had she announced it to her husband and dearest friends?

"You can't take that back now." John angled his chin away and lowered his eyes.

"No siree, that's a Texas-sized promise," Tom chortled.

Seated on the front porch, sipping sweet tea, Susan and John watched as ore boats moved through the Straits in the late afternoon sun. "Dinner last night with Momma went well." Susan and John had been seated next to Alyssa and Romelda, who were excellent company. Momma sat further down the table with another representative and two powerful Michigan constituents. Periodically, she'd catch Susan's gaze and smile. At the beginning and the end, hugs and kisses had been exchanged. Nothing unusual. And the government Secret Service and her caregiver were exceptionally discreet.

"No drama. Gotta love that." John stroked her arm.

Her phone pinged a text message. She read it and then held her cellphone so John could read the screen. "Momma has summoned us."

"You sure she sent this and not one of her cronies?"

She re-read the message. "Regardless, it's her phone. Small reception tonight in the Roosevelt Room. Semi-formal attire. Bring ID."

In the yard, some of the medical retreat guests played frisbee on the lush verdant lawn.

"She seemed in good shape last night." John drank his tea.

"I don't know." She sighed. "Ever since Colby received those meds for her, when he visited, I keep wondering what else we can do."

"Of course, she denied they were hers."

She gave a curt laugh. "Her name was on the prescription bottles."

"Colby heard that half the old-timers on Capitol Hill have their pharmacies send those drugs to their offices."

"Which is shocking." She wrapped her hand around the cold glass.

"Seems about right. So many decrepit people in office." He waved off a fly. "At least my favorite old person is going to retire."

She playfully slapped at him. "I'm going to tell Momma that I'm retiring and suggest, yet again, that she do the same."

"Good luck with that."

"You better go lay your suit out and tell Tamara we'll be gone."

John rose and saluted her. "Will do."

She cast him a stern look. He whistled some Navy tune as he headed off. *I'm in the Navy now.*

When she found Tamara, she learned Momma had texted them too.

"That was so sweet of your mother to remember me and reach out."

Susan shook her head. "Or does she think it's the nineties still and you and I are running up the road to one of her tea parties at the Capitol?"

Tamara pressed her hands to her face. "Remember the gals we were talking with for a long time and finally they up and left our table?"

"We were talking at them, not to them. Those poor ladies from Guatemala didn't understand half of what we said."

"It was still fun. And fancy." Tamara did jazz hands and rocked her hips. "We sure were young then, weren't we?"

"We aren't anymore, so we both better get working on our outfits and hair."

"And makeup and jewelry."

"No hats!" they both said in unison and laughed.

"No more tea hats, thank you, Jesus." Susan gave a little wave as she headed off to her room.

Several hours later, John and Susan walked down the sidewalk to the Grand Hotel, hand-in-hand. "This is a beautiful night for a walk." She gestured toward the Straits of Mackinac.

"Smooth as glass out there. And prettier than the Atlantic, isn't it?" Her husband squeezed her hand.

"It's got a lot more blue than gray, and sometimes I'd swear we were in the Caribbean with the turquoise color it turns."

John pointed to Round Island lighthouse. "We better do that lighthouse ferry tour before the summer is over and we're back in Virginia."

"This Saturday?"

"They're only offered certain days. I'll check tomorrow."

"Thanks. I'm sure you'll be an excellent date."

"I bet you say that to all your husbands."

"I do." She leaned in to kiss him.

They reached the red-carpeted stairway at the side entrance to the hotel. A tall, slim, dark-haired man wearing tinted glasses strode toward them. "Mr. and Mrs. Mullen?"

They nodded.

"Take the elevator up to the second floor. Then follow the signs with purple arrows."

"Okay." John escorted Susan up the steps. The doorman opened the glass side door to the hotel, and John and Susan entered.

Tom and Tamara had been instructed to arrive earlier so they could be verified as guests before entering the event. Susan's phone pinged. She read their message.

"Tam and Tom are up there. They had to get patted down. Can you believe that?"

"I can. Take a look at this bunch—not your average tourist group." John's dark eyes widened as he escorted Susan into the Grand Hotel's parlor, which was filled with people—most attired in evening dress. Diamond necklaces or bracelets on many of the ladies glittered from the chandelier lighting overhead.

She spotted a half dozen Secret Service agents in the crowd.

"You sure you're ready for this?" John leaned in. "A little different from last night."

She inhaled his spicy aftershave. "You smell good. Maybe we should just go hide out down one of the inner hallways and smooch."

He laughed. "Probably one of those agents would stop us and ruin our fun."

"Better get this over with." She huffed a sigh. "Momma will probably give us two minutes of her time, three at best."

Once inside the reception room, the scents of perfume, a sweet fruity drink, and men's aftershave mingled and made Susan want to sneeze.

Tamara, attired in a sequin-embellished maxi dress, waved from a counter height table by the wall. Tom, in a tailored suit with a Texas-style bolo-tie at his neck, and a white Stetson hat, extended his cowboy-booted heel.

John led her to them.

"Howdy, John. Howdy Susan." Tom's mega-watt smile and those good looks should have made him a movie star not a cancer surgeon.

Tamara hugged Susan and whispered, "The Grand Dame is at three o'clock—if the back wall is high noon."

Susan pulled away. "You're making this sound like a bad Western."

"Well, this reception kind of is, isn't it?"

"Are you Miss Kitty, then?" Susan gestured from head-to-toe.

Tamara feigned shock. "You know Miss Kitty was, well, shall we say not all she seemed to be?"

"The few times I watched Gunsmoke I was pretty certain respectable ladies didn't run a bar back then."

"I'm not Miss Kitty, but if I were, I'd probably sashay through this crowd to your mom." Tamara inclined her head toward John. "I'll bet this guy knows how to get you through to your mother."

John extended his arm. "Come on, now, we're doing this."

The next thing she knew, John was weaving them through the ill-formed lines that led to her mother. When they got near the security guards surrounding her, one huge corn-fed linebacker type and the other surely a member of the WWF, John headed straight to the linebacker guard.

He pointed at Susan. "This here is Congresswoman Daniels daughter, Susan Daniels Mullen, and I'm her husband, John."

Corn-fed looked John up and down, then focused on his face, and then Susan's. "Yeah, I recognize you two." He jerked a thumb for them to go behind him, apparently to approach Momma, who was seated on a raised high-backed velvet chair. He led them to where two female officers stood, their guns bulging beneath trim navy suit jackets.

"Susan and John!" Momma's caregiver waved at them from where she was standing about six feet behind the female agents. She held onto Momma's empty wheelchair.

John shook hands with the woman. "Good to see you here."

Corn-fed jabbed his hand in Momma's direction. "She's ready for you."

He led them to her mother, who frowned. "What're y'all doing here?"

Oh no. Yesterday was a good day, was today a bad one? From the blank look in Momma's eyes, and confusion written on her face, she'd not remembered she'd invited them. Which is why the neurologist had pleaded with Momma to step down from her public office. Not that Momma ever listened to experts, who she always claimed were catastrophizing or hysterical. Name calling of anyone disagreeable was Momma's main tactic.

The caretaker hurried around to Momma and whispered in her ear.

A slow, fake smile blossomed on her mother's wrinkled face. She gestured for them to come forward. "Come give your Momma a kiss!"

"Best talk with her helper sooner rather than later," John murmured as they joined her mother.

The sound of cameras clicking assaulted Susan's ears. John held a hand in front of his face. This was why they'd raised Colby out of the spotlight. This was why she never shared with people, other than her closest friends, that her mother was "the" Mrs. Daniels of Washington.

Representative Daniels who'd outlasted all the representatives who'd ever served in Congress.

As Susan bent and kissed her, Momma's eyes widened in full recognition. A genuine smile lit her face.

Love.

That's why Susan was here. That's why she and John had done everything that they could to keep her very independent mother protected—even from herself. Sometimes to no avail. Momma clasped her hand.

"Look at all these people here for little ol' me!" Mama gestured toward the massive group of glitterati. "You know I can't retire now and disappoint them. My constituents need me."

Susan bit her tongue. She wasn't going to point out that these were not her Virginia constituents. She and John might be the only two people in the room who were voters from her own district.

Mama angled her head. "You understand, girl?"

"Yes, Momma, I know." The only way her mother would stop would be when they placed her in her coffin. Until then, Susan had to accept that this was how things would be.

John bent and kissed her mother's cheek. "I know you'll never retire, but we've got to get Susan to turn in her retirement papers."

Mama pointed to John. "With a man this fine and already retired and at home—what are you waiting for, child?"

Susan's heart swelled and tears pricked her eyes at both her mother's clarity in recalling that John had indeed retired and with the realization that her mother was exactly right.

"I'm not waiting anymore, Momma."

"Good. Y'all go on now while I talk a little while with these folks. They're ponying up good money to have a chat with me."

More photographs ensued, and Susan and John made their way to Tamara and Tom.

A young guy with an oversized professional camera joined them. He locked eyes on Susan and John. "Can I get your names? And your relationship to Representative Daniels."

Dr. Austin stood to his full height and tipped the front of his Stetson back and looked down. "These two folks here are my cowpokes. Cowboy Johnny Mustang and Cowgirl Susie Pinto. Representative Daniels only rides bareback with these two. And only at midnight."

The photographer blinked his green eyes a few times and then headed off.

Tamara elbowed her husband. "Susie Pinto? That's your best shot?"

"Yeah, Tom, you made me sound like a bean." Susan crossed her arms.

Tom straightened his Stetson. "First thing that came to mind. A Pinto horse is a fine thing to behold—just as you were up there. I could tell your momma didn't recognize you at first or something was wrong. But you recovered immediately."

"Susie Pinto best not become my nickname." Susan uncrossed her arms and shook her finger at him. "You're right though, Momma wasn't quite sure who we were."

Tam cringed. "I saw her caregiver come up there, and I figured that's what happened. My heart went out to you."

John slapped Tom's shoulder. "I don't mind being Johnny Mustang. Might have my wife call me that from now on."

"Only if we're riding bareback at midnight."

Tom slid his hands into his pocket. "I can arrange that. Come on out with me and Tamara to the ranch this winter."

"I'm retiring. I just might." She fluffed her hair back. "No bareback riding unless I wear a cowgirl hat."

Tamara made a referee time-out motion with her hands. "Don't tell him that—you'll soon find a lady's Stetson delivered to your room."

"Okay, cancel the bareback riding. But I wouldn't mind learning how to ride."

Tom scratched his cheek. "You'd be a greenhorn or a tenderfoot by my reckoning."

"Not for long." John thrust out his chest. "Not with Cowboy Johnny Mustang by her side."

"You've created a monster." Tamara grabbed Tom's Stetson and passed it to John.

"Yeehaw!" John donned the hat.

"Looking good, honey."

John passed the Stetson back to Tom.

Music began at the front of the room and a microphone squealed. Susan flinched.

"Freshly back from his European tour, the acclaimed tenor, Colby of New York City, will serenade his grandmother and her guests."

Susan's jaw could have dropped and bounced back into her face.

"He kept that on the down low, didn't he?" John kissed her forehead.

"He sure did." She didn't know whether to be angry that her son hadn't kept her informed, or thrilled that he'd be performing. Her heartbeat ratcheted up as excitement won out.

As her son launched into a beautiful rendition of Respect, by Aretha Franklin, motherly pride swallowed whole any resentment she had.

All eyes were on Colby, but Susan didn't miss Momma's caregiver and a Secret Service agent transferring her from the chair to her wheelchair. Alyssa and Romelda appeared in a hidden doorway at the back of the room. While Colby continued to sing, Momma was wheeled toward the back, as Alyssa held the exit door. Had this short meet-and-greet worn her out? Were Romelda and Alyssa called in to rescue her?

Poor Momma.

Not poor Momma. Dedicated, sacrificing, long-serving public servant Momma who, despite her failing cognitive skills, pushed through. Pride swelled in her heart for her mother, too. Momma's decision to continue serving wasn't tied to Susan's choices. She could retire in good conscience.

I've never acknowledged that I didn't want to fail Momma. But she had to own it now. She'd never be a Representative Daniels, but she'd done the best she could at her job. And the only One she had to please was a power much higher than any of them.

Thy will be done, not mine.

John leaned in. "Was your momma heading off with her chum to the Cupola bar upstairs?"

Her phone vibrated. Text from her mother.

Bring Colby upstairs when he's done. Top Cupola. You and your pals too.

When Colby finished the song, the audience erupted in applause.

She showed John the phone message and waved Tamara and Tom to accompany her toward the stage.

Poor Momma, indeed—she still had a half dozen tricks up her sleeve.

And she was still owed respect.

Chapter Twenty-Two

Alyssa waved at the repainted walls in Tandem Cottage's nursery. "Looks like nothing was ever there."

"Grandpa Gianni's recommended crew took care of it." Carter slid his top horizontal hand over his lower hand in a swooshing movement.

"In under three days. Wow." She'd returned the previous night, while her great-grandmother entertained her board of directors at the Grand Hotel.

A smirk tugged at his lips. "You shoulda seen Shane's face."

"Aw, come on." She elbowed him. "He's a dad, like you."

"Nothing alike." He made a foul motion. "Bad call."

She laughed. "Any guy who could save hometown girl, Shalley Woods, from her past gets points from her former cafeteria worker." She splayed her fingers below her neck.

"We better get up to the Grand for the buffet while Maria is here." Carter checked his Apple watch. "And not keep your great-grandmother waiting."

"You got a lot accomplished this morning on your project. You earned this long lunch." She nibbled her lower lip.

"Agreed. Let's go."

They stepped out into the cool mid-morning air to the sounds of birds chirping. Sounded like someone had turned their volume up today.

Carter trotted past her toward the bikes.

Alyssa slowly followed him. "She said to meet her in the dining hall."

"It's kinda cool seeing all the tourists in there for the huge buffet."

"Noisy?"

"Oh yeah. Makes Kelsey's loudest screams sound pretty quiet."

"Might give us a decibel reset?"

"Yeah. It could."

"Might be helpful for those fussy nights she's been having with her teeth." Lately, poor Kelsey had to be rocked for what seemed like hours.

They got onto the tandem bike and Carter directed them out onto the road. They pedaled past the houses on West Bluff, both waving at the horse on the Jeffries' porch—their new tradition—as they passed.

"Do you think he'll ever wave back at us?" she called up to Carter.

He turned his head. "What makes you think that's a he? Could be a mare."

"You have a point."

"We'll have to ask the owner later."

What? No. She hoped he didn't plan on stopping and asking. But he knew so many people on the island—it was probably like stopping at a neighbor's house, for him.

"I'll ask Linda. She's finished their mural and should be over at our house. . ." Had she really called it their house? *Yikes.* "At Tandem Cottage, this afternoon."

On the right, the Straits of Mackinac, dotted with low whitecaps, beckoned her toward the mainland. Now that her parents were bringing Sammy soon for a visit, she imagined how she'd get on a ferry and run off to find her boy waiting for her. Tears blurred her vision and she blinked rapidly.

Within a few minutes, they arrived. They parked the bike and headed up the side stairs.

Ahead of them stood two tall, dark-suited men. When one turned, an earpiece was visible. *Security?* "Representative Daniels is here, too. Those could be her bodyguards."

"Right." Carter cringed. "I hope they don't hassle us."

"They were fine the other night when Grandma Romelda and I hung out with the congresswoman."

The two men swiveled and glanced toward a crowd of tourists entering the Grand's beautifully appointed parlor. She and her great-grandmother had enjoyed after-dinner music there the nights she'd stayed. What a fun time. She hadn't gotten to speak with her great-grandmother as much as she wished because there were always people around. And when there weren't, Romelda was preparing for her next sermon. She had a huge revival meeting scheduled in Detroit the following week.

An elderly woman flanked by two more bodyguards entered the huge room. Attired in a billowing ruby-colored gown embroidered in gold, her matching turban glittered with crystals arranged in a wave.

Beyond Representative Daniels, a line of people with cameras shot pictures.

"Carter, that's Grandma Romelda's best friend. And the senior-most member of Congress." Some called Mrs. Daniels a national treasure.

"My dad says she's a fossil who should retire."

She frowned. "I can't believe you said that."

He shrugged. "I say she's like most elderly government workers—retired in place."

Alyssa cocked her head to the side. "Do you believe that?"

"The Representative is in her late eighties. Elder abuse by her constituents might be the right way to frame it. They should let that poor woman step down."

"You have a point." Alyssa quirked her lips to the side. "But didn't you vote for her in Virginia?"

"Um, well, yeah."

She laughed. "My own great-grandmother's ministry viewers would want her to work until she'd dropped dead at the pulpit."

"I agree about Romelda. Won't stop till she drops." He offered a cocky smile.

"The first woman to hold the position of pastor in her denomination." Pride in her great-grandmother was chased by the knowledge of the cost. "Of course, my dad then got harassed by the other kids—and the parents in his small community."

"But your dad's a pastor, too."

"But Grandma was in a very progressive church whereas Dad chose a completely conservative path."

"One where no women are allowed to preach?"

"Good guess."

"I bet her viewers know how Romelda felt about that." Carter brought his hands together and splayed his fingers open and apart.

"Yeah. Not happy and also very sad for us. My sister and I never got to see her growing up. And, because I live with my parents, I couldn't reach out to her before now."

"I don't think God would like that—not that I know God's mind."

"I've thought the same thing." They exchanged a quick glance. She had the sudden urge to slip her arm through his.

Carter took her arm, surprising her. He guided her across the hall to a corridor. "Come on. Let's go find your great-grandmother."

Just then, Grandma Romelda waved to them from the hallway. Attired in similar fashionable clothing she wore on her show, and matching costume jewelry, she looked ready to go onscreen.

She gestured for people behind her to come forward. A group of about ten older men and women complied and gazed wide-eyed at Alyssa and Carter. These were different folks than when she'd stayed there.

Romelda waved her hand in a circle as they hurried down the hall. When they reached her, Grandma gave her a big hug. When she released her, she pointed to the others. "Y'all this is my great-granddaughter who I've been bragging about, and that means she's kin to y'all, too!"

These people were all related to her? Overwhelmed, tears pricked her eyes.

As she was introduced to each relative, Carter stood back, talking with Grandma.

"Well, butter my biscuit! I finally get to meet you." A tall man with a shock of white hair shook her hand firmly. "I'm Buck, your great-grand uncle, your great-grandma's brother."

"Good to meet you. Wonderful, actually."

"Well, I pray your pa says the same thing. 'Cause we need you to rustle him on over to meet up with all of us."

She tapped her toes. "I've got an idea."

But first she should tell Carter about her boy. She cast him a quick glance.

She was leaving soon. Why not enjoy these last moments of being "just Alyssa" not "that poor single mom Alyssa"?

I'm not ready to leave this island world. She wasn't ready to say goodbye to Carter and his family.

But she did need to greet all of these members of her own family.

Chapter Twenty-Three

St. Ignace

The hum of the motor, subtly vibrating through the ferry's floor, replicated the buzz of Alyssa's nerves. Her son would be waiting in St. Ignace. The grief of their separation, that she'd successfully held back all these weeks, broke its chains. Tears overflowed. Thank God, she'd worn her oversized sunglasses—cheap but they did their job.

She hunched in the rear seat on the lower level of the ferry. Seated on the left, she'd be able to see the mainland as it came into view. This being mid-day, the main returnees on board were from the island hotels and most were seated up top for the view. But there were a few handfuls of people seated below deck.

She'd be with her boy soon. She pulled her phone from her purse, hands shaking.

On my way, she typed and sent the message.

Her parents had told her that they'd need to talk with her alone, so they wanted to go down by the beach at the park and let Sammy play.

Soon she'd move with her boy to the Soo and begin her new life.

God bless Carter Parker.

Her sweet boss had made it possible for her to complete a verified internship. When he signed off in a few weeks, she could submit that to the school district. She could hardly wait to work with others in her field.

Others in my field—like Carter.

Her cheeks heated. This was a summer job and only made possible because Gino had demanded visitation and had threatened her.

But now he could never take her boy away.

She sniffed and choked back a sob.

My son. She pulled tissue from her purse and dabbed at her wet cheeks.

And Jennifer had left Gino. And had notified his commanding officer about the circumstances of Gino's son. He could face charges and possibly be discharged from the military.

Jennifer and Gino had tried to force the impression of a stable family home. But it was all a lie and had come crashing down on them.

Two rows in front of her sat a family of four. The father sported a baseball cap on his blond hair. Beside him sat a dark-haired boy with a matching cap. The mother's hair was the exact tint and style of Alyssa's and clipped up like hers usually was but no cap. She shifted a child in her arms and a smiling toddler with ginger hair looked over the woman's shoulder at Alyssa, wide-eyed. A slow smile blossomed on her adorable face and then she raised a pudgy hand to wave.

Alyssa waved back and made a silly face. The mother jostled the child a bit then set her back on her lap.

That family—that could be. . .

No. Not going there. Stop right now!

She was moving to the Soo where she'd be employed full time as a computer technology specialist.

The ferry moved past the Mackinac Bridge and the mainland came into view. Most of her trips to St. Ignace had been for Dad's church events. Those had slowed way down after Alyssa had given birth.

Shame knocked on the door of her soul, but she wouldn't answer. God didn't send that shame. The Lord had forgiven her as soon as she'd asked Him to do so. Her sin was as far as the East was from the West, just like the Bible said. And after the conversations she'd had with Mom this summer, it seemed she, too, was refusing that unwelcome visitor.

Outside the window, water sprayed. The ferry bounced and she grabbed the seatback in front of her. Another ferry surged past. She couldn't help but grin. This had been a surprisingly beautiful summer so far. How funny that God would interrupt her one-time fantasy of being a child-free twenty-something to have her care for someone else's baby. A perfect baby. *Well, not perfect—only one baby had ever been truly perfect.* But Kelsey had grabbed onto Alyssa's heart in a big way.

She drew in a steadying breath. In a month she'd have to leave that precious girl behind and begin a brand-new journey. But no fantasies of being carefree—she just wanted her son with her.

The St. Ignace cliffside, dotted with pretty homes, came into view and then the park where soon she'd be meeting with her son and parents. She placed her hand on the inexpensive nylon bag she'd filled with little gifts for her parents and son. Hopefully, they'd like what she'd picked. And she prayed Dad wouldn't freak out when he saw who awaited them at the park.

Soon, the ferry's engine slowed. The increased vibration again matched her internal state.

Alyssa gazed out the window, hoping to catch sight of her family, but the wharf was too full of passengers awaiting departure.

No doubt Dad made Mom and Sammy wait in the parking lot, anyways.

In what seemed both like no time and yet forever, Alyssa and the rest of the passengers disembarked. She cast a quick glance at the family who'd hinted at what she might have with Carter—which was plain silliness to imagine. The man motioned for the boy to go ahead of him, and he took the little girl in his arms. Then he kissed the woman tenderly. Alyssa quickly averted her gaze.

Crazy to imagine that could be her. Hadn't she put aside those dreams years earlier? Not too many guys interested in a woman with a child. And Carter was a widower and her boss. And not interested in her anyway, not *that* way. Not only that, but if he knew she had a child, a nine-year-old at that, and with Aspergers. . .

Should have told him. Too late now.

She exited the ferry and disembarked onto the dock. A long queue of passengers wound back and forth. No Mom and Dad, no Sammy waiting. She continued toward the parking lot.

Standing beneath a tall oak tree, a handsome blond man, about thirty, with a large leather duffel checked his cellphone. Another tall blond man jogged up from the parking lot.

Carter.

Alyssa froze, but then stepped aside so people could walk past her. She watched as he embraced the other man and held on for what looked like dear life. Then the other man lifted him off the ground. *Brothers.*

She'd known Carter had gone to the mainland. She'd assumed for shopping. He'd said nothing about his brother, Parker, being there. And now there they both were. And Carter was about to know her secret.

She didn't care. *I do, but I just want to be with my boy—even if for only a few hours.*

The ferry workers announced passenger boarding.

"Mom!" Her boy. Her beautiful son ran toward her, and Alyssa's heart pounded in her chest. She jogged in and out of the straggling passengers and soon had her son in her arms—right where he belonged. She kissed the top of his head and held him so close she could feel the buttons on his shirt. When she released him, she stepped back. Tears rolled down his cheeks and she wiped them away.

"Look at you. I think you've grown an inch or two this summer."

Mom and Dad walked slowly toward them. Thoughtful of her parents to give her and Sammy some space.

"I don't want to go back!" Sammy threw his arms around her again and buried his face in the middle of her chest. She patted his back.

"It'll be okay."

He began to sob, his body shaking.

"Alyssa?" Carter's voice carried from nearby.

Carter's face held concern as he and his brother moved toward them.

Not now. Not here. This wasn't how she wanted to tell him about her beloved boy.

Her shirt was soaking up tears, and soon she'd have a wet spot that wasn't spit-up caused by baby Kelsey.

She kissed the top of Sammy's head. "We'll work things out."

She rolled her lips together. Sammy stepped back just as Carter joined them. His brother remained back a few paces.

"Mom, can I come stay with you?"

Carter's eyebrows drew together as he glanced between her and her son.

She placed an arm around Sammy's shoulder and turned him to face her boss. "Carter Parker, let me introduce my amazing son, Sammy Teann." She kissed the top of his head.

Sammy sniffed.

When Carter extended his hand, Sammy shook it vigorously.

"You're my mom's boss?" His voice sounded a little too eager.

"Sure am. I'd like to think I'm her friend, too." The muscle jumping in his jaw was a tell that he was ticked. "We share a lot of things with each other."

Should have told him about my precious boy.

"He's baby Kelsey's dad." She gave her son a tight smile. "And he's an awesome dad."

Sammy's nose crinkled. "Too bad mine isn't."

Her raised eyebrows matched Carter's. She pulled her son closer. "Well, that's not something we're discussing right now."

He pulled free. "Mom! I'm never going back to him not even for a visit." He turned and ran from the dock to her parents.

Alyssa brought her hands together and then raised them to wipe the tears from her face.

Carter took two steps closer and clasped her shoulders. She stiffened. When she met his gaze, she saw only concern and maybe a little hurt.

"Alyssa, I don't know what's going on. I don't know. . ." He clamped his mouth shut.

"I don't either. But obviously my son's upset."

Carter dipped his chin. "As are you."

She nodded.

"But if you need to bring him to the island, I'm sure we can work something out." His voice sounded world-weary. He was so young to have gone through everything he'd suffered.

His brother stepped forward. "Everything okay?"

Up close, Parker was even more handsome than the picture she'd seen. He pulled off his sunglasses revealing eyes a slightly different shade of blue than Carter's. "I'm Parker, Carter's brother."

Alyssa straightened. "I'm Alyssa Parker, Carter's. . ."

Both Carter and Parker made a strange face. Parker's eyebrows were raised high. What had she just said?

"Alyssa Parker?" Parker glanced between Carter and Alyssa.

Oh, Earth, swallow me up whole right now. Alyssa's face flamed. She opened her mouth wide, but nothing came out.

"Carter, is there something you've forgotten to tell the family?"

"No!" Alyssa and Carter both blurted out. She shook her head. "I'm so sorry, I'm just kinda rattled right now. I'm Alyssa Teann."

Carter inclined his head toward her family. "Alyssa's son isn't happy. And as you'll soon find out—when your child isn't happy, it's hard to think straight."

"Right." Alyssa felt the heat slowly leave her face. *Great cover by Carter.* She'd thank him later. "Speaking of which—I'd better go join him."

"Seems like a nice kid." Carter pulled a business card from his pocket. "If he doesn't end up joining us at Tandem Cottage, give him this emergency contact."

She took the card, that matched one he'd initially given her. "Thanks."

"I mean it." His lips twitched. "Plenty of room and I'm sure Colton and Cassandra won't mind. Especially now that the uninvited physicist has um, left."

Leland had been hospitalized in Virginia, according to Mr. Welling.

"I appreciate that offer more than you know." She turned and smiled at Parker. "Nice to meet you."

Parker slowly surveyed first Carter's face and then Alyssa's and back again. A knowing grin tugged at his full lips. "I'm super glad to meet you, too." There was a tease in his voice. "Even though you aren't technically Mrs. Carter Parker."

Her cheeks burned.

"Knock it off, Parker." Carter elbowed his older brother and then Parker grabbed him and mussed up his hair.

She turned and strode off toward her boy.

As shame for keeping Sammy a secret knocked on her door again, she answered. She'd earned this visit from her old enemy.

When she got back to the island, she'd apologize to her boss.

No. She'd apologize to her friend.

Friends didn't keep secrets.

And maybe he'd forgive her.

Mom and Dad, however, might not forgive what she was about to do. Great-grandma Romelda's plan had better work.

When she reached them, Mom pulled her into a gentle embrace. "Missed you, my sweet girl."

"Missed you, too." And she had.

She turned toward her dad. He gave her a peck on her cheek and a quick hug. "How's my baby?"

Alyssa laughed. "Your baby?"

He gave her a sheepish grin as he headed to the driver's seat.

Alyssa opened the back door of the Dodge Dart. "Dad, you remember where the park is, right?"

"Go left out of here and a left at the base of the hill." Dad slid into the driver's seat while Mom went around to the front passenger's seat.

"That's it." She and Sammy got in the back and buckled up.

Sammy reached for her hand and clutched it tightly as Dad drove up the main street to the park. Like on the island, colorful summer flowers bloomed everywhere.

Mom turned her head. "Have you enjoyed your work? How's the little baby?"

"Oh, she's adorable." She squeezed Sammy's hand. "Of course, not as cute as Sammy was as a baby. But she's a little babbler."

"Oh yeah?" Dad actually sounded interested. He looked at her in his rear-view mirror.

"She's making all kinds of sounds. Says dada all the time." She'd leave out that Kelsey called her mama.

"I like babies a lot." Sammy released her hand and looked out the other window. "I got to help feed them their bottles sometimes."

Mom turned further. "At the summer camp? There were babies? And why would a nine-year-old be feeding them their bottles?"

Alyssa leaned forward and placed a hand on her mother's seatback. "Mom, it wasn't a summer camp."

"Nope, it was a darned daycare," Sammy declared.

"Don't say 'darned'," Dad told him.

"It's okay, Grandpa. It's not a cuss word. My friend told me, and he's sixteen so he should know about things these days."

"What?" Dad clutched the steering wheel so tight that his hands began to shake. "Are you going listen to me, your grandpa an ordained minister, or a teenage stranger?"

"That's a good point, Grandpa. Sorry. But it was a daycare in Marquette, Grandma."

"Last week was summer camp at home in Newberry. No babies there. "

"Right, Grandma. Tahquamenon Summer Camp was tons of fun."

She tapped her dad's shoulder. "That's the turn up there."

Was Dad going to have a fit and make them all leave, or would he accept this God-given opportunity?

"Awful lot of people in the park today." Mom pointed toward the crowd.

"It's a free place, so we can't complain." Dad pulled into the drive.

They parked and got out of the sedan. Alyssa spied Mr. and Mrs. Mullen at the edge of a huge circle of what she knew were her extended family members.

"Oh, I see my friends right over there. Let's go say hello to them."

"I thought we were going to have a little picnic and visit." Mom pulled her purse strap over her shoulder.

"Come on." Alyssa took Sammy's hand and pulled him toward the group.

"What's going on?" Dad asked Mom.

Alyssa leaned in. "Sammy, there are a bunch of people here who are our kin."

"Family?"

"Yup."

"Why don't we know them?"

She sighed. "You know how Grandpa hasn't talked with his grandmother, your great-great-grandmother, in a long time?"

"Yeah, that's wrong." He wiped his arm across his nose. "The Bible says to honor the old people in your family—or something like that."

She laughed. Even a nine-year-old understood the gist of the Scripture.

"Alyssa!" Susan waved.

They joined the couple.

"This is my son, Sammy." If they were surprised, they didn't show it. "Sammy this is Mr. and Mrs. Mullen."

John extended his broad hand. "Good to meet you, Sammy."

Alyssa recognized most of the relatives she'd met at Romelda's luncheon at the Grand.

"Romelda is sort of hiding in the middle of all of those kin of yours." Susan jerked a thumb toward the covered picnic area.

"Good idea."

Dad and Mom caught up and Alyssa introduced them.

"I'm Susan Daniels Mullen—do you remember me, Joey?"

Dad gaped. "Susan Daniels, of course. My grandmother and your mother were thick as thieves."

"Still are." Susan pointed toward the large group. "Momma wants to see you before her contingent swoops her back to Washington."

"She sure was a firecracker." Dad shook his head.

Representative Daniels was wheeled through the group by her caregiver. "Well look at you. Little Joey Teann, you've done grown up real good."

Dad's cheeks turned pink. "Why thank you, Mrs. Daniels, that is Representative Daniels."

"I hear you're gonna atone for your ways and give my best friend Romelda a very nice birthday gift."

Alyssa and her great-grandmother's birthdays were only a few days apart.

"What do you mean?" Dad drew his chin in tight.

The large group parted and Romelda, sporting a navy dotted tunic and white flowing pants, emerged from the crowd.

"Grandma." Dad's complexion paled. Jaw dropped open, he stood there as Romelda moved toward him.

She reached for Dad. "I've missed you more than you can ever know, Joey. I've never stopped praying for this. . ." her voice choked off.

"Grandma." Tears filled Dad's eyes as he bent and pulled Romelda close. "I'm sorry."

"Shhh, we're gonna be all right. God promised me this day, and I knew He'd deliver before He flies me home to heaven."

Dad stepped back and looked at her. "You're healthy, though. Right?"

"Praise the Lord, I am. But I'm no spring chicken, either."

A handful of boys ran from the group toward the playground.

Sammy yanked on Alyssa's hand. He pointed to the boys. "Are they my kin?"

"Go see if they want to play."

He was off like a shot.

Mom leaned her head against Alyssa's shoulder. "Thank you. I don't know what you did, but I know you were behind this."

She pointed heavenward. "Only the good Lord could soften Dad's heart and open him up to this opportunity."

"Well, thank you for letting God use you in that process of reuniting that hard-headed man with a woman who was far ahead of her time." Her mother pressed a slim hand to the buttons on her dresses' neckline.

"I'd love it if they could reforge a relationship, Mom. I don't think my great-grandmother has a whole lot of time left on this earth."

"Maybe this is the sign we've been praying for."

"Sign?"

"Your sister has been begging us to move to Virginia. And Romelda's headquarters is there."

"Virginia?" Gayle lived a two days' drive away.

"Yes, I've been nudging your dad to get nearer to his mom."

"Really?"

"Yes."

So her parents wouldn't be in the next town over? They'd be a thousand miles away? "When would you be moving, if you leave?"

"Depends on if your dad feels led to accept a position he's been offered there. But within six months."

Life was changing. Not the way she thought it might. But her parents weren't a parental unit running in the background on sleep mode, waiting for her to activate them. They were real people with their own lives. And she and Sammy were only part of that.

"Alyssa?"

"Yeah?"

"I think it would be best if you bring Sammy to the island with you, since your boss offered. I'm concerned your dad is going to be more than a little discombobulated after this meetup with his grandmother."

"All right." All her cards would be on the table with Carter.

But were any cards in play?

Mackinac Island

Carter showed Sammy to his room. "You'll be right next to your mom, Sam." He pointed to her door.

Sam looked up at him, his eyes wide. That kid may have Asperger's and people on the spectrum might not show their feelings on their faces—but this boy did. People were individuals. They were not a label, nor a diagnosis. "I'd like to be called Sam by you. My dad called me Samuel, and I didn't like that."

"Cool, Sam." Carter offered a fist bump, and Sam bumped him back.

He opened the door and switched on the light. "This room's theme is—"

"Whoa, it's Dark Sky Park like Mackinaw City has." He jumped up and down, pointing to the deep navy walls and ceiling, painted with stars and planets.

"Check out these lights, little dude." Carter flipped the switch so that lights embedded in constellations lit up. A Northern Lights effect lit on the far wall.

Sam slumped onto the round bed and stared up at the ceiling. "I love astronomy. And we have just as pretty a night sky in Newberry as they have at that park. Now I won't miss it so much."

"Super. Why don't you rest while your mom and I make dinner." And discuss her child.

How did a freshly minted twenty-six-year-old woman have a nine-year-old son? *Okay, okay, I know the answer to that—the question is more why didn't she trust me with that info?*

He headed to the kitchen.

"Look what just got delivered." Alyssa held a Sanders' Bumpy Cake. "I've never had one of these before."

She slid the cake into the freezer.

He rubbed his nose, feeling a little awkward. His childcare worker and intern had a child she'd neglected to mention. "I hope you enjoy it. I ordered it when I realized it was your birthday."

"I gotta say this was my best birthday ever." She must not have picked up on his tense tone. "Having my dad reunited with his grandmother was the best gift I could have been given."

"I imagine having your son with you helped, too." He cocked his head. "I gotta say that's a huge surprise to me."

"You mean like not sharing that your wife died?" She crossed her arms.

"Yeah, you're not the only one keeping secrets. That really wasn't my business anyway about Sam. And he's a cool kid. I like him."

"You said I could have friends or family here if I wanted." Her intense look dared him to contradict her.

"Yes, I did. But is a husband going to show up here soon, too, or an ex?"

Her features hardened. "No. Not applicable. And like you and your limits on discussing your wife, I don't care to talk about it right now."

"Yes, ma'am." He saluted. Why wasn't an ex applicable? There had to have been a dad, obviously. But no relationship? It didn't matter. *Not my business.*

He went to the fridge and pulled out one of Alyssa's favorite meals—chicken enchiladas with rice. "My mom sent this over and asked if she and Dad could join us for cake later, but I told her you'd had a pretty hectic day." He'd leave out the part where they shared that Parker told them she'd called herself Alyssa Parker.

"It would have been fine." She touched his arm. "Are we okay?"

He looked at her a long time. "I shoulda known you were too awesome a mom with Kelsey to not have personal experience." He shook his head.

"I'll take that as a compliment. He's an amazing kid and makes it easy to love him, despite. . ." She chewed her lower lip. "Anyway, Sammy was never supposed to come to the island, and once I finished my work here, I never thought I'd see you again."

Even though he'd harbored similar thoughts about why not to tell Alyssa about Abbi-Renae, hearing her say it made something in his chest hurt.

I can't imagine not seeing her again.

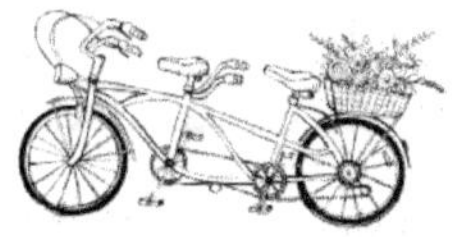

Chapter Twenty-Four

Carter cracked eggs and emptied them into the bowl to scramble them—which is what Alyssa's secret had done to his brain. Still, he was glad some things were out in the open now.

"Can you add two more for Sammy?" Alyssa poured orange juice into glasses and set them on the island. "Better make that three—he's a growing boy."

He grinned. "Will do. And two for you as usual?"

"Yup. Thanks." From the gratitude glowing from her eyes, he understood that she was thanking him for more than making breakfast, which had become their little Sunday tradition.

"De nada." He faux bowed at the waist.

Alyssa's son jogged into the kitchen, dressed in sleep shorts and a T-shirt. He wrapped his arms around his mom's waist and squeezed so hard, that her eyes widened. Carter bit his tongue, wanting to ask Sam to be gentle. Alyssa bent and whispered something in his ear. Maybe saying what he'd just thought to ask him.

"Have you started the bacon?" Alyssa pointed toward the microwave, where they usually heated up the pre-cooked bacon strips.

"Did the first warm-up and we can zap them again once the scrambled eggs are done."

"Thanks. And Sammy will do toast duty." She got out a sleeve of bagels and handed them to her son. "There you go. You know what to do."

Sam divided the bagels and set four halves in the toaster. "Butter for everyone?"

Alyssa grabbed the butter from the fridge and brought it to the microwave. She swapped it out for the bacon. She had almost as many foodie concerns as Carter did. The butter had to be soft, not hard, but not too soft. She cast him a glance and winked, almost like she'd read Carter's mind. He gave her a thumbs-up.

"Dada!" Kelsey cruised around in her playpen nearby.

"Better get her out of 'the enclosure,'" Carter sighed.

Sammy rubbed his nose. "That's funny. It sounds like a Sci-Fi place."

"That's why we call it that, little dude."

Alyssa had ordered the large panels once the baby's crawling rate had skyrocketed, and she needed more space.

"Can I hold her?" Sam surprised Carter with his request.

"Sure."

His face very serious, Sam nodded. "I want to take the Red Cross course on babysitting and childcare."

He sounded so much like Abbi-Renae. That same "little professor" voice. But Carter wasn't going to judge. He'd talk with Alyssa later. What if she didn't realize her son may have Asperger's? Abbi's mother certainly didn't accept that her daughter was a little different. All she cared about was that she was an excellent student. *All A's.*

"You look deep in thought." Alyssa removed the butter from the microwave as Sam crossed the room and lifted Kelsey from the playpen.

"Just thinking about my wife." And her odd behaviors. But he'd come to grips with them after they'd married. She was worth it. Quirky, super quirky, but she was so much fun. And she never lied. Was sober and thoughtful toward his brother and dad. But looking back now, had those been the proper requirements for a good marriage? He'd never know if they could have worked things through. He'd never have left her. He'd made a commitment for life.

"It's gotta be hard losing her."

"Hard being a single parent in your folks' household, too, though." He rocked back on his heels then shook his head. "And only sixteen-years-old."

"You're good at math, boss."

He squelched his frown.

Sam carried Kelsey in his arms. Then he stopped. "Oh no! No, no, no!" He held the baby at arm's length.

Alyssa ran over. "Are you a wettie girl? Did you leak?"

Sam swiped at his clothes, which now sported wet spots. He began flapping his hands by his side, stimming.

"Go change," both Alyssa and Carter called out to Sam at the same time.

She wore a perplexed expression as she hurried Kelsey to the changing pad on top of the Pack 'n Play.

Sam still stood there.

"Little dude, go put some fresh clothes on."

When he didn't move, Carter went to him. "Do you wanta shower off real quick, Sam? Or would washing off with a washcloth be okay?"

The boy chewed his lower lip. "Um, yeah, it's only, like, um urine, right?"

Carter crossed his arms and pretended to give Sam's wet shirt a thorough inspection. He leaned back in and uncrossed his arms. "Just some pee that'll wash right off with some antibac soap in the bathroom. Because if you take a shower your food's gonna get cold, little dude." Abbi-Renae always needed her food to be exactly the correct temp, and detested reheating in a microwave.

Sam nodded. "I'll wash off quickly and put on fresh clothing, sir."

Carter raised his hands. "No sir here. Call me Carter."

"Yes, sir." The boy ran off.

This could be what a typical family breakfast would be like if they were a family. And why was he having those thoughts? He shook his head.

Alyssa sidled up to him. "My son has Aspergers."

"I know."

"Your wife did, too. Right?"

"Yup."

No wonder Carter didn't appear too concerned about Sammy's unusual behaviors. He understood them. Relief shot through Alyssa. Mom and Dad, while supportive, always seemed a little anxious about Sammy.

Alyssa slid the freshly changed baby into her highchair and made sure the tray was firmly attached. "You've got to eat little girl, so we can get ready for church."

"Guys remember, Goughs is sending us a carriage within the hour." Carter tapped his watch.

With Jaycie and Parker installed at her family's Butterfly Cottage in Mackinaw City, it would be only the four of them for the carriage.

Sammy returned and sat at his spot. "My clothes are laid out, Mom. It's all I have for now till Grandma and Grandpa send more."

Carter slid the eggs onto their plates. "My mom has a bunch of my nephews' things to bring over. And the church ladies pitched in with some boys' stuff their kids have outgrown."

Alyssa cringed. That sounded an awful lot like digging in the bottom of the charity barrel. She faced him. "I think he'll be fine. My sister and her family will be coming over soon—they'll bring his things."

"Okay, but on Mackinac Island, we all chip in to help each other out. That's how it is. Especially in winter if you can't get to the mainland."

"All right." Growing up poor and receiving handouts through the church had made her self-conscious. Carter slid her plate of eggs and bacon in front of her. She used a baby fork to grab some eggs for Kelsey. "Here ya go."

"Haha, good luck with that." Carter waggled his eyebrows.

"You have to try different things. Not just fruit and carbs all the time."

"Wait for it. . ." Carter pointed and sure enough, Kelsey spit the eggs back out. "Good try, though."

Sammy quickly got the bagels ready and round robin delivered them. "I like those Sagamore kids across the street. They're gonna be at Sunday School today."

Alyssa had been shocked when the occupants of the farmhouse across from them had sent their kids over to ask Sammy to play after dinner the previous night. All three boys had been out there for a couple of hours: biking, playing catch, jumping on the neighbor's trampoline, and swinging on their swing set. "I'm glad you all got along."

"Oops, I forgot the prayer." Carter waved his hand in a circle, and they bowed. "Dear Lord, thank you for this day, and bless our breakfast and our time in service today. In Jesus's name, Amen."

"Amen." Sammy chowed on his eggs and bacon.

Alyssa peeled a banana and squished some pieces for the baby.

Kelsey reached, grabbing Alyssa's hair. "Mama, nana."

"Did she just try to say banana?" Carter held his bagel aloft.

"She called you mama, Mom."

Her face heated. "She calls me that when she wants something."

"So right now she wants you to give her a banana?"

Again, Kelsey shoved her pudgy hand at Alyssa. "Mama, nana!" she demanded.

"You are a smart little baby, aren't you?" Alyssa handed Kelsey the chopped banana pieces.

Carefully, the little girl picked them up. "Mmmm."

"Mom, she said 'Mmmm' just like you do when you like something."

Carter locked eyes on her and something flickered there.

"The Sagamore boys want to see Kelsey." Sammy scratched his cheek. "All they have is a dog, and they want a baby."

Both Alyssa and Carter burst out laughing.

Shaking her head, Alyssa ate a few bites of her eggs and bacon. Carter rose, went to the coffee maker, and returned with the pot, refilling her mug and then his.

"What did I say that was funny?"

Carter cocked his head. "Sammy, think about it. Are a dog and a baby equal?"

Her boy's lips smooshed in like they did when he was thinking. "Nope."

"Son, what if Mr. Parker here," she gestured to Carter, "went over to the boys' house and said that he wanted to see the dog because he only has a baby and not a dog."

Sammy's mouth widened. "Ah. I get it." He waved his fork at her and Carter. "So, you weren't laughing at me."

"Right. We thought it was funny that you boys put it that way."

Her text message sounded, and she looked at her phone. "The taxi is going to arrive early. I'll go grab my shower and get ready. Carter, I need you to get Kelsey changed and her stuff ready."

Giggling, Sammy rose and brought his empty plate to the sink. "That was funny, Mom."

"What?"

"I get it." Carter carried his plate over, too. He leaned in conspiratorially. "Your mom thinks I don't know how to take care of my own baby and that's pretty funny."

The two high-fived each other.

"Sorry, I'm on full mommy-mode." She emptied her plate into the trash and brought the dirty dish to the sink. "Sammy, get a very quick shower and changed, and I'll do the same."

Somehow, all four of them managed to get ready before the carriage arrived. They headed to church as overcast skies threatened rain.

Sammy turned and waved to his friends. "The Sagamores are biking down. Can we do that next time?"

"Maybe." Alyssa held Kelsey close on her lap.

"We could do the tandem bike for you and your mom, and I'd put Kels in the baby carrier behind my bike."

Sammy threw his arms in the air. "I love this place!"

And soon she'd have to take him away from here to yet another environment.

Lord, help me and help my son with all these changes.

This Monday morning couldn't be any prettier and this afternoon her son would have his first day of Summer VBS at church. She, Sammy, and Kelsey were enjoying the new swing set that the Byrnes had ordered to be installed the previous weekend. Like everything else, it was over the top. The work crew was supposed to return later in the week to build the 'fort' which would be a hundred-foot square log cabin with cutout windows and working shutters. The piece they were enjoying had two baby swings, two regular swings, which Sammy alternated between, and a two-seater adult bench swing.

"Whee!" Alyssa pushed Kelsey in her swing.

The baby laughed and raised her hands.

The back door from the south wing opened, and Linda Anderson-Paine emerged.

She'd arrived early that morning and announced her theme—Garden of Eden meets Northwoods. Sammy had still been in bed while Carter was busy working at his computer station, and the baby had woken early, crying for her bottle.

"I know that lady, Mom!" Sammy crossed the lawn and extended his hand to the artist, who shook it.

He looked like such a little gentleman, and motherly pride welled up.

Sammy stood straighter. "Mrs. Anderson-Paine, I met you at my school."

"I remember you, Sammy Teann—you're the boy who won the contest. You had mixed media representing the new playground the Tahquamenon schools will be building."

Alyssa's cheeks heated at the memory. They'd scrounged for materials for the art project and had used and repurposed material that would have gone in the landfill.

"Not only was it beautiful, but it was eco-friendly and that was part of the task—something other students missed."

Sammy beamed. That blue ribbon still hung on the wall in his bedroom at home. At her parents' home—which wouldn't be his home much longer.

Linda waved to Alyssa. "Would you like to see what I have sketched out in the nursery?"

"Can I see, too?" Sammy looked toward her, and Alyssa gave him a thumbs-up.

The door opened again and Carter looked out. "Care if I join you?"

"We're going to see how Mrs. Anderson is executing her design, Mr. Parker."

Thankfully, Carter didn't laugh at the way her son spoke so formally at times.

Linda waved them inside. "Come on. The more the merrier."

They all headed down the long hallway.

When she opened the door to the nursery, the walls were no longer the pristine white that the paint specialists had left them in, after doing whatever they'd done to cover up the "artwork" the disturbed physicist had produced.

Carter leaned in. "Shane told me that Leland is making good progress at the psychiatric facility."

She dipped her chin slightly. "Good."

Linda pointed to the walls, now outlined in a fantastical woods and water paradise. "Voila! Well," she laughed, "a mini voila, because I still need to paint all this."

Sammy walked slowly around the room, mouth agape. He pointed to a tree. "That looks like a woman reaching for an apple."

"Yes, very good."

Alyssa followed her son's progression. The next wall, near the far window, was etched with all manner of fruits and vegetables with deer, rabbits, and foxes at the edges.

Her boy walked to the back wall, near the closet. He stopped, hands on hips, and tilted his chin upward. "That looks like the woods at home and the Northern Lights."

Anderson-Paine was renowned for her paintings of the Upper Peninsula forests and especially her Northern Lights renderings. The artist patted the boy's back. "That's because Mr. and Mrs. Byrnes especially wanted some Up North charm."

"More than charm." Carter raised his eyebrows. "That's breathtaking."

Alyssa shrugged out the building tension in her shoulders. The woods were her escape—where she and Sammy would hike, sometimes for hours, to get out of their house. *My parents' house, but our home, too. But not for long.*

Alyssa swiveled to look at the wall behind them. Waterfalls, similar to Tahquamenon, overflowed into a wide garden of flowers.

Linda flexed her hands upward. "This fall will spout multicolored water instead of the root beer colored flow we're used to at the Tahquamenon Falls in the Upper Peninsula."

"It's brown because of the tannin in the river," Sammy said. He looked so sure of himself and so comfortable chatting. But often kids on the spectrum were more comfortable with adults.

"That's right, Sam." Carter quirked his eyebrows. "My dad told us it was root beer and that an ogre put a curse on it."

"Oh yeah?" Linda laughed. "What curse?"

"If you tried to take one drink of the root beer, you couldn't stop drinking and then you'd die from it." He stretched his arms overhead and made a writhing motion and laughed.

"Whoa, hadn't heard that one." The artist touched Sammy's arm. "Would you like to help me add an ogre to the edge of the falls?"

"Oooh, what about hiding in the flowers?" Sammy gestured to the bottom.

Linda dipped her chin. "Even better."

"Can I, Mom?"

Carter elbowed her lightly. "I say we put him to work. Make him earn his room and board."

Did he resent her son being there? Horrified, she stared up at him. All she saw was humor and a glint of mischief in his blue eyes. But was he also reminding her that she was here because she was his paid employee?

"You can take any additional costs Sammy incurs from my paycheck," she whispered to him. Then she swept Kelsey from the room, as heat sped up her neck. Instead of heading outside again, she hurried toward the other side of the house to the nursery.

I just need a moment.

She paced back and forth, clutching Kelsey in her arms. She and Sammy wouldn't be here that much longer. She'd just been ungracious. She should have taken Carter's comment in stride. But she'd felt so guilty for withholding information about her son from him. She needed to apologize.

Footfall sounded outside the door and Carter stepped inside.

She locked gazes with him.

"I'm sorry," they both said.

Then they laughed.

"I'm very sorry, I should have let that go."

Carter raised his hands. "I'm more sorry. I was just repeating one of my dad's lame comments he always made to Parker and me—when he had little jobs for us to do at the resort."

Alyssa placed Kelsey on the changing table. "Blue line, Daddy. Do you want to do the honors? Ew!" She turned her face away from the dirty diaper.

"Um, I'm not that sorry."

"Didn't think so."

He laughed as he headed down the hall.

Chapter Twenty-Five

Maybe it was "girly," like Abbi-Renae had mockingly said, but a nice hot cup of mint tea settled Carter's stomach and soul. His "aunt" Rachel had started him on the stuff, and his nightly anxious stomach disappeared. As his tea steeped, he prepared Alyssa's espresso. How she could drink a two-espresso cappuccino at night and still sleep was beyond his understanding, but she did.

It was only the three of them in the house right now. Mrs. Anderson was staying with friends on the West Bluff and wouldn't return until morning. Sammy was biking around the island with his new pals' family. Even though days were beginning to shorten, there was still plenty of light even at eight-thirty at night.

In the living room, Alyssa rocked Kelsey. The beautiful woman's features lit with love and she appeared perfectly relaxed, as though she might nod off with his little girl.

Carter sipped his tea. *Perfect.*

Kelsey's eyes flickered closed. They stayed that way as Alyssa rocked her slower, and slower, and finally came to a stop. They had an agreement that whoever rocked the baby to sleep would carry Kelsey to her crib—to not wake her.

Alyssa rose from the rocker and carried his little love down the hallway to her nursery.

This was getting way too comfortable.

And Carter was falling for an older woman. Only two years. He grinned at the thought. As Alyssa had pointed out to him recently, with all he'd been through, he was probably a lot more like a forty-year-old than a twenty-four-year-old. That made his maturity much older than hers. She'd been through a lot, too. Raising a kid on her own. With her parents' help, but still. . . having a kid as a teen, then going through school and working and trying to take care of Sam. *Sheesh.*

His phone pinged. His mother-in-law had consulted yet another attorney. On impulse, he texted her to come and see Kelsey. *That'll never happen.*

"You look deep in thought." Alyssa headed straight to the espresso machine.

"Oops, ya caught me, and I didn't add your froth."

"No tip for you, boss man."

She still looked remarkably relaxed.

"I got a question for ya." He set his mug down on the counter.

"Yeah?" She poured milk into the frothing cup.

He ran his thumb over his lower lip. "You look like you're in another joy-filled world with Kelsey when you're rocking her—"

"There's a reason." She placed the milk in the microwave. "Because I never got to spend a whole lot of time with Sammy when he was an infant. My mom took care of him. Many times, she'd make me sit at the table doing homework instead of rocking my baby and putting him to bed. She'd say that the schoolwork was what I was *supposed* to be doing."

"Sort of denying you that bonding time with him?"

She tucked her lower lip over her upper lip.

"Sounds like—almost as if she was punishing you for wanting those close snuggles at bedtime. Or am I wrong? I'm wrong a lot." He barked a laugh, then grabbed his mug. *Need to keep my opinions to myself.*

"Well, no, I mean, maybe." She pushed her hair behind her ear. "I guess I never looked at it that way before. But I don't think Mom had any ill intent. When I rock Kelsey to sleep, I love how that feels."

"Pretty good snuggler."

She swiped at her eyes. "I didn't know what I'd been missing all those years ago."

Carter set down his cup, took two steps toward her, and opened his arms. She stepped right into his embrace and hugged him with her face nestled against his chest, with a fierceness that both surprised, yet pleased him.

What have I just done?

What have I done? Alyssa sniffed. She'd stupidly not only accepted her employer's hug, but she'd made a fool of herself clutching him like he was her life raft. Which he was, wasn't he?

She stepped back, hanging her head. "I'm sorry. I shouldn't have done that."

Carter took hold of her hands. "No. Don't say that. I'm the one who reached out."

"But I. . . I shouldn't have—"

"Hey, we'd be fooling only ourselves at this point if we don't acknowledge there's something between us. Everyone else knows." He shrugged.

She stared up at him, her eyes wide. "Like who?"

"Like anyone who has seen us together."

"Hopefully not my son."

"Nah, I don't think Sammy has caught on yet, but it's a matter of time."

She huffed a laugh. "I'm sure it didn't help when I called myself Alyssa Parker when I met your brother." Her cheeks heated at the thought.

He squeezed her hands and cackled like he did when he was tickled about something. "That was pretty funny. Especially since. . ." Sadness dimmed the light in his eyes.

"Since what?"

He dropped her hands and leaned back against the counter. "Oh, well, my wife didn't change her name to mine. Abbi-Renae Kelly. Nor did she want Kelsey to be named Parker."

"Oh? Not even hyphenated?"

"Right. We had to flip for that—and I won the coin toss. We chose the name Kelsey because it's close to Kelly."

"Wow." She couldn't help raising her eyebrows. "Hmm, well in a relationship, as I understand it, there's got to be a lot of giving and taking. At least I know that from Sammy and me—not so much as far as regular, you know, male-female relationships."

He gave her a strange look, his mouth quirked at an odd angle. "Weren't you in a relationship with his father?"

"Nope." She took a fortifying drink of her cappuccino. Some would call it rape because of the circumstances and the age difference. "And, no, I have never dated anyone. I never had time."

"Never?"

She slugged back two more gulps of her coffee, embarrassed. "Nope. No time. Ever. And the few guys who asked me out ditched me as soon as they realized I had a child."

"But what about this Gino, Sammy's dad?"

"You sure you want to hear?"

"Yeah. I do."

After hearing about what that scumbag, Gino, did to sweet Alyssa, Carter smacked his fist hard into his open palm. "I think I'd like to beat Gino up, but I don't want to end up in jail—but you'd take care of Kelsey for me, wouldn't you?"

"Um, I think you're forgetting that your mother-in-law would be waiting for just such a moment like that to grab Kelsey and run."

"Yeah, you're right. And she's a crazy woman. No matter how much I pray for her, I see no difference in her behavior."

"Free will." Alyssa threw her hands up. "That's what we have. Free will to make decisions."

"Then why did your family decide to not press charges?"

"That was me. I felt so embarrassed and responsible for what had happened."

"Have you talked with anyone about it?"

Her front teeth covered her lower lip. "Only God. But I'm going to talk with my sister, Gayle, about it when she and Tony come over before they leave."

"That's a good idea."

Sammy sat on the rug in the main living room, building a Lego house. He was only allowed to use the building blocks in this room if Kelsey wasn't going to be crawling on the floor. "Mom?"

Her heart warmed. How she loved hearing that one simple word loaded with love.

"Yes?"

Her son gazed past her to where Carter, seated on the couch, was bouncing Kelsey on his knee.

"Can I tell you something?"

"Sure."

He rose and ambled toward her, his new moccasin slippers soundless on the carpet. He plopped down next to her and draped an arm around her shoulders. "You know I love you and Grandma and Grandpa, right?"

She leaned her head against his. "Of course."

"But this is how I'd always hoped our family could be," he whispered as he glanced around the room.

Guilt shot through her but was chased by mercy, by a sense of God's provision and of the rightness in their new life.

"It's time for Kelsey's bath." She patted her son's leg. "You want to help?"

"Okay, but I need to stay up and finish my project."

"All right. I have some programming to do, too."

They headed to the bath in Kelsey's nursery. Alyssa readied the water and then tested its temperature. Soon she had the baby in the tub. "Go grab me that new boat by the sink, sweetie."

"Swee-ee," Kelsey repeated.

Sammy jogged off and returned with the pink boat. "Should I wind it up?"

"Definitely."

Just as Sammy bent to place the boat in the water, Kelsey slapped her hands down, splashing him.

"Hey!"

"Sa-sa!" Kelsey giggled.

"Did you call me Sammy?" He placed his hand on his chest. "Me Sammy, you Kelsey."

"Sa-sa!" She splashed again but this time he backed away in time.

"She got me all wet, Mom."

"Yup, babies do that sometimes."

"She's still fun."

"Definitely."

A short while later, with the kids in bed, it was time for email reading, Alyssa's least favorite task on the computer. She'd received an email from the Soo Schools.

> Sault Ste. Marie Public Schools.
>
> Dear Ms. Teann,
>
> As I'm sure you're aware, we have a new superintendent coming on board. Unfortunately, with changes made, I can't issue you a standard contract. We can offer a temporary position until new hiring is approved. You'd attend in-service training for all staff as planned. I apologize for this inconvenience, especially after you've worked so hard to be onboarded. I'm guessing this is a hiccup, and we'll have you squared away soon.
>
> Best regards,
>
> George Ridley

"A hiccup? Temporary?" Alyssa gaped at her computer screen as she reread the message.

She grabbed her stress reliever ball, one that couldn't harm Kelsey, and she squeezed it as hard as she could. She threw it at the fireplace just as Carter entered the room.

"Whoa. What's up?

She hung her head. He'd helped her complete the internship requirements. Had she bullied him into it? No, but it had taken a lot of their nighttime hours. She rolled back from her computer. "You read it."

He bent near her, and she inhaled his fresh woodsy fragrance. "Huh. That's HR speak for this guy doesn't have a clue what his new superintendent is going to do."

"That's my take, too."

"Let's go sit out back and make a fire in the firepit."

Since Sammy had arrived, they'd made a bonfire almost every night after Kelsey was asleep. Sammy was a toasted marshmallow fan and would devour s'mores every night if they let him. He'd already asked if the Sagamore family could join them on the weekend for a campfire.

"We'll only do a one-logger." He pulled his phone from his pocket. "I've got Kels on speaker in case she wakes up."

"Me, too." Alyssa displayed her phone screen, which showed a shadowy image of the baby in her starfish pose.

They headed outside, to the back.

"It's awesome how the Byrnes have this all hardscaped for fire safety, but it's a chore keeping Kels away from all this brickwork."

"This whole place is amazing." Alyssa shook her head. "I've gotten spoiled this summer. I'll soon be living in one of my great-grandmother's homeless shelters."

"Aw, come on, those are converted hotel rooms, not a shelter. And it's temporary."

"And free." She laughed. "It was good of her to offer me the use of the end unit."

"Heck, with your new boss acting like your position is iffy, you might not be there long."

"Well, aren't you a bag of sunshine, encouraging me like that?" She playfully punched his arm.

"I'm getting back my sunrays, thanks to you. But I'm coming up on the anniversary. So, expect major black clouds."

Here she was fussing over her job situation—with a delay in her contract—while he was about to relive the worst moments of his life. "You sure you want to move back into your house in Virginia?" *Did I actually ask that?* A couple special moments together and she got to question his actions? *Sheesh.*

"I put it on the market."

Her heart did a lurch. "What?" Was he staying in Michigan?

He left her side and grabbed a small log and some kindling. "It's listed for sale."

Carter lit the small fire.

She shivered as wind stirred the chill in the air. She went to the storage bench and pulled two cushions and a throw from it. If he was staying in Michigan, then what might that mean?

"What will you do, then?" Could it be possible she factored into his decision?

The fire took and flames leapt on the kindling and log. Carter backed away. He pulled two chairs closer to the firepit, and she joined him.

"Would the Byrnes let you stay on?"

"Nah, I'm just their caretaker. But you're right." He locked eyes on her. "I can't go back into that house."

"I'm so sorry." Once again, she stepped into his arms, and he pulled her close. She rested her face on his firm chest as the sounds of the fire crackled.

"I feel like my whole world got rolled up in a rug and transported to the dump. Sorry for that bad analogy, but what I thought my life would be, has been erased."

She pulled back. "Not erased. You've got Kelsey, you've got your whole family, you've got your whole life ahead of you."

His mouth covered hers, warm, inviting. She tensed. Unbidden tears welled. She trusted him. He'd never hurt her.

He pulled away. "Sorry, I should have asked if I could kiss you."

She placed her hand behind his head and demanded another kiss, surprising herself. She kissed him, covering his cheeks with little kisses before returning to his mouth, savoring the taste of mint tea on his lips.

Carter stepped back and took her hands. A spark sizzled from the log, and he laughed. "We've got our own combustion going here and we'd better be careful."

"Will you take me to the ball at the end of the season? Will you still be here on the island?" She couldn't believe she'd asked him. She wasn't ready to let go of him yet.

"You're asking me on a date?" He bowed at the waist. "Milady, I am your humble servant."

Kelsey's cry pierced the night.

Carter punched the air. "But I must first respond to the little princess, Milady. I will return forthwith."

A flashlight beamed in their direction. "Thought I'd find you here."

"Dad?" Carter jogged toward the house. "What're you doing here?"

"Can't I come see my own son?"

"Sure." Carter slapped his father's back. "Gotta check on Kelsey."

She couldn't hear what Mr. Parker said, but when Carter disappeared inside the house, his dad ambled toward the firepit. She waved at him.

"Hi, Alyssa."

What had he seen?

"Sammy has us roasting marshmallows most nights—just as soon as your granddaughter falls asleep."

Hamp pulled another chair up near theirs and the two of them sat. "Sons get you to do all kinds of things. Like get sober."

That was a pretty heavy statement. She nodded. "Because of my boy, I was determined to get through college and get a job." Possibly a temporary job if the superintendent got a whim to not sign for any new hires.

"That's commendable. I was one of those coattail guys myself. My dad ran our resort and while my wife and I drank our way through life, I floated along doing whatever my folks asked me to do— sometimes badly."

"But you've done great things with the place now."

"Carter had enough of my bad behavior and gave me an ultimatum. Either get sober or I'd never see him again." He gave a curt laugh. "It was a wakeup call. I had to do the hard work of facing my addiction, but he gave me support. I leaned on him a little too heavily and so did his brother—who had his own issues."

Why was he telling her all this?

"Alyssa, my son—who everyone has leaned on—turned to us during his darkest hours. We were glad to be there for him."

"That's beautiful you could help. Family needs to support each other."

"Exactly. But additionally," Hamp leaned back in his chair, "this guy was our sunshine. And that left him. You've got him laughing again."

She raised her hands to protest, but he shook his head.

"We all see it. We're so grateful. I guess what I'm trying to say besides, 'thank you,' is that I think my son is in love with you. And if you break his heart—"

In love with me?

The back door opened. "Here we are!" Carter clutched a bundled-up Kelsey to his chest and play-galloped through the yard.

"Somebody musta known her grandpa was here." Hamp stood and extended his arms.

"I'm not glad she's up, but I'm glad you're here." Carter passed her to his father. "We're not going back to Virginia."

"You're accepting Gianni's offer?"

"Yeah. We'll stay here for now. But Tandem Cottage isn't winter insulated."

"Parker and Jaycie will be on the mainland Butterfly Cottage to be closer to the obstetrician. They'll move to the island after the baby arrives."

"There are two Butterfly Cottages? One by your resort and another in Mackinaw City?" Alyssa frowned. "That must be confusing."

"Not to us. We understand the history." Mr. Parker jostled Kelsey, who kept patting his face.

History. Carter and his family had it in droves here.

She was only beginning to understand her family's history.

"Maria and I will head to Europe as soon as all is safe with Jaycie and the baby." Sorrow washed over his face. Was it from memories of his daughter-in-law or that he was leaving his sons behind and grandchildren?

"We'll miss you."

"Same." Mr. Parker kissed Kelsey.

Dad sang Kelsey a few bedtime songs, forgetting half the lyrics, as he walked her around the backyard. A couple sounded like beer hall lyrics.

"I think it's time," Carter told Alyssa, as she rose from her seat by the fire.

"It's past time." She waved Dad over.

His father pulled the baby close. "Do I really have to let her go?"

Alyssa reached for Kelsey. "Grandpa is a lot of fun, but you're up way past your bedtime. And are those new jammies?"

Carter leaned over and planted a kiss on Kelsey's head. "Her wet diaper soaked her other pair."

"That explains the unicorns instead of bunnies on these pjs."

"Well, we're gonna put those unicorns to sleep. No more frolicking with Daddy and Grandpa." Alyssa carried Kelsey back to the house, singing a Sunday School song to her as they went—no lapses in the lyrics either.

"So, you're lettin' her go?"

"It's her bedtime." Carter sat in the chair and scooted a little closer.

"You know who I meant."

"Yup. I can't control what she does."

"Maybe, but you could influence her."

"So now I'm an influencer—maybe I'll do a TikTok for Alyssa."

"At least invite Alyssa to the ball."

"Why?" He enjoyed goading his dad on. The log shifted, sending up a slew of embers.

"Because you like her, and clearly, she likes you, too."

"Not asking her." He tapped his foot.

"Thought I brought up someone with some smarts."

He faced his dad. "She's already invited me."

Dad's expression morphed from shocked to gleeful. "I knew she had some gumption."

"People don't say gumption anymore. That's archaic."

"I'm archaic. I'm good with that." He placed both hands on his chest. "But I'm archaic and married to a good woman."

"I don't think marriage is on Alyssa's agenda. She's looking to prove herself—show she can take care of Sammy on her own."

Dad huffed a sigh. "Highly overrated. I've done the single parent thing—hardest job I ever had."

"I agree. Don't forget I'm doing it now."

"No, Son." He pointed toward the house. "You're doing it with the help of a fine woman. And she's about to leave this island before long."

"Yup."

"Time for you to stake your claim."

"You've been hanging around Grandpa Wayne too long on his ranch."

"Got some good wisdom from those old cowhands out there."

"Tell me about your favorite times out there."

"Sure."

Dad regaled him with stories about the Stevens' ranch and all the old movie stars who'd shown up and hung out with him and Wayne.

Alyssa emerged from the house, carrying two mugs. "Hot cocoa with marshmallows. No s'mores tonight." She handed a mug to Dad and one to him.

"Where's yours?"

She gestured to her white sweatshirt. "This is a stain magnet—a new kind of fabric which attracts every single drop of coffee, tea, or cocoa."

Dad did a sideways motion with his hand. "Don't wear that tomorrow when you and Carter take a ride around the island. Wear camo."

"We're working."

"Go after work then. Your mom and I are bringing Kelsey and Sammy to see Grandma Kareen and Grandpa Gianni at their new place—and what will be your winter digs."

Carter turned toward Alyssa. "I'll take Kelsey over there once Tandem Cottage gets too cold. It's not set up for cold weather. Not fully insulated."

"Oh."

He should have told her.

"Is it babyproofed?" Alyssa slacked her hip. "She's into everything now that she's crawling."

"Yup, Grandpa Gianni's kids and grandkids have tested it out."

"It's all set then." Dad grinned. "We're sending you two off for some alone time."

"But we'd be together, not alone." A mischievous look glinted in Alyssa's eyes. "What makes you think I'd want my free time to be spent with your annoying son?"

"Two reasons." Dad set his mug down on the side table. "One— I hear you invited him to the ball. Two—I saw you two kiss, so he can't be that annoying."

"All right, you got me then. I'll take your son off your hands for a couple of hours." Alyssa crossed her arms.

"She's gonna fit right in with our family," Dad muttered.

He was correct.

Chapter Twenty-Six

Carter opened another delivery of toddler-sized clothes. His baby girl was growing.

"Look at this adorable outfit." Alyssa pulled out a green and white gingham dress with little matching pants. "And look at the walking shoes." She displayed a tiny white pair of sneakers that fit in the palm of her hand.

He shook his head slowly. "She's gonna be walking soon and the shoes we ordered still haven't arrive."

"Canceled. Sorry I forgot to tell you." She set the clothes and shoes down. "I was ordering her more formula for her bottles, and I checked and they'd canceled the shoes—out of stock indefinitely."

"At least we have those."

Alyssa laughed. "Which might fit her in a year. Way too big."

"But they're so small. I guessed her size."

"Not as small as her little tootsies. I'll order some in her right size. The outfit should fit her now, though."

"Have you shopped for Sammy's school clothes yet?"

"No. We'll wait until we're on the mainland." She stood and took the clothes with her.

"Where you going?"

"Gotta wash this outfit before I put in on our baby girl."

Had Alyssa just called Kelsey *their* baby girl? Was that another slip of the tongue, like calling herself Alyssa Parker? *Has a nice ring to it.*

He followed her to the laundry room. "Hey, you wanta take the kids tonight and go on a ride?" Soon they'd be gone, and he'd miss them.

"Sammy has been bugging me to let him ride your bike and pull Kelsey." She tossed the new outfit into the front-loading washer and then pulled more baby items from the dirty clothes basket.

"You and I can ride tandem. He'll do fine. He's a strong kid. He and his buddies are out there every night riding."

She puffed out a breath, making her bangs fluff on her forehead. Even in a rumpled T-shirt and equally wrinkled shorts, she looked adorable. He took two steps forward. He shouldn't try to kiss her again—but he wanted to.

Alyssa started the washer. "Are you thinking what I'm thinking?"

"Maybe."

"Close the laundry room door then, so no one sees us."

Grinning, he shut the door. With his mom and dad and his grandma and new grandpa wandering in and out and Starr showing up at odd times, they never knew who might be next.

He pulled her into his arms and gently kissed her.

Both of their phones sounded for the front door.

"Seriously? Probably Sammy back for more cookies for the Sagamores' fort."

They both pulled out their phones.

"Who is that at the door?" Alyssa frowned.

"That's Colton Byrnes in the flesh."

"I thought—"

"I thought so too. They weren't supposed to be here until next week."

Carter pressed the sound button. "Dude, you're early."

Colton laughed. "Dude, I own this place."

"Use your key then."

"Just tryin' to be polite and all that."

"Even more polite would have been showing up when you said."

"Cassie sent me here to see the mural and then I'm joining her with my buddy Michael and his wife Willa. We're touring the Great Lakes this week on a charter ship for an HGTV show."

"Cool. See ya in a minute." Carter ended the contact.

"A charter cruise around the Great Lakes for an HGTV show?" Alyssa pressed her index fingers into her cheeks. "Who gets to live like this?"

"Apparently Michael and Willa, who have their own show, and good old Cassie and Colton, too."

"I think I hate them."

"Aw, come on," he pulled her in for a quick hug. "It's not their fault that they are fabulously rich, good looking, and famous."

"It's probably pretty awful. Lousy even. They're probably miserable."

"Right. They cry night and day and are never once happy on any day of the week."

Heavy footfalls carried down the corridor. Carter released his love—yes, he had to be honest with himself—he loved this woman. He opened the door.

Colton waved. "Hey dude, how ya doin'?"

The guy looked like he had no cares, all sunshine and roses. Had it all and then some but Carter wouldn't tell Alyssa that.

On the other hand, Colton had been famously dumped by his ex, Sue Pentland, who left him for the richest guy in Dubai.

He'd tell Alyssa that part.

Susan filled the last of a huge box that she and John were mailing home. "Packing up to leave is so much harder than packing to come up here."

"But at least you've got all the gifts in there." John added a mug embossed with 'Healthcare Retreat—Lilac Cottage' on it. "Tamara gave me that last night when I told her we're both definitely coming back next year."

"I'm glad you're hired, too."

He pulled her into a hug and kissed the top of her head. "I haven't had this much fun in a long time."

She pulled back and looked up at him. "Even with me disclosing confidential info with my client standing there?"

"Former client. It all worked out, didn't it?" He pulled her back into his arms.

"It did. Alyssa recently confided that Carter's mother-in-law is planning a trip to Mackinac in the fall to see baby Kelsey." She looked upward at the swirled pattern on the high plastered ceiling. "I believe there needs to be God's help with that, more than any advice I could dole out."

"Amen to that. God is in everything—whether repairing lives or making big decisions."

There was more than a little nudge to take action. She'd still not notified the school district about her retirement. She'd redirect the topic. "The situation with Leland was something else."

"That absolutely wasn't your fault."

"I'm glad he's getting help."

"Me, too." He kissed her again and released her.

She gestured to the massive room with wide-planked hardwood floors and windows that almost reached the ceiling. "You think we'll get used to our normal-sized room after this place?"

He laughed. "I guess we'll have to."

"It'll be good to get home, though. Back to our own church."

"As much as I've enjoyed the one here, it'll be good to be back in our pew at home."

"And I've got all those in-service trainings to get ready for."

It sounded like he mumbled, "But you didn't have to. . ."

She stepped across the thick wool area rugs to her desk on the far side of the room.

"What're you doing?"

She logged in, opened her email, and began typing.

John joined her and looked over her shoulder. "That's for 2026?"

"The end of the school year. My last contract." She sent the message that she'd not be renewing for the following year.

A text message pinged. "From Colby." She held it up so John could see.

"Our son's going to tour Europe not this winter but next!"

"And we can go over there and see him!"

"Because it's done. You've turned in your notice."

"It's done."

And all kinds of blessings were coming.

"It's almost done," Alyssa told Sammy as she pointed to the calendar. "Auntie Gayle has to get back to Virginia." And she was almost through with her summer job.

"Will Uncle Tony take me and my cousins everyplace today?"

"Um, not everyplace, but some special touristy things."

"The carriage tour?" He bounced up and down.

"Yup."

"Arch Rock?"

"Yup, that's on the tour."

His eyes widened in hope. "Every fudge shop?"

"Nope. Only Joann's because you've been to every single other one of them since you've arrived."

"Awww, I like Murray Hotel's best because they have the orangey one."

"Fine. Two, but that's the limit." Unless Tony decided he wanted to try them all, which was quite likely.

"And if you feel like something is. . ." she mussed his hair, "too much, then what will you do?"

"Code word Grizzly Bear." He pulled his elbows up tight and growled.

"Only growl if Uncle Tony forgets the code, okay?"

"All right."

Their code words had saved them many meltdowns.

Carter entered the living room. "Kels is finally down for her nap. Starr will be here soon and then I'm going for a jog."

"But you're having us all here for pizza tonight, right?" Sammy tapped his fingertips together.

Alyssa exhaled a hard breath. "Like I told you, they won't have time to come up here. Instead, we'll all meet up for pizza in town."

Her boy slumped his head. "I wanted to show them this place."

"Next year." Carter playfully tapped Sammy's shoulder. "But we'll probably be over at Cardinal Cottage then."

Sammy perked up. "It's even better than this place. It's got a hot tub out back and the pool is heated."

"Sammy, go get your backpack."

He ran off like a shot.

She locked eyes on him. "You can't make promises to people on the spectrum that you can't keep."

He went to the coffee pot and refilled his mug. "What makes you think I can't keep that promise? Gianni made me the caretaker." He scrunched his lips together as he wanted to say more.

Oh my heavens, I was assuming he'd meant we'd be married and living there. Alyssa's cheeks flamed. He'd not said that only "we'll probably be" and that could mean him and Kelsey. She'd inferred he'd meant all of them.

Her phone rang. *Gayle.* "I've gotta take this."

Sipping his coffee, he turned and left.

An hour later, she and Gayle were seated outside behind the library. The spot was gorgeous, with a clear view of the beautiful turquoise water. Today, two ferries passed each other as she and her sister grabbed two empty chairs on the deck.

"This is lovely." Gayle gestured to the lawn. "I wish we could get our grass to look like this at home."

"I wonder how Dad did with mowing this summer."

"Not too bad." Gayle laughed. "You've been a real champ to mow for him all these years."

"He's been so good to Sammy and me."

Gayle swiveled in her seat to look at Alyssa. It was hard to see her eyes through those dark sunglasses. "You want to tell me what happened?" She placed her hand on Alyssa's. "With Gino?"

She pulled her visor lower and turned to face the water.

"I've always felt it had something to do with me." Gayle removed her hand and pushed back into her seat. "Because that youth pastor acted like he had the hots for me."

"Maybe he did."

"Why do you say that?"

Alyssa pressed her tongue to the roof of her mouth. "I wish I'd told Gino that I wasn't you."

"What?" Gayle gaped at her.

"When he asked me to go for a ride with him, instead of going into the nursing home with the others, he said something." She tapped her hands on her legs, imitating one of Sammy's nervous habits.

Gayle touched her shoulder. "What did he say?"

"That I was just as gorgeous as the youth pastor had said." She sniffed.

"But you never met Pastor Jimmy." Gayle straightened. "He'd never seen you."

"I know." She swiped at her eyes. "I knew he'd meant you. But hearing Gino say that, I wanted to be the pretty one. Not the studious mouse."

"Oh, Alyssa, you've always been beautiful—inside and out."

"I didn't feel that way. And I should have told him I wasn't who he thought. Because you, being three years older, were eighteen—almost nineteen."

"And away at college. If only I'd been there. I'd have told that guy off and smacked him." Gayle rubbed her shoulder. "But that youth group was only for kids in high school. So he still should have known."

Alyssa shook her head. "I think Pastor Jimmy told him you were eighteen. And that's what he claims." She pulled a tissue from her pocket and blew her nose. "He drove me to that place by the lake where all the popular kids went to make out."

"Oh no. Dad always warned us off there."

"I was curious. And yes, I know about what curiosity did to the cat."

They both laughed, breaking the tension.

"He convinced me I'd be more comfortable in the back seat. And. . ." She clamped her teeth over her lower lip. "I stupidly went along. I can't explain what I was thinking. But I was amazed this handsome older guy thought I was attractive."

Gayle made a clucking sound.

"My first kiss. I thought it would be amazing. But everything happened so fast." She swiped her hand across the air. "I was so stupid. One minute he's kissing me and the next he's pushed my skirt up and—" She leaned over and pressed her wet face into her hands as Gayle patted her back.

"Regardless of your age, that's not giving consent to what happened. That's rape."

That's what Carter had said, too. And he'd offered to start the legal process of charging Gino.

She nodded, feeling the press of her sister's hand against her back.

"Oh! Sorry, we didn't mean to interrupt." Two older ladies, in matching off-white straw hats, stood at the edge of the library building. They headed back around.

"Sheesh, we're in a public space here." Alyssa straightened. It felt like a massive load had been lifted from her. "You're the first person I've told the whole truth. I blamed myself."

"It wasn't your fault."

"Carter also said that."

"He's right."

"I'm going to file charges once I'm back on the mainland." She hugged her sister. "I don't want Sammy thinking I didn't want him, though, or that there's something bad about him."

"Right. I get that."

"Out of something so awful came that beautiful boy. He's a handful, but he's a blessing."

"Both you and Carter might have kids with lots of questions later in life. Baby Kelsey might blame herself for what happened to her mom."

"I won't let her do that."

Gayle leaned away. "Sounds like you have intentions toward Carter."

"Intentions?" She swiped the last of her tears from her face.

"Yeah. And maybe you should let him know you're not just focused on supporting yourself and your son. Maybe you should let him know you're open to a relationship."

"I kissed him!" Alyssa touched her fingertips to her lips.

Gayle's mouth widened into an 'O.' "You did?"

"More than once."

"And he kissed you back?" Gayle's voice held a tease.

"Yes."

"Does this feel like it should be?"

"It does."

"Ah! Ah!" Two young children rounded the corner screaming.

"Ahuh!" An older child followed them. For a split second, she thought it was Sammy, but it wasn't. Then the parents rounded the corner, pushing a stroller.

"Quiet down!" But the dad was even louder than the kids.

Alyssa took her sister's hand. "Come on. I'm gonna take you to get the best coffee around, eh."

"Let's go."

A feeling of lightness enveloped Alyssa as they headed toward Lucky Bean.

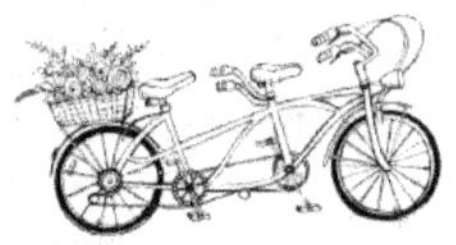

Chapter Twenty-Seven

Sault Ste. Marie, Michigan

Formal Attire Required—three little words that had Alyssa rattled. She scanned the website for the ball again. Heavy hors d'oeuvres, chef's specialty beef Wellington, coffee/tea/soft drinks, assorted desserts—and a cash bar would be available. Carter and his family wouldn't be utilizing the alcohol option, given their AA and Al-Anon memberships.

She'd only moved to the Soo a week earlier and she'd already hit every thrift store, except this one, for a long dress, with no luck. She pulled back the section of large-size dresses, but they were too big after riding a bike around Mackinac Island all summer. The medium-size section included stuff that looked like what her great-grandmother had worn in the 1990s on her television show. *Ack.* But thinking of Grandma Romelda made her grin. They'd reestablished a relationship now with her, her sister's family, and Mom and Dad.

Who was she kidding? Sammy wasn't going to tolerate her staying overnight on the island. Their new church had an overnight kids' event, but the chances of Sammy making it through that without a meltdown were slim to none. *Maybe I should have brought him with me.* But with this being the one-year anniversary of Abbi-Renae's death, Carter had indeed become withdrawn. Their last few conversations were brief, and he'd been, honestly, cranky. Not that she blamed him. Still, he'd wanted her to come over.

She did want to see him and Kelsey.

The thrift store manager came alongside Alyssa. "Something's come in that's a little more contemporary. You could dress it up or down."

"I don't think I'll be able to attend this function anyway." She shrugged.

The woman, slender with wavy silver hair that poufed around her lined face, tilted her head to the side. "And yet you're looking."

"Hope springs eternal?" She shrugged. "I've got a special needs child. I'm not sure he'll be good with me being away overnight."

"I have a boy with special needs, too. Well, not a boy—he's forty now. But he heads up a tech company in Silicon Valley. That's in California, ya know."

"I do know. I'm a computer programmer."

"Here in the Soo?"

"It's a hybrid job with the school district." *And possibly very temporary.*

"I sure miss my son." The lady displayed the simple red dress. "When he was young, we didn't think we could stay away from him. He'd do these. . ." She began flapping her hands and blinking rapidly.

"Stimming?"

"Is that what they call it? We didn't know what to think back then. But he's doing okay now. And before we knew it, he was happily leaving us behind—no stimming involved." She laughed. "Well, maybe his dad and I did that little dance."

Alyssa ran her hand over the gown. "This looks good. But it's kind of bold." She'd really stand out with this color, even if she barely accessorized it.

"Why don't you take it? If it doesn't work out, bring it back and I'll give you a full refund." She went to the register and rang up the sale. "I've got a good feeling, though, that your event will go just fine."

"I pray you're right."

Straits of Mackinac

The ferry was almost empty as Alyssa rode over, except for someone she recognized. Sure looked like the back of Starr's head, with the multicolor glitter in her hair.

Alyssa scooted to the end of the bench seat, pulling her backpack with her. A pack that included the simple long dress and a pair of glossy, but cheap strappy sandals. *Why did I bring them? Sammy will likely call me, crying, and I'll be rushing back home.*

She edged forward. When she came alongside Starr, the pretty young woman looked up. She beamed and scooted over. "Hi there, Mama-girl!"

Alyssa laughed. "Hi there, sparkly gal!"

She slid in and set her backpack on the floor.

Starr swiveled toward her; her knee bent up on the seat. She was impossibly agile. Her body moved more like a child's. "Certain people are so thrilled about you coming that they are telling everybody!" She threw her hands in the air as if celebrating.

Alyssa swallowed hard. Had Carter gone around publicizing her visit? "I'll bet that was Kelsey," she teased.

Starr blinked rapidly. "Well, no, it was baby Leoni."

Alyssa pushed her back into the seat. Starr was known for saying some weird stuff, but surely she didn't imagine that Parker and Jaycie's unborn child, could communicate with her.

Pink streaked Starr's cheeks. "Oh, I mean Leoni's mommy did—Jaycie." She laughed awkwardly.

Why did it disappoint Alyssa that it had been Jaycie celebrating her arrival and not Carter? "Well, it's true I invited Carter to the auction and ball." *Not that I have any intention of staying for it.* Her life had taken such a massive turn that she couldn't have anyone messing with her heart right now.

Their friendship had been fraught with secrets. Was a lie by omission still a lie? The two of them were good at that. But after those kisses and embraces, what was she to think?

Starr pretended a drum roll on her thighs. "You two have all weekend to catch up."

"Oh no." Alyssa waved her open palms toward each other. "I'm only here for the afternoon." *Oops, she'd let her plans slip.*

"If you say so." Starr gave her a knowing grin.

"Until," she didn't want to lie, "until I leave on the ferry later today."

"Last ferry from the island leaves early." Starr winked. "Just remember or you'll be in a pumpkin of a jam."

She laughed. Starr had some interesting expressions. By nine Alyssa would be back in the Soo dreading her son's ire when she picked him up from the overnight event. He'd wanted to sleep over. But Asperger's kids didn't usually do well at such things. She had told him and prepared him. If he needed her at bedtime, then she'd come and get him.

"Are you going to the auction, Starr?"

"I'm working it. Can't you tell?" She motioned downward from her neck to her knees.

"Um, I'm not thinking that glitter leggings, a hot pink velvet stretch shirt, and a neon green miniskirt would be good barista attire."

"Silly girl!" Starr patted Alyssa's knee. "I'm the deejay!"

Carter paced in Cardinal Cottage's circular garden area, awaiting Alyssa's arrival. Although only a week had passed since he'd seen her, it felt like a month. He took a deep breath, startled when the scent of incense wafted his way.

He turned. A man in a hooded brown robe, a monk maybe, was waving a brass incense holder. Was this his brother pulling a prank? But the guy wasn't the right height to be Parker.

Carter waited, as unease built. After the problem with the artist, he sure didn't need oddballs on site, especially with his family inside and Alyssa en route.

"Excuse me!"

The man turned. The smile, the large dark eyes, and the peaceful expression announced the man as Juan Pablo, his friend.

"I haven't seen you in ages."

The pastor waved his arms around. "I've been here."

Was he staying with Grandma and Grandpa but hidden away?

"Didn't know you were a priest." In none of Juan Pablo's sermons had the itinerant preacher indicated that he was a priest.

Juan didn't answer him, but stood there, his right arm raised high with the incense. "I'm here to consecrate a space in this garden."

Consecrate a space? For what? "Oh yeah?" Maybe his grandparents asked him to bless the space.

"This will be a memorial garden. To God be the glory." He continued to walk the garden, waving the incense.

Maybe his grandmother was dedicating it to Grandpa Hampy. Nah, he couldn't see that. But perhaps Gianni was doing something for his deceased wife.

Juan Pablo stopped in the center of the garden and began to sing a song in Latin. He lifted his arms toward heaven, bowed, and then straightened before continuing to sing. The next phrases were about God's glory—that was the limit to Carter's understanding of Latin.

"Private carriage is here!" Gianni called from the back door.

Carter's heartbeat ticked upward. Alyssa had arrived.

"Give her a few minutes alone with the bambino before you join us, okay?" Gianni winked at him.

"Sure."

The door closed and Carter turned to watch Juan Pablo. He was gone. Carter walked to where he'd just been singing. There were footsteps, and in the center a two-foot hole had been dug. But he'd not seen it before. A white shovel lay on a bench.

Maria jogged out the back door to him. "What's going on out here? I thought I heard you speaking to someone a little while ago."

"Juan Pablo was here. My pastor friend."

"Oh, si, Kareen and Gianni have been attending his prayer vigils out at Sunset Rock."

He stiffened. "Haven't heard anything about it."

She shrugged. "Maybe it's a private thing. Come in before Alyssa thinks you're hiding."

"Gianni said to wait."

She waved her hand as if batting away Gianni's suggestion. "Some men have no clue."

One thing Carter did have a clue about was that Abbi-Renae had been brought up as a Roman Catholic.

In his heart, he understood that Juan Pablo's gestures were meant in remembrance of Abbi-Renae.

The spacious room was crammed full of Carter's family as Alyssa entered. It looked more like a family reunion than a Saturday afternoon gathering. But each one greeted her, and some hugged her as she joined them.

"Come on, sit beside Jaycie and Parker." Kareen pointed to an exceptionally long multicolored divan. As soon as Alyssa sat, Baby Kelsey, who was across from her, let go of Hamp's knee and took two steps toward her. "Oh my gosh!" She caught the little darling just before she fell.

"Her first steps!" Maria declared.

Tears welled in Kelsey's eyes. "Mama mama!" Alyssa pulled the baby into her arms and pressed her own wet cheeks to hers.

"That's a smart kid," Gianni mumbled, but she heard him.

She looked up to see Carter enter the room. His family was gathered there in the massive living room. They had welcomed her like she was one of them. They'd all beamed as if she'd left for Mars and had just returned. And she felt the same, too.

Jaycie scooted over and Carter sat next to Alyssa.

They spent time talking about Alyssa's new job, her little apartment and how Sammy missed his buddies on the island. And everyone shared something special Kelsey had done the previous week. Carter was seated so close beside her that his warm muscular shoulder pressed into hers. But since no one else was crammed in like that, this seemed purposeful. Yet he hadn't led her off to talk with her alone.

Carter fluffed the top of Kelsey's hair.

"Isn't her hair so cute?" Kareen grinned. "How it sticks up in the middle like those old Kewpie dolls I used to have."

"It's adorable." Alyssa leaned in and kissed the back of the baby's head.

Carter locked eyes on her, with a gaze so intent, it stole her breath. What was he thinking?

"Phew, you're all gonna need to get ready for the ball." Jaycie glanced around the room.

"You're not going?" Alyssa couldn't help but look at the other woman's belly, which had expanded even in the past few weeks.

"Nah. I'm gonna put the peanut to bed and then go to sleep myself." She pointed to Kelsey. "Aren't Uncle Park and I gonna watch you tonight?" She made jazz hands, and the baby giggled.

"I better get started." Kareen slowly rose, but Gianni jumped up beside her and took her arm.

"We're using the first-floor suite." Hamp told Carter. "And you'll need to show Alyssa the second-floor guest suite where she'll be staying."

She wanted to protest. She should get back to her son. Once she got to the room, she'd check in at Sammy's sleepover and see how he was getting along. But she'd need to get back on the ferry before they stopped for the night.

"You look stunning." Carter watched as Alyssa, attired in a sleek red sleeveless gown descended the stairs. Her hair had been swirled up atop her head. With matching red lipstick and nails, she was elegance personified.

"She's out of your league, dude." Parker cackled from the corner where he leaned against the wall.

Dad, spiffed up in a navy suit, stepped forward. "She invited him, Son. I'm guessing she'd disagree."

An electronic buzz sounded, followed by an Artificial Intelligence voice, "Carriage approaching drive."

"Grover, permission to enter!" Gianni hollered a little too loudly because Alyssa flinched.

Carter shrugged. "His name is A.I. Grover, go figure."

"I like it." Alyssa took his hand as she reached the bottom of the step. "And yes, I did ask you to the ball. But I have to confess I'll have to duck out a little early."

"What?" Dad and Parker bellowed simultaneously, and she cringed.

"I have a little Prince Charming at home who is not so charming if he's overstimulated. There can be meltdowns, and he morphs into Humpty Dumpty broken on the ground."

"Wow, that's a little too many metaphors for my old brain." Gianni pretended to wipe sweat from his brow.

"Carter can be one of the king's horses and try to put him together again." Parker cackled again.

"Come on, everyone."

Soon, they settled into their carriage seats.

"Everybody set back there?" Their driver glanced back at them.

"Off we go." Carter resisted the urge to take Alyssa's hand in his, but to his surprise, she slipped her slim palm into his.

The driver urged the horses forward.

The carriage moved out from the house and down the long, wooded drive to the main road. The leaves, lightly tinged with yellow and orange, hinted at autumn. But within weeks, the leaf peepers would get their reward when vibrant reds colored the maples.

Too bad Alyssa may pull a Cinderella move and attend the event's first part, the auction, and then slip away to the wharf, to catch the last ferry home.

"You should stay." He'd pull the K card. "Kelsey will cry when she realizes you left without saying goodbye."

"I can't believe you just said that." She chuckled. "You put the 'Mom guilt' move to shame."

"Yeah, well, 'Dad guilt' can be even better."

"Sammy is doing fine right now."

"He should be." Gianni smirked. "I messaged him that if he can get through tonight okay, then I'll bring him over to see the Sagamore brothers next week."

Kareen slapped at his leg. "You didn't."

"Yes, I did."

"Wish I'd thought of that," Carter muttered and Alyssa, too, swatted at his leg.

"A little bribery, er, uh, incentive, can go a long way." Gianni tugged on his pale blue tie.

Alyssa checked her phone. "A text from Sammy."

"Read it," Dad encouraged.

"Mom G n I have a deal so can I go see the Ss next weekend?" She quickly explained her son's abbreviations.

"I'm G, yeah?" Gianni squared his shoulders.

"Wait till he's a teenager and see what he calls you." Dad crinkled his nose.

His family was acting like this was a done deal. Like he and Alyssa were a serious item.

Were they?

What did they know that Carter didn't? Or was he not ready to acknowledge where this was going?

Within a half hour they'd arrived at the Grand and passed through the auction hall.

When they hesitated, Alyssa glancing at the items, Dad waved them on.

Grandpa Gianni touched Alyssa's shoulder. "We'll come back and look at the auction items during the first orchestra break."

"Sure." His gorgeous date frowned. "Huh, Starr claimed she was deejay tonight."

They all moved through to the orchestra hall where they grabbed a large table and ordered drinks. The band had already set up on the front stage and the music started.

"I'd like to claim this dance." Carter wasn't letting Alyssa get out of reach. "Can you waltz?"

She blushed as he swept her into his arms and out onto the dance floor. "Believe it or not, my strict father did allow dancing at wedding receptions. He showed me how to waltz."

"That's kinda sweet." He looked down into her warm brown eyes. "Let's see how well Reverend Teann taught you."

With Alyssa so close to him, all seemed right with the world. He took her through the steps and although they hesitated on the turns, they did fine.

Jack and Rachel danced toward them. Jack made a point of bumping into Carter. "Oh, didn't see ya there." Carter scowled at him as Alyssa rolled her eyes.

Why had dancing with Carter felt like rehearsing for a wedding dance? Maybe because while they were on the floor, she kept imagining what that would be like. He felt like the perfect partner in the waltz. Maybe in life.

They danced two more, one to a pop song and the other another slow dance. Maria and Hamp moved gracefully past them. At the song's conclusion, Rachel and Jack, carrying a large rectangular white box, mounted the stairs to the stage.

Rachel looked gorgeous, as usual, attired tonight in a turquoise ensemble that set off her dark hair. The main singer stepped back and Rachel took the microphone.

"Welcome, everyone. For those of you who don't know us, I'm Rachel Dunmara Welling and this is my husband Jack. We host summer medical retreats at Lilac Cottage and for the past several years we've also been blessed to give away an unbelievably generous donation—

A Cassie Browne original gown."

Alyssa and Carter applauded, as did the others.

"We usually announce our winner after the auction, but our recipient has to head back downstate to catch her flight," she paused, "to Montana. Claire Ecker is our winner."

There was a gasp from someone nearby. She turned to see Clark Jeffries bend and kiss the cheek of the woman she'd seen him with earlier in the summer. The brunette, attired in a deep violet gown, strode with efficiency toward the stage. Her sturdy walk perfectly emulated that of a healthcare worker.

"Claire is a neurosurgical floor nurse out west." Jack removed the dress from the box and displayed it.

There was a collective moment of silence followed by chatter about the gorgeous creation.

Carter took her hand and leaned in. "Time to go check out the auction." He pointed toward his parents and grandparents who were exiting the room.

She nodded and they weaved through the crowd and out into the hallway.

Laughter carried from farther down the hall, in the auction area.

"Dad usually bids on at least one thing every year."

She smiled at him.

Carter's blue eyes lit up as he bent to kiss her. "I had to sneak that in before we get down in that crowd."

When the hallway opened into the reception area, it looked like most of the attendees had stopped here before entering the orchestra hall to dance.

"Whoa, that can't be who I think that is." Carter turned her toward a long wall of artwork, most oil paintings, but some sculptures and decorative craft ware. "Let's go this way."

One of the portraits caught her eye. "Oh my goodness, that's one of Linda's."

"Linda?" Carter glanced back toward the entry doors.

"Linda Anderson-Paine, the artist who did the Byrnes' nursery. And it's a version of one she showed Sammy's classroom last year. Oh, I love that painting." She stepped closer and looked at the bids. Absolutely out of her price range. But a girl could dream.

Behind them, near the entrance she heard the security guards preventing a guest from entering.

It sounded like Carter sucked in a breath, just as he swiveled and escorted Alyssa near the entryway.

"Well I never! I have an invite. Just lookie here." The nasal voice sounded vaguely familiar.

"That's from two years ago. See the date." The guard read the past date aloud.

"It's still good. I'm telling you."

Carter's face, especially his ears, were turning red. He stopped and clasped her elbows. "We should get out of here."

"Why?"

"There! That's my son-in-law, Carter Parker. Just ask him if I don't have an invite!"

That woman was Abbi-Renae's mother? Attired casually and wearing tennis shoes and a visor, she waved frantically at Carter.

"Carter Parker, come tell them to let me in."

"What's she doing here?" Alyssa whispered.

He shrugged. "Haven't a clue."

"I thought she was coming in the fall to see Kelsey."

"I'm Nancy Kelly and this guy has kept me from seeing my granddaughter, Kelsey!" Mrs. Kelly's voice rose.

The two security guards were joined by two more men. If Alyssa was correct, those were Gianni's private guards. The biggest man wagged a finger at the petite woman with the loud voice. "You need to leave before we call the police."

"Wait till you have children. Wait till your only child dies, and you can't see your grandchild!" Mrs. Kelly wagged her own index finger back.

Susan Mullen, attired in a burgundy-and-black ensemble, and her husband stepped toward the agitated woman. "Why don't you come with us?"

John jerked his thumb toward a hallway. "We've got a private salon right down here."

Abbi's mother blinked hard.

Alyssa and Carter reached her, and the guards gave them wide-eyed looks.

"Let's go with Mr. and Mrs. Mullen, Nancy. They're my friends." Carter smiled, but a muscle jumped in his cheek.

"All right. That's more like it. And then we can go into the ball and find Abbi-Renae."

Alyssa gasped. She believed her daughter was still alive?

"I know you're hiding her in there."

From behind them, a man's deep voice sounded. "Nancy, honey, what are you doing?"

"My father-in-law," Carter exhaled a sigh.

The heavyset man with dark eyeglasses and a receding hairline carried a black-and-gold enameled box.

Carter took two steps toward the man, anger contorting his features. "What are you doing with that?"

Mrs. Kelly swiveled. "I've got a key to your house, and I let our daughter out of there."

They brought their daughter's remains to this public event? Alyssa began to tremble. Was that a cremation box?

"I can't believe you did this. You had no right." Carter shook his head, his skin mottled red.

Abbi-Renae's dad clutched the box tighter. "Nancy said you wanted us to bring it here—which didn't make sense to me."

"Yeah, well Nancy just said Abbi-Renae was in there at the auction." Carter raised his voice. "I'm guessing she's not making a lot of sense in a lot of realms."

"No. She hasn't been doing well. I just hoped. . ."

"Come on this way, sir." Susan pressed a hand to Mr. Kelly's back while John did the same for the poor man's disturbed wife.

Allowing them to step ahead of them into the private salon, Alyssa grabbed Carter's arm. "You never told me she was mentally ill."

"I didn't realize she was. I just thought. . ." He blew out a breath. "My mother-in-law was always different, but she's gone off the deep end now."

"She can't be around Kelsey."

"I know."

"Maybe if there were a bunch of us there, but Carter, she needs help. Grandma Romelda's ministry sponsors some treatment options in coastal Virginia."

"I'll speak with my father-in-law."

Chapter Twenty-Eight

The sun rose despite it having been the strangest night Carter had experienced in a long time. Nancy had lost it. His father-in-law discovered that she'd not been taking her medications and got her to take them. He'd also promised to bring her back later if she'd start going to her therapy sessions again. Although she'd agreed, Carter wasn't sure Nancy would comply.

A tap sounded at his door. He rose to answer it.

Juan Pablo stood there, attired in his monk's habit again, holding a Bible in one hand and Abbi-Renae's ashes in the other. "It's time for the ceremony."

Was Nancy rubbing off on everyone? And why hadn't the alarm sounded that they'd had a visitor? "What ceremony?"

Juan Pablo, face serene, turned on his heel. "In the garden."

Dressed in T-shirt and knit sleep shorts, Carter padded after the man.

Once outside, he spied Alyssa and Kelsey, attired in matching pink sundresses, standing beside the hole in the ground.

Juan Pablo placed the enamel box into the hole. "Into this consecrated ground, we return our sister in Christ, Abbi-Renae Kelly. Ashes to ashes, dust to dust. God you are eternal. May her spirit dwell with you forever. In Jesus's name, Amen." Then he prayed in Latin.

Alyssa took a shovel from a nearby bench and passed it to Carter. "Are you ready?"

"I am." He blinked back tears as he dug into the pile of dirt near the hole and placed the first mound on the pristine box. She didn't want to return here, and now he was placing her remains on Mackinac Island soil.

"Do not let your soul be troubled." Juan Pablo locked his dark gaze on him. "Our sister Abbi's eternal spirit rests in heaven. One day we will all meet her there again, in God's glory."

Alyssa raised her hands. "Amen. To God be the glory forever and ever."

"Gw-ee," Kelsey said, sounding suspiciously like 'Glory.'

As Carter continued to cover the box, he wished his wife goodbye. *Abbi-Renae, if you could see our precious girl, you'd know part of our love lives on. No matter what happens, even with a future with Alyssa, I will tell our child about her amazing mother. I'm sorry, I wish I could have saved you, but that was not to be. And I know now you wouldn't have blamed me.*

This was holy ground. Consecrated. And Abbi-Renae deserved respect and closure—as did he.

From the side of the house, Starr appeared, attired in a long flowing white dress and carrying baskets of flowers. Juan Pablo pointed to where Carter stood and Starr began to dance toward them, scattering flowers and singing.

"That's really lovely." Alyssa swayed back and forth with Kelsey.

Starr handed Alyssa, Kelsey, and him each a small bouquet of flowers and pointed to where Abbi-Renae's remains were now buried.

Grandpa Gianni, carrying a large brass plaque, and Grandma Kareen came out. She came to his side. "Gianni and I remember that heartbreaking call you made to us at Thanksgiving when you weren't sure what might happen. You decided you and Abbi should marry. You brought some joy out of tragedy at losing your friend. Abbi brought an incredibly beautiful blessing out of her life that she gifted to you. And we're grateful for her life, even as short as it was."

He blinked back tears as Gianni showed him the engraved plaque. Juan Pablo said a blessing and Gianni bent and placed the plaque where Abbi-Renae's remains had been buried.

He wasn't alone. His family had his back. And they had loved her, too.

Carter faced his friends and family. "Thank you, everyone." Words weren't enough, but they'd have to do.

All week long, Sammy had reminded Alyssa of how "good" he'd been and that he would be going to Mackinac Island that coming Saturday. "Son, I hate to say this. I know I'm going to sound just like my mother—but if you say that one more time. . ." She trailed off. His wide eyes showed he understood the unspoken threat.

Now on Saturday morning the two of them arrived on the island. The Sagamore boys broke free from their parents, at the end of the wharf, and ran to Sammy. They grabbed his overnight bag and all the way back to their parents chanted, "Sammy! Sammy! Sammy!"

When Alyssa reached the parents, she rolled her eyes. "You sure you're up to this?"

Bruce Sagamore jerked a thumb to where the boys were still chanting. "That's what I've been hearing all week."

Marney Sagamore cupped her hands around her mouth. "That's enough!"

Apparently, those were the right words, because her sons stopped their chant. "We want to go to the fort first," the older one said.

"Yeah," agreed the younger.

"Sammy?" Bruce pointed at her son.

He shrugged. "As long as I'm with my friends I'll be happy."

"So we'll see you tomorrow at Cardinal Cottage?" Marney grinned. "I've been wanting to look inside that place ever since we got lost down their driveway one summer."

"We got chased off by a security guard." Bruce offered a lopsided smile.

Alyssa laughed. "We'll all head out to church together—no security guards chasing us."

"Super. We'll see you then." Marney pushed her sunglasses further up her nose.

Sammy turned and waved goodbye before heading off the dock with the Sagamores.

A slim dark-haired man with glasses jogged up toward her. Clark Jeffries. Handsome as ever. What had happened with him and his nurse friend? *Not my business.* But meeting with him and Molly about Grandma Romelda's computer needs was the point of her meeting with them this morning.

"Thought that was you, Alyssa!" Clark, dressed in a light blue oxford shirt and tan chinos, exuded polished confidence; while she, in shorts, a T-shirt, and tennis shoes, did not.

"It's me. And while I may not be dressed like a pro, I appreciate you listening to something my great-grandmother wants to pitch."

He cupped his hands around his ears. "Molly and I will be all ears."

They headed off to where his business partner was waiting in front of the restaurant.

Alyssa laughed. "This is where I first met you."

Inside, where Alyssa had first sat with Mrs. Menteur, an older woman with gray hair tied up in a bun, sat bent over a full breakfast, eating with gusto. Attired in faded gray knit slacks and a pullover top with frayed sleeves, the woman had a plastic bag next to her on the bench. No purse visible.

Alyssa slid into the seat next to Molly and shook her hand. "Thanks for meeting with me."

"Good to see you." Molly inclined her head toward the adjacent booth. "I think Menteur has a new victim."

"Really?" She looked homeless, poor thing. "Was she seated with her?"

"Yup, and Menteur got up and walked away. Told that old woman that she had nothing for her this winter."

"Wow. That's heartless, considering her appearance."

"The strange thing was the older lady just laughed."

"All right, you two." Clark shook his head. "Let's select a nice big brunch from the menu because I understand that Romelda is paying."

"That's right." Alyssa tapped the table. "Our time, her dime is what she said."

"I love business lunches like that." Clark grinned.

"Breakfasts, too." Molly opened her menu and patted the image in the middle. "Although this will last me until dinner tonight."

"Not sure we'll have lunch when Carter and I bike around the island." She couldn't wait to see him again.

Clark closed his menu. "Good to hear Carter isn't a complete sad sack this month."

She laughed. "I'm glad, too. I was trying to give him room— since it's the anniversary, but. . ."

"I can't even imagine." Molly slowly shook her head.

A cloud passed over Clark's face. "My friend lost her dad during the pandemic, and I don't think she's ever gotten over it. In fact, I think. . ." He rubbed his thumb over his lips, as though silencing himself.

Was that the nurse?

The waiter bopped up to their table, his dark hair flopping around his tanned face. "My fave customers. What'll it be? Toast and tea or tea and toast?"

"Nope. The full shebang." Molly handed him the menu. "Yooper breakfast feast."

"No way." The young guy leaned back.

"Yes way."

Clark pointed to Alyssa. "She's paying, so give me a lumberjack breakfast. Sausage not bacon."

"High roller here today. And what'll you have?" He raised his thick eyebrows expectantly.

"I'll have the vegetable scrambled eggs with sausage, please." Because Sammy wouldn't eat them, she never cooked them.

"Sure thing."

"Wait." She motioned for him to come closer. "Was the lady at the next table with Mrs. Menteur?"

He huffed a sigh. "Yeah. And Menteur's out of here."

"Put the lady's bill on mine." She didn't want the poor woman to be embarrassed later.

"Yeah?" His skeptical tone had her rethinking.

"Yes." Her great-grandmother would approve.

The waiter added the older woman's order to the bill and then left.

Alyssa steepled her fingers together. "So let me pitch what my great-grandmother is looking for right now."

She laid out for the computer consultants what Grandma Romelda wanted. "And all that is beyond my experience."

"I think Carter could have helped with this." Clark sipped his coffee.

"He's got a full-time job."

Molly placed her napkin on her lap. "Did you ask him?"

She hesitated. "No. When I realized I couldn't pull this off in my free time, I immediately thought it would be great to keep this work in the EUP."

"Absolutely." Clark set his mug down. "That's one reason I kept my business here."

Molly leaned in. "Does that count when you take it remote out west this winter?"

"Uh." He raised his hands. "I plead the fifth."

The waiter arrived and slid their plates from the serving tray onto the table in front of each of them. "Enjoy!"

"Thanks." Alyssa eyed her companions. "Mind if I pray?"

"Please do." Clark closed his eyes, as did Molly.

"Lord, bless this food to the nourishment of our bodies and guide our decisions today and every day. In Jesus's precious name, Amen."

"Amen," the two echoed.

"I'm tucking into my breakfast because this place is beginning to fill up." Molly winked. She proceeded to share about her family.

Clark updated Alyssa about state park happenings. "My father loves his job as director. Our entire family is excited about those new things coming.

At the adjacent booth, the elderly woman waved her coffee cup, and the waiter hurried over to her. She was still sitting there, although she should have finished her breakfast ages ago. Did she have no place to go? Was she waiting for Mrs. Menteur to return?

The woman scootched to the edge of the bench seat and slowly rose. She rocked almost sideways as she walked. If anyone needed a cane, it was this lady. She stopped at their table.

"I'm just heading back to the can. Would you keep an eye on my things?" Her gravelly voice announced her as a longtime smoker.

Alyssa nodded slowly, assuming by things that the woman meant her plastic bag.

"Thanks for paying for my grub."

Clark laughed. "We've seen Mrs. Menteur rip off a lot of people by not paying their bills."

"Oh yeah?" Her hazel eyes twinkled. "She offered me winter on the island and now she's bugged outta here."

"I'm sorry." Alyssa made a sympathetic face.

"Oh, don't be. Now that I know my girl is learning some new tricks she got from me, I feel relieved."

Her girl?

The waiter arrived with a pot of coffee. "These are the kind folks who paid your bill."

The woman cackled. "I left my daughter here at fourteen to earn her keep, and I'm glad to hear she's learned her way around these tourists."

"Is Mrs. Menteur your daughter?" Clark's deep brown eyes widened.

"Don'tcha know it, bub?" She clucked her tongue. Then she ambled off toward the bathroom.

"Seriously?" Molly held her mug toward the waiter, who stood there blinking.

He poured the coffee. "Mrs. Menteur told me she only hires people who refuse to pay the bill and walk away. She emails them later."

"No way." Alyssa extended her coffee cup, too.

"I'm a pre-law student on a year's break. I went to her office and quoted her the legal violation she'd made with her scam. She hired me on the spot."

"She's a piece of work." Clark covered his mug as the waiter moved the carafe in his direction.

"The apple doesn't fall too far from the tree, it seems." Alyssa's dad loved that quote.

"Left her here at fourteen?" Molly cringed. "Unbelievable."

"And by all accounts I've heard, she met her wealthy husband and married him a couple of years later."

"At sixteen?" Alyssa couldn't help but feel some compassion for Mrs. Menteur. It still didn't make the woman's little game right.

Lord, soften her heart and make her stop.

Meet him at the jeweler's, Carter had texted her. Why that location? Maybe because it was right at the end of the block and next to a good bike rack. But as Alyssa headed down the sidewalk, the sounds of horses' hooves clip-clopping along with her heart, she considered what a lifetime with him could mean.

A seagull squawked overhead, as if mocking her thoughts.

She went into the jewelry store, and spied Carter at the case, leaning over. Was he? He swiveled and grinned, waving her over.

He gave her a side hug. "Take a look at this and tell me what you think."

Was it a huge diamond that she wouldn't dare wear? Was it a modern ring covered with smaller diamonds in an arch? She held her breath as she looked over the lit interior of the velvet-lined case.

Tiny gold charms of girls' and boys' silhouettes as well as other charms were arranged in a crescent.

"I thought I'd buy one for her great-grandma and grandma—in honor of Kelsey's birthday. I didn't do that when she was born, and it's a family tradition."

She'd seen his Grandma Kareen's hefty traditional gold charm bracelet and Maria's Pandora-style one. "Oh, that's sweet." Her voice came out disappointed, so she forced some cheer. "They'll love that. And can you get them engraved here?"

The salesman nodded. He pulled three charms from the case. "If you'll just enter your information on that form, we'll have them this afternoon."

"Thanks."

What had she been thinking?

Carter wrote on the small form. "You ready for our trip around the island?"

"I am." She couldn't help eyeing the solitaires in the next case. One had an eternity loop in the middle with two diamonds flanked by two smaller diamonds on either side. It made her think of her and Carter with each child adjacent. The matching wedding ring was inset with several more diamonds and a swoop of metal that attached to the engagement ring. When she saw the price, she nearly swallowed her tongue.

"See something you like?" Carter's gaze locked on her, and her face flushed.

"They have some beautiful jewelry in here."

"I intend to buy many more items here over the years." He set the slip and pen on the counter and took her hand. "Come on. We better head out."

"You act like we'll be late for something." She laughed. "I'm a lady of leisure until your daughter wakes up from her nap in two hours."

They headed out and soon were away from town.

They stopped at the Cannonball Oasis and parked their bikes. In September it was still busy, with lots of tourists stopping.

"You look decidedly not cranky and mournful." Alyssa took his hand.

He laughed. "I called Mrs. Mullen this morning and she said, 'Carter, you don't have to follow someone else's grief path.' She was right."

"I agree."

"Come on. Hamburgers, fries, and ice cream await." He released her hand and jogged to the restaurant's counter.

She caught up with him. "I'm still full."

"You can have some of mine, then."

"Ask for a kids' cone for me."

Soon they sat at a picnic table.

"Are you having fun?" Carter kissed her cheek.

"Of course. I'm with you." Were the Sagamores and Sammy having fun, too?

"Mom! Mom!" She turned around; the voice sounded like her son's. A thin young teen with curly red hair was hopping in place, like Sammy did when he was stimming. "They have fried pickles!"

The mom, thin with jet black hair and oversized sunglasses, danced in place. The man with her, with graying hair, high-fived the boy. They looked happy. There was no embarrassment about their son's behavior. That was one of the things she absolutely loved about Carter. He never acted like Sammy's stimming was a problem.

Carter lifted his water bottle. "Those parents understand their son. I wish I'd had that. I see that with you and Sammy, and I want to be that kind of dad."

"I think you already are."

"Thank you."

They sat for a bit as the leaves slowly drifted down onto the picnic area. They were dropping their leaves at a quicker rate than usual. They reminded her of Linda's painting and the clock in the background.

Time didn't wait on anyone.

When Alyssa had gazed with longing at the wedding sets earlier, he'd almost dropped down on one knee. He had so much he wanted to say, and he'd almost forgotten how difficult it was to talk and ride at the same time. "This time apart has made me realize how much I. . . I want you near me. I want us, me and Kels, near you and Sam."

Tears built in her eyes as he grabbed her hands and clasped them.

She didn't say anything.

"I respect what you're trying to do with your job. I wish I could do something more. I asked my boss if they could make a spot for you, but they've frozen hiring."

She nodded.

He rubbed his thumb pads along her cheeks. "You've helped me get my head on straight."

She leaned back and feigned examining his head. "Looks like it's on there cockeyed."

"Haha. No, it's much better than when you met me."

"You sure?"

"Yeah. Not only that but you helped with more."

"Oh? As your intern? New job skill to add to my resume then?"

"Yup. Head straightener and heart mender."

"Um, I'm not gonna take God's job from Him." She pointed upward. "Only He can help with that."

"Okay, well great job being God's minion. Will you accept that?"

"God's minion. Great job title. I think. . ." She frowned. "Gosh, I think Starr said that's the name of her deejay business."

Carter tilted his head back and laughed hard. "Well, God's Minion no-showed at the ball."

Horses nearby neighed almost in response.

The driver shot a glare at them.

He wiped her hands off with his napkin and picked up the remnants of lunch. "Alyssa, do you like me at least a little?"

"Maybe a little." She put her fingertips and thumb a fraction apart.

He stood. "And my daughter, too?"

She opened her arms wide. "A lot."

"Okay, now I know where we stand." He tossed the garbage in the nearby can.

Alyssa rose and stretched. "Do you?"

"I'd hoped those kisses sent the message."

"Oh, they sent a message all right." She made a dirty look. "A very mixed message."

"I know." He bent his head and swiped his hand across his brow. "The shame of it."

"Don't start shame with me. I don't do that well. I gave that up."

"Good."

"And you helped with all that, Mr. Parker."

He jerked his head toward her. "Are you gonna start calling me 'Sir' again?"

"Nah." She waved as if shooing the notion.

The two of them headed toward their bikes.

He made a motion to include the two of them. "We're a mutually helpful computer geeks society."

"Does that group include our children?"

"Of course. Do you realize that we'd have a family of four if we. . . If we—"

"Married?" her voice squeaked out.

This would be way too soon to be walking down the aisle.

Yet here he was, talking about it.

And it felt good.

Chapter Twenty-Nine

Straits of Mackinac

Two long weeks since he'd seen Alyssa and both he and Kelsey had felt the absence. He'd been disappointed when he'd missed her the previous weekend in Newberry. She was supposed to have helped with packing up her parents' belongings. But Sammy had been sick, and she hadn't come. Then, she'd refused for Carter to come check on them in the Soo, in case he caught what her son had and passed it on to the baby.

That morning, Carter caught the first ferry over to St. Ignace, after he'd read the *Sault Evening News*. The headline read, 'School Superintendent and School Board Agree to Hiring Freeze.' *No new contracts.* All temporary employees given thirty days' notice.
He needed to see Alyssa.

What was she going to do when he showed up on her doorstep?"

On impulse, he texted Alyssa's great-grandmother. She'd told him to reach out if Alyssa needed anything. Given what Reverend Teann answered the previous Sunday, Carter would ask Romelda the same question.

On the mainland, he accessed his family's vehicle storage area and unlocked the truck. He started his GPS and headed north to the Soo.

Carter arrived over forty minutes later to find Alyssa was about to close the door behind Sammy as they stepped into the driveway. He parked adjacent to her small sedan.

She looked confused. But then a smile lit her face.

"Carter! What a surprise," she cried out as he exited the truck. "I'm taking Sammy to the church."

Sam ran to him and hugged him. "They have Saturday Fun Day."

"Great! Can I drive you?"

"Yeah. I want to go in your truck. Can we, Mom?"

"Sure." She shrugged.

When Sam ran to the truck, he pulled Alyssa in for a quick hug. "Missed you."

"Missed you more." She tipped her head back, and he obliged her with a kiss. "What brings you here?"

"I saw the newspaper."

"Ah. Yeah, that."

After dropping off Sammy at the church, she had Carter drive them toward the Soo Locks Park. They got out and headed toward the entrance and went through the checkpoint.

They headed down the sidewalk. She pointed to the maples. "The leaves are spectacular this year." No doubt Cadotte Avenue on Mackinac was also gorgeous.

"Sure thing. And you're looking pretty spectacular, too."

She laughed. "I'm wearing a Mackinac Island T-shirt from Sammy's favorite store."

"Ah, the Big Little store."

"Correct. Very affordable. And I've got shorts that haven't fit me in years and probably won't again soon, since I'm not biking around the island." She could already feel the waistband tightening in this past month.

"Come back to the island then." He covered her hand with his. "I am really sorry about your job."

"The Lord giveth and the Lord taketh away."

"No kidding He does, but it doesn't mean you can't have some feelings about it."

She pushed her bangs off her forehead. "I kinda got a bad vibe almost immediately at my new job."

"Yeah?"

"Balancing IT work with small programming assignments. A little tricky wearing two hats."

"I think it would be. I'm not good at the IT part."

"Yeah, me neither it turns out, and I'm a little sad about that."

"It's okay. You tried it."

"Yup. And I'm glad you've come, because I wanted to talk with you about this in person. My great-grandmother asked me to come on board with her programming team. They're expanding their apps. Some of it is for overseas use, but she hasn't lined up her language translators yet."

"You could still work on the apps, though."

"Right, she had other work that I discussed with Clark and Molly a couple of weeks back. I told you about that on the phone." And he hadn't been happy that she'd not told him. "For this, though, she mentioned us moving to Virginia to be near headquarters."

"Where your folks are moving to?"

"Yes, but Sammy is struggling here. He's met a few nice kids at church who, shall we say, tolerate him?" And would it be even worse being a newcomer in Virginia and adjusting to a new environment?

"That's no good. He needs some genuine buds like the Sagamore boys."

"He misses them."

"Kelsey is off. She keeps asking for you."

"For me?"

"She calls for 'Mama' off and on through the day." He took her hand in his and led her to a bench beneath a scarlet maple tree.

From the look in his eyes, this was something serious.

He couldn't be. Not this soon. Her heartbeat ratcheted up.

"I met with your father last weekend, and he's given me permission to court you."

She blinked at him. "Court me?"

"Yup."

"Who says court anymore?"

"Well. . ." he drew out the word. "I guessed the good Reverend Teann would want to know that our dating was going to lead somewhere. He'll permit courtship, with the intention of marrying you later."

"You do realize we've only had one of what I'd call an," she made air quotes, "official date."

"Exactly. Yeah, your dad would frown upon more until he knew where this was going." He shrugged. "He struck me as that kind of pastor."

"Which he is." Seriously? He'd told Dad he wanted to date her with the intention of marrying her?

"But you might not want to be courted by me." He ran his hand along his jawline.

"Because?"

This was a huge 'because' for him. "I don't think I could handle having any more children after what I went through." He whooshed out a breath.

She touched his face. "That's understandable. But things happen."

He nodded. Abbi-Renae was pregnant almost immediately after they married.

"Carter, you'd need to be in a place where you could deal with that possibility."

He wouldn't blame her for putting him on standby. He pressed his spine against the bench's seatback. "Do you mean no dating?"

"I mean no marriage ideas until you could deal with that scenario. It's only been a year since your wife's tragic death."

He lowered his eyebrows and swiped his hand across his forehead. "It feels like a lifetime ago, sometimes." He shook her hand lightly. "But you and Sammy will still hang out with me and Kels?"

"Sure. My name isn't Reverend Joseph Teann." She leaned in and kissed him.

His heartbeat ticked upward as he returned the kiss and pulled her closer.

His cellphone rang. He still held her tight, not wanting to let go.

"You better check that. Could be Kelsey."

He pulled out his phone. *Dad.* "Everything okay?"

"Kelsey is fine, but your niece is on her way."

"My niece. Leoni? Jaycie's having the baby?" His voice shook. Nothing better happen to either of them.

"Yup. And they sent her to the Soo because there's a terrible accident en route to Petoskey. Can you go meet them there?"

Carter froze. No way was he going to the hospital. "Um, I don't think so." No way was he going to relive what he'd been through. His entire body began to shake as a dark mental fog drifted down on him.

"Son. It's gonna be alright, Son. I know what you're thinking. You'll be okay. Baby Leoni is gonna be fine."

He swallowed hard.

Alyssa leaned in. "What's going on? Is Kelsey okay?"

He nodded and mouthed, "Baby is coming."

She clapped her hands as a huge smile spread across her beautiful face. The warmth of that joy melted the ice that had been chilling his heart only moments before. Having her at his side would bolster him.

"I'll go over to the hospital now, Dad. Let me tell Alyssa." He covered the speaker. "She's at the hospital here."

"In the Soo?"

"Change in plans." Life was like that.

By the time Carter and Alyssa got there, the nurse explained that the baby had arrived quickly. She was being bathed, and he could go on to her room. "Only two family members at a time, though."

"I'll wait in the cafeteria." Alyssa gave him a quick kiss.

He headed down the hall as a piercing cry sounded nearby. Was that her? His niece?

Abbi-Renae was fine at the hospital. It wasn't until later that she'd hemorrhaged. He wanted so badly to beg the hospital to keep Jaycie there for a week. He knew they'd never do it. He pasted a smile on his face as he entered the spacious room.

Jaycie sat up in the hospital bed, her dark hair plastered to her forehead. Parker stood beside her holding their baby to his shoulder.

"You're a mama! And I'm an uncle." Carter swaggered in like their biological grandfather would have done in one of his Old West movies. He knew they'd be worried that he'd have a meltdown, but Carter would rein that in—with God's help. For surely the Lord was there with them in this room.

Tears streamed down Jaycie's flushed cheeks. "Finally. Our own baby."

Parker leaned in and kissed his wife's forehead.

Alyssa carried a small vase of pink carnations and white roses as she headed to Jaycie's room. She reached the room and rapped on the door.

Carter opened it. "I'll let Parker know he should go eat. Only two of us in here at a time."

In a moment, Parker exited the room.

"Congratulations!"

To her surprise, he leaned in and gave her a big hug. "We're so very blessed I can't even put it into words."

After so many pregnancy losses, it was no wonder he was so emotional. "Go get some food and make some calls. Carter and I will stay here with Jaycie."

"Thanks." He headed off, shoving his hand through his thick sandy hair like Carter did.

"Come on." Carter brought her into the room. "Wash your hands and use the sanitizer."

"Sure."

Jaycie held her baby, whose little eyes were wide open.

"Congratulations, Mommy Jaycie! I see your darling is awake." She went to the sink and quickly washed and then pumped antibacterial gel into her hands.

"She's surprised us, but the nurse said she'll conk out soon and will probably sleep for a long time." Jaycie yawned.

"I bet you're exhausted."

"I am but she's so worth it. Aren't you, Leoni?"

Alyssa gave a thumbs-up. "Good job."

"She looks like Kelsey did." Carter moved closer.

"She looks just like her own unique self." Warmth flowed through Alyssa. "Leoni is a precious gift from God."

"Absolutely." Jaycie leaned back against her pillow and closed her eyes, her dark hair plastered against her neck.

Whoa, what was happening here? Was Jaycie all right? Carter moved closer to her and watched as the machine beside her showed her pulse, oxygen, and something else to be normal.

Alyssa didn't seem to notice him. Her attention was fixed on little Leoni. She hurried toward the bedside and pressed a hand beneath the bundled baby.

Carter leaned closer to Jaycie and examined the white sheets covering her. No blood leaking out. She seemed to be breathing normally. When she began to snore, he stepped away from the bed.

"Poor Mommy needs to sleep," Alyssa said softly as she took the baby in her arms. "I wasn't going to pick her up but. . ."

But because I was more worried about Jaycie dying, I hadn't grabbed my own niece.

Alyssa cuddled the baby to her shoulder and jostled her, pacing back and forth, talking in a soothing voice the whole time.

"Dr. and Mrs. Austin, Jaycie's mom and stepdad, will come in the morning to see the baby," he whispered. "After the Petoskey traffic clears out. Maria and Hamp are on their way, and Starr will watch Kelsey."

Alyssa sat in the rocking chair and rubbed the infant's back. She looked perfectly content, the picture of motherly devotion and love. Warmth spread through his chest. He could imagine the two of them welcoming their own child one day—if God blessed them both with another.

He went to the side and peeked at Leoni. "Eyes closed," he whispered, "like her mommy's."

"Go tell Daddy Parker that his wifey and baby are sleeping and to be quiet when he returns," she whispered back.

Leoni was in good hands. He couldn't resist checking on Jaycie one more time before he searched out Parker. But when another gentle snore came from her direction, he left.

God, she's in your hands. Please protect her.

Trust me, God whispered to his heart.

That's what he had to do. He didn't know why God let Abbi-Renae leave so soon and so tragically. Didn't know why he and Kelsey were left alone. Didn't know what would come of his relationship with Alyssa.

But he did know he could trust God. The Lord had brought him through so much already.

Jireh, You are enough.

Chapter Thirty

Mackinac Island, December

If this was the Parkers' notion of a bridal shower, then what was Christmas going to be like? And that was only weeks away. They were all settled in the main living room at Cardinal Cottage with a fire going in the fireplace. They'd gone down to the Christmas tree lighting and admired the wreaths lining the main street on their way back. Now they were warming back up and celebrating.

Alyssa leaned in toward her fiancé. "Are we really doing this?"

"Having a shower or getting married?" He touched the double infinity engagement ring on her left ring finger.

"Both." She kissed him.

"Ahem, first gift coming up." Gianni opened a large squarish box and removed a painting.

"Alyssa, we grabbed this at the auction, and the artist signed an additional sentiment on the back." Kareen clasped her hands together as Gianni passed her and Carter the gift.

"Linda Anderson-Paine's tandem bicycle and clock painting!" Her jaw dropped.

"Oh my goodness, Sammy, come see this!" But her son and the Sagamore boys were filling their plates with snacks at the food table.

Gianni chuckled. "Who do you think told us about this special painting you admired?"

"Of course, we saw you eyeing it at the auction, too." Kareen sipped her drink.

Carter extended his hand. "Stay there, Sam, you can see it later." In a lower voice he said, "When his hands aren't covered with orange Cheeto dust."

Jaycie passed her another gift wrapped in glossy deep brown paper. "Lucky Bean package sent by Carolyn and her husband."

Alyssa opened it and found Love Potion #9 coffee, two adorable matching mugs, and chocolate dipped shortbread cookies.

"Just for me, I see." Carter grabbed the cookies, and Alyssa stretched her arm for them.

Mom gave her the stink eye, and Alyssa stopped reaching for the treat.

"Honey, your dad and I want to be involved with the wedding ceremony, and I will make my famous tea cakes."

"Did you just brag, Mom? I can't believe that."

Dad shifted closer to the edge of the sofa. "It's a fact. Grandma Romelda put the recipe on her show and her viewers went nuts over them. *Woman's World Magazine* is interviewing your mom and including those in their upcoming Easter issue."

Easter? That seemed far away, but in the publishing industry it probably wasn't.

"And we have this for you. Your own family Bible which has all your names in it." Mom gestured around the room while Dad rose and brought the Bible, in a gold embossed box, to them.

"Thank you, Reverend and Mrs. Teann." Carter opened the box and flipped the cover over to where it was dedicated to them.

"Beautiful. Thanks, Mom and Dad."

Carter waved a postcard. "Our friend, Starr Bourne, sent us a card from Montana, where Rachel and Jack are vacationing. Says Rachel is pregnant."

"Really?" Maria clapped her hands together. "They are such a sweet couple."

Carter continued. "Starr and Juan Pablo are doing what she calls 'chocolate ministry' out there."

"What's that?" Alyssa leaned in. "Looks like they're working for an internationally known chocolatier. Wow."

"And I believe I saw a box from her and Juan over there." Carter pointed and his dad grabbed the rectangular box from the table. He leaned toward her, "By the way, she claims she and Juan Pablo were at the ball and auction, but I sure never saw them."

She shrugged. If those two were angels, as she believed, then they could have been.

Carter made a big show of sniffing the box. "It's world-class chocolate and I'm not sharing."

"Not even with your *prometida*?" Maria glared at him.

"His fiancé might want him to have it." Hamp offered.

Alyssa made a grab for it but he held it out of reach.

"They can arm wrestle for it." Jaycie laughed as she handed Leoni off to Parker. "We're offering a honeymoon in Switzerland this April, which is when we're heading back."

Clark Jeffries raised his mug of cappuccino. "Molly and I will hold down the fort for you while you're gone, Alyssa."

She'd left her job one week and started contract work with Clark and Molly the next, heading up her great-grandmother's project. "That would be great."

Molly handed her a card. "In addition to what's in there, Clark and I will babysit Sammy for your honeymoon."

"Oh no!" Marney Sagamore stood. "We have first dibs."

"The boys would reprogram the locks on the house and keep us out if we don't have Sammy stay with us." Bruce Sagamore grabbed his mug of hot cocoa.

"Sorry, Molly, the Sagamores won with their highest bid. Ding, ding, ding." Carter opened the envelope. "Oh, wow, thanks, Molly and Clark. We love the Mustang Lounge and that'll be a great date night."

Molly stood, hands on hips, facing Bruce and Marney. "I call dibs on babysitting Sammy that night."

Bruce crossed his arms and held them up as if holding off a vampire. "Fine, fine."

Sammy turned. Cheese crud pillowed around his mouth. "Are you fighting over me?"

"Maybe not, Son." Alyssa huffed a sigh, rose, and brought a napkin to her boy. She leaned close to him. "Go in and wipe your face off. You're a mess."

He ran off to the nearest bathroom and slammed the door.

Hamp and Maria Parker started laughing. "Our gifts are outside in the memorial garden."

A twinge of pain tamped down Alyssa's emotions. They'd named the garden the Abbi-Renae Garden of Light, planted several hundred white bulbs, and installed some wonderful lighting.

"We got all three of you some fat-tire bikes for this winter." Maria handed Alyssa a pink basket and Carter a blue one. "And your own new tandem bikes so you don't have to keep using the ones from Tandem Cottage."

"Yay!" Sammy exclaimed as he rejoined them. "Do you have other wedding gifts for me?

She couldn't believe that he'd just said that.

"Well, we have a gift for all of us for this winter." Marney Sagamore passed an envelope to them. "But it's in our garage for right now."

"Interesting." Carter squeezed Alyssa's hand.

"A small llama?" Alyssa asked.

Jaycie raised her hand like a schoolgirl. "Camel?"

"Some mongooses or is that mongeese?" Parker frowned.

The computer flickered on with a Zoom call just as Hamp was hollering "Water buffalo!" and punching at the air.

Grandpa Gianni, seated closest to the computer, made a funny face as his image came onscreen. "What? Do I look like a water buffalo?" He leaned away.

"No, Grandpa Gianni, we're guessing what our friends the Sagamores gifted us with."

"Easy peasy," Grandma Kareen repositioned the laptop. "They own a hiking shop, or did, down near Asheville. I'm betting outdoor gear."

"Aw, Grandma, you have no imagination."

She crossed her arms. "Okay. I'm wrong. It's probably a crate full of bananas from Doud's."

Carter opened the envelope and removed the card. "Grandma Kareen, how did you know that?"

Alyssa grabbed the cute card. *Bananas?* She smirked when she saw they were gifting them a toboggan and a baby-friendly sled. Kareen could be blunt but she was a smart lady. "Thanks for the bananas, Marney and Bruce."

The couple laughed. "No prob."

Romelda's face cut in on the Zoom screen. She waved. "Hey, y'all. I'm here in sunny Virginia. I bet it's cold up there. Brrrr." She pretended to shiver.

Dad waved at the screen. "Hi, Grandma."

"Hello, Sonny!" She did air kisses. She and Dad talked every other day.

"Whatcha got for the kids?" Dad clapped his hands together looking like a little boy himself.

"Well since I can't give 'em a good old-fashioned pounding—"

"A pounding?" Kareen's eyes grew wide.

"It's where you gift the couple with a pound of this and a pound of that. It's real fun." Romelda tilted her head.

Alyssa looked around the room. Everyone but Clark looked dubious.

"It's an old colonial custom." Clark shrugged.

With his father being a historic parks director, it didn't surprise her that Clark knew.

"Anyhoo, after the wedding, but before epiphany, I'm going to take the whole family to Busch Gardens for Christmas Town. I'll even have it shut down for two hours for privacy's sake."

Sammy threw his arms overhead. "Yay! Grandma Romelda, I've read about that place."

Gianni leaned in. "I can fly them down and back on my private jet."

On his private jet? Alyssa stared at Gianni and then at her great-grandmother on the screen. A private viewing at the park and a private jet? And to think only a few months earlier, she'd wondered how she could afford the trip to and from the island for her interview.

"I'm so sorry I can't perform the ceremony for y'all, but I plan to do my own blessing of your marriage while you're here in Virginia."

Blessing, upon blessing, upon blessing.

God had given her back triple fold what the enemy had stolen from her.

Alyssa would remember that every day for the rest of her life.

The End

Author's Notes

First the artists! Linda Anderson-Paine is a well-known artist from the Eastern Upper Peninsula of Michigan who'd shared with me that she had painted murals at cottages on Mackinac Island. That was the inspiration for the muralist in this novel! Mary Lou Peters is indeed a renowned artist from Mackinac City. I'm blessed to own several of her pieces but even more blessed to call her friend! After this story was well underway, with a cover developed, I saw Lorna Bricco's gorgeous submission for the Mackinac Island Art Council's Lilac Festival poster contest. It won the People's Choice Award! I felt led to contact Lorna and with many submissions from locations far and wide, I wasn't sure if I'd even find her. Truth is stranger than fiction. I located her online in the Soo, where I graduated college. I messaged her and we spoke on the phone. Not only did she also attend Lake Superior State, like I had, but she was from my hometown of Newberry! I was flabbergasted further to learn she was related to many people who I knew and who'd had an impact on my life. Lorna agreed to allow me to use her original artwork as cover art. So I tossed the cover I had and am so blessed to have Lorna's painting on my cover! Lorna exhibits at many art fairs in the Mid-West.

Next locations! This is fiction but many places mentioned in this novel are factual. Tandem Cottage as a Frank Lloyd Wright creation hidden in Hubbard's Annex is pure fiction. Hubbard's Annex, however, is a real location. Cardinal Cottage is fictional as are the Parkers' Resort and the Butterfly Cottage on Mackinac Island (located adjacent to fictional Parkers' Resort.). Lilac Cottage is inspired by a cottage often referred to as the Wedding Cake Cottage on West Bluff and the Canary/Welling/Swaine Cottage owned by Maria is inspired by Cairngorm Cottage on West Bluff. If you have visited Mackinac Island, you know that the Grand Hotel is a real place as are Fort Mackinac and Marquette Park. Lucky Bean is my favorite coffee shop on the island (or anywhere!) and is owned by beautiful

Carolyn May. Doud's grocery is a great place and the oldest family-run grocery in the country. "The Soo" is home to the world-famous Soo Locks and to Lake Superior State University. This is a very old French-settled city surrounded by the Saint Mary River and cut through by old canals. It's the largest town in the Eastern Upper Peninsula.

Finally, characters/people. The hemorrhage that Abbi-Renae suffered was inspired by the story of a local lady. Thank God, that lovely mom survived, like the nurse who speaks to Carter about her experience of everything being "just right" and God delivered her. The mentally disturbed "artist" Leland was loosely inspired by a real-life person. Sadly, many women, like fictional Alyssa, experience sexual assault and don't report it for many reasons. When I was working on Alyssa's character, I wondered—what if not only your child was the result of rape but also struggled with being on the spectrum. That young woman would need a strong faith, her own relationship with the Lord not based on religious rules, to get her through. It's very difficult raising a child with special needs, as many of us know. But if someone tried to take that child away, momma bear instinct would certainly take over. Carter Parker's character was inspired by a young ferry worker my son and I met in 2018. I put my fictional Carter through a lot in the past seven years, some of which we all endured (Pandemic), and some which only some of us did (death of a parent from drugs, death of a spouse). As a former psychologist, tagline "Overcoming with God," I want to show that God can get us through.

Acknowledgements

I always thank God first. Without Him I would not even be here and without Him there would be no story. Thank you to my family for their support and my granddaughter, Lorelai, for inspiring the baby Kelsey character.

Thank you to my critique partner, Sheila Stovall, for her insight. Much appreciation to my editor, Melissa Main. Kudos to Ivy Sterling Lasley, who stepped in as a copy editor for this novel. Mother-daughter beta readers, Robin Auten and Andrea Selaty, were so much help! Thank you to beta readers: Tina St. Clair Rice and Gail Mundy.

Much appreciation to my Advance Copy Readers: Diana Flowers, Rory Lemond, Susan Marie Johnson, Paula Ecker Shreckhise, Rebecca Tellez, Joy Roberts Gibson, Linda Matson Thomas, Beverly Duell-Moore and Teresa S. Mathews. Thank you to the other members of my Tandem Cottage Promo Team for all your help!

As usual, I "borrowed" many names. Cassandra and Colton Byrnes are my daughter and son-in-law. Susan Mullen, who is a social worker, is my dear friend and John is her husband, Colby her son. Kareen is my cousin's first name. Cassie Browne is my cousin. There are many more as well!

Much appreciation to The Island Bookstore owners, Mary Jane Barnwell and Diane Brandonisio, manager Tamara Tomac and longtime staff members Jill Sawatzki and Jeremy for their support and encouragement! It's always so fun to sign books at the store, too!

Thank you to my readers and those who encourage my Christian Fiction writing. I'm grateful for my Pagels' Pals Team members especially. Also blessed by the Avid Christian Fiction Readers group and administrator Martha Artyomenko Hurley!

With gratitude to the Addicted to Mackinac Island Facebook group and to the administrators—Linda Borton Sorensen, John Hubel, Lynn Anderson, and Camella Mendenhall Walker—for their encouragement and love of all things Mackinac!

Mackinac Island Cottages Series

Butterfly Cottage – Book 1

Selah Awards 2nd Place Winner in Women's Fiction

Three generations of women unexpectedly head out to the family's cottage at the Straits of Mackinac for a small-town Michigan summer together. Jaycie begins an Archeology internship on Mackinac Island. Her mother, Tamara, takes a break from teaching kindergarteners. And her grandmother, Dawn, struggles with a decision to sell her successful travel agency and possibly retire.

Each has her own journey to pursue during this short respite time from "normal" life. One of them has a secret that will change all of their lives. Can she make this one special summer to remember or will all be devastated? Faith for family and friends will be tested, with some finally able to put the past behind them and begin anew. (Set in 2018, pre-Pandemic.)

Lilac Cottage – Book 2

Selah Award 2nd Place Winner in Women's Fiction

Out of options, Rachel Dunmara 'camps out' at her deceased Grandmother's cottage on Mackinac Island. Next door, her childhood nemesis, Jack Welling, is overseeing his family's remodeling of their home on the West Bluff. When Rachel's new boss, at a local coffee shop, pushes her to work as Jack's assistant, for her second job, can they mend their rift?

Kareen Parker, widowed in the past year, returns to the island to share long-held information with her son and to transition ownership of her resort to her son. Her grandson befriends Rachel, who was banned by her family from associating with the Parkers. In a summer full of secrets that are finally revealed, can three families be healed?

Associated Novel
in the Mackinac Island Cottages Series

Behind Love's Walls
The Grand Hotel Slowly Reveals Her Secrets

Visit historic American landmarks through the Doors to the Past series. History and today collide in stories full of mystery, intrigue, faith, and romance.

Two successful women, a hundred and twenty years apart, build walls to protect their hearts. Modern-day Willa, a successful interior decorator, is chosen to consult for the Grand Hotel's possible redesign. She discovers a journal detailing the struggles of a young woman, Lily—which reveals dark secrets. The renowned singer wasn't who she pretended to be. As Willa reaches out to Lily's descendant, a charismatic and prominent landscape artist, she lets down her guard. Should she share the journal with him, or once again erect a wall as she struggles to redesign both the Grand and her life?

Biographies

CARRIE FANCETT PAGELS, Ph.D., had a twenty-seven-year career as a school and clinical psychologist. Although Carrie misses being a psychologist, she brings her expertise, as well as her faith, into each story she writes. She is now the multi-award-winning and bestselling author of over twenty-five Christian fiction books. She has two series set on Mackinac Island—a historical series and a contemporary—and a third series set at the Straits of Mackinac. Her novel *My Heart Belongs on Mackinac Island* won the Maggie Award and was chosen as a Romantic Times Top Pick. Her book *The Fruitcake Challenge* was a Selah Award finalist and was chosen by Women's World Magazine as a recommended Michigan Christmas Read selection.

Carrie grew up in Michigan's beautiful Eastern Upper Peninsula. Although she now resides with her family in Virginia, she vacations most summers at the Straits of Mackinac—where many of her stories are set. She has a new granddaughter to spend time with and spoil! She's a tea addict with an overflowing tea cart. The family dog, an Aussie Kelpie, tries to walk his granny daily and often succeeds.

Social Media:
You can find Carrie on her author page on Facebook, on Instagram, goodreads, BookBub, Pinterest, LinkedIn, and don't forget to 'Like' her Amazon author page!

LORNA BRICCO is a high energy artist with a love of vintage, decorating, painting and family! Bricco's Art & Design became her favorite job after retiring from the State of Michigan in 2021. Lorna's watercolors are all originals. Lorna also creates cards, ornaments, jewelry, mugs & tumblers and more using her original artwork! Lorna's heart goes into all her artwork. She's an award-winning artist and a popular artist at events across the Mid-West. She's on multiple social media outlets.

If you enjoyed this novel, a review is very
much appreciated!

Book Clubs:

For questions for you book clubs or to arrange a
virtual visit with the author, contact me online!

www.ingramcontent.com/pod-product-compliance
Lightning Source LLC
Chambersburg PA
CBHW061921130726
47908CB00016B/624